To Glory We Steer

Alexander Kent

arrow books

First published by Arrow Books in 1970

This edition published by Arrow Books in 2006

1 3 5 7 9 10 8 6 4 2

First published in the United Kingdom
by Hutchinson in 1969

Arrow Books
The Random House Group Limited
20 Vauxhall Bridge Road, London, SW1V 2SA

www.rbooks.co.uk

Addresses for companies within The Random House Group Limited
can be found at:
www.randomhouse.co.uk/offices.htm

The Random House Group Limited Reg. No. 954009

A CIP catalogue record for this book
is available from the British Library

ISBN 9780099527862

The Random House Group Limited supports The Forest Stewardship
Council (FSC), the leading international forest certification organisation.
All our titles that are printed on Greenpeace approved FSC certified paper
carry the FSC logo. Our paper procurement policy can be found at:
www.rbooks.co.uk/environment

Mixed Sources

Product group from well-managed
forests and other controlled sources
www.fsc.org Cert no. TT-COC-2139
© 1996 Forest Stewardship Council

Typeset in Times by SX Composing DTP, Rayleigh, Essex
Printed and bound in Great Britain by
Cox & Wyman Limited, Reading, Berkshire

The stirring story of the life and times of Richard Bolitho is told in Alexander Kent's bestselling novels.

1756   Born Falmouth, son of James Bolitho

1768   Entered the King's service as a Midshipman on *Manxman*

1772   Midshipman, *Gorgon (Midshipman Bolitho)*

1774   Promoted Lieutenant, *Destiny*: Rio and the Caribbean *(Stand into Danger)*

1775-7   Lieutenant, *Trojan*, during the American Revolution. Later appointed prizemaster *(In Gallant Company)*

1778   Promoted Commander, *Sparrow*. Battle of the Chesapeake *(Sloop of War)*

1782   Promoted Captain, *Phalarope*; West Indies: Battle of Saints *(To Glory We Steer)*

1784   Captain, *Undine*; India and East Indies *(Command a King's Ship)*

1787   Captain, *Tempest*; Great South Sea; Tahiti; suffered serious fever *(Passage to Mutiny)*

1792   Captain, the *Nore*; Recruiting *(With All Despatch)*

1793   Captain, *Hyperion*; Mediterranean; Bay of Biscay; West Indies *(Form Line of Battle!* and *Enemy in Sight)*

1795   Promoted Flag Captain, *Euryalus*; involved in the Great Mutiny; Mediterranean; Promoted Commodore *(The Flag Captain)*

1798   Battle of the Nile *(Signal – Close Action!)*

1800   Promoted Rear-Admiral; Baltic; *(The Inshore Squadron)*

1801   Biscay. Prisoner of war *(A Tradition of Victory)*

1802   Promoted Vice-Admiral; West Indies *(Success to the Brave)*

1803   Mediterranean *(Colours Aloft!)*

1805   Battle of Trafalgar *(Honour This Day)*

1806-7   Good Hope and the second battle of Copenhagen *(The Only Victor)*

1808   Shipwrecked off Africa *(Beyond the Reef)*

1809-10   Mauritius campaign *(The Darkening Sea)*

1812   Promoted Admiral; Second American War *(For My Country's Freedom)*

1814   Defence of Canada *(Cross of St. George)*

1815   Killed in action *(Sword of Honour)*

Contents

The thundering line of battle stands,
  And in the air Death moans and sings:
But Day shall clasp him with strong hands,
  And Night shall fold him in strong wings.

JULIAN GRENFELL

1

The Phalarope

The New Year of 1782 was only three days old but already the weather had made a decided change for the worse. Steady drizzle, pushed by a freshening southerly wind, explored the narrow streets of Portsmouth Point and made the stout walls of the old fortifications gleam like polished metal. Moving threateningly above the huddled buildings the cloud was unbroken and the colour of lead, so that although it was all but midday the light was feeble and depressing.

Only the sea was really alive. Across the normally sheltered expanse of the Solent the surface quivered and broke with each eager gust, but in the distorted light the wave crests held a strange yellow hue in contrast with the dull grey hump of the Isle of Wight and the rain-shrouded Channel beyond.

Captain Richard Bolitho pushed open the door of the George Inn and stood for a few moments to allow the drowsy heat to enfold him like a blanket. Without a word he handed his cloak to a servant and tucked his cocked hat beneath his arm. Through a door to his right he could see a welcoming fire in the coffee room, where a noisy throng of naval officers, interspersed with a few bright scarlet uniforms of the military, were taking their ease and keeping their worries and demands of duty beyond the low, rain-slashed windows.

In another room, grouped in contemplative silence around several small tables, other officers studied their playing cards and the faces of their opponents. Few even glanced up at Bolitho's entrance. In Portsmouth, and at the George Inn in particular, after years of war and unrest, only a man out of uniform might have warranted attention.

Bolitho sighed and took a quick glance at himself in a wall mirror. His blue coat and gold lace fitted his tall figure well, and against the white shirt and waistcoat his face looked unusually tanned. Even allowing for a slow voyage back from the West Indies, his body was still unprepared for an English winter, and he forced himself to stand a little longer to clear the aching cold from his limbs.

A servant coughed politely at his elbow. 'Beg pardon, sir. The admiral is waitin' on you in his room.' He made a small gesture towards the stairway.

'Thank you.' He waited until the man had hurried away to answer some noisy demand from the coffee room and then took a final glance at the mirror. It was neither vanity nor personal interest. It was more of a cold scrutiny which he might offer to a subordinate.

Bolitho was twenty-six years old, but his impassive features and the deep lines on either side of his mouth made him appear older, and for a brief instant he found himself wondering how the change had come about. Almost irritably he pushed the black hair away from his forehead, pausing only to allow one rebellious lock to stay in place above his right eye.

Neither was that action one of vanity. More perhaps one of embarrassment.

Barely an inch above his eye, and running deep into his hair-line, was a savage diagonal scar. He allowed his fingers to touch it momentarily, as a man will let his mind explore an old memory, and then with a final shrug he walked briskly up the stairs.

Vice-Admiral Sir Henry Langford was standing, feet

well apart, directly in front of the highest log fire Bolitho had ever seen. His glittering uniform shone in the dancing flames, and his thick shadow seemed to reach out across the spacious room to greet Bolitho's quiet entrance.

For several seconds the two men stood looking at each other. The admiral, in his sixties, and running to bulkiness, his heavy face dominated by a large beaked nose above which his keen blue eyes shone like two polished stones, and the slim, tanned captain.

Then the admiral stirred into life and stepped away from the fire, his hand outstretched. Bolitho felt the heat from the fire released across the room, as if a furnace door had been flung open.

'I am glad to see you, Bolitho!' The admiral's booming voice filled the room, sweeping away the years and replacing the image of an overweight old man with that of Bolitho's first captain.

As if reading his thoughts the admiral added ruefully, 'Fourteen years, isn't it? My God, it doesn't seem possible!' He stood back and studied Bolitho critically like a plump bird. 'You were a scraggy midshipman, twelve years old, if I remember correctly. Hardly an ounce of flesh on you. I only took you aboard because of your father.' He smiled. 'You still look as if a good meal would not come amiss!'

Bolitho waited patiently. Those fourteen years of service had taught him one thing at least. Senior officers had their own ways of getting round to the reasons for their actions. And it usually took time.

The admiral moved ponderously to a table and poured two generous glasses of brandy. 'With most of the world against us, Bolitho, brandy has become somewhat of a luxury.' He shrugged. 'However, as I am more troubled by rheumatism than gout, I look upon it as a last remaining necessity.'

Bolitho sipped carefully and studied his superior over

the rim of the glass. He had arrived back from the West Indies just three days earlier, as one year faded and gave way to the next. His ship, his beloved *Sparrow*, had been handed over to the dockyard for a well-earned refit, while her less fortunate company were scattered through the ever-hungry fleet to replace the growing gaps left by death and mutilation. Most of the sloop's crew had been away from their homeland for six years, and with a little well-earned prize money they had been hoping to see their loved ones again, if only for a short while. It was not to be, but Bolitho knew that his feeling of resentment and pity would be as useless as a ship without sails.

The pale eyes fixed suddenly on Bolitho's face. 'I'm giving you the *Phalarope*, Bolitho.' He watched the brief shaft of emotion play across the young captain's features. 'She's lying out at Spithead right now, rigging set up, yards crossed, a finer frigate never floated.'

Bolitho placed the glass slowly on the table to give his mind time to deal with the admiral's words. The *Phalarope*, a thirty-two-gun frigate, and less than six years old. He had seen her through his glass as he had rounded the Spit Sand three days ago. She was certainly a beautiful ship, all that he could ever have hoped for. No, more than he could have dreamed of.

He pushed the *Sparrow* to the back of his thoughts. It was part of yesterday, along with his own hopes of taking a rest at his home in Cornwall, and getting to know the firm feel of the countryside, of so many half-remembered things.

He said quietly, 'You do me a great honour, sir.'

'Nonsense, you've more than earned it!' The admiral seemed strangely relieved. As if he had been rehearsing this little speech for some time. 'I've followed your career, Bolitho. You are a great credit to the Navy, and the country.'

'I had an excellent teacher, sir.'

4

The admiral nodded soberly. 'They were great days, eh? Great days.' He shook himself and poured another brandy. 'I have told you the good news. Now I will tell you the other part.' He watched Bolitho thoughtfully. 'The *Phalarope* has been attached to the Channel Fleet, mostly on blockade duty outside Brest.'

Bolitho pricked up his ears. Being on blockade duty was no news at all. The hard-pressed fleet needed every frigate like gold in its constant efforts to keep the French ships bottled up in their Channel ports. Frigates were maids of all work. Powerful enough to trounce any other vessel but a ship of the line in open combat, and fast enough to out-manoeuvre the latter, they were in permanent demand. What caught his immediate attention was the way the admiral had stressed *has been attached* to the Channel Fleet. So there were new orders. Maybe south to help relieve the beleaguered garrison in Gibraltar.

The admiral continued harshly, 'Most ships go rotten from without. Wind and sea are cruel masters, even to the best timbers.' He stared at the rain splattering across the windows. '*Phalarope* has received her rot from within!' He began to pace angrily, his shadow crossing and recrossing the room like a spectre. 'There was almost a mutiny a month back, and then when her squadron was engaged in battle with some blockade runners she avoided action!' He halted and glared at Bolitho with something like shock. 'Can you believe that? A King's ship, and she failed to engage!'

Bolitho bit his lip. Mutiny was always a threat. Men pressed from life ashore, a handful of troublemakers, even one stupid officer, could turn a well-drilled ship into a living hell. But it rarely occurred with other ships in company. Usually this sort of madness broke out in a ship becalmed under a relentless tropical sun, with fever and disease the main instigators. Or during a long voyage out of sight of land, when a ship seemed to shrink in size with

5

each dragging day, as if to force the men at each others' throats.

Sir Henry Langford added sharply, 'I've relieved her captain of his command, of course.'

Bolitho felt a strange warmth for this tired, irritable old man, whose flagship, a massive three-decker, was even now taking on stores in the harbour and preparing to carry her master back to his squadron off the hostile French coast. He had said '*of course*'. Yet Bolitho knew that many admirals would have backed up their captains even knowing them to be both guilty and incompetent.

The admiral gave a small smile. 'I am afraid your honour is double-edged! It is never easy to take over an unhappy ship, especially in time of war.' He pointed at a sealed envelope on his desk. Its seals glittered in the firelight like fresh blood. 'Your orders. They require you to take command forthwith and proceed to sea.' He weighed his words carefully. 'You will seek out Sir Samuel Hood's squadron and place yourself under his orders.'

Bolitho felt dazed. Hood was still in the West Indies whence he had just returned. He had a brief picture of the same thousands of miles of empty sea, in command of a strange ship, with a crew still seething in discontent.

'So you see, Bolitho, I am still a hard taskmaster!' The admiral shuddered as a squall hit the window. 'I am afraid you are nearly one hundred men under strength. I had to remove many of the troublemakers, and replacements are hard to come by. Some I will have to hang, as soon as a court martial can be convened. You have barely enough men to work the ship under way, let alone in action.' He rubbed his chin, his eyes glittering. 'I suggest you make sail at once and head for the West Country. I understand that the fishing fleets are mostly in port in Devon and Cornwall. The weather it seems is not to their liking.' His smile broadened. 'I see no objection to your visiting

6

Falmouth, Bolitho. While your officers are ashore pressing some of these fishermen into the King's service, you might well find the time to call upon your father. You will give him my kind regards, I hope.'

Bolitho nodded. 'Thank you, sir. I will do that.' All at once he wanted to get away. There was so much to attend to. Stores and cordage to be checked, food and provisions for the long voyage. Above all, there was the *Phalarope*, waiting for him, ready to judge or condemn him.

The admiral picked up the canvas envelope and weighed it in his hands. 'I will not advise you, Bolitho. You are young, but have more than proved yourself. Just remember this. There are bad men and good aboard your ship. Be firm, but not too hard. Do not regard lack of knowledge as insubordination, like your predecessor.' There was a bite to his tone. 'If you have difficulty in remembering all this, try and recall what you were like when you came to serve me as midshipman.' He was no longer smiling. 'You can give the ship back her rightful place by returning her pride. But if you fail, even I cannot help you.'

'I would not expect you to, sir.' Bolitho's eyes were hard grey, like the sea beyond the harbour.

'I know. That is why I held the command for you.' There was a murmur of voices beyond the door and Bolitho knew the audience was nearly over. The admiral added, 'I have a nephew aboard the *Phalarope*, he is one of your young gentlemen. His name is Charles Farquhar, and he might yet make a good officer. But do him no favours for my sake, Bolitho.' He sighed and handed over the envelope. 'The ship is ready to sail, so take advantage of this southerly wind.' He held Bolitho's hand and studied his face intently. 'We may not meet again, Bolitho, for I fear my days are numbered.' He waved down the other man's protest. 'I have a responsibility, and I have certain rewards for my duty. But youth I cannot have.'

Bolitho hitched up his sword and tucked his hat under his arm once more. 'Then I will take my leave, sir.' There was nothing more he could say.

Almost blindly he walked through the door and past the little group of whispering officers, awaiting their admiral's pleasure.

One officer stood apart, a captain of about his own age. There the similarity ended. He had pale, protruding eyes and a small, petulant mouth. He was tapping his fingers on his sword and staring at the door, and Bolitho guessed him to be the man who had been taken from the *Phalarope*. But he seemed unworried, merely irritated. He probably had influence at Court, or in Parliament, Bolitho thought grimly. Even so, he would need more than that to face Sir Henry.

As he crossed to the stairway the other captain met his stare. The pale eyes were empty of expression yet vaguely hostile. Then he looked away, and Bolitho reached the foot of the stairs where a marine orderly waited with his cloak.

Outside the inn the wind howled in his face and the rain dashed across his skin like ice rime. But as he walked slowly towards the Sally Port he noticed neither.

When he reached the Hard, Bolitho noticed that the high-water garland of slime and weed was all but covered by the angry, hissing wavelets, and he knew that the tide was nearing the flood. With luck he could get his new ship under way on the ebb. Nothing made a ship's company settle down to a fresh master more quickly than routine and work.

As he left the shelter of the last line of buildings he caught sight of the boat which waited to carry him away from the land. The oars were tossed, and swayed like twin lines of bare trees as the small craft rocked uneasily in the swell, and he guessed that each man in the boat was watching his slow approach. At the top of the stone ramp, his thick body framed against the cruising wavelets, was the familiar shape of Stockdale, his personal coxswain. Aboard the *Phalarope* there would be one friend at least, he thought grimly.

Stockdale had followed him from ship to ship. More like a trusting dog than a man. Bolitho often found time to wonder at the bond which had held them together, a link which was beyond explanation in words.

As a young and very junior lieutenant Bolitho had been sent ashore with a recruiting party during the uneasy peace, when he had considered himself more than fortunate to be spared the indignity of so many of his fellows, that of being beached and unwanted on half-pay. Volunteers had been few, but when about to return to his ship to face the wrath of his captain Bolitho had seen Stockdale standing miserably outside a local inn. Stripped to the waist he had made a truly imposing figure, his thickset body a mass of muscle and power. A loud-mouthed barker at his side had called to the small naval recruiting party that Stockdale was a prizefighter of great repute, and that a golden guinea would be immediately awarded to any one of Bolitho's men who could lay him low. Bolitho had been weary, and the thought of a cool drink at the inn while his men tried their luck overcame his normal objections to what he thought to be a degrading spectacle.

As it happened, he had had in his party a gunner's mate who was not only a very proficient fist-fighter but a man quite used to maintaining discipline by that and any other means which came his way. He had thrown aside his jacket, and encouraged by the other sailors had gone to the attack.

Exactly what had happened next Bolitho was not quite sure. It was said that one of the sailors had managed to trip Stockdale, and that seemed likely, as Bolitho had never seen him beaten since that day, but the next instant, even as Bolitho had been reaching for his ale, there had been a scream of rage from the barker and a great bellow of laughter from the sailors.

Bolitho had found the gunner's mate pocketing his guinea while the infuriated barker had proceeded to beat Stockdale with a length of chain, interspersed with threats and curses.

It was then that Bolitho had discovered that Stockdale accepted loyalty like a manacle. He never flinched from the unjust beating, although he could have killed his tormentor with one blow.

Pity or disgust drove Bolitho to stop the beating, and the look of dumb gratitude on Stockdale's battered face only helped to make things worse. Watched by the grinning sailors and the flint-eyed barker he had asked Stockdale to volunteer for the King's service. The barker had raised a storm of protest at the thought of his living being removed for all time.

Stockdale had given a brief nod and picked up his shirt without a word. Even now he hardly ever spoke, his vocal cords having been damaged over the years of fighting in one town after another.

Bolitho had imagined that his angry gesture had ended the matter. But it was not so. Stockdale had settled down aboard ship in a manner born. For all his strength he was gentle and patient, and only one real object seemed to alter his placid way of life. Wherever Bolitho went, so did he.

At first Bolitho decided to ignore this fact, but when at length he had his own command and required a personal coxswain, Stockdale just seemed to be there, ready. As he was now.

He was staring emptily at the sea, his body motionless in the wind, his wide white trousers and blue jacket flapping around his limbs like pennants on a heavy ship of the line. He turned at Bolitho's approach and knuckled his forehead, his deep brown eyes watching his captain with silent concern.

Bolitho gave a tight smile. 'Is everything ready, Stockdale?'

The man nodded slowly. 'I've stowed your boxes in the boat, sir.' He glared at the waiting boat's crew. 'I've had a word with this lot about how things should be done from now on!'

Bolitho stepped down into the boat and gathered his cloak tightly around him. Stockdale grunted an order and the boat idled clear of the stonework.

'Out oars! Give way together!' Stockdale swung the tiller and squinted between the oarsmen as the boat turned and bit into the first angry swell.

Bolitho watched the oarsmen through narrowed eyes. Each man was careful to avoid his scrutiny. The new captain, any captain, was second only to God. He could promote and flog, reward and hang any man aboard, and when a ship was out of company, alone on the high seas, the powers were exercised according to a particular captain's temperament, as Bolitho well knew.

As the boat pushed into open water he forgot the straining seamen and concentrated his full attention on the distant frigate. Now that he was closer he could see the steady pitch and roll of the graceful hull as she strained at the taut cable in the freshening wind. He could even see the flash of bright copper as she showed her bilges, and then as she canted to the opposite side he could make out the busy activity on the maindeck below her tall, tapering masts and furled sails. Aft by the entry port there was a neat scarlet rectangle of marines already drawn up to greet him, and momentarily in the wind he caught the sound of twittering pipes and the hoarse bellow of orders.

She was a fine ship, he thought. One hundred and forty feet of power and living grace. From the high gilt figurehead, a strange bird mounted on the back of a dolphin, to her carved poop with the rippling ensign above she was the proof of a shipbuilder's art.

Now he could see the group of officers waiting on the quarterdeck, more than one with his glass raised and trained on the tossing boat. He set his face in an impassive mask, forcibly dampening down the excitement and the sense of challenge which the ship had given him.

'Boat ahoy!' The hail was caught by the wind and tossed to the screaming gulls above.

Stockdale cupped his hands and yelled, '*Phalarope!*' There was no doubt now for the waiting officers. No doubt at all that their new overlord was approaching.

Bolitho opened his cloak and threw it back across his shoulders, the feeble light glinting on his gold lace and the hilt of his sword. Still the frigate grew bigger and bigger, until at last she towered above the boat, blotting out all else.

As the oarsmen manoeuvred towards the entry port Bolitho ran his eye slowly along the masts and yards and the taut black rigging. There was no sign of slackness, everything was as it should be. The hull was well painted, and the amount of gold leaf around the figurehead as well as the broad-windowed stern was proof that her last captain had spent a good deal of his own money to make her so.

The thought of money well spent made him glance briefly at his boxes in the sternsheets. He had brought over a thousand pounds of prize money back from the Indies, yet apart from the new uniforms and a few small luxuries he had little to show for it. And now he was off to sea again, where a mutineer's knife might end his life as quickly as a French cannon ball, unless he was constantly vigilant. He suddenly recalled the admiral's warning, 'If you fail, even I cannot help you!'

The boat lurched alongside and almost threw him from his feet as he jumped clear of the gunwale and began to climb up the spray-dashed side.

He tried to shut his ears to the crash of sound which greeted him. The trilling pipes from the side party, and the slap of muskets as the marines presented arms; it was too easy and too dangerous to let his guard slip even for an instant. Even to allow himself to enjoy this moment to the full, for which he had been waiting for so long.

A tall, heavily built lieutenant stepped forward and removed his hat. 'Lieutenant Vibart, sir. I am the senior here.' He had a thick, rasping tone, and his face was unsmiling.

'Thank you, Mr. Vibart.' Bolitho stared past him along the full length of his ship. The gangways on either side of the hull which connected the forecastle with the quarterdeck were crowded with silent men, and others had climbed into the shrouds so that they could see their captain better. His eye moved on, across the neat lines of guns, firmly lashed behind closed ports, the spotless decks and well-flaked lines. Lieutenant Vibart was a good first lieutenant as far as smartness and outward appearance was concerned, he thought.

Vibart was saying gruffly, 'Mr. Okes and Mr. Herrick, the second and third lieutenants, sir.'

Bolitho nodded, keeping his expression noncommittal. He had a quick impression of two young officers, nothing more. Later the men would emerge from behind the strange faces. Right now it was more important that his own impression on them was made quite clear.

'Have the hands lay aft, Mr. Vibart.' He drew his commission from inside his coat and unrolled it as the men were urged towards him. They looked healthy enough, but their bodies were clad in rags, and some of them seemed to be dressed in the remains of what they had been wearing when pressed into service. He bit his lip. That would have to be changed, and at once. Uniformity was all important. It killed envy amongst the men, if only for poor remnants of clothing.

He began to read himself in, his voice carrying crisply above the sigh of wind and the steady thrumming of stays and rigging.

It was addressed to Richard Bolitho, Esquire, and required him forthwith to go on board and take upon him the charge and command of captain in His Britannic Majesty's frigate *Phalarope*. He finished reading and rolled the scroll in his hands as he looked down at the assembled faces. What were they thinking and hoping at this moment?

He said: 'I will address the men further, Mr. Vibart.' He thought he saw a gleam of resentment in Vibart's deepset eyes, but ignored it. The man looked old for his rank, maybe seven or eight years older than himself. It could not be pleasant to see a chance of command moved back another pace by his sudden arrival. 'Are you in all respects ready to proceed to sea?'

Vibart nodded. 'Yes, sir.' He sounded as if he meant to say '*of course*'. 'We were warped out here a week ago, and the fresh water came aboard this forenoon by lighter. We are fully provisioned in accordance with the admiral's orders.'

'Very good.' Bolitho turned back to the crew. Sir Henry Langford had taken no chance, he thought dryly. With the ship fully provisioned and safely anchored away from the shore there was little chance of contaminating the fleet with her unhappiness. He longed for a few minutes alone so that he could read fully the extent of his orders. They might give him a further clue to the puzzle.

He cleared his throat. 'Now, men, I just want to tell you of our destination.' They would know he had had no time to inform his officers, and this immediate show of confidence might well help to bridge the gulf between quarterdeck and forecastle.

'England is fighting for her life! Even as we lie here, anchored and impotent, our country is at war with France

14

and Spain, with the Dutch and the rebellious colonialists in the Americas. Every single ship is needed to win the day, each man amongst you is vital to our just cause!' He paused and waited a few seconds. In the *Sparrow* his men would have cheered, would have shown some animation. Suddenly, as he stared along the packed expressionless faces he felt a pang of longing and loneliness. In his mind's eye he could see the little sloop's cheerful, tanned company, like a lot of carefree pirates. The healthy faces, the feeling of oneness which was totally absent here. He saw Stockdale standing by the lee rail and wondered what he thought about his new shipmates.

He allowed a note of hardness to creep into his voice. 'Today we sail for Falmouth.' He steeled himself. 'And from thence to the West Indies to join Sir Samuel Hood against the French and their allies!'

No individual called out, but something like a moan of pain transmitted itself through the packed figures below him. A petty officer snarled, 'Silence on deck! Keep quiet, you scum!'

Bolitho added flatly, 'I ask nothing but your loyalty. I will do my duty, and I would wish you to do the same!' He turned on his heel. 'Carry on, Mr. Vibart. We will make sail in one hour. See that all boats are secured, and then be so good as to have the anchor hove short.' His tone was cold and formal, but the lieutenant blocked his way, his mouth working angrily.

'But, sir! The West Indies!' He struggled for words. 'God, we've been on the blockade for two years!'

Bolitho let his voice carry to the other officers. 'And I have been away for *six*, Mr. Vibart!' He walked aft where Stockdale soundlessly marked the cabin hatch for his retreat. 'I want all officers, and senior warrant officers in my cabin in ten minutes!'

He ran lightly down the ladder, his head automatically bowed beneath the low deck beams. Right aft, below a spiralling lantern, a red-coated marine snapped to attention outside his cabin door. Beyond it would be his haven, the only place aboard a crowded ship where he could think and dream alone.

Stockdale held open the door and stood aside as Bolitho entered the cabin, which after *Sparrow*'s cramped and spartan quarters seemed almost spacious.

The sloping stern windows ran the whole width of the main cabin, and the thick glass gave a wide, panoramic picture of tossing water and the hostile, grey sky. The air was heavy and damp, and once again he was conscious of the cold in his limbs. It would be good to get back to the sun, he thought. To see blue and gold through those windows, and know again the peace of a friendly sea.

A partition hid his sleeping quarters, and another concealed the small chart room. The main cabin itself contained a good table and matching chairs, as well as a bulkhead desk and a hanging wardrobe for his uniforms which even now Stockdale was unpacking from the boxes.

The previous captain had done well for himself, Bolitho thought. On either side of the cabin, discreetly hidden in a canvas cover, was a big twelve-pounder, lashed down like some leashed beast, so that even here, in the captain's own domain, the air would be filled with smoke and death when action found the frigate.

He made himself sit quietly on the padded bench below the windows, and ignoring Stockdale's furtive movements and the shipboard noises above and beyond the door began to read his orders.

But apart from the usual directions the orders told him nothing. There were extra marines aboard, with a full captain in charge of them instead of the original sergeant. That was interesting. Sir Henry Langford obviously considered that if all else failed Bolitho could defend himself with the afterguard.

He slammed the thick papers on the table and frowned.

He did not want protection. He had meant what he had said. He wanted loyalty. No, he *needed* loyalty!

The deck canted beneath him and he heard the patter of bare feet overhead. In spite of everything he was glad to be leaving the land. At sea you had room to think, and space to act. Only time was at a premium.

Exactly ten minutes after Bolitho had left the quarterdeck the officers filed through the door into his cabin.

Vibart, his head lowered beneath the deck beams, introduced each one in order of seniority in the same rasping tone.

Okes and Herrick, the two other lieutenants, and Daniel Proby, the master. The latter was old and weathered like carved wood, his body round-shouldered beneath his well-worn coat. He had a lugubrious, heavy-jowled face, and the most mournful eyes Bolitho had ever seen. Then there was Captain Rennie of the marines, a slim and languid young man with deceptively lazy eyes. Bolitho thought that he at least would guess that there might still be trouble in the offing.

The three midshipmen stood quietly in the background. Farquhar was the most senior, and Bolitho felt a small pang of uneasiness as he studied the youth's tight lips and haughty expression. The admiral's nephew might be an ally. He could equally be the admiral's spy. The other young gentlemen, Neale and Maynard, seemed pleasant enough, with the usual crumpled cheekiness which most midshipmen reserved as their defence against officers and seamen alike. Neale was minute and chubby, and could not be more than thirteen, Bolitho thought. Maynard, on the other hand, was keen-eyed and as skinny as a pike, and watched his captain with a fixed and intent expression which might mean anything.

Then there were the senior warrant officers. The professional men. Evans, the purser, a small ferret in a plain dark coat, dwarfed by Ellice, the surgeon, brick-red and perspiring, with anxious rheumy eyes.

Bolitho stood with his back to the windows, his hands clasped behind him. He waited until Vibart had finished speaking and then said, 'We shall get to know each other better very soon, gentlemen. For the moment let me say that I shall expect all of you to do your best to pull the ship's people together into one efficient company. When I left the Indies things were not going well for England. It is likely, indeed it is more than probable, that the French will take full advantage of our military commitments in that area for their own ends. Action will certainly seek us out, and when that happens I want this ship to give a good account of herself.' He watched their faces, trying to pierce their guarded expressions. His gaze fell on Herrick, the third lieutenant. He was a round-faced, competent looking officer, but there was an air of assumed attentiveness about him, like one who had been betrayed in the past and no longer trusted a first impression.

He dropped his eyes to the deck as Vibart said, 'May I ask if we're being despatched to the Indies because of the trouble we had aboard, sir?' He stared unflinchingly at Bolitho's grey eyes, his voice challenging.

'You may ask.' Bolitho watched him narrowly. There was something dominant about Vibart. A sense of inner force which seemed to cow all the others into mere spectators. He said calmly, 'I have studied the reports and the logs. I consider that the near-mutiny,' he let his voice hang on the last word, 'was caused as much by negligence as anything else.'

Vibart replied hotly, 'Captain Pomfret trusted his officers, sir!' He pointed to the books on the table. You can see from the log books that the ship did all which could be expected of her!'

Bolitho pulled a book from beneath the others and saw Vibart look momentarily off guard.

'I often find that this, the punishment book, is a better gauge of a ship's efficiency.' He turned the pages idly, forcibly hiding the disgust he had felt when he had first examined it. 'In the past six months over a thousand lashes were awarded to the crew.' His voice was cold. 'Some men received four dozen at a time. One apparently died after punishment.'

Vibart said thickly, 'You can't win men by weakness, sir!'

'Nor by senseless cruelty, Mr. Vibart!' His tone was like a whip. 'In future I will have more attention to leadership than to brutality in my ship!' He controlled his voice with an effort. 'Also, I want every man fitted out with proper clothing from the slop chest before we reach Falmouth. This is a King's ship and not a Spanish slaver!'

There was a sudden heavy silence, so that ship and sea intruded into the cabin. The clatter of deck gear, the sluice of the tide around the rudder, and the distant bark of commands added to Bolitho's sense of isolation.

He continued evenly, 'At Falmouth we will make efforts to increase our company to full strength. I will send parties of trusted hands ashore to press suitable men for service. Not cripples and young boys, but *men*. Do I make myself clear?'

Most of them nodded. Lieutenant Okes said carefully, 'I have often read of your exploits in the *Gazette*, sir.' He swallowed painfully and glanced quickly at Herrick. 'I think the whole ship will be happy to have you as captain.' His voice trailed away miserably and he fidgeted with his sword.

Bolitho nodded. 'Thank you, Mr. Okes.' He could not afford to add anything else. Okes might be seeking favouritism, or making haste to cover up some old misdemeanour. But still, it was a beginning.

He added, 'I cannot alter what Captain Pomfret did or did not do. I have my own ways, and I expect them to be

19

considered at all times.' From the corner of his eye he saw the master shaking his head doubtfully. 'Do you wish to say anything, Mr. Proby?'

The old man looked up with a jerk, his jowls shaking. 'Er, no, sir! I was just thinking it will make a change to navigate in some deep water instead o' all these shoals an mudbanks!' He smiled, the effort only adding to his mournful appearance. 'The young gentlemen will benefit from a long voyage, no doubt?'

It was meant in all seriousness, but the midshipman Neale nudged his companion Maynard and they both tittered. Then Neale saw Vibart's frown and hurriedly looked at his feet.

Bolitho nodded. 'Very well, gentlemen, prepare to get under way. I will come on deck in ten minutes.' He met Vibart's eye. 'I shall be interested to see the men at their stations, Mr. Vibart. A bit of sail drill might take their minds off their troubles for a while!'

The officers filed away and Stockdale firmly closed the door. Bolitho sat down and stared at the piles of books and papers. He had tried to find an opening and had failed. There was a barrier, a shield of resentment, or was it fear? He had to find out himself. He could trust no one, confide in nobody until he was sure of his ground. He looked at Stockdale and asked quietly, 'Well, how do *you* like the *Phalarope*?'

The ex-fighter swallowed hard, as he always did to clear his maimed chords. 'She's a good craft, Captain.' He nodded slowly. 'But I don't care much for the meat inside the bones!' He placed Bolitho's sword carefully beside the pistol rack and added meaningly, 'I should keep these by you, Captain. Just in case!'

Richard Bolitho climbed the ladder to the quarterdeck and made himself walk slowly to the weather rail. The frigate was alive with fresh activity, and he could see men standing at the capstan bars, while others waited below the masts with their petty officers. He gauged the wind against his cheek and glanced quickly aloft at the masthead pennant. The ship tugged at her cable eagerly and fretfully, as if she too wanted to be free of the land once again, and Bolitho curbed his own impatience as he watched and waited the final preparations for sea.

The decks gleamed with blown spray and drizzle, and he realised with a start that he was already soaked to the skin. But perhaps it was just as well that his seamen should see him unshrouded in watchcoat and unprotected from the weather as indeed they were themselves.

He caught sight of the midshipman Maynard hovering by the lee rail, and again thanked God for his ability to remember names after hearing or reading them but once.

'You are in charge of signals, Mr. Maynard?' The youth nodded, his thin body looking like a scarecrow against the angry water alongside. 'Very well. Make a signal to the Flag. "Ready to proceed".'

He saw the flags soaring aloft and immediately forgot them as Vibart strode aft, his face set in a grim frown.

'Anchor's hove short, sir!' He touched his hat. 'All stores secured!'

'Very well.' Bolitho lifted his glass and watched the flags blowing out from the shore signal tower. Maybe, just to the right, from his warm room at the inn, the admiral would be watching.

Maynard yelled, 'Reply, sir! "God speed and good luck"!'

Bolitho handed his glass to Stockdale and thrust his hands beneath the tails of his coat. 'Get the ship under way if you please. Lay a course to weather the headland.' He would take no part in it. He would watch every man. And every man would know it.

The boatswain's mates took up the cry, 'Hands aloft! Loose tops'ls!'

The rigging and shrouds were suddenly alive with swarming figures as the topmen ran aloft as surefooted as cats, the laggards urged on mercilessly by the petty officers with fists and ropes ends alike.

'Break out the anchor!' Mr. Quintal, the barrel-chested boatswain, swung his cane over the straining forecastle hands. 'Heave! Put yer backs into it, you whimperin' old women!' His cane whacked down and a man cried out. 'Heave! Heave!' The capstan jerked and then cranked steadily as the dripping cable came inboard.

'Loose heads'ls!' The cry was passed along the deck like a chant. High above, the released canvas flapped and banged in the wind, and the men strung out along the swaying yards like ants kicked and grappled with each growing area of rebellious sail.

Bolitho ignored the flying spray and watched the men dashing from one job to the next. The shorthandedness was all the more apparent now with the topmen aloft.

Herrick called from the bows, 'Anchor's aweigh, sir!'

Like a released animal the frigate paid off into the wind, her deck heeling sharply as the gust found and held her.

Vibart grated, 'Man the braces there! Look alive!'

The men at the braces laid back heaving and panting until the great yards began to squeak round. Then the wind filled the sails and the billowing canvas thundered out hard and full as the *Phalarope* went about and gathered way.

By the time the anchor was catted and made fast the land was already drawing away on the starboard quarter, the Isle of Wight quite invisible in a curtain of drizzle and spray.

Everything creaked and banged as the ship continued to swing on course, with shrouds and rigging whining like the strings of some mad orchestra.

Bolitho watched the unwanted men sliding down the stays and adding their weight to the men at the braces.

'Lay her on the port tack, Mr. Vibart.' He looked back across the taffrail and tried to recall what was so terrible about Captain Pomfret. He remembered the man's cold eyes, and the cowed faces of his men.

Proby was standing hump-backed beside the quartermaster, his battered old hat over his ears like a candlesnuffer. Bolitho said, 'Let her run freely, Mr. Proby. There may be need for reefing down later, but I want to reach Falmouth as soon as possible.'

The master watched the captain's slim figure beside the rail and sucked his teeth. Pomfret had never let the frigate have her head. Now she was flying like a mad thing as more and more canvas crept along her yards and exploded, full-bellied before the wind. When he looked at the spiralling mastheads he could almost imagine they were bending. But his eyesight was not so good now, so he made no comment.

Vibart stood at the quarterdeck rail, one foot on a carronade slide, his eyes slitted as he watched the men at their stations. Once he looked back too, towards Portsmouth, where Pomfret had left the ship under orders. Where Bolitho had come aboard to replace him, and by so doing had killed Vibart's own chance of promotion.

He watched Bolitho's profile and felt the anger running through him like fire. It was five thousand miles to Hood's squadron. A lot could happen before that.

He awoke with a start as Bolitho said crisply, 'Dismiss the watch below, Mr. Vibart, and double the lookouts. He gestured towards the open channel. 'Here, everyone is an enemy.' He gave Vibart a meaning glance and went below.

2

Beware, the Press!

The gig's crew pulled steadily towards the stone jetty and then gratefully tossed their oars as Stockdale growled an order and the bowman jabbed at a ringbolt with his boathook,

Bolitho turned his head to look back at the frigate and smiled slightly to himself. The *Phalarope* was anchored well out in Falmouth Bay, her sleek shape black and stark against the sea and watery sunlight which had at last managed to break through the scudding clouds. The ship had made a slow approach towards the headland, and he had no doubt that her presence had long since been reported, and every able-bodied man in the town would have taken full advantage of the warning to make himself scarce from the dreaded press.

By his side, huddled in his boat cloak, Lieutenant Thomas Herrick sat in silence, his eyes watching the rain-soaked hills beyond the town and the grey, timeless bulk of the castle above Carrick Roads. There were several small craft moored in the safety of the Roads, coasters and tubby fishing boats enjoying the shelter and the protection of the anchorage.

Bolitho said, 'A brisk walk will do us good, Mr. Herrick. It may be the last chance we get for a while.' He stepped stiffly from the boat and waited until Herrick had followed him up the worn steps. An ancient sailor with a grey beard called, 'Welcome, Captain! It is a fine ship you have out there!'

Bolitho nodded. A Cornishman himself, and a native of Falmouth, he knew well enough that it was unlikely any younger men would dare to stay and pass idle remarks to a King's officer. Frigates were too busy to enter port unless for one thing. To gather men.

Vibart had voiced that very thing as the *Phalarope* had swooped through the night, her sails thundering to the wind, her bow throwing back the spray in an unbroken white wake. But when Bolitho had outlined his plan even he had lapsed into silence.

As a boy Bolitho had often seen the approach of a ship of war, and had heard the news shouted down the narrow streets, the cry carried from house to house like a distress signal. Young men had dropped their work, bid hasty farewells to their friends and families, and made for the safety of the hills, where they could watch and wait until the ship had made sail and dipped towards the horizon. There was a rough coast road above the cliffs which led north-east away from Falmouth towards Gerrans Bay and St. Austell. No press gang would take the time and trouble to follow them. Hampered by weapons and the short breath left by lack of exercise, they would know such efforts to be wasted. No, there were few who were slow or stupid enough to allow the King's men an easy catch.

In pitch darkness Bolitho had turned the ship inshore and heaved to, the deck canting savagely to the stiff wind and the swift offshore currents. Old Proby had been at first doubtful, and then had openly showed his admiration. There were no beacons, and apart from a dull shadow of land there was nothing to show that Bolitho had found the exact point below Gerrans Bay where the chart displayed a tiny crescent of beach.

A landing party had been detailed soon after leaving Portsmouth, and below the quarterdeck, their faces pale in a shaded lantern, the selected men had listened to Bolitho's instructions.

'I am putting you ashore here in the two cutters. You will be in two parties. Mr. Vibart and Mr. Maynard with one, and Mr. Farquhar with the second.' He had sought out the severe face of Brock, the gunner. 'Mr. Brock will also accompany the second party.' Farquhar might be too eager if left alone, he thought. Brock's experience and self-contained efficiency would make a nice balance.

'If I know Falmouth, as soon as the ship appears in the Bay at first light the sort of men we are after will make their way along the coast road as fast as they can go. If your parties keep up a steady march along that road as soon as you leave Pendower Beach, they should run right into your arms. It saves selection, I believe.' He had seen Brock nod his narrow head approvingly. 'The boats will return to the ship and you can march straight on to Falmouth.' A few of the men sighed, and he had added calmly, 'It is only five miles. It is better than tramping around the town for nothing.'

With Herrick at his side he walked briskly up the sloping road towards the neat houses, his shoes slipping on the well-remembered cobbles. By now Vibart must have made some catches, he thought. If not, if he had made his first misjudgement, it would only help to add to the tension in the *Phalarope*.

Lieutenant Okes was still aboard in charge of the ship until his return, and Captain Rennie's marines would be able to deter anyone who still hoped to desert. Even a desperate man would find it hard to swim the long stretch of tossing water from the anchored frigate.

He glanced sideways at Herrick and said abruptly, 'You have been aboard for two years, I believe?' He watched the guard drop behind the lieutenant's eyes. He had an open, homely face, yet there was this reserve, this caution, which seemed to symbolise for Bolitho the attitude of the whole ship. It was as if they were all cowed to a point where they neither trusted nor hoped. He added, 'According to the log you were officer of the watch when the trouble started?'

Herrick bit his lip. 'Yes, sir. We were beating up from Lorient. It was during the middle watch and quiet for the time of year.'

Bolitho watched the uncertainty crossing the man's face and felt a touch of pity. It was never easy to be the junior lieutenant in a ship of war. Promotion was slow and hard without either luck or influence. He thought of his own first chance, how easily it might have gone against him. One piece of luck had followed hard upon another. As a lieutenant in a ship of the line, at the very time of the American rebellion, he had been sent away in charge of a prize crew in a captured brig. While heading towards Antigua he had fallen upon a privateer and had fooled her captain into believing that his brig was still an ally. A rush of boarders, a swift and savage clash of steel, and the second ship had been his. Upon arrival at Antigua he had been welcomed by the Commander-in-Chief like a hero. Victories had been scarce, and reverses only too many.

So at the age of twenty-four he had been given command of the *Sparrow*. Again luck had guided his footsteps. The sloop's original commander had died of fever, and her first lieutenant was too junior for the coveted post.

He forced the sympathy to the back of his mind. 'How many men were in the mutiny?'

Herrick replied bitterly, 'No more than ten. They were trying to release a seaman called Fisher. Captain Pomfret had had him flogged for insubordination the previous day. He had been complaining about the foul food.'

Bolitho nodded. 'That is not uncommon.'

'But Captain Pomfret was not satisfied!' The words burst from his lips in an angry flood. 'He had him lashed to the bowsprit, without allowing the surgeon even to treat his back!' He shuddered. 'In the Bay of Biscay, with frost on the rigging, and he left him lashed there like so much meat!' He controlled himself with an effort and muttered, 'I am sorry, sir. I keep thinking about it.'

Bolitho thought back to Pomfret's neat, matter-of-fact recording in the log. The protesting seaman had rushed the quarterdeck and overpowered the quartermaster and master's mate at pistol point. Only Herrick, a man who obviously agreed with everything the seamen had offered as a grievance, stood between them and a full-scale mutiny. Somehow or other he had cowed them with words. He had ordered them back to the forecastle and they had obeyed because they trusted him, The next day Pomfret's vengeance had broken over the ship in a wave of ferocity. Twenty floggings, and two men hanged. He would not wait until the *Phalarope* rejoined the fleet, nor would he wait for higher authority to gauge his actions. Herrick's bitterness was well founded, or was it? On the face of it, Pomfret was within his rights. Perhaps Herrick should have shot down the mutineers, or even have foreseen the coming danger. He could have summoned the afterguard, given his life if necessary. Bolitho chilled at the thought of what might have happened if Herrick too had been overcome while he tried to reason with the desperate seamen. The sleeping officers would have been slaughtered, the ship thrown into chaos in enemy waters. It did not bear thinking about.

He persisted, 'And then later, when you rejoined the fleet off Brest and came to action with those French ships. Why was the *Phalarope* not engaged?' Again he saw the wretched emotions, the uncertainty and anger.

Then it dawned on him. Herrick feared him almost as much as Pomfret. He was captain. He had taken over the ship where Herrick's own misery and shame moved like a ghost between decks. Gently he added, 'I take it that the crew were making their own protest?'

Herrick sunk his chin into his neckcloth. 'Yes, sir. There was nothing you could put a name to. Sails were badly set. Gun crews slow in responding.' He laughed sharply. 'But it was wasted. Quite wasted!' He looked sideways at Bolitho, a brief spark of defiance in his eyes. 'Pomfret usually avoided action if possible!'

Bolitho looked away. You fool, he thought angrily. You have allowed this man to act as a conspirator. You should silence him now, before everyone aboard knows you have accepted an open criticism of Pomfret, a selected captain, without a murmur.

He said slowly, 'When you have a command of your own, Herrick, you may feel otherwise. The right course of action is not usually the easiest.' He thought of Vibart's hostility and wondered what *he* had been doing during the mutiny. 'I know that every officer must *earn* his men's loyalty.' He hardened his tone. 'But a captain has the loyalty of his officers as a right, do I make myself clear?'

Herrick looked straight ahead along the street. 'Aye, aye, sir!' The guard was restored. His expression wooden and controlled.

Bolitho halted below the church wall and looked up the familiar street which ran beside the churchyard. At the top of the road was the house, its square, uncompromising shape, the familiar grey stonework as enduring as his memory of it.

He stood looking up at it, suddenly apprehensive, like an intruder. He said, 'Carry on, Mr. Herrick. Go and see the garrison victualling officer and arrange to have as many fresh eggs and butter sent over to the ship as you can manage.'

Herrick was looking past him towards the big house, his eyes suddenly wistful. 'Your home, sir?'

'Yes.' Bolitho began to see Herrick in a different light again. Away from the order and discipline of the frigate and framed by the rain-washed building behind him he looked vaguely defenceless. Bolitho knew from his own methodical study of the ship's papers that Herrick came of a poor, middle-class Kentish family, his father being a clerk. For that reason he would be without influence when he most needed it, and unless he was very fortunate in battle his chances of advancement were slight.

The sight of his home, the confusion of judgement and ideas angered him, and he said sharply, 'After you have dealt with the Army perhaps you would care to join me for a glass of wine before we sail, Mr. Herrick?' He gestured up the road. 'My father will welcome you.'

Herrick opened his mouth, an unspoken refusal caught in mid-air. He tugged at his cross-belt and said awkwardly, 'Thank you, sir.' He touched his hat as Bolitho turned away towards the house.

Herrick stood quite still, the wind tugging at his boat-cloak, until Bolitho reached the gates. Then, chin sunk on chest, he walked slowly towards the castle, his brow creased in a deep frown.

Lieutenant Giles Vibart cursed as his feet skidded on loose stones and a seaman cannoned into his back. The grey morning light showed the extent of the previous night's wind, and the long grass and gorse was flattened and glittering with rain. He pulled his watch from inside his coat and then held up his hand.

'We'll stop here for a bit!' He saw his order passing down the small party of men, and waited until they had squatted beside the crude track before he crossed to the two midshipmen and the gunner.

'We'll give these idlers ten minutes and then move off again.' He looked round as a shaft of frail sunlight touched his cheek. 'Then you can take a party further inland, Mr. Farquhar, in case of stragglers.'

Farquhar shrugged and kicked at a pebble. 'Suppose nobody comes, sir?'

Vibart snapped, 'Just do as you're told!'

Maynard, the other midshipman, readjusted his dirk and looked anxiously towards the resting seamen. 'I hope none of 'em try and desert. The captain would be very displeased!'

The gunner gave a lazy grin. 'I picked them myself. They're all old hands.' He picked up a piece of grass and pulled it between his uneven teeth. 'All pressed men, too. Much better than volunteers for this job!'

Vibart nodded. 'Quite right, Mr. Brock. There's nothing better to give an edge to the press. No sailor likes to think others are getting away with it!'

Brock frowned. 'An' why should they? It's not right that the fleet is expected to fight bloody battles and keep the country free of the Frogs without help from these lazy, pampered civilians! They make money and live happily with their wives while we do all the hard work!' He spat out the grass. 'To hell with 'em, I say!'

Vibart walked away from them and stared down at the rocky beach below the cliff What did it matter what anybody said? They needed men, and the sooner the better.

He watched the wind hissing through the tangled grass and thought again of the frigate's dash through the night. How unlike Pomfret, he thought. He had always liked and expected a smart ship. But to him it had been more like a possession than a weapon of war. He lorded it in his fine cabin, enjoying his choice wines and well-stocked food store while he, Vibart, ran the ship and did all the things of which he was totally incapable. He moved restlessly on his thick legs as the old fire of resentment and injustice explored his mind like a drug.

Pomfret had been full of promises. A word in the right quarter and his first lieutenant would receive recognition and promotion when the time was right. All Vibart had to do was take care of the ship and her discipline and he would do the rest.

The captain had no interest in prize money. He was rich beyond Vibart's imagination. He was equally indifferent to glory. He was inefficient as he was cowardly.

Vibart would have been able to manage Pomfret's indulgences but for the captain's real weakness. Like many cowards he was a bully and a sadist. To Vibart harsh discipline was a necessity, but senseless cruelty seemed to be pointless. It weakened or maimed men who would be better employed on duty, it damaged the blind trust of men required to obey without question.

But Vibart was only a lieutenant, and was thirty-three years old. Unlike most of the other officers he had not entered the Navy as a boy, but had come the hard way, having served in merchant vessels the length and breadth of the world. His last three years at sea, prior to entering the Navy as a master's mate, had been aboard an African slaver where he had soon learned that senseless brutality had meant loss of profit at the end of a voyage, with stinking holds as full of useless carcasses as prime, saleable bodies.

He turned angrily and shouted, 'Right! We'll move off now!' He watched with brooding eyes as the men picked up their weapons and shambled down the track, while that arrogant young monkey Farquhar strode up the hillside to head inland. He was typical, Vibart thought viciously. Eighteen years old, pampered and well bred, with a powerful admiral to watch over his progress like a nurse. He glared at the lanky Maynard: 'Don't stand there gaping. Go ahead of the party!'

Well, in spite of their advantages of breeding and influence he, Giles Vibart, had shown them. He allowed the knowledge to stir his insides like rum. He had realised that Pomfret's weakness could not be changed, just as he had soon understood that to oppose him would have finished any hope he might have had left for personal reward. He had managed to overcome his own objections.

After all, did it really matter that men were unjustly flogged? They might be flogged later for a real cause, so where was the difference?

He had had one ally aboard the unhappy frigate. David Evans, the purser, had kept him fully informed of what was going on between decks. Evans was an evil man even by the standards of his trade. Whenever his ship touched land he would be ashore negotiating for stores and food, using his keen brain and ready tongue to purchase the very worst, the most rancid stock available, and adjusting the price to his own pocket. Vibart, as first lieutenant, was well aware of this trick, but used his knowledge to his own advantage. Evans had useful toadies on the lower deck, reliable men who would inform readily on their messmates for small reward.

Carefully and methodically Vibart had put ruthless pressure on the crew. But floggings were all in the captain's name, never in his own. He was always careful to show off his own seamanship and prowess at navigation whenever Pomfret was not there to see it. Whatever happened when the pressure broke through the men's resistance, Vibart had to be sure that he was ready and blameless at any enquiry.

Evans had told him about the proposed mutiny, and Vibart had known that the moment had at last arrived. When he had suggested to Pomfret that the flogged seaman, Fisher, should be lashed to the bowsprit like some flayed figurehead, he had known that it was the last thing needed to fan alive the flame of anger and mutiny.

The ringleaders had chosen their time well, he conceded. If Okes had been officer-of-the-watch he might have panicked and raised an almighty row which even Pomfret, half sodden with drink in his bunk, would have heard. But Herrick was a different matter. He was a thinker. He would be bound to reason with the men, to prevent an uprising rather than to crush it by brute force.

33

Knowing all these things, even to the chosen time, Vibart had waited breathlessly in his cabin. Squeezed in the wardroom had been the ship's full complement of marines, their sergeant another of Vibart's willing helpers. It was such a straightforward plan that Vibart had wanted to laugh at its simplicity.

The mutineers would rush the quarterdeck and overpower the watch. Herrick, rather than raise the alarm and drive Pomfret to another bloody frenzy, would try to quieten them, to listen to their complaints. But the men would kill him, and then Vibart would rush on deck and blanket the quarterdeck with musket fire.

At the court of enquiry even the most biased admiral would not fail to see that Vibart had saved the ship, when one officer lay dead with his watch and the captain slept in a drunken stupor.

Even now on the wet hillside Vibart could remember the sound of his own breathing in that sealed cabin. Then the stealthy approach of the mutineers even as two bells pealed out from forward. But there were no shots, and no cries. No rasp of steel, or the sound of Herrick's last gasp for life.

When at last, unable to control his anxiety, he had crept on deck he had found Herrick at his post, the maindeck deserted.

The young lieutenant had reported the incident as a 'deputation' concerned with the welfare of the dying Fisher. That was all. When Vibart had pushed him further, Herrick had still stood his ground, his anger giving way to contempt as his eyes had fallen on Vibart's loaded pistols and the marine sergeant at the cabin hatch.

The next morning Pomfret had been almost as beside himself as if an actual mutiny had broken out. 'Complaints?' He had screamed at Vibart across the wide cabin. 'They *dare* to complain?' Even without much prompting he had seen the men's actions as a real challenge to his own authority.

When at last the frigate had been ordered to Portsmouth to face an enquiry, Vibart had known fresh hope. Things had moved fast, The ship had been stripped of known troublemakers and had been fitted out for another long spell of service. Pomfret had stayed in his cabin, sulky and brooding up to the time he was ordered from the ship. But no new commission had arrived for Vibart. No command of either the *Phalarope* or any other ship.

He was back exactly as he had been when he had first joined the frigate under Pomfret, except that the new captain, Bolitho, was another kind of person entirely.

He jerked from his thoughts as Maynard called breathlessly, 'Sir! One of the men is signalling from the hillside!'

Vibart drew his sword and slashed sharply at a small bush. 'So the captain guessed right, did he?' He waved his arm in a half circle. 'Right, you men! Get to either side of the road and wait for Mr. Farquhar's party to work round behind them. I don't want anyone to escape!' He saw the men nod and shuffle to the bushes, swinging their clubs and readjusting their cutlass belts.

When the moment of contact actually came, even Vibart was taken off guard.

It was more like a carefree procession than a party of men avoiding the press gangs. Some fifty or more men tightly bunched on the narrow track, talking, some even singing as they strolled aimlessly away from Falmouth and the sea.

Vibart saw Farquhar's slim silhouette break the skyline and stepped out from the bushes. His appearance could not have affected them more deeply had he been something from another world. He held up his sword as his men stepped out across the road behind him.

'In the King's name! I charge you all to line up and be examined!' His voice broke the spell. Some of the men turned and tried to run back along the road, only to halt gasping at the sight of Farquhar's men and the levelled muskets. One figure bolted up the hillside, his feet kicking the grass like some terrified rabbit.

Josling, a bosun's mate, lashed out with his cudgel. The man screamed and rolled down the slope and lay in a puddle clutching his shin. Josling turned him over with his foot and felt the man's bleeding leg. Then he looked at Vibart and said offhandedly, 'No eggs broken, sir!'

Shocked and dazed the men allowed themselves to be pushed into line on the road. Vibart stood watching and calculating. It had been so easy that he wanted to grin.

Brock said, 'Fifty-two men, sir. All sound in wind and limb!'

One of the uneven rank dropped on to his knees and whimpered, 'Please, *please*, sir! Not me!'

There were tears on his cheeks, and Vibart asked harshly, 'What is so special about you?'

'My wife, sir! She's *ill*! She needs me at home!' He rocked on his knees. 'She'll die without my support, sir, in God's name she will!'

Vibart said wearily, 'Stand that man on his feet. He makes me sick!'

Another at the end of the rank said in a tight voice, 'I am a shepherd, I'm excused from the press!' He stared round challengingly until his eye fell on Brock. 'Ask him, sir. The gunner will bear me out!'

Brock sauntered across to him and held up his cane. 'Roll up your sleeve.' He sounded bored, even indifferent, and several of the watching men forgot their shocked misery to lean from the rank and watch.

The man in question took a half-pace away, but not quickly enough. Like a steel claw Brock's hand fastened on his rough shirt and tore it from his arm to display an interwoven tattoo of crossed flags and cannon.

Brock stepped back and swayed on his heels. He looked along the rank. 'No man has a tattoo like that unless he is

36

a seaman.' His voice was slow and patient, like a schoolmaster with a new class. 'No man would recognise me as a gunner unless he had served in a King's ship!'

Without warning his cane flashed in the weak sunlight. When it returned to his side the other man had blood on his face where it had cut almost to the bone.

The gunner looked at him levelly. 'Most of all, I dislike being taken for a fool!' He turned his back, dismissing the man from his mind.

A seaman yelled, 'Another signal, sir! One more group comin' down the road!'

Vibart sheathed his sword. 'Very well.' He looked coldly at the shivering line of men. 'You are entering an honourable service, You have just learned the first lesson. Don't make me teach you another!'

Maynard fell into step beside him his face troubled. 'It seems a pity that there is no other way, sir?'

Vibart did not reply. Like the man who had begged for his wife, such statements lacked both purpose and meaning.

Only aboard the ship did anything count for any of them.

Bolitho sipped at his port and waited until the servant girl had cleared away the table. His stomach had long grown used to meagre and poorly cooked shipboard food, so that the excellent meal of good Cornish lamb left him feeling glutted and uncomfortable.

Across the table his father, James Bolitho, drummed impatiently on the polished wood with his one remaining hand and then took a long swallow of port. He seemed ill at ease, even nervous, as he had been from the moment of his son's arrival.

Bolitho watched him quietly and waited. There was such a change in his father. From his own boyhood days to the present time Bolitho had seen his father only on rarely spaced occasions when he had returned here to the family home. From foreign wars and far-off countries, from exploits which children could only guess at. He could remember him as tall and grave in his naval uniform, shedding his service self-discipline like a cloak as he had come through that familiar doorway beside the portraits of the Bolitho family. Men like himself, like his son, sailors first and foremost.

When Bolitho had been a midshipman under Sir Henry Langford he had learned of his father's wounds whilst he had been engaged in fighting for the fast-advancing colonies in India, and when he had seen him again he had found him suddenly old and embittered. He had been a man of boundless energy and ideas, and to be removed from the Navy List, no matter how honourably, was more than the loss of an arm, it was like having his life cut from within him.

Locally in Falmouth he was respected as a firm and just magistrate, but Bolitho knew in his heart that his father's very being still lay with the sea, and the ships which came and went on the tide. Even his old friends and comrades had stopped coming to visit him, perhaps unable to bear what their very presence represented. Interest changed so easily into envy. Contact could harm rather than soothe.

Bolitho had a brother and two sisters. The latter had now both married, one to a farmer, the other to an officer of the garrison. Of Hugh, his older brother, nothing had yet been said, and Bolitho made himself wait for what he guessed was uppermost in his father's mind.

'I watched your ship come in, Richard.' The hand drummed busily on the table. 'She's a fine vessel, and when you get to the West Indies again I have no doubt you will bring more honour to the family.' He shook his head sadly. 'England needs all her sons now. It seems as if the world must be our enemy before we can find the right solution.'

It was very quiet in the house. After the pitch of a deck, the creak of spars, it was like another world. Even the smells were different. The packed humanity, and the varied aromas of tar and salt, of cooking and damp, all were alien here.

It felt lonely, too. In his mind's eye he could still picture his mother, young and vivacious as he remembered her. Again, he had been at sea when she had died of some brief but final illness. Now there was no companion for James Bolitho, and nobody to sit enraptured or amused by stories of the family's past exploits.

Bolitho glanced at the great clock. 'My men will have found new people for the crew by now or not at all,' he said quietly. 'It is a sad necessity that we have to get seamen like this.'

His father's face came alive from his inner thoughts. 'I believe that their duty is more important than their passing comfort! Every week I have to sign deportation orders for the colonies, or hang useless thieves. Life in a King's ship would have spared them the indignity of life ashore, would have saved them from petty greed and temptation!'

Bolitho studied his father's face and remembered himself as he had appeared in the mirror of the George Inn at Portsmouth. It was there in his father, as it was in the portraits along the walls. The same calm face and dark hair, the same slightly hooked nose. But his father had lost his old fire, and his hair was grey now, like that of a man much older.

His father stood up and walked to the fire. Over his shoulder he said gruffly, 'You have not yet heard about your brother?'

Bolitho tensed. 'No. I thought he was still at sea.'

'At sea?' The older man shook his head vaguely, 'Of course, I kept it from you. I suppose I should have written to you, but in my heart I still hoped he might change his ways and nobody would have known about it.'

Bolitho waited. His brother had always been the apple of his father's eye. When last he had seen him he had been a lieutenant in the Channel Fleet, the next in line for this house and for the family inheritance. Bolitho had never felt particularly close to Hugh, but put it down to a natural family jealousy. Now, he was not so sure.

'I had great hopes for Hugh.' His father was talking to the fire. To himself. 'I am only glad his mother is not alive to know of what he became!'

'Is there something I can do?' Bolitho watched the shoulders quiver as his father sought to control his voice.

'Nothing. Hugh is no longer in the Navy. He got into debt gambling. He always had an eye for the tables, as I think you know. But he got into *deep* trouble, and to end it all he fought a duel with a brother officer, and killed him!'

Bolitho's mind began to clear. That explained the few servants, and the fact that over half the land belonging to the house had been sold to a local farmer.

'You covered his debts then?' He kept his voice calm. 'I have some prize money if . . .'

The other man held up his hand. 'That is not necessary. It was my fault for being so blind. I was stupid about that boy. I must pay for my misjudgement!' He seemed to become more weary. 'He deserted the Navy, turned his back on it, even knowing how his act would hurt me. Now he has gone.'

Bolitho started. 'Gone?'

'He went to America. I have not heard of him for two years, nor do I want to.' When he turned Bolitho saw the lie shining in his eyes. 'Not content with bringing disgrace on the family name, he has done this thing. Betrayed his country!'

Bolitho thought of the chaos and death at the disaster of Philadelphia and answered slowly, 'He may have been prevented from returning by the rebellion.'

'You know your brother, Richard. Do you really think it likely? He always had to be right, to hold the winning cards. No, I cannot see him pining away in a prison camp!'

The servant girl entered the room and bobbed in a clumsy curtsy. 'Beggin' pardon, zur. There's an officer to zee you.'

'That'll be Herrick, my third lieutenant,' said Bolitho hurriedly. 'I asked him to take a glass with us. I'll tell him to go if you wish?'

His father stood up straight and flicked his coat into position again. 'No, boy. Have him come in. I will not let my shame interfere with the real pride I have in my *remaining* son.'

Bolitho said gently, 'I am very sorry, Father. You must know that.'

'Thank you. Yes, I do know. And you were the one I thought would never make your way in the Navy. You were always the dreamer, the unpredictable one. I am afraid I neglected you for Hugh.' He sighed. 'Now it is too late.' There was a step in the hallway and he said with sudden urgency, 'In case I never see you again, my boy, there is something you must have.' He swallowed. 'I wanted Hugh to have it when he became a captain.' He reached into a cupboard and held out his sword. It was old and well tarnished, but Bolitho knew it was of greater value than steel and gilt.

He hesitated. 'Your father's sword. You always wore it!'

James Bolitho nodded and turned it over carefully in his hands. 'Yes, I always wore it. It was a good friend.' He held it out. 'Take it! I *want* you to wear it for me!'

His father suddenly smiled. 'Well then, let us greet your junior officer together, eh?'

When Herrick walked uncertainly into the wide room he saw only his smiling host and his new captain, one the living mould of the other.

41

Only Bolitho saw the pain in his father's eyes and was deeply moved.

It was strange how he had come to the house, as he had always done in the past, seeking comfort and advice. Yet he had mentioned nothing about the difficulties and danger of his new command, or the double-edged responsibility which hung over his head like an axe.

For once, he had been the one who was needed, and he was ashamed because he did not know the answer.

At dawn the following day the frigate *Phalarope* unfurled her sails and broke out her anchor. There were no cheers to speed her parting, but there were many tears and curses from the women and old men who watched from the jetties.

The air was keen and fresh, and as the yards creaked round and the ship heeled away from the land Bolitho stood aft by the taff rail, his glass moving slowly across the green sloping hills and the huddled town below.

He had his ship, and all but a full complement. With time the new men would soon be moulded into sailors, and given patience and understanding they might make their country proud of them.

St. Anthony's Light moved astern, the ancient beacon which was the returning sailor's first sight of home. Bolitho wondered when or if he would see it again. He thought too of his father, alone in the old house, alone with his memories and shattered hopes. He thought of the sword and all that it represented.

He turned away from the rail and stared down at one of the ship's boys, a mere infant of about twelve years old. The boy was weeping uncontrollably and waving vaguely at the land as it cruised away into the haze. Bolitho asked, 'Do you know that I was your age when I first went to sea, boy?'

The lad rubbed his nose with a grubby fist and gazed at

the captain with something like wonder.

Bolitho added, 'You'll see England again. Never you fear!' He turned away quickly lest the boy should see the uncertainty in his eye.

By the wheel old Proby intoned, 'South-west by south. Full and by, quartermaster.'

Then, as if to cut short the agony of sailing, he walked to the lee rail and spat into the sea.

3

Beef for the Purser

Twenty days after weighing anchor the frigate *Phalarope* crossed the thirtieth parallel and heeled sickeningly to a blustering north-west gale. Falmouth lay three thousand miles astern, but the wind with all its tricks and cunning cruelties stayed resolutely with the ship.

As one bell struck briefly from the forecastle and the dull copper sun moved towards the horizon the frigate ploughed across each successive bank of white-crested rollers with neither care nor concern for the men who served her day by day, hour by hour. No sooner was one watch dismissed below than the boatswain's mates would run from hatch to hatch, their calls twittering, their voices hoarse in the thunder of canvas and the never ending hiss of spray.

'All hands! All hands! Shorten sail!'

Later, stiff and dazed from their dizzy climb aloft, the seamen would creep below, their bodies aching, their fingers stiff and bleeding from their fight with the rebellious canvas.

Now, the men off watch crouched in the semi-darkness of the berth deck groping for handholds and listening to the crash of water against the hull even as they tried to finish their evening meal. From the deck beams the swinging lanterns threw strange shadows across their bowed heads, picking out individual faces and actions like scenes from a partially cleaned oil painting.

Below the sealed hatches the air was thick with smells. That of bilge water mixing with sweat and the sour odour of seasickness, and the whole area was filled with sound as the ship fought her own battle with the Atlantic. The steady crash of waves followed by the jubilant surge of water along the deck above, the continuous groaning of timbers and the humming of taut stays, all defied the men to sleep and relax even for a moment.

John Allday sat astride one of the long, scrubbed benches and gnawed carefully at a tough piece of salt beef. Between his strong teeth it felt like leather, but he made himself eat it, and closed his mind to the rancid cask from which it had come. The deep cut on his cheek where Brock's cane had found its mark had healed in an ugly scar, and as his jaws moved steadily on the meat he could feel the skin tightening painfully where blown salt and cold winds had drawn the edges together like crude stitching.

Across the table, and watching him with an unwinking stare, sat Pochin, a giant seaman with shoulders like a cliff. He said at last, 'You've settled in right enough, mate.' He smiled bleakly. 'All that squit when you was pressed came to nothin'!'

Allday threw a meat bone on to his tin plate and wiped his fingers on a piece of hemp. He regarded the other man with his steady, calm eyes for several seconds and then replied, 'I can wait.'

Pochin glared through the gloom, his head cocked to listen to some of the men retching. 'Lot of bloody women!' He looked back at Allday. 'I was forgettin', you are an old hand at this.'

Allday shrugged and looked down at his palms. 'You never get rid of the tar, do you?' He leaned back against the timbers and sighed. 'My last ship was the *Resolution*, seventy-four. I was a foretopman.' He allowed his eyes to

45

close. 'A good enough ship. We paid off just a few months before the American Revolution, and I was clean away before the press could lay a finger on me!'

An old, grey-haired man with washed-out blue eyes said huskily, 'Was you really a shepherd like you told 'em?'

Allday nodded. 'That, and other things. I had to stay out in the open. To keep away from the towns. I would choke to death under a roof!' He gave a small smile. 'Just an occasional run into Falmouth was enough for me. Just enough for a woman, and a glass or two!'

The old seaman, Strachan, pursed his lips and rocked against the table as the ship heeled steeply and sent the plates skittering across the deck. 'It sounds like a fair life, mate.' He seemed neither wistful nor envious. It was just a statement. Old Ben Strachan had been in the Navy for forty years, since he had first trod deck as a powder-monkey. Life ashore was a mystery to him, and in his regimented world appeared even more dangerous than the privations afloat.

Allday looked round as a hunched figure rose over the table's edge and threw himself across his arms amongst the litter of food. Bryan Ferguson had been in a continuous torment of seasickness and fear from the very moment Vibart's figure had appeared on that coast road. In Falmouth he had been a clerk working at a local boatyard. Physically he was not a strong man, and now in the swinging lantern's feeble light his face looked as grey as death itself.

His thin body was bruised in many places, both from falling against unfamiliar shipboard objects and not least from the angry canes of the bosun's mates and petty officers as the latter sought to drive the new men into the mysteries of seamanship and sail drill.

Day after day it had continued. Harried and chased from one part of the ship to the next with neither let-up nor mercy. Quivering with terror Ferguson had dragged his way up the swooping shrouds and out along the yards, until he could see the creaming water leaping below him as if to claw at his very feet. The first time he had clung sobbing to the mast, incapable of either moving out along the yard or even down towards the safety of the deck.

Josling, a bosun's mate, had screamed up at him, 'Move out, you bugger, or I'll have the hide off you!'

At that particular moment Ferguson's tortured mind had almost broken. With each eager thrust of the frigate's stem, and with every passing hour, Ferguson's home fell further and further astern. And with it went his wife, sinking into the wave-tossed distance like a memory.

Over and over again he had pictured her pale, anxious face as he had last seen her. When the *Phalarope* had been sighted heading for Falmouth Bay most of the young townsmen had headed for the hills. Ferguson's wife had been ill for three years, and he had seen her get more frail and delicate, and on that day she had been more than unwell and he had begged to stay with her. But gravely she had insisted.

'You go with the others, Bryan. I'll be all right. And I'm not wanting the press to find you here!'

The nightmare became worse when he considered that if he had stayed with her he would still be safe and able to protect and help her.

Allday said quietly, 'Here, take some food.' He pushed a plate of dark meat across the boards. 'You've not eaten for days, man.'

Ferguson dragged his head from his forearms and stared glassily at the relaxed looking seaman. Unbeknown to Allday, Ferguson had almost jumped from the swaying mainyard rather than face another hour of torture. But Allday had run inboard along the yard, his feet splayed and balanced, one hand held out towards the gasping Ferguson. 'Here, mate! Just follow me an' don't look down.' There had been a quiet force in his tone, like that of a man who expected to be obeyed. He had added harshly, 'Don't give that bugger Josling a chance to beat you. The bastard enjoys making you jump!'

He stared now at the man's dark features, at the scar on his cheek, and at his calm, level eyes. Allday had been accepted immediately by the frigate's seamen, whereas the other newly pressed men were still kept at arm's length, as if on trial, until their merits or shortcomings could be properly measured. Perhaps it was because Allday was already hardened to a life at sea. Or maybe it came from the fact he never showed his bitterness at being pressed, or boasted about his life ashore like some of the others.

Ferguson swallowed hard to bite back the rising nausea. 'I can't eat it!' He peered wretchedly at the meat. 'It's swill!'

Allday grinned. 'You'll get used to it!'

Pochin sneered. 'You make me spew! I suppose you used to take your wife up to the 'eadland and go moist-eyed at the sight of a King's ship! I'll bet you used to feel so holy, so almighty proud as the ships sailed safely past!'

Ferguson stared at the man's angry face, mesmerised by his hate.

Pochin glared across the canting deck where the other crowded seamen had fallen silent at his outburst. 'You never had a thought for the poor buggers who manned 'em, nor what they was doin'!' He turned back to Ferguson with sudden malice. 'Well, your precious woman'll be out on the 'eadland now with some other pretty boy, I shouldn't wonder.' He made an obscene gesture. 'Let's 'ope she finds the time to be proud of *you*!'

Ferguson staggered to his feet, his eyes wide with a kind of madness. 'I'll kill you for that!'

He swung his fist, but Allday caught his wrist in midair. 'Save it!' Allday glared at Pochin's grinning face. 'His wife is sick, Pochin! Give him some rest!'

48

Old Ben Strachan said vaguely, 'I 'ad a wife once.' He scratched his shaggy grey beard. 'Blessed if I can remember 'er name now!'

Some of the men laughed, and Allday hissed fiercely, 'Get a grip, Bryan! You can't beat men like Pochin. He envies you, that's all!'

Ferguson hardly heard the friendly warning in Allday's voice. Pochin's goading tone had opened the misery in his heart with renewed force, so that he could see his wife propped in her bed by the window as clearly as if he had just entered the room. That day, when the press gang had pushed him down the hillside, she would have been sitting there, waiting for his return. Now he was never going back. Would never see her again.

He staggered to his feet and threw the plate of meat down on the deck. 'I can't!' He was screaming. 'I *won't*!'

A horse-faced fo'c's'leman named Betts jumped to his feet as if shaken from a deep sleep. 'Don't jeer at 'im, mates!' He stood swaying below one of the lanterns. 'He's 'ad enough for a bit.'

Pochin groaned. 'Lord save us!' He rolled his eyes in mock concern.

Betts snarled, 'Jesus Christ! What do you have to suffer before you understand? This man is sick with fear for his wife, and others here have equal troubles. Yet all some of you can do is scoff at 'em!'

Allday shifted in his seat. Ferguson's sudden despair had touched some hidden spring in the men's emotions. Weeks, and in some cases years at sea without ever putting a foot on dry land were beginning to take a cruel toll. But this was dangerous and blind. He held up his hand and said calmly, 'Easy, lads. *Easy*.'

Betts glared down at him, his salt-reddened eyes only half focusing on Allday's face. 'How can you interfere?' His voice was slurred. 'We live like animals, on food that was rotten even afore it was put in casks!' He pulled his knife from his belt and drove it into the tables. 'While those pigs down aft live like kings!' He peered round for support. 'Well, ain't I right? That bastard Evans is as sleek as a churchyard rat on what he stole from *our* food!'

'Well, now. Did I hear my name mentioned?'

The berth deck froze into silence as Evans, the purser, moved into a patch of lamplight.

With his long coat buttoned to his throat and his hair pulled back severely above his narrow face he looked for all the world like a ferret on the attack. He put his head on one side. 'Well, I'm waiting!'

Allday watched him narrowly. There was something evil and frightening about the little Welsh purser. All the more so because any one of the men grouped around him could have ended his life with a single blow.

Then Evans' eye fell on the meat beside the table. He sucked his teeth and asked sadly, 'And who did this. then?'

No one spoke, and once more the angry roar of the sea and wind enclosed the staggering berth deck with noise.

Ferguson looked up, his eyes bright and feverish. 'I did it.'

Evans leaned his narrow shoulders against the massive trunk of the foremast which ran right through both decks and said,' "I did it, *sir*." '

Ferguson mumbled something and then added, 'I am sorry, sir.'

Allday said coldly, 'It was an accident, Mr. Evans. Just an accident.'

'Food is food.' Evans' Welsh accent became more pronounced as his face became angrier. 'I cannot hope to keep you men in good health if you waste such excellent meat, now can I?'

Those grouped around the table stared down at the shapeless hunk of rancid beef as it lay gleaming in a patch of lamplight.

Evans added sharply, 'Now, you, whatever your bloody name is, *eat it*!'

Ferguson stared down at the meat, his mind swimming in nausea. The deck was discoloured with water and stained with droppings from the tilting table. There was vomit too, perhaps his own.

Evans said gently, 'I am waiting, boyo. One more minute and I'll take you aft. A touch of the cat might teach you some appreciation!'

Ferguson dropped to his knees and picked up the meat. As he lifted it to his mouth Betts pushed forward and tore it from his hands and threw it straight at Evans. 'Take it yourself, you bloody devil! Leave him alone!'

For a moment Evans showed the fear in his dark eyes. The men had crowded around him, their bodies rising and falling like a human tide with each roll of the ship. He could feel the menace, the sudden ice touch of terror.

Another voice cut through the shadows. 'Stand aside!' Midshipman Farquhar had to stoop beneath the low beams, but his eyes were steady and bright as they settled on the frozen tableau around the end table. Farquhar's approach had been so stealthy and quiet that not even the men at the opposite end of the deck had noticed him. He snapped, 'I am waiting. What is going on here?'

Evans thrust the nearest men aside and threw himself to Farquhar's side. With his hand shaking in both fear and fury he pointed at Betts. 'He struck me! *Me*, a warrant officer!'

Farquhar was expressionless. His tight lips and cold stare might have meant either amusement or anger. 'Very well, Mr. Evans. Kindly lay aft for the master-at-arms.'

As the purser scurried away Farquhar looked round the circle of faces with open contempt. 'You never seem to learn, do you?' He turned to Betts, who still stood staring at the meat, his chest heaving as if from tremendous exertion. 'You are a fool, Betts! Now you will pay for it!'

Allday pressed his shoulders against the frigate's cold, wet timbers and closed his eyes. It was all happening just as he knew it would. He listened to Betts' uneven breathing and Ferguson's quiet whimpers and felt sick. He thought suddenly of the quiet hillsides and the grey bunches of sheep. The space and the solitude.

Then Farquhar barked, 'Take him away, Mr. Thain.'

The master-at-arms pushed Betts towards the hatch ladder adding softly, 'Not a single flogging since we left Falmouth. I knew such gentleness was a bad mistake!'

Richard Bolitho leaned his palms on the sill of one of the big stern windows and stared out along the ship's frothing wake. Although the cabin itself was already in semi-darkness as the frigate followed the sun towards the horizon, the sea still looked alive, with only a hint of purple as a warning of the approaching night.

Reflected in the salt-speckled glass he could see Vibart's tall shape in the centre of the cabin, his face shadowed beneath the corkscrewing lantern, and behind him against the screen the slim figure of Midshipman Farquhar.

It took most of his self-control to keep himself immobile and calm as he considered what Farquhar had burst in to tell him. Bolitho had been going through the ship's books again trying to draw out Vibart's wooden reserve, to feel his way into the man's mind.

Like everything else during the past twenty days, it had been a hard and seemingly fruitless task. Vibart was too careful to show his hostility in the open and confined himself to short, empty answers, as if he hoarded his knowledge of the ship and her company like a personal possession.

Then Farquhar had entered the cabin with this story of Betts' assault on the purser. It was just one more thing to distract his thoughts from what lay head, from the real task of working the frigate into a single fighting unit.

He made himself turn and face the two officers.

'Sentry! Pass the word for Mr. Evans!' He heard the cry passed along the passageway and then added, 'It seems to me as if this seaman was provoked.'

Vibart swayed with the ship, his eyes fixed on a point above the captain's shoulder. He said quickly, 'Betts is no recruit, sir. He knew what he was doing!'

Bolitho turned to watch the open, empty sea. If only this had not happened just yet, he thought bitterly. A few more days and the damp, wind-buffeted ship would be in the sun, where men soon learned to forget their surroundings and started to look outboard instead of watching each other.

He listened to the hiss and gurgle of water around the rudder, the distant clank of pumps as the duty watch dealt with the inevitable seepage into the bilges. He felt tired and strained to the limit. From the moment the *Phalarope* had weighed anchor he had not spared himself or his efforts to maintain his hold over the ship. He had made a point of speaking to most of the new men, and of establishing contact with the regular crew. He had watched his officers, and had driven the ship to her utmost. It should have been a proud moment for him. The frigate handled well, lively and ready to respond to helm and sail like a thoroughbred.

Most of the new men had been sorted into their most suitable stations, and the sail drill had advanced beyond even his expectations. At the first suitable moment he intended to exercise the guns' crews, but up to this time he had been prevented from much more than allocations of hands to the various divisions by the unceasing wind.

Now this, he fumed inwardly. No wonder the admiral had asked him to watch young Farquhar's behaviour.

There was a tap at the door and Evans stepped gingerly into the cabin, his eyes flickering like beads in the lamplight.

Bolitho gestured impatiently. 'Now then, Mr. Evans. Let me have the full story.'

He turned to stare at the water again as Evans launched into his account. To start with he seemed nervous, even frightened, but when Bolitho allowed him to continue without interruption or comment his voice grew sharper and more outraged.

Bolitho said at length, 'The meat that Betts threw at you. What cask did it come from?'

Evans was caught off guard. 'Number twelve, sir. I saw it stowed myself.' He added in a wheedling tone, 'I do my best, sir. They are ungrateful dogs for the most part!'

Bolitho turned and tapped the papers on his table. 'I checked the stowage myself, too, Mr. Evans. Two days ago when the hands were at drill!' He saw a flicker of alarm show itself on Evans' dark face and knew that his lie had gone home. A feeling of sudden anger swept through him like fire. All the things he had told his officers had been for nothing. Even the near-mutiny seemed to have made no impression on the minds of men like Evans and Farquhar.

He snapped, 'That cask was in the low stowage, was it not? And how many others were down there, do you think?'

Evans peered nervously around the cabin. 'Five or six, sir. They were some of the original stores which I . . .'

Bolitho slammed his fist on the table. 'You make me sick, Evans! That cask and those others you have suddenly remembered were probably stowed two years ago before you began the Brest blockade! They most likely leak, and in any case are quite rotten!'

Evans looked at his feet. 'I—I did not know, sir.'

Bolitho said harshiy, 'If I could prove otherwise, Mr. Evans, I would have you stripped of your rank and flogged!'

Vibart stirred into life. 'I must protest, sir! Mr. Evans

was acting as he thought fit! Betts struck him. There is no way of avoiding that fact.'

'So it appears, Mr. Vibart.' Bolitho stared at him coldly until the other man looked away. 'I will certainly back my officers in their efforts to carry out my orders. But senseless punishment at this time will do more harm than good.' He felt suddenly too tired to think clearly, but Vibart's anger seemed to drive him on. 'In another two weeks or so we will join the fleet under Sir Samuel Hood, and then there will be more than enough to keep us all occupied.'

He continued more calmly, 'Until then, each and every one of you will translate my standing orders into daily fact. Give the men your leadership and try to understand them. No good will ever come of useless brutality. If a man still persists in disobedience, then flogged he will be. But in this particular case I would suggest a more lenient experiment.' He saw Vibart's lower lip quivering with barely controlled anger. 'Betts can be awarded extra duties for seven days. The sooner the matter is forgotten, the sooner we can mend the damage!' He gestured briefly, 'Carry on with your watch, Mr. Farquhar.'

As Evans turned to follow the midshipman Bolitho added flatly, 'Oh, Mr. Evans, I see no reason for me to mention your neglect in the log.' He saw Evans watching him half gratefully, half fearfully. He finished, 'Provided I can show that you purchased the meat for your own purposes, your own mess perhaps?'

Evans blinked at Vibart and then back to Bolitho's impassive face. 'Purchase, sir? Me, sir?'

'Yes. Evans, *you*! You can make the payment to my clerk in the forenoon tomorrow. That is all.'

Vibart picked up his hat and waited until the door had closed behind the other man. 'Do you require me any more, sir?'

'I just want to tell you one thing more, Mr. Vibart. I

have taken fully into consideration that you were under considerable strain during your duty with Captain Pomfret. Maybe some of the things you had to do were not to your liking.' He waited, but Vibart stared woodenly across his shoulder. 'I am not interested in the past, except as a lesson to everyone of what can happen in a badly run ship! As first lieutenant you are the key officer, the most experienced one aboard who can implement my orders, do you understand?'

'If you say so, sir.'

Bolitho dropped his eyes in case Vibart should see the rising anger there. He had offered Vibart his due share of responsibility, even his confidence, and yet the lieutenant seemed to accept it like a sign of weakness, of some faltering uncertainty. The contempt was as plain in his brevity as if he had shouted it to the ship at large.

It could not be easy for Vibart to take orders from a captain so junior in age and service. Bolitho tried once more to soften his feelings towards Vibart's hostility.

The latter said suddenly, 'When you have been aboard the *Phalarope* a little longer, sir, then maybe you will see it different.' He rocked back on his heels and watched Bolitho's face with a flat stare.

Bolitho relaxed his taut muscles. It was almost a relief that Vibart had shown him the only way to finish the matter. He eyed him coldly. 'I have read every log and report aboard this ship, Mr. Vibart. In all my limited *experience* I have never known a ship so apparently unwilling to fight the enemy or so incapable of performing her duty.' He watched the expression on Vibart's heavy features altering to shocked surprise. 'Well, we are going back to war, Mr. Vibart, and I intend to seek out and engage the enemy, *any* enemy, at every opportunity!' He dropped his voice. 'And when that happens I will expect to see every man acting as one. There will be no room for petty jealousy and cowardice then!'

56

A deep flush rose to Vibart's cheeks, but he remained silent.

Bolitho said. 'You are dealing with men, Mr. Vibart, not *things*! Authority is invested with your commission. Respect comes later, when you have earned it!'

He dismissed the first lieutenant with a curt nod and then turned back to stare at the creaming wake below the windows. As the door closed the tension tore at his body like a whip, and he gripped his hands together to prevent their shaking until the pain made him wince. He had made an enemy of Vibart, but there was too much at stake to do otherwise.

He slumped down on the bench seat as Stockdale pattered into the cabin and began to spread a cloth across the table.

The coxswain said, 'I've told your servant to bring your supper, Captain.' There was mistrust in his tone. He disliked Atwell, the cabin steward, and watched him like a dog with a rabbit. 'I don't suppose you'll be havin' any officer to dine with you, sir?'

Bolitho glanced at Stockdale, battered and homely like an old piece of furniture, and thought of Vibart's seething bitterness. 'No, Stockdale. I will be alone.'

He leaned back and closed his eyes. Alone and vulnerable, he thought.

Lieutenant Thomas Herrick tightened the spray-soaked muffler about his neck and shrugged his shoulders deeper into his watchcoat. Above the black, spiralling masts the stars were small and pale, and even in the keen air he could sense that the dawn was not far away.

The labouring ship herself was in darkness, so that the shapes around the deserted decks were unreal and totally unlike they appeared in daylight. The lashed guns were mere shadows, and the humming shrouds and stays seemed to go straight up to the sky, unattached and endless.

But as Herrick paced the quarterdeck deep in thought, he was able to ignore such things. He had seen them all too often before, and was able to pass each watch with only his mind for company. Once he paused beside the ship's big double wheel where the two helmsmen stood like dark statues, their faces partly lit in the shaded binnacle lamp as they watched the swinging compass or stared aloft at the trimmed sails.

Three bells struck tinnily from forward, and he saw a ship's boy stir at the rail and then creep, rubbing his eyes, to trim the compass lamp and adjust the hourglass.

Time and again he found his eyes drawn to the black rectangle of the cabin hatch, and he wondered whether Bolitho had at last fallen asleep. Three times already during the morning watch, three times in an hour and a half the captain had appeared momentarily on deck, soundless and without warning. With neither coat nor hat, and his white shirt and breeches framed against the tumbling black water, he had seemed ghostlike and without true form, with the restlessness of a tortured spirit. On each occasion he had paused only long enough to peer at the compass or to look at the watch-slate beside the wheel. Then a couple of turns up and down the weather side of the deck and he had vanished below.

At any other time Herrick would have felt both irritated and resentful. It might have implied that the captain was too unsure of his third lieutenant to leave him to take a watch alone. But when Herrick had relieved Lieutenant Okes at four o'clock Okes had whispered quickly that Bolitho had been on deck for most of the night.

Herrick frowned. Deep down he had the feeling that Bolitho had acted more by instinct than design. As if he was driven like the ship, by mood rather than inclination. He seemed unable to stand still, as if it took physical force to hold himself in one place for more than minutes at a time.

A figure moved darkly at the quarterdeck rail and he heard Midshipman Neale's familiar treble in the darkness.

'Able Seaman Betts has just reported, sir.' He stood staring up at Herrick, gauging his mood.

Herrick had to tear his thoughts back to the present with a jerk. Betts, the man who had apparently escaped a flogging or worse only at Bolitho's intervention, had been ordered to report at three bells for the first part of his punishment. Vibart had made it more than clear what would happen if he failed to execute the orders.

He saw Betts hovering behind the small midshipman and called, 'Here, Betts. Look lively!'

The man moved up to the rail and knuckled his forehead. 'Sir?'

Herrick gestured upwards towards the invisible topmast. 'Up you go then!' He kept the harshness from his tone. He liked Betts, a quiet but competent man, whose sudden flare of anger had surprised him more than he cared to admit. 'Get up to the main topmast, Betts. You will stand lookout until the first lieutenant orders otherwise.' He felt a touch of pity. One hundred and ten feet above the deck, unsheltered from the cold wind, Betts would be numb within minutes. Herrick had already decided to send Neale up after him with something warm to eat as soon as the galley fire was lit for breakfast.

Betts spat on his hands and replied flatly, 'Aye, aye, sir. Seems a fair mornin'?' He could have been remarking on something quite normal and unimportant.

Herrick nodded. 'Aye. The wind is dropping and the air is much drier.' It was true. Betts' instinct had grasped the change as soon as he had emerged from the packed, airless berth deck where eighteen inches per man was the accepted hammock space.

Herrick added quietly, 'You were lucky, Betts. You could have been dancing at the gratings by eight bells.'

Betts stood staring at him, unmoved and calm. 'I'm not sorry for what 'appened, sir. I'd do it again.'

Herrick felt suddenly annoyed with himself for mentioning the matter. That was his trouble, he thought angrily. He always wanted to know and understand the reason for everything. He could not leave matters alone.

He snapped, 'Get aloft! And mind you keep a good lookout. The dawn'll be awake soon.' He watched the man's shadow merge with the main shrouds and followed him with his eye until he was lost in the crisscross of rigging against the stars.

Again he found himself wondering why Bolitho had acted as he had over a man like Betts. Neither Vibart nor Evans had mentioned the matter, which seemed to add rather than detract from the importance of the affair. Perhaps Vibart had overstepped his authority again, he pondered. Under Pomfret the first lieutenant's presence had moved over the ship, controlling every action and day-to-day happening. Now he seemed hampered by Bolitho's calm authority, but the very fact that their disagreement was close to showing itself openly only made things worse. The ship seemed to split in two, divided between the captain and Vibart. Pomfret had remained a frightening force in the background, and Herrick had found his work cut out to stay impartial and out of trouble. Now it appeared as if such neutrality was impossible.

He thought back to the moment he had gone to the big house in Falmouth. Before he had imagined he would find only envy there. His own poor beginnings were hard to shake free. He recalled Bolitho's father, the great pictures along the walls, the air of permanence and tradition, as if the present occupants were merely part of a pattern. Compared with his own small home in Rochester, the house had seemed a veritable palace.

Herrick's father had been a clerk in Rochester, working for the Kentish fruit trade. But Herrick, even as a small child, had watched the ships stealing up the Medway, and had allowed his impressionable mind to build his own future accordingly. For him it was the Navy. Nothing else would do. It was odd because there was no precedent in his family, all of whom had been tradesmen, sprinkled with the occasional soldier.

His father had pleaded in vain. He had warned him of the pitfalls, which were many. Lack of personal standing and financial security made him see only too clearly what his son was attempting to challenge. He even compromised by suggesting a safe berth aboard an Indiaman, but Herrick was quietly adamant.

Quite by chance a visiting warship had been laid up near Rochester while repairs had been carried out to her hull. Her captain had been a friend of the man who employed Herrick's father, a grave senior captain who showed neither resentment nor open scorn when the eleven years old boy had waylaid him and told him of his desire to go to sea in a King's ship.

Faced by the captain and his employer, Herrick's father had given in. To do him full justice he had made the best of it by using his meagre savings to send his son on his way, outwardly at least, a young gentleman as good as any of his fellows.

Herrick was now twenty-five. It had been a long and arduous journey from that time. He had learned humiliation and embarrassment for the first time. He had faced unequal opposition of breeding and influence. The starry-eyed boy had been whittled away and hardened like the good Kentish oak beneath his feet. But one thing had not changed. His love of the sea and the Navy stayed over him like a protecting cloak or some strange religion which he only partly understood.

This timeless thing was the same to all men, he decided. It was far above them. It controlled and used everyone alike, no matter what his ambition might be.

He smiled at himself as he continued his endless pacing. He wondered what young Neale, yawning hugely by the rail, would think of his grave faced senior. Or the helmsmen who watched the swinging needle and gauged the pull of the sails. Or Betts, high overhead on his precarious perch, his own thoughts no doubt full of what he had done and what might lie in store for him behind Evans' vengeance.

Maybe it was better to be unimaginative, he thought. To be completely absorbed in day-to-day worries, like Lieutenant Okes for instance. He was a married man, and that was obstacle enough for any young officer. Okes spent his time either fretting about his distant wife or treading warily to avoid Vibart's eye. He was a strange, shallow man, Herrick thought, unsure of himself, and afraid to unbend even with his own kind. It seemed as if he was afraid of becoming too friendly, and nervous of expressing an opinion outside the necessities of duty. As if by so doing he might awake suspicion elsewhere or give a hint of misplaced loyalty.

Herrick moved his stiff shoulders inside his coat and pushed Okes from his thoughts. He might after all be right. Aboard the *Phalarope* it often seemed safer to say nothing, to do nothing which might be wrongly interpreted later.

He stared at the weather rail and noticed with a start that he could see the carved dolphin above the starboard ladder and the fat, ugly cannonade nearby. His thoughts had carried him through another half hour, and soon the dawn would show him an horizon once more. Would bring another day.

Harsh and clear above the hiss of spray he suddenly heard Betts' voice from the masthead. 'Deck there! Sail on the starboard bow! Hull down, but it's a ship!'

Snatching his glass from the rack Herrick scrambled up into the mizzen shrouds, his mind working on the unexpected report. The sea was already gathering shape and personality, and there was a finger of grey along where the horizon should be. Up there, high above the swaying deck, Betts would just be able to see the other ship in the dawn's cautious approach.

He snapped, 'Mr. Neale! Up you go and see what you can discover. If you give me a false report you'll kiss the gunner's daughter before you're much older!'

Neale's face split into a grin, and without a word he scampered like a monkey towards the main shrouds.

Herrick tried to stay calm, to return to his pacing as he had seen Bolitho do. But the newcomer, if there was indeed a ship, filled him with uncertainty, so that he stared at the dark sea as if willing it to appear.

Betts called again. 'She's a frigate, sir! No doubt about it. Steerin' south-east!'

Neale's shrill voice took up the call. 'She's running before the wind like a bird, sir! Under all plain sail!'

Herrick breathed out noisily. For one brief instant he had imagined it might be a Frenchman. Even out here, alone and unaided, it was not impossible. But the French rarely sailed fast or far by night. Usually they lay to and rode out the darkness. This was no enemy.

As if to open his thoughts Betts yelled, 'I know that rig, sir! She's an English ship right enough!'

'Very well, keep on reporting!' Herrick lowered the speaking trumpet and peered back along the quarterdeck. Even in minutes the place had taken more shape and reality. The deck was pale and grey, and he could see the helmsmen again as familiar faces.

There might be new orders in the other frigate. Maybe the American war was already over and they would return to Brest or England. In his heart Herrick felt a sudden twinge of disappointment. At first the prospect of another long commission in the unhappy *Phalarope* had appalled him. Now, with the thought that he might never see the West Indies at all, he was not so sure.

Neale slithered straight down a backstay, disdaining shrouds and ratlines, and ran panting to the quarterdeck.

Herrick made up his mind. 'My respects to the captain, Mr. Neale, and tell him we have sighted a King's ship. She will be up to us in an hour, maybe much less. He will wish to prepare himself.'

Neale hurried down the hatchway and Herrick stared across the tumbling waste of water. Bolitho would be even more concerned, he thought. If the *Phalarope* was ordered home now, all his plans and promises would be without meaning. He would have lost his private battle before he had had time to begin.

There was a soft step beside him and Bolitho said, 'Now, Mr. Herrick, what about this ship?'

4

The Signal

Bolitho steadied his glasses against the weather rigging and waited for the other ship to leap into focus. In the time it had taken him to walk from his cabin to the quarterdeck and listen to Herrick's excited report, the dawn sun had slowly clawed its way over the horizon so that already the endless waste of tossing whitecaps was touched with pale gold, the shadows gone from the short, steep waves.

The other vessel made a fine sight in the strengthening light, he thought, with her tall pyramids of full sails and the unbroken curtain of spray bursting around the high bow. She was moving fast, her topmast glittering in the weak sunlight like crucifixes.

Over his shoulder he called, 'You have a good lookout, Mr. Herrick! He is to be complimented for such an early sighting.'

Even for a trained seaman it was not easy to pick out a ship from the shadows of night and dawn and identify her. She was English right enough, and there was a certain familiarity about her.

Vaguely in the background he could hear the boatswain's mates calling the hands, the shrill twitter of pipes.

'All hands! All hands! Show a leg!'

He could imagine the sleep-dazed men tumbling from their hammocks groaning and protesting, while from forward came the usual mixture of smells from the galley. Another day, but this time it would be different. The sea was no longer empty and hostile. The other ship might make the men remember that they were part of something real and important.

He saw the frigate's big yards begin to change shape and heard Herrick say, 'She's going about, sir. She'll be up to us shortly!'

Bolitho nodded absently. The stranger would swing round to run parallel, keeping the *Phalarope* down to leeward. As Herrick had suggested, it might mean new orders.

He climbed down from the rigging suddenly chilled and tired. The keen spray had moulded his shirt to his body and his hair felt wet against his cheek. He noticed that his ship had changed yet again. The quarterdeck seemed thronged with figures, the officers keeping to the lee side, but with their glasses raised and watching the other frigate.

Midshipman Maynard looked anxiously towards the stranger and strained his eyes through his big telescope. As he was in charge of signals he knew that Bolitho would be watching him.

The maindeck was also alive with newly awakened seamen, and the bosun's mates had to use their ropes ends more than usual to drive them away from the bulwark as they peered across the water at the frigate's approach. Chattering and excited they stowed their hammocks in the nettings and still staring abeam moved reluctantly towards the galley hatch.

Bolitho lifted his glass again as tiny black balls soared to the other ship's yards and broke out to the wind.

Vibart leaned against the binnacle and growled at Maynard, 'Come on then! Read it out!'

Maynard blinked the spray from his wet eyes and flicked rapidly through his book. 'She's made her number, sir! She's the *Andiron*, thirty-eight, Cap'n Masterman.'

Bolitho closed his glass with a snap. Of course. He should have known her immediately. When in *Sparrow* he had often seen her on patrol off the American coast. Masterman was an old hand at the game. A senior captain, he had chalked up many successes against the enemy.

The *Andiron* had completed her manœuvre and was settling down on the same course as the *Phalarope*. Her sudden wide turn had taken her across the *Phalarope*'s beam, but as her sails bellied and filled once more she began to overhaul to windward.

Bolitho watched Maynard's signal party hoisting the *Phalarope*'s number and wondered what Masterman would say when he eventually discovered that he was now in command. The signal books would still show Pomfret as captain.

Maynard shouted, 'Signal, sir! *Andiron* to *Phalarope*. Heave to, have despatches on board.'

The sunlight glittered along the *Andiron*'s closed ports as she swung slightly down on the other ship.

Herrick said, 'She'll not need to lower a boat, sir. She could drift a raft across.' He rubbed his hands. 'I wonder if she has any fresh vegetables aboard?'

Bolitho smiled. This was just what he had hoped for. A distraction to take their minds off themselves if only for a passing moment.

'Carry on, Mr. Vibart. Heave to, if you please!'

Vibart lifted his speaking trumpet. 'Main tops'l braces! Look alive there!'

Stockdale appeared at Bolitho's side holding his captain's blue coat and cocked hat. He squinted at the other ship and grinned. 'Like old times, Captain.' He peered forward as Quintal, the boatswain, let loose a stream of curses and obscenities. The men had been slow to respond to the sudden orders, and already there was chaos on the crowded deck where off-duty idlers collided with others who were struggling with spray-swollen braces.

Maynard said hoarsely, 'Signal, sir!' His lips moved slowly as he spelled out the message. 'Have you news of Hood's squadron?'

Quintal had at last got his men sorted out, and with sails flapping and thundering the *Phalarope* began to swing heavily into the wind.

Bolitho had half slipped his arms into his coat, but pushed Stockdale aside as Maynard's words chilled his mind like ice. Masterman would never ask such a question. Even if he had lost his squadron he would certainly know that *Phalarope* was a stranger and had never served in these waters before. His mind rebelled, and he stared mesmerised as his ship continued to swing until the *Andiron*'s bowsprit seemed to point at right-angles across his own.

Vibart turned startled and confused as Bolitho yelled, 'Belay that order, Mr. Vibart! Stand by to go about!'

He ignored the surprised gasps and the fresh clamour of orders and concentrated his reeling thoughts on the other ship. Suppose he had made a mistake? It was too late now. Perhaps it had been too late from the moment the *Andiron* had appeared.

Then he saw the other frigate's bows beginning to swing round still further. With her yards turning as one she altered course and charged down towards the helpless *Phalarope*. A few more seconds and the way would have been lost from the *Phalarope*'s sails, and the *Andiron* would have crossed her unprotected stern, unchallenged and overwhelming.

Bolitho felt his ship labouring round, his ears deaf to the cries and curses from officers and men alike. The weeks of sail drill in all weathers were taking charge, and like puppets the seamen tugged at sheets and braces, their minds too dazed by their captain's behaviour to

68

understand what was happening.

Vibart yelled. 'My God, sir! We'll collide!' He stared past Bolitho's tense figure towards the onrushing frigate. Still the *Phalarope* wallowed round, her bowsprit following the other ship like a compass needle.

Bolitho snapped, 'Steer south-east! Out second reefs!' He did not listen to his repeated orders but walked briskly towards the scarlet-coated marine drummer boy beside the cabin hatch.

'Beat to quarters!'

He saw the boy's dull expression giving way to something like horror. But again training and discipline took charge, and as the drum began to stutter its warning tattoo the tide of men on the maindeck swayed, faltered and then surged in opposite directions as gun crews rushed madly to their weapons.

Vibart gasped, 'Her ports are opening! My God, she's running up her colours!'

Bolitho saw the striped flag breaking to the crosswind and followed Vibart's shocked stare as the frigate's ports opened and the concealed guns trundled outwards like a row of shining teeth.

He said harshly, 'Clear for action, Mr. Vibart! Have the guns loaded and run out immediately!' He checked Vibart as he ran to the rail. 'It will take all of ten minutes. I will try to give you that amount of time!'

The deck canted as the ship steadied on her new course around and away from the other frigate. But the *Andiron* was already turning on the same circle, her sails flapping as she headed into the wind in an effort to close the range. From her peak the new American flag made a patch of bright colour against the tan sails, and Bolitho had to tear his mind back to the present to stop himself thinking of what would have happened but for that one stupid signal.

Andiron would have crossed the *Phalarope*'s unprotected stern and her gunners, hitherto concealed behind the bulwark and sealed ports, would have poured shot after shot through the big cabin windows. The balls would have screamed and torn the full length of his command, and with half the men still below, helpless and unprepared, the disaster would have been over within minutes.

Even now it might be too late. *Andiron* was the bigger ship, and her deep keel was better for this sort of handling. Already she was cutting across the *Phalarope*'s stern and beating rapidly up to windward to regain her first advantage. In another fifteen minutes she would try the same manœuvre again, or she could be content to close the range from the larboard quarter. With the wind in her favour action could not be avoided.

He made himself walk to the taffrail and stare back at the other ship. The pretence had gone now, and he could see the crouching gunners, the clusters of officers on the canting quarterdeck. What had happened to Masterman? he wondered. He were better dead than know his proud ship to be a privateer.

He turned his back on the *Andiron*'s dark hull and looked along his own command. The chaos had gone, and to the unpractised eye the ship looked ready and eager for battle.

On both sides the guns had been run out and the gun captains were testing their trigger lines and passing hoarse orders to their men. Boys ran the length of the deck throwing down sand to give the gunners a firm grip when the time came, while others scuttled from gun to gun with water buckets for the swabs and to damp down any sudden fire.

Vibart stood below the quarterdeck rail and yelled, 'Cleared for action, sir! All guns loaded with double shot and grape!'

'Very well, Mr. Vibart.' Bolitho walked slowly towards the rail and ran his eye along the larboard side guns. They would be the first to engage. His heart sank as he picked out faults in the pattern like flaws in a painting.

At one gun a captain was even having to put a rope fall into the hands of one of his men, as the poor wretch stared at it without comprehension. His mind was too full of fear, his eyes too mesmerised by the overtaking frigate with her long row of guns to heed what the petty officer was saying. At each gun there were men like this. With so many new hands, pressed from unwarlike jobs ashore, this danger was inevitable.

Given time, he could have trained each and every one of them. Bolitho banged his fist slowly on the rail. Well, there was no more time. *Andiron* not only had more guns, but they were eighteen-pounders, against *Phalarope*'s twelve pounders. Most of her crew would no doubt be made up of English deserters and seasoned sailors who were no strangers to battle. Any crew which could take the *Andiron* from Captain Masterman was a force to be feared.

At his back Captain Rennie stood nonchalantly by the hammock nettings, his sword looped to his wrist with a gold lanyard, as he watched Sergeant Garwood dressing his men into neat scarlet ranks. There was something very reassuring about the marines, Bolitho thought grimly, but their muskets would not be much use against eighteen-pounders!

All at once the remorse and despair he had been enduring since the *Andiron*'s first treachery had shown with her flag gave way to something like blind rage. It was too late for the 'if onlys' and the 'maybes'. He had brought his ship and his men to this. His was the sole respon-sibility. He had recognised the American's trap just in time to save them all from the first blow, but he should have seen it earlier.

He walked to the rail and shouted along the deck, 'Now listen to me, men! In a few moments we are going to give battle to that ship!' He saw every face turned towards him,

71

but already they had lost meaning and personality. They were a crew. Good or bad, only time would show. But that they should all trust him was essential.

'Just take your time and obey orders, no matter what is happening around you! Each gun is fitted with the new flintlock, but make sure there is a slow-match at hand in case of failure!'

He saw Okes look across from the starboard battery to where Herrick waited by his own guns. A quick exchange of glances which might have meant anything.

He felt Stockdale slipping the coat over his shoulders and then the firm clasp of the swordbelt around his waist. He watched the powerful frigate plunging over towards the larboard quarter, his eyes gauging the speed and the distance.

'One more thing!' He leaned forward as if to will them to listen. 'This is a King's ship! There will be no surrender!'

He thrust his hands beneath the tails of his coat and walked slowly to the weather rail. It would not be long now. He looked across to Proby's shabby outline beside the wheel. 'In a moment we will beat to windward, Mr. Proby.' He heard a mumbled assent and wondered what the master would make of his order.

The American captain would no doubt expect the smaller ship to turn again and try to slip downwind, and as soon as she turned he would pour a full broadside into the *Phalarope*'s stern, as he had first intended. Bolitho's manœuvre would bring the *Phalarope* round towards the other ship, and with luck Herrick might be able to get in the first blood.

He saw the flash of sunlight on a telescope from the *Andiron*'s quarterdeck and knew the other captain was watching him.

'Stand by, Mr. Proby!' He lifted his hat and yelled along the maindeck, 'Right, lads! A broadside for old England!'

With a protesting groan the yards came round, while overhead the canvas thundered like a miniature battle. Bolitho found that his mouth was as dry as sand, and his face felt chilled into a tight mask.

This was the moment.

John Allday crouched beside the second gun of the larboard battery and stared fixedly through the open port. In spite of the cool morning breeze he was already sweating and his heart pumped against his ribs like the beating of a drum.

It was like being a helpless victim of a nightmare, with every detail clear and stark even before it happened. Somehow he imagined it would be different this time, but nothing had changed. He could have been sailing into battle for the first time, new and untried, with the agony of suspense tearing him apart.

He tore his eyes from the open square of water and glanced back across his shoulder. The same men who had jeered Ferguson or ringed Evans in menacing silence now stood or crouched like himself, slaves to their guns, their faces naked and fearful.

Standing a little apart from the battery, his back to the foremast, Lieutenant Herrick was watching the quarter-deck, his fingers resting on his sword, his bright blue eyes unwinking and devoid of expression.

Allday followed the officer's stare and saw the captain at the quarterdeck rail, his palms resting on the smooth wood, his head jutting slightly as he watched the other ship. The latter was almost hidden from Allday by the high bulwark and gangway and the other guns, but he could see her topmasts and straining sails as she bore down on the larboard quarter, until she seemed to hang over the *Phalarope* like a cliff.

Pryce, the gun captain, slung the powder horn over his hip and squatted carefully behind the breech, the trigger line in his hands. Through his teeth his voice sounded strange and taut. 'Now, lads, listen to me! We'll be firing a broadside first.' He looked at each man in turn, ignoring the other gunners at the next port. 'After that it will all depend on how quickly we load and run out. So move sharply, and as the cap'n said, take no notice of the din about you, got it?'

Ferguson clung to the rope tackle at the side of the gun and gasped, 'I can't take it! God, I can't stand this waiting!'

Pochin on the opposite side of the breech sneered, 'Just as I said! It takes more than pretty clothing to make men of the likes o' you!' He jerked savagely at the tackle. 'If you'd seen what I'd seen you'd *die* of fear, man.' He looked around at the others. 'I've seen whole fleets at each other's throats.' He let his words sink in. 'The sea covered in masts, like a forest!'

Pryce snapped, 'Hold your noise!'

He cocked his head as Herrick called, 'Gun captains! As soon as we engage on the larboard side send your best men to back up the other battery under Mr. Okes!'

The captains held up their hands and then turned back to watch the empty sea.

Allday looked across at Okes and saw the officer's face gleaming with sweat. He looked white. Like a corpse already, he thought.

Vibart's voice rang hollowly through his speaking trumpet. 'Braces there! Stand by to wear ship!'

Allday ran his fingers along the cold breech and whispered fervently, 'Come *on*! Get it over with!'

The *Phalarope* was outclassed and outgunned, even he could see that. With half her men already too terrified to think it was just a matter of how soon her colours would fall.

He glanced down at his legs and felt a chill of terror. It never left him, and the years on the quiet Cornish hillside amongst the sheep had done nothing to dispel it. The fear of mutilation, and the horror of what followed.

Old Strachan called softly from the next gun, ''Ere, you lads!' He waited until his words had penetrated the minds of the new men. 'Wrap a neckscarf around yer ears afore we start to blow! You'll 'ave no eardrums else!'

Allday nodded. He had forgotten that lesson. If only they had been prepared and ready. Instead they had stumbled out from their hammocks and almost at once the nightmare had begun. First the excitement of a friendly ship, fading instantly in the drummer's roll as the men ran gasping and wide-eyed to quarters. He could just see the same little drummer boy beside one rank of marines. He was staring across at the captain as if to read his own fate.

Pryce muttered, 'Never bin a fight like this afore.' He looked up at the billowing sails. 'Too much wind. It'll be hit hard an' run, you mark my words!'

There was a rasp of steel as Herrick drew his sword. He lifted it above his head, the blade holding the sun like firelight.

'Stand by in the larboard battery!'

Ferguson moaned softly. 'Oh, Grace! Where are you, Grace?'

From aft Vibart bellowed, 'Put the helm down! Hard down there!'

They all felt the deck begin to cant further as the seamen forward let go the headsail sheets and allowed the plunging frigate to swing wildly across the wind.

Allday swallowed hard as the gunports suddenly darkened and the other ship's raked bow pushed across his vision. She filled the port, her guns and spray-soaked hull leaning at an angle as if to reach out and smash the *Phalarope* as she swung impudently towards her.

Herrick dropped his sword. '*Fire!*'

The captains jerked their lines and the whole world fell apart in the staggering, uneven broadside. Choking smoke billowed back through the ports, rasping the lungs and filling every eye as the guns lurched angrily back on their tackles. It was like hell, too terrible to understand.

But already the gun captains were yelling like fiends, urging and hitting at their stunned gunners as the powder monkeys ran forward with fresh cartridges and new, gleaming balls were lifted from the racks.

Pryce knocked down a man's arms and screamed, 'Sponge out, you bastard! Remember what I taught you! You'll blow us all up if you drop a charge into a burning gun!' The man mumbled dazedly and obeyed him as if in a trance.

Herrick shouted, 'Reload there! Lively, lads!'

Allday waited a few more minutes and then threw his weight on the tackles. Squealing like angry pigs the gun trucks rumbled forward again, the muzzles racing each other to be first through the ports.

But the *Phalarope* was almost into the *Andiron*'s bow. A few more feet and it seemed as if both ships would smash into each other, to die together in locked combat.

'Fire!'

Again the savage roar of a broadside, the deck yawing away beneath them with its force. But this time more ragged, less well aimed. Through the din of shouts and groaning spars Allday heard some of the balls strike home, and saw Maynard, one of the midshipmen, waving his hat in the streaming smoke and yelling to the sky, his words lost in the guns' roar.

The *Andiron* must have fired simultaneously with the *Phalarope*, her gunfire lost in the general thunder of noise. There was more of a feeling than a sound, like a hot wind, or sand blasted across a parched desert.

Allday looked up as the sails jerked and twisted as if in agony. Holes were appearing everywhere, and from high aloft came a falling tangle of severed halyards and ropes. A block dropped on to the breech with a loud clang, and

Pryce said without looking up from his priming, 'The bastards fired too soon! The broadside went right over our 'eads!'

Allday peered through the port, still dazed, but understanding at last what Bolitho had done. The *Phalarope* had not turned away, had not offered her stern for punishment. Her sudden swing to attack had caught the enemy off balance, and rather than risk a senseless collision he had hauled off so that his first broadside had failed to make real contact.

He heard Herrick call across to Lieutenant Okes, 'By God, Matthew, that was a close thing!' Then in a wilder tone, 'Look at the masthead pendant! The wind's veering!'

There was bedlam as the enemy ship swung rapidly clear of the charging *Phalarope*. But so sudden or so unexpected was the attack that the *Andiron*'s captain had failed to notice what Bolitho must already have seen even as he steered towards possible disaster.

Instead of beating back to windward the *Andiron* met the full wind hard across her larboard bow. For a moment it looked as if she would rally and at worse come crashing back alongside.

Herrick was jumping with excitement. 'My God, she's *in* irons! She's in irons!'

Men were standing beside their guns calling the news along the deck while across the water, framed in a rolling bank of gunsmoke, the *Andiron* rolled helplessly up wind, unable to pay off on either tack. Already men were running along her yards, and across the shadowed water they could hear the blare of commands through a speaking trumpet.

Herrick controlled himself. 'Over to the starboard battery. Jump to it!'

Pryce touched the men he needed and scampered across the deck.

From aft came the call, 'Stand by to go about! Man the braces!'

Allday threw himself down beside the opposite gun and showed his teeth to the crouching men.

Old Strachan croaked, 'The cap'n can certainly 'andle the ship well enough.'

Okes shouted, 'Silence there! Watch your front!'

Herrick walked to the centre of the deck and watched the carpenter and the boatswain hurrying to repair the brief damage. Men were already climbing aloft to splice the severed lines, and others were at last rigging nets above the maindeck to give some protection from falling blocks or spars.

Round came the yards once more, sails thundering, braces screaming through the blocks as the men ran like goats to obey the constant demands from the quarterdeck.

It did not seem possible. Caught and surprised one instant, and the next moment they were not only attacking, but hitting the enemy again and again.

Bolitho must have thought it all out. Must have planned and schemed during his lonely walks up and down the night-darkened deck, waiting for just an eventuality.

He could see him now, calm-eyed and stiff-backed behind the rail, his hands behind his back as he watched the other ship. Once during the waiting Herrick had seen him wipe his forehead, momentarily brushing away the lock of dark hair and displaying the deep, savage scar. He had seen Herrick watching him and had jammed on his hat with something like anger.

Herrick ran his eye along his own guns, now manned by depleted crews and blind to the enemy as the *Phalarope* tacked round to close the range. He had heard Pochin's bitter remarks and had seen the way Allday had rallied to help the new men. It was strange how they all forgot their other worries when real danger was close and terrible.

It was true that the ship was different under Bolitho.

And it went deeper than the uniform clothing now worn by all hands, issued on Bolitho's order to replace the stained rags which had been commonplace in Pomfret's time. There was this violent uncertainty instead of sullen acceptance, as if the men wanted to draw together to match the young captain's enthusiasm, yet had forgotten how to go about it.

Okes said sharply, 'She's under way again! She's swinging round!'

The *Andiron*'s sails were flapping and banging in apparent confusion, but Herrick could see the difference in her outline and the new angle of her yards.

Bolitho's voice cut through their speculations. 'Another salvo, lads! Before she completes her turn!'

Herrick breathed out sharply. 'He's going to try and cross her stern! He'll never make it. We'll be broadside to broadside in minutes!'

The wild confidence which their successful attack had brought him changed to the chill of uncertainty as the *Phalarope* gathered way, her masts and spars quivering under the press of sail. He gripped his sword more tightly and gritted his teeth as once more the enemy top-sails showed above the hammock nettings. The masts were no longer in line, she was swinging fast and well. There was nothing else for it but to take what had to come.

Okes could only stare at the oncoming ship, his jaw open as the distance was swallowed up in the gap of tossing water between them. He held up his sword. 'Stand by starboard battery!' But his voice was lost in a savage ripple of gunfire from the other ship as gun after gun belched fire and smoke from aft to forward as each one came to bear.

This time there was no mistake.

Herrick felt the hull shudder beneath his feet and reeled against the foremast as smoke blotted out the deck and the air became full of splintering woodwork and falling rigging. Above and around him the air quivered and shook with the crash of guns, and the nerve jarring scream of cannon balls as they whipped through the smoke like things from hell.

The scream of passing shots mingled with closer, more unearthly sounds as flying splinters ripped into the packed gunners and bathed the smooth decks with scarlet. Herrick had to bite his lip to retain control of himself. He had seen men bleed before. In an occasional skirmish, and under the cat. From a fall or a shipboard accident. But this was different. It was all around him, as if the ship was being painted by a madman. He could see specks of blood and gristle across his white breeches, and when he looked across at the nearest gun he saw that it had been upended and one of its crew had been pulped into a scarlet and purple mass. Another man lay legless, a handspike still gripped and ready, and two of his companions were clinging together screaming and tearing at each other's terrible wounds in the insane torment.

The enemy frigate must have reloaded almost at once, and another ragged volley thundered and crashed in the *Phalarope*'s side.

Men cried and yelled, cursed and fumbled blindly in the choking smoke, while above their heads the nets jerked and danced madly to the onslaught of falling gear from aloft.

A powder monkey ran weeping towards the magazine hatch, only to be pushed away by one of the marine sentries, He had dropped his cartridge carrier and was running below, to the safety of darkness. But the sentry yelled at him and then struck at him with his musket. The boy reeled back and then seemed to come to his senses. With a sniff he picked up his carrier and made for the nearest gun.

There was a scream of shot, and Herrick turned biting back vomit as the eighteen-pound shot cut the boy in half.

The head and shoulders remained upright on the planking for several seconds, and before he turned away Herrick saw that the boy's eyes were still open and staring.

He cannoned into Okes who still stood with upraised sword, his eyes fixed and glassy as he gaped at the remains of his battery.

Herrick shouted, 'Fire, Matthew! Give the order!'

Okes dropped his sword and here and there a gun lurched back adding its voice to the dreadful symphony,

Okes said, 'We're done for! We'll have to strike!'

'Strike?' Herrick stared at him. All at once the reality was cruel and personal again. Death and surrender had always been words, a necessary but unlikely alternative to victory. He looked towards the quarterdeck at Bolitho's tall figure and the marines beyond. The latter must have been firing their muskets for some while, yet Herrick had not even noticed. He saw Sergeant Garwood with his half-pike dressing one rank where two red-coated bodies had left gaps in the line, while he called out the time and numbers to his men as they reloaded and fired another volley into the smoke. Captain Rennie had his back to the enemy and was staring across the other rail as if seeing the sea for the first time,

Pryce, the gun captain, gave one long scream and fell backwards at Herrick's feet. A long splinter had been torn from the deck and had embedded itself in the man's shoulder. Through the blood Herrick could see the thick stump of jagged timber sticking out like a tooth, and knew that the other end would be deep inside. The splinters were always the most dangerous and had to be cut out from the flesh in one piece.

Herrick gestured towards the men by the main hatch, 'Take this one below to the surgeon!' They had been staring at a pulped corpse beside the hatch, its teeth white against the flayed flesh, and Herrick's harsh tone seemed to give them strength to break the spell.

Pryce began to scream. 'No! Leave me here by the gun! For God's sake, don't take me below!'

One of the men whispered, ' 'E's a brave 'un! 'E don't want to leave 'is station!'

Pochin spat on the gun and watched the spittle hissing on the barrel. 'Squit! 'E'd rather die up 'ere than face the butcher's knife.'

There was a splintering crack, like that of a coach whip, high overhead, and as Herrick squinted up through the drifting smoke he saw the maintopgallant quiver, and then as the wind tore jubilantly at the released canvas it began to slide forward.

Herrick cupped his hands. 'Look alive, you men! Get aloft and cut those shrouds! It'll foul the foremast otherwise!'

He saw Quintal and some seamen running up the shrouds and then winced as another cannon ball ploughed along the deck by his feet and smashed into two wounded gunners beside the lee bulwark. He looked away, sickened, and heard Vibart yell, 'Heads below! The t'gallant is falling!'

With a jarring crash the long spar pitched over the bulwark and remained trapped and tangled in a mass of rigging, the torn sail ballooning in the water alongside and dragging at the ship like a sea anchor.

To add to the horror, Herrick could see the man, Betts, the one who had first sighted the other frigate, pinned in the trailing rigging like an insect in a web.

Vibart yelled, 'Axes there! Cut that wreckage adrift!'

Betts stared up at the frigate with glazed eyes, his voice short and painful between his teeth. 'Help me! Don't let me go to the bottom, lads!'

But already the axes were at work, the men driven half mad by the din, too dazed to care for the suffering of one more seaman.

Okes seized Herrick's arm. 'Why doesn't he strike? For

Christ's sake *look* what he's doing to us!'

Herrick's mind was dulled and refused to work clearly any more. But he could see what Okes was trying to show him. The heart had gone out of the men, what heart there had been. They crouched and whimpered as the enemy balls thundered all around them, and only occasionally did a single gun reply. Then it was usually a small handful of men led by one seasoned and dedicated gun captain which kept up a one-sided exchange with the enemy.

Herrick shut his ears to the screaming wounded as they were dragged below and closed his eyes to everything but the small open patch of quarterdeck where Bolitho stood alone by the rail. His hat had gone and his coat was stained with powder and blown spray. Even as he watched Herrick saw a messenger run towards the captain, only to be cut down by musket fire from the other vessel as she loomed sideways out of the smoke. Musket balls were thudding against the hammock nettings and biting across the deck, yet Bolitho never budged, nor did he alter his expression of detached determination.

Only once did he look up, and then to glance at the large scarlet ensign which streamed from the gaff, as if to reassure himself that it still flew.

Herrick shook his head. 'He'll not strike! He'll see us all dead first!'

5

Rum and Recriminations

The deck slewed over as the *Phalarope*'s helm went hard down and she swung blindly on to her new course. Bolitho had lost count of the number of times his ship had changed direction, or even how long they had been fighting.

Of one thing he was sure. The *Andiron* was out-manœuvring him, was still holding to windward and keeping up a steady barrage. His own gunners were hampered by yet another hazard. The wind was falling away, and his men were now firing blindly into an unbroken bank of thick smoke which rolled down from the other ship and mingled with their own intermittent firing. The smoke seemed to writhe with many colours as the American privateer continued the attack. Once, when a freak wind had blown the smoke skywards like a curtain Bolitho had seen the *Andiron*'s battery belching long orange flames as each gun was trained and fired singly across the bare quarter mile between the two frigates. They were firing high, the balls screaming through the rigging and slashing the remaining sails to ribbons. Ropes and stays hung from above like weed, and every so often heavy blocks and long slivers of wood would fall amongst the labouring gunners or splash in the clear water alongside.

She intended to dismast and cripple the *Phalarope*. Maybe her captain had plans for using another captured ship, just as he had the *Andiron*.

The long nine-pounders on the quarterdeck recoiled as one, their sharp, barking detonations penetrating the innermost membranes of Bolitho's ears as he stared through the smoke and then back at his own command. Only on the quarterdeck was there still some semblance of unity and order. Midshipman Farquhar stood by the taffrail, his eyes bright but determined as he passed his orders to the gun captains. Rennie's marines were standing fast, too. From their smoke-blinded position behind the hammock nettings they kept up a steady musket fire whenever the other ship showed herself through the choking fog of powder smoke.

But the maindeck was different. Bolitho let his eyes move slowly over the chaos of scarred planking and grisly remains which marked every foot of deck space. The guns were still firing, but the intervals were longer, the aim less certain.

At first Bolitho had been amazed at the success of that opening broadside. He had known that later the lack of training would slow down the barrage, but he had not dared to hope for such a good opening. The double-shotted guns had fired almost as one, the ship staggering from the combined recoil. He had seen the bulwarks jump apart on the other frigate, had watched the balls tear through the packed gunners and gouge into her spray-dashed hull. It had seemed momentarily that the battle might still be contained.

Through the streaming smoke he saw Herrick moving slowly aft along the starboard battery checking the gunners and aiming each weapon himself before allowing the gun captain to jerk his trigger line. It should have been Okes on the starboard side, but perhaps he was already dead, like so many of the others.

Bolitho made himself examine each part of the agonising panorama which the *Phalarope* now represented. His body felt sick and numb from the constant battering, but his eye and mind worked in cold unison, so that the pain and suffering was all the more apparent.

Small pictures stood out from the whole, so that wherever he looked there was a pitiful reminder of the cost and the price still to be paid.

Many had died. How many he had no way of knowing. Some had died bravely, serving their guns and yelling encouragement and curses up to the moment of death. Some died slowly and horribly, their mutilated and broken bodies writhing in the blood and flesh which covered the deck as in a slaughterhouse.

Others were less brave, and more than once he had seen men shamming death, even cowering in the stench and horror of the discarded corpses until dragged and kicked back to their stations by the petty officers.

Some had escaped below in spite of Rennie's sentries, and would now be covering their ears and whimpering in the bilges to face drowning rather than the onslaught from the *Andiron*'s guns.

He had seen the little powder monkey cut in half, and even above the roar of battle he had heard his own words to that same boy just three weeks ago:

'You'll see England again! Never you fear!'

Now he was wiped away. As if he had never been.

And there had been the seaman Betts, trapped and writhing on the severed topgallant. The man he had used to try to prove his authority. The axes had cut the spar away, and with a sigh it had bobbed clear of the ship before moving away in the smoke in a trail of rigging. The spar had idled past the quarterdeck, and for a brief instant he had seen Betts staring up at him. The man's mouth had been open like a black hole, and he had shaken his fist. It was a pitiful gesture, but it felt like a curse from the whole world. Then the spar had rolled over, and before it had faded astern Bolitho had seen Betts' feet sticking out of the water, kicking in a futile dance.

He tore his eyes from the carnage as more balls slapped through the main course and whined away over the water. It could not last much longer. The *Andiron* had hauled off slightly to windward. He could see her upper yards and punctured sails moving above the smoke bank as if detached from the hidden ship beneath, and guessed she was drawing clear to pound the *Phalarope* into submission with slow, carefully aimed shots.

He did not recognise his own voice as he gave his orders automatically and without pause. 'Tell the carpenter to sound the well! And pass the word for the boatswain to send more men aloft to splice the mizzen shrouds!' There was little point any more, but the game had to be played out. He knew no other way.

His eye fell on an old gun captain at the nearest twelve-pounder below the quarterdeck. The man showed fatigue and strain, but his hoarse voice was unhurried, even patient as he coaxed his crew through the drill of reloading. 'That's right, my buys!' He peered through the haze as one of his men rammed home the cartridge and another cradled the gleaming ball into the gaping nuzzle. A splinter flew from the gun port and laid open his arm, but he merely winced and tied a filthy rag around his biceps before adding, 'Ram that wad well home, bucko! We don't want the bugger to fall out agin!' He saw Bolitho watching him and showed his stained teeth in what might have been either pain or pride. Then he bawled, 'Right then! Run out!' The trucks squeaked as the gun lumbered up the canting deck and then roared back again as the old man pulled his trigger.

Vibart loomed across the rail, his figure like a massive blue and white rock. He looked grim but unflinching, and waited for the nine-pounders to fire and recoil before he shouted, 'No water in the well, sir! She's not hit below the waterline!'

Bolitho nodded. The American obviously felt sure of a

capture. It would not take long to refit a ship in one of the dockyards left by the British retreating from the American colonies.

The realisation brought a fresh flood of despairing anger to his aching mind. The *Phalarope* was fighting for her life. But her men were failing her. He was failing her. He had brought the ship and every man aboard to this. All the hopes and promises were without meaning now. There was only disgrace and failure as an alternative to death.

Even if he had contemplated flying from the *Andiron*'s attack it was too late now. The wind was falling away more and more, and the sails were almost useless, torn like nets by the screaming cannon balls.

A marine threw up his hands, clawing at the gaping scarlet hole in his forehead before pitching back into his comrades,

Captain Rennie drawled, 'Fill that space! What the hell do you think you're doing?' To Sergeant Garwood he added petulantly, 'Take the name of the next man who dies without permission!'

Surprisingly, some of the marines laughed, and when Rennie saw Bolitho looking at him he merely shrugged, as if he too understood it was all part of one hideous game.

The ship staggered, and overhead the sails boomed in protest as the fading wind sighed against the flapping canvas. Bolitho snapped, 'Watch your helm, quartermaster! Steady as you go!'

But one of the helmsmen had fallen, a pattern of scarlet pouring from his mouth and across the smooth planking. From somewhere another seaman took his place, his jaw working steadily on a wad of tobacco.

Vibart growled, 'The starboard battery is a shambles! If we could engage the opposite side it would give us time to reorganise!'

Bolitho eyed him steadily. 'The *Andiron* has the advantage. But I intend to try and cross her stern directly.'

Vibart peered abeam, his eyes cold and calculating. 'She'll never allow it. She'll pound us to shavings before we get a cable's length!' He looked back at Bolitho. 'We will have to strike.' His voice shook. 'We can't take much more.'

Bolitho replied quietly, 'I did not hear that, Mr. Vibart. Now go forrard and try and get the full battery into action again!' His tone was cold and final. 'When two ships fight, only one can be the victor. I will decide on the course of action!'

Vibart seemed to shrug. As if it was not his concern. 'As you say, sir!' He strode to the ladder adding harshly, 'I *said* that they did not respect weakness!'

Bolitho felt Proby shaking his arm and turned to see the anxiety etched on his mournful face. 'The wheel, Captain! It don't answer! The yoke lines have parted!'

Bolitho stared dully over Proby's rounded shoulders to where the helmsman pulled vaguely at the wheel, the squeaking spokes responding in empty mockery as the ship paid off and began to sidle suggishly downwind.

The sudden movement brought more cries from the maindeck as the frigate rolled her gunports skyward in a dizzy, uncontrollable elevation.

Bolitho ran his fingers through his hair, realising for the first time that his hat had been knocked from his head. The masthead pendant was barely flapping now, and without power in her sails the ship would drift at the mercy of the sea until her surrender or destruction. It would take all of an hour to re-rig the rudder lines. By then . . . he felt a cold shudder moving across his spine.

He cupped his hands. 'Cease firing!'

The sudden silence was almost more frightening than the gunfire. He could hear the chafe and creak of spars, the gurgle of water below the counter, and the swaying clatter of loose rigging. Even the wounded seemed quelled, and lay gasping and staring at the captain's still figure at the quarterdeck rail.

Then across the water, drifting with the smoke like a final insult, he heard a wild cheering. It was more like a baying, he thought bitterly. Like hounds closing for the kill.

A V-shaped cleft broke in the smoke, and through it came the *Andiron*'s raked bow and the long finger of her bowsprit. Filtered sunlight played across her figurehead and glinted on raised cutlasses and boarding pikes. As more and more of the other ship glided into view Bolitho saw the press of men running forward to the point where both ships would touch. Others were crawling out along the yards with grapnels, ready to lash the two enemies together in a final embrace. It was nearly finished.

He heard Stockdale mutter at his elbow, 'The bastards! The *bastards*!'

Bolitho saw that there were small tears in the man's eyes, and knew that the battered coxswain was sharing his own misery.

Above his head the flag whipped suddenly in a small breeze, and he knew that he dare not look at it. A defiant patch of scarlet. Like the red coats of the marines and the great glittering pools of blood which seeped through the scuppers as if the ship herself was bleeding before his eyes.

A new wildness moved through his mind, so that he had to lock his fingers around his swordbelt to prevent his hands from shaking.

'Get Mr. Brock! At the double!'

He saw Midshipman Maynard lope forward, and then forgot him as his glance strayed again to the watching men. They were exhausted and smashed down with the fury of battle. There was hardly a spark amongst them. His fingers settled on the hilt of his sword and he felt the painful prick of despair behind his eyes. He could see his father, and so many others of his family, ranked with his crew, and watching in silence.

Proby said hoarsely, 'I've sent a party to splice the yoke lines, Captain.' He waited, plucking the buttons of his shabby coat. 'It were not your fault, sir.' He shifted beneath Bolitho's unwavering stare. 'Don't you give in, sir. Not now!'

The gunner reached the quarterdeck and touched his hat. 'Sir?' He was still wearing the felt, spark-proof slippers he always wore in the dark magazine, and he seemed dazed by the sudden silence and the litter of destruction about him.

'Mr. Brock, there is a task for you.' Bolitho listened to his own voice and felt the strange wildness stirring him like brandy. 'I want every starboard gun loaded with chain shot.' He watched the *Andiron*'s slow, threatening approach. 'You have about ten minutes, unless the wind returns.'

The man nodded and hurried away without another word. His was not to question a meaningless order. A command from the captain was all he required.

Bolitho looked down at the maindeck, at the dead and wounded, and the remaining gunners. He said slowly, 'There will be one final broadside, men.' The words swept away his own illusion of making a last empty gesture. He continued, 'Every gun will have chain shot, and I want each weapon at full elevation.' They began to stir, their movements brittle and vague like old men, but Bolitho's voice seemed to hold them as he added sharply, 'Load, but do not run out until the word!' He saw the gunner's party carrying the unwieldy chain shot to each gun in turn. Two balls per gun, and each ball linked together with thick chain.

Captain Rennie said quietly, 'They're getting close, sir. They'll be boarding us very soon now.' He sounded tense.

Bolitho looked away. All at once he wanted to share the enormity of his decision, but at the same instant he knew the extent of his own loneliness.

91

His last effort might fail completely. At best it would only drive the enemy to a madness which only the death of the whole of his crew would placate.

Herrick looked aft, his eyes steady. 'All guns loaded, sir!' He seemed to square his shoulders, as if to project some strange confidence over his battered men.

Bolitho pulled out his sword. Behind him he heard the marines fixing their bayonets and shuffling their booted feet on the stained planking.

He called, 'Stand by the starboard carronade, Mr. Farquhar! Is it ready?' He watched narrowly as the other ship's bowsprit swung over the *Phalarope*'s bulwark, her forechains and rigging alive with shouting men. Her captain must have stripped his guns to get such a large boarding party. Once aboard, they would swamp the *Phalarope*, no matter how desperate the resistance.

Farquhar swallowed hard. 'Loaded, sir. Canister, and a full charge!'

'Very good.' The *Andiron* was barely twenty feet clear now, the triangular patch of trapped water between them frothing in a mad dance. 'If I fall, you will take your orders from Mr. Vibart.' He saw the young officer's eyes seeking out the first lieutenant. 'If not, then watch for my signal!'

The *Andiron*'s bow nudged the main shrouds and a great yell of derision broke from the waiting boarders.

Bolitho ran down the ladder and leaped on to the starboard gangway, his sword above his bare head. A few pistols banged across the gap and he felt a ball pluck at his sleeve like an invisible hand.

'Repel boarders!' He saw the gunners staring up at him, uncertain and shocked, their guns still inboard and impotent.

Herrick jumped up beside him, his eyes flashing as he shouted, 'Come on, lads! We'll give the buggers a lesson!'

Somebody voiced a faint cheer, and the men not employed at the guns surged up to the gangway, their cutlasses and pikes puny against the great press of boarders.

Bolitho felt a man drop screaming at his side, and another pitched forward to be ground between the hulls like so much butcher's meat. He could see the privateer's officers urging their men on and pointing him out to their marksmen. Shots banged and whistled around him, and the cries and jeers had risen to one, terrifying roar.

The hulls shuddered once more and the gap began to disappear. Bolitho peered back at Farquhar. The quarterdeck with its dead marines seemed a long way away, but as he waved his sword in a swift chopping motion he saw the midshipman jerk the lanyard and felt the gun's savage blast pass his face like a hot wind.

The canister shot contained five hundred closely packed musket balls, and like a scythe the miniature bombardment swept through the cheering boarders, cutting them down into a bloody tangle of screams and curses. The boarders faltered, and a young lieutenant who had climbed up on the *Andiron*'s bowsprit dropped unsupported on to the *Phalarope*'s gangway. His scream was cut short as a big seaman lashed out and down with an axe, and then his body was pinned between the hulls and forgotten.

Bolitho shouted wildly, 'Come on, you gunners! Run out! *Run out!*'

He held out his sword like a barrier in front of his men. 'Back there! Get back!'

His small party fell back, confused by this turn of events. They had faced certain annihilation, and had accepted it. Now their captain had changed his mind. Or so it seemed.

But Herrick understood. Almost choking with excitement he yelled, '*All guns run out!*'

Bolitho saw the survivors from the carronade's single blast falling back towards their guns, shocked and dismayed as the *Phalarope*'s muzzles trundled forward and upwards towards them.

'Fire!' Bolitho almost fell overboard, but felt Stockdale catch his arm as the whole battery exploded beneath his feet.

The air seemed to come alive with inhuman screams as the whirling chain shot cut through sails and rigging alike in an overwhelming tempest of metal. Foremast and maintopmast fell together, the great weight of spars and canvas smashing down the remaining boarders and covering the gunports in a whirling mass of canvas.

The recoil of *Phalarope*'s broadside seemed to drive the two ships apart, leaving a trail of wreckage and corpses floating between them.

Bolitho leaned against the nettings, his breath sharp and painful. 'Reload! Carry on firing!' Whatever happened next, the *Phalarope* had spoken with authority, and had hit hard.

The frigate's proud outline was broken and confused in tangled shrouds and sails. Where her foremast had been minutes before there was only a bright-toothed stump, and the resonant cheers had given way to screams and confusion.

But she pushed forward across the *Phalarope*'s bows, followed by a further ragged salvo and a single angry bark from a forecastle nine-pounder. Then she was clear, gathering her tattered sails like garments to cover her scars, and pushing downwind into the rolling bank of smoke.

Bolitho stood watching her, his heart thumping, his eyes watering from strain and emotion.

The minutes dragged by, and then the insane realisation came to him. The *Andiron* was not putting about. She had taken enough.

Half stumbling he returned to the quarterdeck where Rennie's marines were grinning at him and Farquhar was leaning on the smoking carronade as if he no longer trusted what he saw.

Then they started to cheer. It was not much at first. Then it gathered strength and power until it moved above and below decks in an unbroken tide.

It was part pride and part relief. Some men were sobbing uncontrollably, others capered on the blood-stained decks like madmen.

Herrick ran aft, his hat awry, his blue eyes shining with excitement. 'You did for them, sir! My God, you scuppered 'em!' He clasped Bolitho's hand, unable to stop himself. Even old Proby was grinning.

Bolitho controlled his voice with one last effort. 'Thank you, gentlemen.' He looked along the littered decks, feeling the pain and the blind exultation. 'Next time we will do better!'

He swung round and pushed through the whooping marines towards the dark sanctuary of the cabin hatch.

Behind him, as if through a fog, he heard Herrick shout, 'I don't know about *next* time, lads! This will do me for a bit!'

Bolitho stood breathing hard in the narrow passageway listening to their excitement and laughter. They were grateful, even happy, he realised dully. Perhaps the bill would not be too high after all.

There was so much to do. So many things to prepare and restore before the ship would be ready to fight again. He fingered the worn sword hilt and stared wearily at the deck beams. But it would wait a moment longer. Just a short moment.

Herrick leaned heavily on the forecastle rail and wiped his forehead with the back of his hand. Only the slightest breeze ruffled the calm sea ahead of the gently pitching bows, and as he watched he saw the sun dipping towards the horizon, its glowing reflection already waiting to receive it and allow night to hide the *Phalarope*'s scars.

Herrick could feel his legs shaking, and again he tried

95

to tell himself it was due to fatigue and the strain of a continuous day's working. Within an hour of the privateer's disappearance Bolitho had returned to the quarterdeck, his dark hair once more gathered neatly to the nape of his neck, his face freshly shaved, and the dust of battle brushed from his uniform. Only the lines at the corners of his mouth, the grave restlessness in his eyes betrayed any inner feelings as he passed his orders and began the work of repairing the damage to his ship and crew.

At first Herrick had imagined the task impossible. The men's relief had given way to delayed shock, so that individual sailors lay aimlessly about the stained decks like marionettes with severed strings, or just stood and stared listlessly at the aftermath of the nightmare.

Bolitho's sudden appearance had started a train of events which nobody could really explain. Every officer and man was too spent, too dulled by the brief and savage encounter to spare any strength for protest. The dead had been gathered at the lee rail and sewn into pathetic anonymous bundles. Lines of kneeling men had moved from forward to aft working with heavy holystones to scrub away the dark stains to the accompaniment of clanking pumps and the indifferent gurgle of sea-water.

The tattered and useless sails were sent down and replaced with fresh canvas, while Tozer, the sailmaker, and his mates squatted on every available deck space, needles and palms moving like lightning as they patched and repaired anything which could be salvaged and used again.

Ledward, the carpenter, moved slowly around the splintered gun battery, making a note here, taking a measurement there, until at length he was ready to play his part in restoring the frigate to her original readiness. Even now, as Herrick relived the fury of the bombardment and heard the screams and moans of wounded men, the hammers and saws were busy, and the whole new areas of planking were being tamped neatly into place to await the pitch and paint of the following morning.

He shivered again and cursed as his knees nearly gave under him. It was shock rather than mere fatigue. He knew that now.

He thought back to his impressions of the battle, to his own stupid relief and loud-voiced humour when the enemy had hauled away. It had been like listening to another, uncontrollable being who had been incapable of either silence or composure. Just to be alive and unharmed had meant more than anything.

Now as the sky grew darker astern of the slow moving ship he examined his true feelings and tried to put his recollections into some semblance of order.

He had even tried to regain some of the brief contact he had made with Bolitho. He had crossed the quarterdeck where the captain had been staring down at the labouring sailors and had said, 'You saved us all that time, sir. Another minute and she'd have been into us with a full broadside! It was a clever ruse to ask us to heave to. That privateer was a cunning one and no mistake!'

Bolitho had not lifted his gaze from the maindeck. When he had replied it had been as if he was speaking to himself. '*Andiron* is an old ship. She has been out here for ten years.' He had made a brief gesture towards the maindeck. '*Phalarope* is new. Every gun is fitted with the new flintlock and the carronades are almost unknown except in the Channel Fleet. No, Mr. Herrick, there is little room for congratulations!'

Herrick had studied Bolitho's brooding profile, aware perhaps for the first time of the man's constant inner battle. 'All the same, sir, she outgunned us!' He had watched for some sign of the Bolitho he had seen waving his sword on the starboard gangway while shots had hammered down around him like hail. But there had been nothing. He had ended lamely, 'You'll see, sir, things will be different after this.'

Bolitho had straightened his back, as if throwing off some invisible weight. When he had turned his grey eyes had been cold and unfeeling. 'I hope you are right, Mr. Herrick! For my part I was disgusted with such a shambles! I dread to contemplate what might have happened in a fight to the finish!'

Herrick had felt himself flushing. 'I was only thinking . . .'

Bolitho had snapped. 'When I require an opinion from my third lieutenant I will let him know! Until that moment, Mr. Herrick, perhaps you would be good enough to make your people get to work! There will be time later for suppositions and self-adulation!' He had swung on his heel and recommenced his pacing.

Herrick watched the surgeon's party carry another limp corpse from the main hatch and lay it beside the others. Again, another picture of Bolitho sprang to his mind.

Herrick had been between decks on a tour of inspection with the carpenter. There were no shot holes beneath the water-line, but it had been his duty to make sure for his own satisfaction. Still dulled by the noise of battle he had followed Ledward beneath the massive, curved beams, his tired eyes half mesmerised by the man's shaded lantern. Together they had stepped through a screen and entered a scene from hell itself.

Lanterns ringed the deck space, to allow none of the horror to escape his eyes, and in the centre of the yellow glare, strapped and writhing like a sacrifice on an altar, was a badly wounded seaman, his leg already half amputated by Tobias Ellice, the surgeon. The latter's fat, brick-red face was devoid of expression as his bloody fingers worked busily with the glittering saw, his chins bouncing in time against the top of his scarlet-daubed apron. His assistants were using all their strength to restrain the struggling victim and pin his spread-eagled body on top of the platform of sea chests, which sufficed as an operating table. The man had rolled his eyes with each nerve-searing thrust of the saw, had bitten into the leather strap between his teeth until the blood had spurted from his lips, and Ellice had carried on with his amputation.

Around the circle of light the other wretched wounded had awaited their turn, some propped on their elbows as if unable to tear their eyes from the gruesome spectacle. Others lay moaning and sobbing in the shadows, their lives ebbing away and thereby spared the agony of knife and saw. The air had been thick with the stench of blood and rum, the latter being the only true way of killing the victims' senses before their turn came.

Ellice had looked up as the man had kicked out wildly and then fallen lifeless even as the severed limb had dropped into a waiting trough. He had seen Herrick's face stiff with shock and had remarked in his thick, tipsy voice, 'A day indeed, Mr. 'Errick! I sew an' I stitch, I saws an' I probes, but still they rushes to join their mates aloft!' He had rolled his rheumy eyes towards heaven and had reached for a squat leather bottle. 'Maybe a little nip for yerself, Mr. 'Errick?' He had lifted it against the light. 'No? Ah well then, a little sustenance for meself!'

He had given the merest nod to his loblolly boy, who in turn had pointed out another man by the ship's rounded side. The latter had been immediately seized and hauled screaming across the chests, his cries unheeded as Ellice wiped his mouth and had then ripped away the shirt from the man's lacerated arm.

Herrick had turned away, his face sweating as the man's scream had probed deeper into his eardrums. He had stopped in his tracks, suddenly aware that Bolitho was standing slightly behind him.

Bolitho had moved slowly around the pain-racked figures, his voice soothing but too soft for Herrick to comprehend. Here he had reached to touch a man's hand as it groped blindly for comfort or reassurance. There he had stopped to close the eyes of a man already dead. At one instant he had paused beneath a spiralling lantern and had asked quietly, 'How many, Mr. Ellice? What is the bill?'

Ellice had grunted and gestured to his men that he had completed his ministrations with the limp figure across the sheets. 'Twenty killed, Cap'n! Twenty more badly wounded, an' another thirty 'alf an' 'alf!'

It was then that Herrick had seen Bolitho's mask momentarily drop away. There had been pain on his face. Pain and despair.

Herrick had immediately forgotten his anger and resentment at the captain's remarks earlier on the quarterdeck. The Bolitho he had seen on the ship's side waving his sword had been real. So, too, was this one.

He stared down at the canvas-shrouded corpses and tried to remember the faces to fit against the names scrawled on each lolling bundle. But already they were fading, lost in memory like the smoke of the battle which had struck them down.

Herrick started as he caught sight of Lieutenant Okes' thin figure moving slowly along the shadowed maindeck. He had hardly seen Okes at all since the action. It was as if the man had been waiting for the hard-driven sailors to finish their work so that he could have the deck to himself.

There had been that moment immediately after the sound of the last shot had rolled away in the smoke. Okes had staggered up through a hatchway, his eyes wild and uncontrolled. He had seemed shocked beyond understanding as he had looked around him, as if expecting to see the enemy ship alongside. Okes had seen Herrick watching him, and his eyes had strayed past to the smoking guns in the battery which he had left to fend for themselves.

He had clutched Herrick's arm, his voice unrestrained and desperate. 'Had to go below, Thomas! Had to find those fellows who ran away!' He had swayed and added wildly, 'You believe me, don't you?'

Herrick's contempt and anger had faded with the discovery that Okes was terrified almost to a point of madness. The realisation filled him with a mixture of pity and shame.

'Keep your voice down, man!' Herrick had looked round for Vibart. 'You damn fool! Try and keep your head!'

He watched Okes now as the man skirted the corpses and then retraced his steps to the stern. He too was reliving his own misery. Destroying himself with the knowledge of his cowardice and disgrace.

Herrick found time to wonder if the captain had noticed Okes' disappearance during the battle. Perhaps not. Maybe Okes would recover after this, he thought grimly. If not, his escape might be less easy the next time.

He saw Midshipman Neale's small figure scampering along the maindeck and felt a touch of warmth. The boy had not faltered throughout the fight. He had seen him on several occasions, running with messages, yelling shrilly to the men of his division, or just standing wide-eyed at his station. Neale's loss would have been felt throughout the ship, of that Herrick was quite sure.

He hid a smile as the boy skidded to a halt and touched his hat. 'Mr. Herrick, sir! Captain's compliments and would you lay aft to supervise burial party!' He gulped for breath. 'There's thirty altogether, sir!'

Herrick adjusted his hat and nodded gravely. 'And how are you feeling?'

The boy shrugged. 'Hungry, sir!'

Herrick grinned. 'Try fattening a ship's rat with biscuit, Mr. Neale. As good as a rabbit any day!' He strode aft, leaving Neale staring after him, his forehead creased in a frown.

Neale walked slowly past the bow chasers, deep in thought. Then he nodded very slowly. 'Yes, I might try it,' he said softly.

Bolitho felt his head loll and he jerked himself back against his chair and stared at the pile of reports on his table. All but completed. He rubbed his sore eyes and then stood up.

Astern, through the great windows he could see moonlight on the black water and could hear the gentle sluice and creak of the rudder below him. His mind was still fogged by the countless orders he had given, the requests and demands he had answered.

Sails and cordage to be repaired, a new spar broken out to replace the missing topgallant. Several of the boats had been damaged and one of the cutters smashed to fragments. In a week, driving the men hard, there would be little outward sign of the battle, he thought wearily. But the scars would be there, deep and constant inside each man's heart.

He recalled the empty deck in the fading light as he had stood over the dead men and had read the well-tried words of the burial service. Midshipman Farquhar had held a light above the book, and he had noticed that his hand had been steady and unwavering.

He still did not like Farquhar, he decided. But he had proved a first-class officer in combat. That made up for many things.

As the last corpse had splashed alongside to begin its journey two thousand fathoms deep he had turned, only to stop in surprise as he had realised that the deck had filled silently with men from below decks. Nobody spoke, but here and there a man coughed quietly, and once he had heard a youngster sobbing uncontrollably.

He had wanted to say something to them. To make them understand. He had seen Herrick beside the marine guard, and Vibart's massive figure outlined against the sky at the quarterdeck rail. For a brief moment they had all been together, bound by the bonds of suffering and loss. Words would have soiled the moment. A speech would have sounded cheap. He had walked aft to the ladder and paused beside the wheel.

The helmsman had stiffened. 'Course south-west by south, sir! Full an' by!'

He had returned here. To this one safe, defended place where there was no need for words of any sort.

He looked up angrily as Stockdale padded through the door. The man studied him gravely. 'I've told that servant o' yours to bring your supper, Captain.' Stockdale peered disapprovingly at the litter of charts and written reports. 'Pork, sir. Nicely sliced and fried, just as you like it.' He held out a bottle. 'I took the liberty of breaking out one o' your clarets, sir.'

The tension gripped Bolitho's voice in a vice. 'What the hell are you jabbering about?'

Stockdale was undaunted. 'You can flog me for sayin' it, sir, but today was a victory! You done us all proudly. I think you deserve a drink!'

Bolitho stared at him lost for words.

Stockdale began to gather up the papers. 'An' further, Captain, I think you deserves a lot more!'

As Bolitho sat in silence watching the big coxswain laying the table for his solitary meal, the *Phalarope* plucked at the light airs and pushed quietly beneath the stars.

From dawn to sunset she had given much. But there would be other days ahead, thanks to her captain.

6

A Sight of Land

Bolitho walked to the starboard side of the quarterdeck and rested his hands on the sun-warmed hammock netting. He did not need either chart or telescope now. It was like a homecoming.

The small island of Antigua had crept up over the horizon in the dawn's light, and now sprawled abeam shimmering in the forenoon sunlight.

Bolitho felt the old excitement of a perfect landfall coursing through his limbs, and he had to make himself continue in his interrupted pacing, if only to control it. Five weeks to a day since the *Phalarope* had showed her stern to the mist and rain of Cornwall. Two weeks since the clash with the privateer, and as he looked quickly along his ship he felt a quick upsurge of pride. All repairs had been completed, and the remaining wounded were well on the mend. The death roll had risen to thirty-five, but the sudden entry into warmer air, with sun and fresh breezes instead of damp and blustering wind, had worked wonders.

The frigate was gliding gently on the port tack, making a perfect pair above her own reflection in the deep blue water. Above her tapering masts the sky was cloudless and full of welcome, and already the eager gulls swooped and screamed around the yards with noisy expectancy.

Antigua, headquarters and main base of the West Indies

squadron, a link in the ragged chain of islands which protected the eastern side of the Caribbean. Bolitho felt strangely glad to be back. He half expected to see the crew and deck of the *Sparrow* when he looked across the quarterdeck rail, but already the *Phalarope*'s company had grown in focus to overshadow the old memories.

'Deck there! Ship of the line anchored around the headland!'

Okes was officer of the watch and he looked quickly towards Bolitho.

'That will be the flagship most likely, Mr. Okes.' Bolitho glanced up to the new topgallant where the keen-eyed lookout had already seen the tall masts of the other vessel.

The frigate slowly rounded Cape Shirley with its lush green hills and the tumbled mass of rocky headland, and Bolitho watched his men as they thronged the weather side, clinging to shrouds and chains as they drank in the sight of the land. To all but a few of them it was a new experience. Here everything was different, larger than life. The sun was brighter, the thick green vegetation above the gleaming white beaches was like nothing they had ever seen. They shouted to one another, pointing out land-marks, chattering like excited children as the headland slipped past to reveal the bay and the landlocked waters of English Harbour beyond.

Proby called, 'Ready to wear ship, sir!'

Bolitho nodded. The *Phalarope* had every sail clawed up except topsails and jib, and on the forecastle he could see Herrick watching him as he stood beside the anchor party.

He snapped his fingers. 'My glass, please.'

He took the telescope from Midshipman Maynard and stared fixedly at the two-decker anchored in the centre of the bay. Her gunports were open to collect the offshore breeze, and there were awnings across her wide quarter-deck. His eye fastened on the rear-admiral's flag at her masthead, the gleam of blue and scarlet from watching figures at her poop.

'Mr. Brock! Stand by to fire salute! Eleven guns, if you please!' He closed the glass with a snap. If he could see them, they could see him. There was no point in appearing curious.

He watched the nearest point of land falling away and then added, 'Carry on, Mr. Proby!'

Proby touched his hat. 'Lee braces there! Hands wear ship!'

Bolitho glanced quickly at Okes and waited patiently. At length he said evenly, 'Clear those idlers off the side, Mr. Okes. That is a flagship yonder. I don't want the admiral to think I've brought a lot of bumpkins with me!' He smiled as Okes stuttered out his orders and the petty officers yelled at the unemployed men by the rail.

The salute began to pound and re-echo around the hills as the frigate swung slowly towards the other ship, and more than one man bit his lip as the saluting guns brought back other more terrifying memories.

'Tops'l sheets!' Proby mopped the sweat from his streaming face as he gauged the slow approach to the anchorage. 'Tops'l clew lines!' He looked aft. 'Ready, sir!'

Bolitho nodded, only half listening to the salutes and the staccato bark of orders.

'Helm a' lee!' He watched the quartermaster pulling steadily at the polished spokes and saw the nearest hillside begin to swing across the bows as the *Phalarope* turned into the wind and began to lose way.

Now there was no sound but for the gentle lap of water as the ship glided slowly towards the shore.

Bolitho called, 'Let go!'

There was a splash from forward followed by the jubilant roar of cable as the anchor plunged into the clear water.

Maynard said excitedly, 'Signal, sir! From *Cassius* to

Phalarope. Captain to repair on board.'

Bolitho nodded. He had been expecting it and was already changed into his best uniform. 'Call away the gig, Mr. Okes, and see that its crew is properly turned out!' He saw the harassed lieutenant hurry away and wondered momentarily what was worrying him. He seemed strained. His mind only half on his duty.

Vibart came aft and touched his hat. 'Any orders, sir?'

Bolitho watched the boat being swayed out, the petty officer in charge using his cane more than usual, as if he too was well aware of the watching flagship.

'You can stand by to take on fresh water, Mr. Vibart. We will no doubt be warping through into English Harbour directly, and the men can go ashore and stretch their legs. They've earned it.'

Vibart looked as if he was going to argue but merely replied, 'Aye, aye, sir. I'll see to it.'

Bolitho looked across at the two-decker. The *Cassius*, seventy-four, flagship of Rear admiral Sir Robert Napier. He was said to be a stickler for promptness and smartness, although Bolitho had never actually met him before.

He climbed down the ladder and walked slowly towards the entry port. It was strange to realise that he had been in command for only five weeks. It seemed as if he had been aboard for months. The faces of the side party were familiar now, and already he was able to pick out the personalities and the weaknesses.

Captain Rennie saluted with his sword and the guard presented arms.

Bolitho removed his hat and then replaced it as the gig idled alongside with Stockdale glaring from the tiller. The pipes twittered and shrilled, and as he stepped into the gig he looked up at the ship's side, at the fresh paint and neat repairs which hid the clawing scars of battle. Things might have been a lot worse, he thought, as he settled himself in the sternsheets.

The oars sent the little boat scudding across the calm water, and when Bolitho looked astern he saw that his men were still staring after him. He held their lives in his hands. He had always known that. But before the short battle some might have doubted his ability. They might even have thought him to be like Pomfret.

He thrust the thought to the back of his mind as the flagship grew and towered above him. They did not have to like him, he decided. But trust him they must.

Rear-Admiral Sir Robert Napier did not rise from his desk but waved Bolitho towards a chair by the broad stern gallery. He was a small, irritable-looking man with stooping shoulders and sparse grey hair. He seemed bowed down by the weight of his dress coat, and his thin mouth was fixed in an expression of pernickety disapproval.

'I have been reading your reports, Bolitho.' His eyes flickered across the younger man's face and then returned to the desk. 'I am still not quite clear about your action with the *Andiron*.'

Bolitho tried to relax in the hard chair, but something in the admiral's querulous tone sparked off a small warning.

Bolitho had been met at the flagship's entry port with due ceremony and greeted courteously by the *Cassius*'s captain. The latter had appeared uneasy and worried, as well he might with a man like Sir Robert aboard, Bolitho thought dryly. The first sign that all was not well had been when he had been ushered into a cabin adjoining the admiral's quarters and told to wait for an audience. His log and reports had been whisked away, and he had stayed fretting in the airless cabin for the best part of an hour.

He said carefully, 'We made a good voyage, in spite of the engagement, sir. All repairs were carried out without loss of sailing time.'

The admiral eyed him coldly. 'Is that a boast?'

'No, sir,' Bolitho replied patiently. 'But I imagined that the need for frigates is still acute out here.'

The other man ruffled the documents with a wizened hand. 'Mmm, quite so. But the *Andiron*, Bolitho? How did she manage to escape?'

Bolitho stared at him, caught off guard. 'Escape, sir? She nearly laid us by the heels, as I have stated in my report.'

'I read that, dammit!' The eyes glowed dangerously. 'Are you trying to tell me that she ran away?' He looked aft through a window to where the *Phalarope* swung at her anchor like a carved model. 'I see little sign of combat or damage, Bolitho?'

'We were well supplied with spare spars and canvas, sir. The dockyard foresaw such an eventuality when they fitted her out.' The admiral's tone was getting under his skin and he could feel his anger smouldering, ignoring the warning in the man's eyes.

'I see. Captain Masterman lost *Andiron* after engaging two French frigates four months back, Bolitho. The French gave the captured ship to their new allies, the Americans.' The contempt was clear in his voice. 'And you state that although your ship was disabled and outgunned she made off without attempting to press home her advantage?' There was anger in his voice. 'Well, *are* you?'

'Exactly, sir.' Bolitho controlled his answer with an effort. 'My men fought well. I think the enemy had had enough. If I had been able to give chase I would have done so.'

'So you say, Bolitho!' The admiral put his head on one side, like a small, spiteful bird. 'I know all about your ship. I have read Admiral Longford's letter and all that he had to say about the trouble there was aboard when with the Channel Fleet. I am not impressed, to say the least!'

Bolitho felt the colour rising to his cheeks. The

admiral's insinuation was obvious. In his view the *Phalarope* was a marked ship and unacceptable, no matter what she achieved. He said coldly, 'I did not run away, sir. It happened just as I stated in the report. In my opinion the privateer was unwilling to sustain more damage.' He had a sudden picture of the crashing broadside, the chain shot ripping away the enemy's sails and rigging like cobwebs. Then another picture of the silent dead being dropped overboard. He added, ' My men did as well as I had hoped, sir. They had little time to defend themselves.'

'Please don't take that tone with me, Bolitho!' The admiral stared at him hotly. '*I* will decide what standards your people have reached.'

'Yes, sir.' Bolitho felt drained. There was no point in arguing with this man.

'See that you remember it in future.' He dropped his eyes to the papers and said, 'Sir George Rodney has sailed to reorganise his fleet. He will be returning from England at any time. Sir Samuel Hood is away at St. Kitts, defending it from the French.'

Bolitho said quietly, 'St. Kitts, sir?' It was barely one hundred miles to the west of his chair aboard the flagship, yet the admiral spoke as if it was the other side of the world.

'Yes. The French landed troops on the island and tried to drive our garrison into the sea. But Admiral Hood's squadron retook the anchorage, and even now is holding all the main positions, including Basseterre, the chief town.' He glared at Bolitho's thoughtful face. 'But that is not your concern. I am in command here until either the Commander-in-Chief returns or Admiral Hood sees fit to relieve me. You will take your orders from *me*!'

Bolitho's mind only half attended to the other man's irritable voice. In his mind he could see the tiny island of St. Kitts and knew exactly what its safety meant to the harassed British. The French were strong in these waters, and had been more than instrumental to the British defeats at the Chesapeake the previous year. Driven from the American mainland, the British squadrons would depend more and more on their chain of island bases for supplies and repairs. If they fell, there would be nothing to prevent the French or their allies from swallowing up every last possession in the Caribbean.

The French fleet in the West Indies was well trained and battle hardened. Their admiral, Count de Grasse, had more than once out-guessed and outfought the hard-pressed ships of the British. It had been de Grasse who had driven a wedge between Admiral Graves and the beleaguered Cornwallis, who had assisted the rebel general, Washington, and had organised the American privateers into useful and deadly opponents.

Now de Grasse was testing the strength of individual British bases with the same sure strategy which had made him his country's most valuable commander. Using Martinique to the south as his main base, he could attack every island at will or, the thought brought a chill to Bolitho's mind, he could speed to the west and fall upon Jamaica. After that there would be nothing to sustain the British. They would have the Atlantic behind them, and nothing to keep them from complete destruction.

The admiral was saying smoothly, 'I will require you to carry out patrols to the westward, Bolitho. I will draft my orders immediately. The enemy may try and transport more troops down from the American mainland to the Leeward Islands, or even further south to the Windward Islands. You will keep contact with the rest of my squadron, and with Admiral Hood at St. Kitts *only if absolutely necessary*!'

Bolitho felt the cabin closing in on him. The admiral had no intention of trusting *Phalarope* with the fleet. Once again the frigate seemed doomed to isolation and suspicion.

111

He said, 'The French will be reinforced by privateers, sir. My ship would be well employed closer inshore, I would have thought.'

The admiral smiled gently. 'Of course, Bolitho, I had almost forgotten. You are no stranger out here. I think I read somewhere of your little exploits.' His smile vanished. 'I am sick and tired of hearing stories of privateers! They are nothing but scavengers and pirates, and no match for one of *my* ships! You will do well to remember that, too! *Andiron*'s capture was a disgrace which should have been forestalled! If you meet her again, I would suggest you summon help to avoid another lamentable failure to capture or destroy her!'

Bolitho stood up, his eyes flashing. 'That is unfair, sir!'

The admiral studied him bleakly. 'Hold your tongue! I am tired of young, hot-headed officers who cannot understand strategy and discipline!'

Bolitho waited for his breathing to return to normal.

'Privateers are just one part of the pattern. The French are the real danger!'

There was a long silence, and Bolitho heard the distant thud of marines' boots and the muted blare of a bugle. The two-decker was like a small town after a frigate, but Bolitho could not wait to get away from it and the admiral's insulting remarks.

The latter said offhandedly, 'Keep a close watch on your patrol, Bolitho. And I would suggest you watch your fresh water and supplies very closely. I cannot say exactly when you will be relieved.'

'My men are tired, sir.' Bolitho tried once more to get through the admiral's cold rudeness. 'Some of them have not been ashore for years.' He thought of the way they had watched the green hills and gasped at the sight of the smooth, deserted beaches.

'And I am tired of this interview, Bolitho.' He rang a small bell on the desk. 'Just do your allotted duty, and remember that I will brook no deviation from it at any time. Foolhardy schemes are useless to me. See that you do not allow your apparent sense of self-importance to mar your judgement.' He waved his hand and the door opened silently behind Bolitho.

He stood outside in the passageway, his hands shaking with suppressed anger and resentment. By the time he had reached the entry port his face was again an impassive mask, but he hardly trusted himself to reply to the quiet words of the *Cassius*'s captain as the latter saw him over the side.

The older man said softly, "Watch your step, Bolitho! Sir Robert lost his son aboard the *Andiron*. He will never forgive you for letting her get away, *whatever* the reason, so you must try and ignore his words, if not his warning!'

Bolitho touched his hat to the guard. 'I have had a lot of warnings of late, sir. But in an emergency they are rarely of any use!'

The flagship's captain watched Bolitho step into the gig and move clear of the *Cassius*'s long shadow. In spite of his youth, Bolitho looked as if he might make trouble for others as well as himself, he thought grimly.

'Deck there! The cap'n's returnin'!'

Herrick moved out of the shade of the mizzen mast and hurried towards the entry port. He brushed some crumbs from his neckcloth and hastily tugged his cross-belt into position. He had always been able to tolerate the dull and badly prepared food aboard ship in the past, but with the *Phalarope* riding at her anchor and the ample provisions of English Harbour lying within cannon shot, it had been all that he could do to swallow his lunch. He squinted across the glittering water, his keen eyes immediately picking out the returning gig, its small crew clean and bright in their check shirts, the oars rising and falling like gulls' wings. Herrick stiffened as Vibart joined him by the rail.

The first lieutenant said, 'Well, now we shall see!'

'I'll wager the admiral was delighted to see our captain.' Herrick darted a hasty glance to make sure that the side party was properly fallen in. 'It will do a power of good for our people.'

Vibart shrugged. 'What do admirals know about anything?' He seemed unwilling to talk and unable to drag his eyes from the approaching gig.

Herrick could see Bolitho's square shoulders in the stern-sheets, the glitter of sunlight on his gold lace.

A master's mate said suddenly, 'Two water lighters shoving' off from the shore, sir. Deep laden by the looks of 'em!'

Herrick glanced in the direction of the man's arm and saw the two ugly craft moving clear of the land. They crawled ponderously towards the frigate, their great sweeps making heavy work of the journey.

Herrick muttered, 'I thought we would wait until we warped through into the harbour?'

Vibart slammed his hands together. 'By God, I knew this would happen! I just *knew* it!' He moved his heavy body violently and pointed towards the blue sea. 'That's for us, Mr. Herrick. No cream for the *Phalarope*, either now or ever!' He added angrily, 'Not until the ship is used as she was meant to be used!'

A boatswain's mate called, 'Stand by!'

Again the pipes shrilled their salute and the sweating guard slapped their muskets to the present.

Herrick touched his hat and watched Bolitho's face as he climbed up through the port. His features were calm and empty of expression, but his eyes as he glanced briefly along the maindeck were cold and bleak, like the North Atlantic.

Vibart said stiffly, 'Water lighters making for us, sir.'

'So I see.' Bolitho did not look round, but stared instead

at the newly scrubbed decks, the quiet atmosphere of order and readiness. He added after a moment, 'Carry on with immediate loading, and tell the cooper to prepare extra casks.'

Herrick asked cautiously, 'Are we to sea again, sir?'

The grey eyes fixed him with a flat stare. 'It would appear so!'

Vibart stepped forward, his eyes hidden in shadow. 'It's damned unfair, sir!'

Bolitho did not answer, but seemed entirely pre-occupied in his thoughts. Then he said sharply, 'We will be making sail within two hours, Mr. Vibart. The wind seems light, but good enough for my purpose.' He looked round as Stockdale padded on to the quarterdeck. 'Oh, tell my servant I will require some food as soon as possible. Anything will do.'

Herrick stared at him. Bolitho had been away for the best part of two hours, yet the admiral had not even bothered to entertain him or offer him lunch. What the hell could he be thinking of? A young, courageous captain, fresh from England with news, as well as a fine addition to the fleet, should have been welcomed like a brother!

He thought of his own feelings while he had eaten his meagre meal in the wardroom. Each mouthful had nearly choked him as he had imagined Bolitho dining with the admiral and enjoying the full fare which a flagship could provide in harbour. Poultry, fresh lean pork, even roast potatoes perhaps! The climate was unimportant to Herrick where good, familiar food was concerned.

Now he realised that Bolitho had received nothing. The same feeling of shame and pity moved through him that he had earlier felt for Okes. A slur on Bolitho was an insult to every man aboard, yet the captain carried the full brunt of it. It was so unfair, so calculated in its cruelty that Herrick could not contain himself.

'But, sir! Did the admiral not congratulate you?' He fumbled for words as Bolitho shifted to watch him. 'After all you have done for this ship?'

'Thank you for your concern, Herrick.' For a brief moment Bolitho's expression softened. 'Things are not always what they first appear. We must be patient.' There was not a trace of bitterness in his answer, nor was their any warmth either. 'But in war there is little time for personal understanding.' He turned on his heel adding, 'We will have gun drill as soon as we get under way.' He disappeared down the cabin hatch and Herrick looked round in dull amazement.

So Vibart had been right. *Phalarope* was a marked ship, and would remain one.

The master's mate came aft. 'Boat shovin' off from the *Cassius*, sir!'

Herrick felt suddenly angry. It was all so pointless, so stupid. 'Very well. It will be bringing despatches. Man the side, if you please.'

He was still angry when a debonair lieutenant climbed up through the port and after removing his hat stood and stared curiously around the deck, as if expecting to see some sort of spectacle.

'Well?' Herrick scowled at the visitor. 'Have you had a good look?'

The officer blushed and then said, 'My apologies, sir. I was expecting something rather different.' He held out a bulky canvas envelope. 'Orders for Captain Bolitho from Sir Robert Napier, Rear-Admiral of the Red.'

It sounded so formal after their first exchange that Herrick could not help smiling. 'Thank you. I'll take 'em aft in a moment.' He studied the officer's tanned face. 'How goes the war out here?'

He shrugged. 'A hopeless muddle. Too much sea and too few ships to cover it.' He became serious. 'St. Kitts is under siege, and the rebels are consolidating up in the north. Everything will depend on how much the French can bring to bear.'

Herrick turned the heavy envelope over in his hands and wondered if he would ever be opening his own orders. In command of his own ship.

'If the privateers are as good as the one we fought then the battle will be a hard one.' Herrick studied the man's face intently, just waiting for some sign of doubt or amusement.

But the lieutenant said quietly, 'We heard about the *Andiron*. A bad business to lose her so. I hope you get a chance to even the score. What with that renegade John Paul Jones playing hell with our communications, it is only to be expected that others will follow his example.'

Herrick nodded. 'I don't see why it should be a disgrace for Captain Masterman to lose his ship in combat.'

'You have not heard?' The officer dropped his voice. 'She fought two French frigates at once. At the height of the battle the *Andiron* was hailed by some American officer aboard one of the enemy ships. He called on the *Andiron*'s people to go over to his side!'

Herrick's jaw dropped. 'And you mean that is what happened?'

He nodded. 'Exactly! They would never surrender to Frogs, but this American made it sound like a new life, so what did they have to lose? And of course they will fight all the better *against us*! Every man-jack knows it will be flogging round the fleet and the gibbet if they are caught now.'

Herrick felt sick. 'How long had *Andiron* been in commission?'

'I'm not sure. About ten years, I believe.' He saw Herrick's mind working and added grimly, 'So *watch* your own people. Out here, thousands of miles from home and surrounded by the King's enemies, emotions play a big part in a man's loyalty.' He added meaningly, 'Especially in a ship where trouble has already felt its way!'

117

He broke off as Vibart strode back from the maindeck. He touched his hat to the first lieutenant and said formally 'I have twenty-five men for you in my cutter, sir. The admiral requested they be used as replacements for the ones killed in battle.' He watched as Vibart climbed down to the port where the marines were already mustering a growing rank of lean-looking sailors.

The officer said quickly, 'I have already spoken enough, my friend. But these men are outcasts. Nearly all have been in serious trouble of one kind or another. I think Sir Robert is more concerned in ridding his flagship of their influence than he is of helping your captain.' With a hurried glance at the distant two-decker he made towards his waiting boat. He whispered finally, 'Sir Robert watches everything. No doubt it will soon be common knowledge that I have spent ten minutes in conversation with *you*!' Then he was gone.

Vibart clumped aft, his face wrinkled in a scowl. 'We will read in those men immediately, Mr. Herrick. I suppose the captain will want them dressed like the rest of his precious company?' He sniffed. 'In my opinion they look more at home in rags!'

Herrick followed his angry glance and felt his spirits drop even further. These replacements were not men raw from the press. They were hardened and professional and at any other time would have been worth their weight in gold. But now they stood idly and insolently watching with all the arrogance of wild animals as the master's mate and Midshipman Maynard sorted them into order and seniority. Curses and beatings would not impress their sort. Even floggings had changed them little, Herrick thought.

Vibart muttered, 'We'll see how the captain deals with this pretty bunch!'

Herrick did not speak. He could imagine the difficulties which seemed to be piling up hour by hour. If the captain tried to separate these troublemakers from the rest of the crew he would lose any respect he had gained. If he did not, their influence could wreak havoc on the crowded berth deck.

On patrol, out of touch with help, the *Phalarope* would need all her resources and skill to stay intact and vigilant.

Herrick had a sudden picture of the *Andiron* as she must have been when Masterman's crew had surrendered. He stared round the sunny quarterdeck and felt chilled in spite of the glare. He imagined himself, suddenly alone, in a ship where discipline and loyal seamen had become strangers and mutineers.

Midshipman Maynard was watching him anxiously. 'Signal, sir. Flag to *Phalarope*. Complete lightering and proceed to sea with all despatch.'

Herrick said wearily, 'Acknowledge, Mr. Maynard.'

Herrick stared over the rail where the seamen toiled with the fresh-water casks and then across at the tallmasted flagship. Almost to himself he muttered, 'You bastard! You just can't wait, can you.'

Grumbling and cursing, the duty watch climbed down the various ladders and into the already crowded berth deck. Both air and lighting came through the central hatchways, and in addition several canvas chutes had been rigged to help ventilate the overpopulated living spaces. At each scrubbed mess table men sat and made use of their time to their own best advantage. Some repaired clothing, heads bent to catch the filtered sunlight on their needles and coarse thread. Some worked on small model ships, and others merely sprawled yarning with their companions.

There was a brief lull in the buzz of speculation and rumour as some of the new men pattered down a ladder followed by Belsey, the duty master's mate. All of the men had been read in, had taken the regulation shower under the deck pump, and now stood blinking in the

119

shadows, their bodies pale and naked against the ship's dark sides. Each man carried a new shirt and a rolled pair of trousers, as well as his own small possessions.

Belsey spun his cane and pointed to the corner mess table where Allday and old Strachan watched the procession in silence. He barked, 'You two! You'll be in this mess, got it?' He glared into the dark corner of the berth deck. 'You've been given your watch and action stations, so just get settled in, and look sharp about it!' He raised his voice. 'Show these replacements where to sling their hammocks, and then get this deck cleared up!' He wrinkled his thick nose. 'It's like a bloody pigsty down here.'

One of the men detailed dropped his bundle on the table and looked down at Strachan and the others. He was tall and well muscled, and his broad chest was covered in a deep mat of dark hair. He seemed quite unconcerned about his nakedness and the rasp of Belsey's introduction.

He said calmly, 'Harry Onslow is the name, mates.' He looked over his shoulder. 'An' this is Pook, another good topman from the *Cassius*!' He spat out the name of the flagship, and Belsey who was hovering nearby strode across to the crowded table.

'Pay attention!' He stared round the watching faces. 'Don't you start thinking that you've got a real fine fellow here, my friends!' He gave a short grin. 'Turn round, Onslow!' He moved his cane menacingly. 'Just get a bit o' sunlight over you!'

Onslow turned his body obediently so that the light played across his back. Something like a hollow groan came from the packed sailors, and Belsey added coldly, 'Take a good look, afore you start listening to the like o' this scum!'

Allday tightened his lips as he saw the savagely mutilated skin on Onslow's body. He could not imagine how many times the man had been flogged, but that he had survived was surely a miracle.

The whole of his back, from the nape of the neck to the top of his buttocks, was ugly with broken and uneven weals, pale and obscene against his tanned arms and legs.

Ferguson looked away, his mouth quivering.

Even Pochin, a hard spectator at many floggings, said thickly, ''Ere, mate, put yer shirt on!'

The other man, Pook, was thin and wiry, and although his back also displayed the clawing embrace of the cat, it was nothing compared with Onslow's.

Belsey sauntered away followed by the other new seamen.

Onslow pulled the shirt over his head and shook, out the clean new trousers. Calmly he remarked, 'What is so different about your captain? Does he like his men to look pretty?' He had a lazy Norfolk accent, and seemed quite unmoved by the horror his scars had unleashed.

Ferguson said quickly, 'He's different. He stopped Betts being flogged.' He tried to smile. 'You'll be all right aboard this ship, Onslow!'

Onslow looked him over without expression. 'Who asked *you* then?'

'All captains are swine!' Pook was tugging on his trousers, and then strapped a wicked-looking knife around his waist. 'We've had a bellyful in the *Cassius*!'

Onslow said, 'Betts, did you say? What happened to him?'

'He attacked the purser.' Pochin looked thoughtful. 'Cap'n Bolitho refused to 'ave 'im flogged.'

'Where is he now?' The man's eyes were dark and unwinking.

'Dead. Went over the side with a main t'gallant!'

'Well, then.' Onslow pushed Ferguson off the bench and squatted in his place. 'It didn't do him much good, did it?'

Old Strachan folded his carving in a piece of sailcloth and said vaguely, 'But the lad's right. Cap'n Bolitho promised that he would see us fair if we pulled our weight. We'll be taking a run ashore soon.' He squinted towards the hatch. 'Just think of it! A walk through them hills, and maybe a drop o' somethin' from a friendly native!'

Ferguson tried again. As if he had to believe in some-body to retain his own sanity. 'And Mr. Herrick said he would try and get a letter put aboard the next homebound ship for me. Just to tell my wife I'm alive and well.' His expression was pitiful.

'You can read and write, can you, little man?' Onslow studied him calmly. 'You could be very useful to me.'

Allday smiled to himself. Already the noise and rumble of voices was returning to the messes. Maybe Ferguson was right. Things might be better from now on. He hoped so, if only for Ferguson's peace of mind.

Pochin asked sourly, 'How did you get the lash, Onslow?'

'Oh, the usual.' Onslow was still watching Ferguson, his face deep in thought.

Pook said ingratiatingly, ''E kicked a bosun's mate! An' afore that he . . .'

Onslow's mouth opened and shut like a trap. 'Stow it! It's what happens from now on that counts!' Then he became calm again. 'I was a boy when I came out here ten years back. For years I've been waiting for that last voyage home, but it never comes. I've been shipped from one captain to the next. I've stood my watches, and I've faced broadsides more times than I can remember. No, mates, there's no let-up for our sort. The only way out is sewn up in a hammock, or take our own course like the lads in the *Andiron*.'

He had every man's attention now. He stood up, his face set and brooding. 'They chose to leave the King's service. To make a new life for themselves out here, or in the Americas!'

Strachan shook his grey head. 'That's piracy!'

122

'You're too old to matter!' There was a bite in Onslow's voice. 'I've yet to find a fair captain, or one who thought beyond prize money and glory for himself!'

At that moment shadows darted across the hatches and the air was filled with twittering pipes.

Pochin groaned. 'Blasted Spithead nightingales! Do they never get tired of blowin' 'em?'

The voices of the bosun's mates echoed round the berth deck. 'All hands! All hands! Stand by to make sail! Anchor party muster on the fo'c's'le!'

Ferguson stared blankly at the sunlight on the ladder, his mouth hanging open. 'He promised! He promised me I could get a letter home!'

Onslow clapped him on the shoulder. 'And he'll promise a lot more, I shouldn't wonder, lad!' He faced the others, unsmiling. 'Well, mates! Do you understand now what I was saying?'

Josling, a bosun's mate, appeared on the ladder, his face running with sweat. 'Are yew deaf? Jump to it there! A taste of my little rope for the last on deck!'

There was a stampede of running feet as the men came to their senses and surged up to the sunlight.

'Stand by the capstan!' The orders clouted their ears. 'Hands aloft! Loose tops'ls!'

Allday saw Ferguson staring wildly at the green, inviting island with its low, undulating hills. He felt a lump in his own throat now. It was not unlike Cornwall in the summertime, he thought.

Then he touched Ferguson's arm and said kindly, 'Come on, lad. I'll race you aloft!'

Vibart's booming voice filled the air. 'Loose heads'ls! Man the braces!'

Allday reached the mainyard and ran quickly along the footrope to join the others lying across the thick spar. Below him he could see the busy deck, and over his shoulder he could identify Bolitho's tall figure by the taffrail.

From forward Herrick yelled, 'Anchor's aweigh, sir!'

Allday dug his toes into the footrope as the sail billowed and filled beneath him and the great yard moved ponderously to catch the wind. Already the land was sliding away, and by the time the sails were set and trimmed it would be lost in the haze. Perhaps for ever, he thought.

7

A Spanish Lugger

Herrick moved slightly around the mizzen mast in an effort to remain in the shadow cast by its thick trunk. He found that his eyes were constantly slitted against the harsh glare, his tongue continually moving across his parched lips as the forenoon watch dragged slowly to its conclusion.

Above his head the sails hung limp and lifeless, and there was not a breath of wind to ruffle the flat, empty expanse of sea, upon which the becalmed frigate lay motionless and hushed.

He plucked at his grubby shirt, immediately irritated by the futility of his action. It felt sodden with sweat, yet his whole being seemed to cry out for moisture. He could feel the deck seams gripping stickily at his shoes, and once when he had inadvertently rested his hand on one of the quarterdeck nine-pounders he had almost cried out with pain. The barrel had been as hot as if it had been firing without pause. His lip curled bitterly at the thought. There had been no action, nor was there likely to be under these impossible conditions.

After leaving Antigua the *Phalarope* had sailed directly to her allotted station, but apart from sighting another patrolling frigate and then later the bulky shape of the *Cassius*, she had kept the sea to herself.

And now, to top it all, the frigate was becalmed. For

twenty-four hours she had idled aimlessly above her reflection, carried at will by the sluggish currents, the lookouts worn and weary from staring hopefully for a squall to break the spell. Seven long days since they had sailed with such haste from Antigua, seven days of watching the burnished horizons and waiting.

Herrick glanced forward where the duty watch lay like dead men below the dark shadow of the bulwark. Their half-naked bodies had already lost their pallor, and more than one unseasoned sailor bore savage burns on his skin from the sun's relentless glare.

Midshipman Neale leaned against the nettings, his round face for once devoid of mischief or interest. Like the rest, he seemed crushed and defeated by the inactivity and heat.

It was hard to believe that anything else existed outside their own enclosed world. St. Kitts lay some fifty miles to the south-east, and the Anegada Passage which separated the Virgin Islands from the disputed Leewards was spread in an eye-searing haze across the motionless bowsprit.

Of Hood's efforts to hold St. Kitts they had heard nothing, and for all Herrick could guess even the war might have ended. When they had met the flagship, Bolitho had made a signal requesting the latest information, but the reply had been unhelpful to say the least. The *Phalarope* had been carrying out gunnery practice, using several old and useless casks as targets. Herrick knew that Bolitho had done it more to break the monotony than with any hope of improving the standards of markmanship by such methods.

Cassius's flags had soared angrily to her yards, and soon Maynard had reported warily that the admiral was demanding an immediate cease-fire. 'Conserve powder and shot', the signal had ordered curtly. So that was that.

Bolitho had made no comment, but Herrick knew his captain well enough now to understand the sudden anger in his grey eyes. It was as if the admiral had gone out of his way to isolate the *Phalarope*, as a doctor would separate a leper from his fellow humans.

He jerked from his thoughts as Bolitho's head and shoulders appeared through the cabin hatch. Like the other officers, he was dressed in shirt and white breeches, and his dark hair was clinging to his forehead with sweat. He looked strained and edgy, and Herrick could almost feel the restlessness which was making Bolitho fret at the inaction around him.

Herrick said, 'Still no wind, sir.'

Bolitho shot him an angry glance and then seemed to control himself. 'Thank you, Mr. Herrick. So I see.' He walked to the compass and glanced at the two listless helmsmen. Then he moved to the starboard rail, and Herrick saw him wince as the sun smote his shoulders like a furnace.

Bolitho said quietly, 'How are the men?'

Herrick replied vaguely, 'Not happy, sir. It is bad enough out here, without short water rations!'

'Quite so.' Bolitho nodded without turning. 'But it is necessary. God knows how long we will be pinned down like this.'

His hand moved vaguely to the scar beneath the rebellious forelock of hair. Herrick had seen him touch the livid mark on several previous occasions, usually when he appeared to be entirely wrapped in his own thoughts. Once Herrick had questioned Stockdale about it, and learned that it had happened when Bolitho, as a junior lieutenant, had been sent ashore to an island with a small party of seamen to refill water casks.

Unknown to the captain or anyone else, the island had not been uninhabited, and almost as soon as the launch had grated up the beach the party had been ambushed by a horde of yelling natives. One had snatched up a cutlass from a dying sailor and attacked Bolitho as he had tried to rally his outnumbered men. In his thick, jolting voice Stockdale had described the scene around the launch, with half the sailors butchered or dying and the others falling back desperately in a frantic effort to regain the safety of the sea. Bolitho had fallen, separated from his men, his face masked in blood from the cutlass slash which should have killed him. The sailors who survived were all for leaving their officer, whom they supposed to be dead anyway, but at the last minute they rallied, and as more boats pulled to their aid Bolitho was dragged to safety.

Herrick knew there was a lot more to it than that. Just as he guessed that it had been Stockdale's massive right arm which had held the men from panic and had saved the man he now served like a devoted dog.

Bolitho walked forward to the quarterdeck rail and stared towards the bows. 'The haze, Mr. Herrick. It looks not unlike a Channel mist.'

Herrick's dry lips cracked into a rueful smile. 'I never thought I would miss the Channel Fleet, sir. But how I would like to hear the wind and feel the cold spray again.'

'Maybe.' Bolitho seemed lost in his thoughts. 'But I have a feeling the wind will return soon.'

Herrick stared at him. It was not a boast or an empty statement of hope. It was like another small picture of the man's quiet confidence, he thought.

There was a step on the deck behind them and Vibart said harshly, 'A word, Captain.'

Bolitho replied, 'What is it?'

'Your clerk, Mathias, sir.' Vibart watched Bolitho's impassive face as he continued, 'He's had a bad fall in the hold, sir.'

'How bad?'

Vibart shook his head. 'He'll not see another day, I'm thinking.' There was no pity in his voice.

Bolitho bit his lip. 'I sent him down there myself to check some stores.' He looked up suddenly, his face clouded with concern. 'Are you sure nothing can be done for him?'

'The surgeon says not.' Vibart sounded indifferent. 'Apart from his ribs, which are badly stove in, he's got a split in his skull you could put a marlin-spike through!'

'I see.' Bolitho stared down at his hands on the rail. 'I hardly knew the man, but he was a hard worker and tried to do his best.' He shook his head. 'To die in action is one thing, but this . . .'

Herrick said quickly, 'I will get another clerk, sir. There is a new man, Ferguson, one of those pressed in Falmouth. He can read and write, and is more used to that sort of work.' Herrick recalled Ferguson's wretched expression as the ship had left Antigua. He had promised to help him get a letter away to his wife. Perhaps this release from the heavy duties of seamanship and the harsh control of the petty officers would make up for the omission in some way.

Herrick watched Bolitho's grave face and wondered how the captain could find the time to grieve over one man when he himself was burdened with such bitter responsibility.

Bolitho said, 'Very well. Detail Ferguson and tell him his duties.'

A yell came from the maintopmast. 'Deck there! Squall comin' from the starboard bow!'

Herrick ran to the rail, one hand shading his eyes. Incredulously he saw the gentle ripple pushing down towards the becalmed ship and heard the rigging stirring itself as the inert sails moved slowly into life.

Bolitho stood upright and clasped his hands behind him. 'What are you all staring at? Stir those men, Mr. Herrick, and get the ship under way!'

Herrick nodded. He had seen the excitement beneath Bolitho's outburst. As the sails filled and flapped overhead Bolitho's expression was almost boyish with pleasure.

It was not much of a wind, but sufficient to get the *Phalarope* moving once more. The water gurgled around her rudder, and as the braces squeaked in the blocks the sails swung to embrace every last ounce of air, eager for the life it had given them.

Bolitho said at length, 'Keep her north-west by north, Mr. Herrick. We will remain on this leg until sunset.'

'Aye, aye, sir.' Herrick watched him walk back to the taff rail and peer down at the small wake. There was no sign of the anxiety he must be feeling, he thought. The wind was a small respite and no way a recompense for the endless, meaningless patrol, yet Bolitho acted as if everything was normal, outwardly at least.

Again the masthead lookout was to prove that nothing could be taken for granted.

'Deck there! Sail fine on the starboard bow!'

Herrick lifted his glass but Bolitho snapped, 'You'll not see anything from here! The haze is like a blanket to the north of us!'

Vibart muttered, 'Mr. Neale, get aloft!'

'Belay that!' Bolitho sounded dangerously calm. 'You go, Mr. Herrick. I want an experienced eye at this moment!'

Herrick ran to the main shrouds and began to climb. He quickly realised how out of condition his body had become, and by the time he had reached the topmast trestle and crosstrees his heart was pounding like a drum. The bearded lookout moved over for him and pointed with a tarry hand.

'Over yonder, sir! Can't make her out yet!'

Herrick ignored the ship swinging like a toy beneath his legs and opened his glass. At first he could see nothing but bright sunlight across the low-lying haze with the million glittering mirrors of the sea beneath. Then he saw the sail and felt a tinge of disappointment. The hull was well shrouded in mist, but from the sail's strange dorsal shape he guessed it was small, probably a coasting lugger of some sort. Not worth taking as a prize, and hardly worth sinking, he decided angrily. He yelled the information to the deck and saw Bolitho staring up at him.

'A lugger, you say?' Bolitho sounded interested. 'Keep watching her!'

'She's not seen us.' The lookout squinted towards the sail. 'Reckon us'll be up to 'er afore she spots us.'

Herrick nodded and then looked down as Vibart called, 'Pipe all hands! Stand by to wear ship!'

So Bolitho was going to close her anyway. Herrick watched the sudden burst of activity on the decks below. He had not seen such a sight since he was a midshipman. The scampering, apparently aimless figures, which surged from between decks and then merged as if by magic into recognisable patterns of discipline and purpose. He could see the petty officers checking their watch bills as they bawled names and orders. Here and there the officers and warrant officers stood like little isolated rocks against the surging tide of running seamen.

Again the yards moved round, flapping indignantly as the frigate altered course two points to starboard. Herrick felt the mast tremble, and tried not to think of the time it would take to fall to the deck.

But the breeze which had found the *Phalarope* had reached the other sail, and as the mist glided away in its path the lugger gathered way and heeled jauntily, another tan sail already creeping up her stumpy mainmast.

The lookout champed on a wad of tobacco and said calmly, 'Her's a Spaniard! Oi'd know that rig anywhere.'

Bolitho's voice cut through his speculation. 'You may come down now, Mr. Herrick! Lively there!'

Herrick reached the deck gasping and sweating to find Bolitho waiting for him, his face deep in concentration.

'She'll have the edge on us, Mr. Herrick. She can make better use of these light airs than we can.' He gestured impatiently towards the forecastle. 'Clear away the two chasers and fire across her bows!'

Herrick got his breath and gasped, 'Aye aye, sir! It would only take one ball to shatter her timbers!'

He saw something like amusement in the grey eyes as Bolitho replied, 'She may have the most precious cargo of all time, Mr. Herrick!'

Herrick stared at him dazedly. 'Sir?'

Bolitho had turned to watch the gunners scampering forward towards the two long nine-pounders on the forecastle. '*Information*, Mr. Herrick! Out here, the lack of it could lose a war!'

One shot was enough. As the tall waterspout fell in a splatter of spray beyond the lugger's bows, first one sail and then the other crumpled and fell, leaving the boat rocking dejectedly to await the *Phalarope*'s pleasure.

Bolitho's wide cabin seemed almost cold after the furnace heat of the quarterdeck, and he had to force himself to stand quite still by the stern windows to steady his racing thoughts and plan the next move. With real effort he closed his ears to the muffled shipboard noises and distant shouts as a boat was dropped alongside to take a boarding party to the lugger, which now rode uneasily under the frigate's lee. It had been all Bolitho could do to remain outwardly unruffled as his orders were passed and carried out, so that in the end he could no longer face the watchful glances of his officers or avoid the buzzing speculation of the upper-deck idlers.

His casual guess about the coming of a wind had seemed like a miracle, and when the lookout had reported the lugger in the haze he had felt his pent up emotions churning around like raw alcohol. The waiting and petty irritations were momentarily put to one side, even the shame he felt for the admiral's attitude to *Phalarope* could be overlooked, if not forgotten.

There was a tap at the door, and he swung round, caught off guard. 'Enter!'

He stared for a few seconds at the pale-faced seaman who hovered uncertainly in the doorway. He wrenched his mind away from the lugger and nodded towards the desk by the bulkhead,

'You must be Ferguson? You will be working here when I require you.' His tone was terse, his thoughts still following the invisible boarding party.

Ferguson stared round the cabin and blinked. 'Yes, sir. I mean—aye, aye, sir.' He seemed confused and nervous.

Bolitho studied him kindly. 'I will tell you more of your duties later. At the moment I am rather busy.' He looked round with a jerk as little Neale panted up to the door.

'Captain, sir!' He fought for breath. 'Mr. Okes has taken the lugger!'

'So I should hope!' Bolitho added dryly, 'Her skipper has a whole broadside staring down his throat.'

Neale considered the point. 'Er, yes, sir.' He stared up at Bolitho's calm face, obviously wondering how the captain could bear to leave the upperdeck when something was at last happening. He added, 'The boat is returning now, sir.'

'That was what I wanted to hear, Mr. Neale.' Bolitho looked through the stern windows towards the empty sea, its surface still ruffled by a small but steady breeze. 'When the boat comes alongside tell Captain Rennie with my compliments to keep the lugger's officers apart until I can question them. Mr. Okes can carry on with his search of the lugger and report when he finds anything.'

'The lugger's *officers*, sir?' Neale's eyes were like saucers.

'They may be dressed in rags, boy, but they are still officers!' Bolitho watched the midshipman patiently. 'And make no mistake, they will know these waters like their own faces.'

The midshipman nodded and scurried away. Bolitho paced restlessly around the cabin and then paused by his table where his personal chart of the Caribbean lay in readiness. The complex mass of islands and soundings, the vague surveys and doubtful descriptions were like the clues of a giant puzzle. He frowned and tugged at his chin. Somewhere amongst the tangle of scattered islands lay the key to the whole campaign. The first to find it would win the day. The loser would be driven from the Caribbean for ever.

With the points of his brass dividers he traced the *Phalarope*'s course and halted at the small pencilled cross. Out here he was doing no good. Fifty miles away St. Kitts might still be fighting a siege, whilst just over the horizon Count de Grasse's great fleet could be mustering for a final attack on the scattered British naval units. With the British driven from these islands, the French and their allies would unroll the South Americas like a chart. Would command the North and South Atlantic and reach for the rich rewards of Africa and beyond.

He pushed the apprehension from his mind as he heard the clatter of feet above and the thuds of muskets on the deck planks.

Vibart appeared in the doorway. 'Prisoners aboard, sir.' He glared at Ferguson who seemed to be trying to curl into a ball beside the desk. 'The lugger is Spanish well enough. Twenty men aboard all told, but no resistance. I have the master and two mates under guard outside, sir.'

'Good.' Bolitho stared at the chart. 'Twenty men, you say? That is a large crew for such a small craft. The Spaniards are usually more sparing when they man a vessel of any kind!'

Vibart shrugged. 'Mr. Farquhar says that the lugger has been used for coastal trading. Not much use for us.'

'I'll see the master first. You can go on deck and keep

an eye on Mr. Okes' progress in the lugger. Let me know if he has found anything.'

The lugger's skipper was small and swarthy, dressed in a tattered shirt and wide canvas trousers. Two gold earrings bobbed from beneath his lank hair, and his dirty, bare feet completed the picture of neglect and poverty.

Beside him, Midshipman Farquhar seemed elegant and unreal.

Bolitho kept his eyes on the chart, conscious of the Spaniard's uneven breathing and the shuffling movements of his bare feet on the deck. He said at length, 'Does he speak English?'

'No, sir.' Farquhar sounded impatient. 'He just gabbles.'

Still Bolitho kept his eyes on the chart. Almost offhandedly he said, 'Then take him on deck and tell the master-at-arms to run a halter up to the mainyard.'

Farquhar fell back startled. 'Halter, sir? Do you mean to hang him?'

'Of course I do!' Bolitho put a rasp in his tone. 'He is no further use to me!'

The Spaniard's legs buckled and he pitched forward at Bolitho's feet. Sobbing and weeping he pulled at Bolitho's legs, the words flooding from his lips in a wild torrent.

'Please, Captain! No hang, *please*! I am a good man, sir, I have wife and many poor children!' His cheeks were running with tears. 'Please, sir, no *hang*!' The last word was almost a shriek.

Bolitho stepped from the man's grasp and said calmly. 'I had an idea that your knowledge of English might return.' To Farquhar he added crisply, 'You may try that ruse on the two mates. See what you can find out!' He turned back to the whimpering man on the deck. 'Now stand up and answer my questions, or indeed I *will* hang you!'

He waited a few more moments, his mind half dwelling on what might have happened if the Spaniard really had been unable to speak English. Then he asked, 'Where were you heading and with what cargo?'

The man stood swaying from side to side, his grubby hands clasped as if in prayer. 'I go to Puerto Rico, Captain. I take small cargo of timber, a little sugar.' He wrung his hands. 'But you can take it all, excellency! Just spare my life!'

'Hold your tongue!' Bolitho peered at the chart. The story was possible. These small trading boats were as common as fleas in the Caribbean. He added sharply, 'From where did you come?'

The man smiled ingratiatingly. 'I go all around, Captain.' He waved his hands vaguely. 'I carry only small cargoes. I reap a living where I can. It is a hard, hard life, excellency!'

'I will ask you once more!' Bolitho fixed him with a hard stare.

The man shifted wretchedly. 'Martinique, Captain. I has small work there. But I *hate* the French, you understand?'

Bolitho dropped his eyes to hide the excitement he now felt. Martinique, the headquarters of all French naval operations, the most heavily protected fortress in the whole Caribbean.

'You hate the French? Your gallant allies?' Bolitho's sarcasm was not lost on the Spaniard. 'Well, never mind that. Just tell me how many ships were there in the anchorage.' He saw the man's eyes glitter with fright and guessed he understood which anchorage he meant.

'Many ships, excellency!' He rolled his eyes. 'Many *big* ships!'

'And who commands these many big ships?' Bolitho could hardly keep the anxiety from his voice now.

'The French admiral, excellency!' The Spaniard puffed out his cheeks as if to spit on the deck, but caught sight of the marine sentry watching from the doorway and swallowed noisily. 'He is a French pig, that one!'

'The Count de Grasse?'

The man nodded violently. 'But you know everything, Captain! You are blessed by the Almighty!'

Bolitho looked up as Farquhar entered the cabin. 'Well?'

'Only a little English between them, sir.' He seemed angry with himself. 'But I gather they were heading for Puerto Rico.'

Bolitho gestured at the sentry. 'Take this prisoner out and keep him closely guarded.' Then he said absently, 'He was lying. He sailed from Martinique. The French would never allow him to carry on trading when they too might be under siege at any time!' He tapped the chart. 'No, Mr. Farquhar, he was at Martinique well enough, but his destination is elsewhere!'

Vibart entered and bowed his head beneath the deck beams. 'Mr Okes reports that the cargo is much as you already know, sir. But there are new ship's spars and casks of salt meat stowed beneath the main load.' He sounded doubtful. 'There is also a great deal of spare canvas and cordage.'

'As I thought!' Bolitho felt strangely relieved. 'The lugger was taking supplies from Martinique' – his finger moved along the charted islands – 'to where?' He looked from Vibart's brooding face to Farquhar's baffled one. 'Get that Spanish skipper back here at once!'

Bolitho walked slowly to the stern windows and leaned out over the water as if to clear his brain. The Spaniard had seemed pleased to tell him about the French ships at Martinique, when he must have known that patrolling British ships would already know this information. He must have imagined that Bolitho had missed the main item.

He swung round as the man was pushed through the

door. 'Now listen to me!' His voice was still controlled, but the harshness made the lugger's master start to quiver uncontrollably. 'You lied to me! I warned you what would happen, did I not?' He dropped his voice still further. 'Now just once more. Where were you bound?'

The man swayed. 'Please, excellency! They kill me if they know!'

'And I will kill you if you keep me waiting!' He saw Herrick's face watching him from the doorway with fixed fascination.

'We sail for Mola Island, Captain.' The man seemed to have shrunk in size. 'The cargo was for ship there!'

Herrick and Farquhar exchanged mystified glances.

Bolitho bent over his chart. 'Mola Island is Dutch.' He measured the distance with his dividers. 'Thirty miles to the nor'-east of our present position.' He looked up, his eyes hard and devoid of pity. 'How many such voyages have you made?'

'Many, excellency.' The Spaniard looked as if he wanted to be sick. 'There are soldiers there. French soldiers. They come from the north. They have ships also.'

Bolitho breathed out slowly. 'Of course! De Grasse would never attempt to move his ships against Jamaica or anywhere else unless he could be sure of a diversion elsewhere and full support from the military!' He stared at the others. 'Our fleet watches Martinique to the south and waits for the French to move, and all the time they are filtering down from the American mainland, gathering for a big, final assault!'

Vibart said bleakly, 'We must inform the *Cassius*, sir.

Herrick spoke from the doorway, his voice eager. 'We could send the lugger to find the flagship, sir, and stay here in readiness!'

Bolitho did not seem to hear them. 'Sentry, take this prisoner and lock him up with the others. My compliments to the boatswain, and tell him to select any of the lugger's crew he thinks could be sworn into our company. I would imagine that even the *Phalarope* would seem better than a prison hulk!'

The marine grinned. 'Aye, aye, sir!' He jabbed the Spaniard with his musket and hustled the man away.

'It will be two days before we meet up with the *Cassius* again.' Bolitho was thinking aloud. 'By then it may be too late. That Spaniard has told us a good deal, but he cannot know the whole truth. If the French have been gathering a force of men and ships in this small island they must be expecting to move, and soon. I consider it our duty to investigate, and do our utmost to stop them.'

Vibart swallowed hard. 'Do you intend to leave the patrol area, sir?'

'Do you have any objections, Mr. Vibart?' Bolitho eyed him calmly.

'It is not *my* responsibility, sir.' Vibart dropped his gaze before Bolitho's cool stare.

Herrick said quickly, 'It is a great risk, if I may say so, sir.'

'As is everything worthwhile, Mr. Herrick.' Bolitho straightened his back and added briskly: 'My compliments to Mr. Proby. Tell him to wear ship and steer northeast. We will be sailing close to the wind so it will be nightfall before we reach Mola Island. Before that time there is much to be arranged, gentlemen!'

He looked around their faces and continued, 'Put a prize crew aboard the lugger, and ask Mr. Okes to search for the recognition signals. It is my guess that this island will be heavily guarded. The lugger will be too useful to spare for finding the admiral.'

Vibart said sulkily, 'The admiral will not be too pleased by your acting like this, sir.'

'And my conscience would never rest if I allowed my own prestige to come before this obvious duty, Mr. Vibart!'

His eyes moved to Herrick and Farquhar. 'This will be a good opportunity for each of you.' He paused and looked around the cabin. 'For the ship, too.'

He waited until the cabin had emptied and then walked to the windows again. For one more minute he allowed the nagging doubts to play havoc with his thoughts. He had acted impetuously and without pausing to consider the possible consequences. Skill and ability were only half the battle. There always had to be a good amount of luck. And if he was mistaken now, there would not be that amount of luck in the whole world.

He saw Ferguson watching from the desk like a mesmerised rabbit and realised that he had forgotten all about his being there. But the story he might repeat on the berth deck might do good for the ship's dwindling morale, he thought vaguely. If the *Phalarope* was lucky this time it would make all the difference.

And if not? He shrugged. There would be few survivors to dispute the matter.

Above his head he heard the afterguard tramping with the braces and felt the deck canting slightly as the frigate went about. Momentarily framed in the stern windows he saw the small lugger swinging round to keep station on the quarter, and wondered how many men had already cursed the keen-eyed lookout for sighting her.

Aloud he remarked, 'You will have something to tell your wife now, Ferguson. She will be proud of you perhaps?'

Bolitho heaved himself from the cutter's sternsheets and allowed groping hands to pull him unceremoniously up and over the lugger's low bulwark. For several seconds he stood swaying on the unfamiliar deck to allow his eyes to get accustomed to the gloom and the packed figures around him.

Already the cutter had shoved off, and apart from the

140

gleam of white spray around the oars it was lost in the enfolding darkness. Bolitho tried to see where the *Phalarope* now lay, but she, too, was well hidden, with not one glimmer of light to betray her presence. He tried to hold on to the mental picture of the chart and of the island which now lay somewhere across the lugger's blunt bows.

Captain Rennie loomed out of the darkness and said in an unnecessary whisper, 'I've packed the marines below, sir. Sergeant Garwood will keep 'em quiet until they are required.'

Bolitho nodded and tried to remember once again if he had left anything to chance. 'You have made sure that all muskets and pistols are unloaded?'

Rennie nodded. 'Yes, sir.' He sounded as if he meant, 'Of course, sir.' A primed musket exploding at the wrong moment, a trigger pulled by an over-excited marine, and their lives would be worth even less than they were now.

'Good.' Bolitho groped his way aft where Stockdale stood straddle-legged beside the crude tiller bar, his head cocked towards the loose flapping sails. Midshipman Farquhar squatted by a shapeless bundle on the deck which Bolitho managed to recognise as the luckless Spanish skipper. He had been brought along as both guide and surety.

Rennie asked flatly, 'Do you think we will get inshore without trouble?'

Bolitho glanced up at the high, bright stars. There was the merest sliver of silver for a moon floating above its reflection in the flat water. The night was dark enough to hide anything. Maybe too dark.

He said, 'We shall see. Now get under way, and make sure the compass light is well shaded.' He walked clear of Rennie and his questions and brushed past the crouching sailors whose eyes gleamed like marbles as they watched him pass. Occasionally he heard the rasp of a cutlass or a dull clink from the bows where McIntosh, a gunner's

141

mate, was making a last-minute examination of his hastily rigged swivel gun. It was loaded with canister, and at close range would be quite deadly. It had to be perfect, Bolitho thought grimly. There might be no time for a second shot.

He wondered what Vibart was thinking, left in charge of the frigate, with hours to wait before he could play his part in the raid. He thought, too, of Herrick's face when he had told him he was taking Lieutenant Okes with him in the lugger. Herrick had known there was no other choice in the matter. Okes was his senior, and it was only fair that he should get the chance of making a name for himself. Or dying before Herrick, Bolitho thought dryly. Vibart's position and seniority made him the obvious choice for taking charge of the *Phalarope*, and if both Bolitho and Vibart were killed, Herrick could still move his way up the chain of command.

Bolitho scowled in the darkness and cursed himself for his morbid thoughts. Perhaps he was already too tired, too worn out by planning and preparation to think any more. All day long, while the frigate had beaten her way towards Mola Island, things had moved at a swift pace. Men and weapons had been transferred to the lugger, and the latter's cargo had been either dropped overboard or rowed across to the *Phalarope* for their own use. The lugger's cramped hold was now packed with marines, each man too busy fighting back the nausea thrown up by the stench of fish oil and sour vegetables to care much about what might lie ahead.

Mathias, Bolitho's clerk, had died and had been dropped overboard with a brief prayer, his death and passing hardly making a break in the frantic preparations. Looking back, it was hard even to recall his face.

Lieutenant Okes stumbled along the side deck, his shoulders hunched as if he expected to be struck by some unseen object. He peered at Bolitho's watchful shape and muttered, 'All – all the men are ready, sir.' He sounded taut and nervous.

Bolitho grunted. Okes' behaviour had been worrying him for some time. He had even offered to stay aboard the frigate in Herrick's place, which was odd, in spite of the danger. Okes, he knew, was not a rich man, and any extra promotion, a glowing report in the *Gazette*, would make all the difference to his career. He was probably frightened. Well, so was anyone but a raving maniac, Bolitho thought.

He replied, 'We shall see the headland soon. There should be plenty of surf to show its position.' He screwed up his eyes to will himself to see the picture he had built of the island in his mind.

It was shaped something like a rough horseshoe, with the deep anchorage lying snugly between the two curved headlands. But the village was on the seaward side of the nearest headland, that being the only beach on the whole island. According to the chart and what he had wrung from the lugger's skipper, the village was connected to the anchorage by a rough road which crossed a steep ravine by way of a wooden bridge. The tip of the headland was therefore isolated by the ravine, and on its highest point there was said to be a powerful battery of guns, probably twenty-four-pounders, which could easily defend the whole anchorage. A sandbar and several isolated reefs completed the hazardous approach. In fact, the approach was impossible without consent from both battery and good daylight. No wonder the French had chosen this place as their strongpoint.

''Eadland, sir!' A seaman pointed abeam. 'There, sir!'

Bolitho nodded and walked aft again. 'Steer close, Stockdale. There is a beach about a quarter of a mile ahead, and a wooden pier, if this Spaniard's word is worth anything!'

From the bow a seaman dropped his leadline overboard and then said hoarsely, 'By the mark two, sir!'

Two fathoms under the keel, and still a long way to go. There was no chance of a surprise attack here either, except by craft as small as the lugger. The only thing in their favour was surprise. Nobody in his right mind would expect a single small boat to approach a heavily guarded island in total darkness.

Belsey, the master's mate, said gruffly, 'I can see th' pier, sir. Look, over yonder!'

Bolitho swallowed hard, conscious of a prickling in his spine. He readjusted his sword and made sure that his pistol was ready at his waist.

'Get the Spaniard up here!' The tension was making his voice harsh, and he heard the prisoner's teeth chattering like dice.

He gripped the man's arm, smelling his fear. Now was the time to make the Spaniard more afraid of *him* than of anything the enemy could do. 'Listen to me!' He shook the man slowly with each word. 'When we are challenged, you know what to do?'

The Spaniard nodded violently. 'Show lantern. Give the signal, excellency!'

'And if they ask why you are coming in at night tell them you have despatches for the garrison commander.'

'But, excellency! I never get despatches!'

'Hold your tongue! *Just tell them!* If I know anything about sentries, they'll be satisfied for long enough!'

The pier crept out of the darkness like a black finger, and as the sails were lowered swiftly and the lugger glided gently towards the tall piles a lantern flickered into life and.a voice yelled, '*Qui va la?*'

The Spaniard opened the shutter of his own lantern. Two long flashes and two short ones. In a quavering voice he began to stutter his message, his words broken up by great gulps for breath. He was shaking so badly that Farquhar had to hold him upright against the mast like a corpse.

The sentry called something to another man, as yet hidden by a small hut in the middle of the pier, and Bolitho heard him laugh. There was a click of metal and then another as the sentries uncocked their muskets.

The bow swung against the pier, and Bolitho saw the sentry leaning forward to watch the lugger bump alongside. He had slung his musket over his shoulder, and his tall shako shone briefly in the glow from a long clay pipe. Bolitho held his breath. This was the time to see if he had chosen his men correctly.

He saw a sailor, moving with elaborate calm, climb nimbly up the nearest wooden ladder, the mooring rope in his hand. The sentry called after him, his voice muffled as he turned his back to watch the man looping the rope's eye over a bollard.

The next sailor, who had been crouching on the stern, leapt straight upwards like a cat. For a moment the two figures swayed together in a macabre dance, but there was hardly any sound. Only when the sailor released his grip and lowered the dead sentry carefully on the pier did Bolitho realise it was time to act.

He snapped, 'Next man up!'

Belsey, the master's mate, slipped over the bows, and followed by the other seaman who was wiping his knife blade on his trousers, disappeared around the side of the hut.

This time there was a little more noise. A clatter of a falling musket, and something like a gurgle. But nothing more.

Bolitho scrambled up to the pier, his body shaking with suppressed excitement. 'Right, Mr. Okes, get your party ashore and up to the end of the pier at the double!' He stopped an onrushing seaman with the back of his hand and snarled, 'Quietly there! There's a guardhouse at the far end!'

Rennie's marines were already pouring gratefully from

the hold, their white crossbelts bright and eerie against their uniforms. Rennie had not forgotten his part, and within minutes he had split his men into two parties, and with a single command had both files trotting briskly along the pier towards the silent village.

Stockdale was the last to leave the lugger, his cutlass swinging from his hand like a toy.

Bolitho took a last look round and checked his bearings. 'Very well, Stockdale, let us go and take a look!'

8

The Raid

Bolitho lifted his hand, and behind him the file of sailors shuffled to a standstill. 'We will wait here for ten minutes! Pass the word down the line!'

He waited until silence had again fallen over the steep roadway and then added quietly to Lieutenant Okes, 'We'll push on a bit further and have a look at the bridge. We can't help Rennie's marines by standing here worrying, and it's already near two o'clock. There is a lot to do before dawn finds us.'

He walked on without waiting for Okes to comment. He could feel the loose stones crunching beneath his shoes, and was conscious of a new sense of light-headedness. Everything had gone so well that the strain was all the more telling. Surely the luck could not last?

It had been less than an hour since the lugger had tied up to the pier. After killing the two luckless sentries, Captain Rennie's marines had gone on to capture the small guard-house at the end of the coast road with hardly a scuffle. The sleeping soldiers, all ten of them, had been gleefully clubbed into deeper slumber, or worse, and the duty N.C.O. had been seized and trussed like a terrified chicken.

Bolitho had left Rennie to spread his men along the roadside and occupy the high ground above the village. From there they should be able to withstand anything but a really heavy assault until the raiding party had completed its work.

Bolitho dropped on one knee and strained his eyes into the darkness. He could just see the spidery outline of a high wooden bridge and the isolated headland beyond, where the sleeping gun battery lay as yet unaware of what was happening. It was quite a solid bridge, Bolitho thought. Wide and heavy enough for guns and stores, for shot, and all the materials for building breastworks and embrasures. It would take a long time to replace once destroyed.

A boot crunched at his side and Sergeant Garwood peered down at him. 'Cap'n Rennie's respects, sir. The marines is all in position. We've 'ad the lugger warped to the end o' the pier so that we can cover our withdrawal with the swivel gun.' He stared towards the bridge. 'I'd like to have a crack at that lot, sir!' He sounded envious.

'You get back to Captain Rennie and tell him to hold the road until we fall back.' Bolitho smiled in the darkness. 'Don't worry, Sergeant, you'll get your pennyworth of fighting before the night's done!'

He saw the man's white crossbelt fading in the shadows and then said sharply, 'Right, Mr. Okes, call up the rest of the party and keep them quiet! A flogging for the first man to make a sound!' He turned back to the bridge. There was probably a sentry at one end, if not both. It would all have to be very quick.

Okes returned breathing heavily. 'All here, sir.'

Farquhar was close behind him, his face pale in the faint moonlight. He said, 'I have picked Glover for the job, sir.'

Bolitho nodded. He recalled that the seaman in question was the one who had so neatly killed the first sentry.

'Very well. Send him forward.' He watched the man slide over the rim of stones and bushes and fade immediately into the deep patch of shadow before the bridge. Then he added slowly, 'Now remember, men, if

Glover fails to find that sentry and the alarm is given, we will have to make a rush for it.' He drew his sword and saw the lethal glitter of cutlasses along the roadside.

To Okes he whispered, 'Mr. Farquhar will take five men to deal with the guns and magazine. McIntosh, the gunner's mate, will lay a good charge to blow the bridge when we fall back, understood?'

Okes nodded. 'I – I think so, sir!'

'You must be *sure*, Mr. Okes!' Bolitho eyed him keenly. Suddenly he wished it was Herrick at his side. Should he be killed before the raid was finished, how would Okes manage? He continued evenly, 'According to our captive Spaniard, there is a rough track down from the battery to the inside of the anchorage. I intend to go down there as soon as the battery is taken and see what can be done about the ships in the harbour. I will try and set fire to one or more of them, and *Phalarope* can deal with any which make a dash for it!' He swung round as Stockdale, dragging the whimpering Spaniard behind him, strode through the bushes, his teeth white in his face.

'Sir! Glover's just whistled! 'E's done for the sentry!'

Bolitho stood up. If only he had a thousand men instead of sixty, he thought vaguely. They could take and hold the whole island intact until help arrived. He tugged his hat down firmly over his eyes and glanced back at his men. He was thankful that every one of them was hand-picked. There had not been a single incident so far to warrant either punishment or anger.

'Now then, lads! Quickly and quietly, and no fuss!' He waved his sword, aware suddenly that his face was fixed in a wild grin. 'Follow me!'

In two files the sailors padded towards the bridge. Bolitho kept just ahead of the nearest men, his eyes straining ahead towards the deserted bridge, which all at once seemed a long way off and vulnerable.

Pad, pad, pad went the feet, and Bolitho knew without

149

turning his head that the orderly approach was already changing into a charge. Then his shoes were booming hollowly on the wooden boards of the bridge, and from the corner of his eye he saw the angry swirl of surf, and heard the roar of a tide-race between the steep walls of the ravine. He almost fell over the spread-eagled corpse of a uniformed sentry, and saw Glover waiting to greet him, a captured musket in his hands.

Bolitho did not pause but gasped, 'Well done, Glover! Now follow me!'

A semi-circular wall pitted with square gunports ran around the far side of the headland, and as his feet slipped on the stubble of gorse and dried grass Bolitho counted seven or eight large guns facing seaward. A high mound was built well behind the guns, and he guessed that these earthworks had been thrown up to protect the magazine.

There was a startled cry from the shadows below the wall and a soldier seemed to rise out of the ground at Bolitho's feet. He saw the bared teeth and heard the man's quick intake of breath as he lunged forward and upward with his bayonet.

Glover, who was pressing close on Bolitho's heels, gave a terrible scream and fell back pinioned on the blade like a slaughtered pig. Bolitho slashed out wildly and felt the shock jar up the sword blade and along his arm like a blow. The soldier seemed to crumple, his arm almost severed from his body by the force of the stroke.

He was lost and forgotten underfoot as the sailors surged wildly along the flattened ground, their eyes staring like madmen as they looked for further victims.

There were only six more French soldiers sleeping in a small stone hut beside a great earth furnace, which even now glowed malevolently and cast an eerie light across the garlands of bright round shot and the cutlasses of the jubilant sailors.

One soldier sat up gaping, as if he no longer trusted

what he saw. A cutlass cut him down before he could even cry out, and two more died screaming even as they struggled for their weapons.

Bolitho ignored the gruesome sounds from the hut and leaned across the breastworks to stare down at the great shimmering mirror of the anchorage. There were two big ships anchored well out in the centre and two smaller ones near the foot of the cliffs. He could see the riding lights like fireflies on the still water. There was no alarm. Nothing to break the quiet night watch. Bolitho felt the sweat cold on his brow and realised that his body was shaking uncontrollably.

Farquhar climbed up beside him, his dirk glinting faintly against his dark coat. 'The battery is ours, sir.' He sounded less controlled than usual, and Bolitho knew that he was suffering the same insane wildness as the rest of them.

Farquhar added in a calmer tone, 'Eight guns, sir. Two of them are thirty-two pounders!' He sounded impressed. 'If they heated the shot in the furnace the Frogs would be able to sink any attacker with ease. A ship would be ablaze in no time from that sort of hammering!'

Bolitho nodded and pointed at the anchored ships. 'I'd like to use the guns on them! But the din would bring the whole island down on us!' He gestured towards the two large craft. 'They'll be troopships, but the soldiers will be sleeping under canvas ashore somewhere. The French would have no use for soldiers too cramped and seasick to march when the time came!'

Okes ran up to him, his sword held across his body like a shield. 'What now, sir?'

Bolitho glanced at the stars. 'It will be getting light in two hours. By that time I want every gun either spiked or pushed over the edge of the cliff. The latter if at all possible. The last thing will be to blow the magazine.'

Farquhar nodded. 'I have put my men to work with

hand-spikes already. I think all the guns will go over the edge well enough, sir.'

'Very well.' Bolitho watched Okes' quick breathing. 'You take charge of the bridge and deal with that, Mr. Okes. Seize anyone who comes down the road, although I imagine it would take an eager spy to get past Rennie's pickets!'

Belsey, the master's mate, said, 'I've found the cliff path, sir. It leads right down to the sea. There are two longboats moored at the foot.' He waited. 'Shall I carry on, sir? I got my men ready.'

Bolitho nodded and watched the man lope away. Belsey had already shown he was well able to manage his part in the proceedings.

He walked back past the hut and then said sharply, 'Get those men out of there. There's a lot to be done yet!' The sharpness of his tone was more to cover his disgust than his anger. He had seen three of his men gleefully stripping the butchered corpses and crowing together like ghouls at a sacrifice.

He continued quietly, 'Get everything ready, Mr. Okes, but do not pull back until I give the signal. If I fall, then you must take command and use your own discretion.' He tapped the ground with his sword. 'But the guns must be destroyed and the battery blown, no matter what else is happening. Have a good fuse put on the bridge, and make sure the men know what they are doing.' He clapped Okes across the shoulder, and the man all but fell to his knees. 'It has been well worth our visit, Mr. Okes! Those two troopships alone could carry enough men to storm Antigua itself if necessary!'

Bolitho walked quickly towards the edge of the cliff where Stockdale waited for him, leaning on his cutlass. He paused and looked back. He felt a sudden surge of pride at the way things had gone so far. Men were working busily in the darkness, and already one of the giant guns had been trundled clear of its mounting. He could see Farquhar and McIntosh stooping over the box of fuses, entirely absorbed in their work of destruction, and other men loading their muskets and watching the captured bridge.

He turned on his heel and followed Stockdale down the steep, roughly hewn steps. If only he could enlarge this feeling of pride and purpose to the rest of the *Phalarope*'s company, he thought. It could be done. He had shown these men *how* it could be done.

It was dark and very cold at the foot of the steps, and he saw the small group of armed seamen already squatting in one of the longboats. He said to Belsey, 'Mark how the nearest ship swings at her anchor, Belsey!' He pointed at the small sloop which was riding less than two cables from the crude jetty below the cliff. Her stern was pointing towards the centre of the anchorage, her bowsprit towards the narrow span of water between the headlands.

Belsey nodded and rubbed his chin. 'Aye, sir! The tide's a-comin' in!' He stooped and dipped his arm underwater along the edge of the steps. 'I can feel no weed 'ere, sir. It must be well on the make.'

'It is.' Bolitho squinted his eyes in concentration. 'We'll go for the sloop there. There'll not be much of a watch kept. They'll think themselves safe enough below the battery. I know *I* would!'

Belsey nodded doubtfully. 'An' *then*, sir?' He sounded as if he would accept anything now.

'We'll set fire to her and let her drift into the nearest troop transport. She'll burn like dry grass!'

The master's mate bared his teeth. 'That'll raise the alarm well enough, sir!'

Bolitho laughed shortly. 'You can't get *everything* without payment!'

He clambered over his men and into the sternsheets. 'Get those oars muffled and be sharp about it! Use your shirts, anything!' He glanced quickly at the stars. Was it imagination, or were they paler than the last time he had looked? He snapped, 'Shove off! And pull handsomely!'

The oars rose and fell, the men holding their breaths as the boat sidled clear of the cliffs. The current gurgled impatiently around the counter and sent the hull swinging crazily into the mainstream.

Bolitho laid his hand on Stockdale's arm. 'Let her run. The tide is an ally tonight.'

He could see the sloop clear across the longboat's bow now, her slender bowsprit pointing directly above his head. He whispered, 'Easy, lads! *Easy*!' He could see a lantern aft by the taffrail and another small glow beside the foremast. That was probably the crew's hatch left open because of the warm night.

'Boat your oars!' He gritted his teeth as the heavy oars were laid carefully across the thwarts. Every sound seemed like a thunderclap. 'Steer with the current, Stockdale.' He leaned forward. 'You, in the bow! Have a grapnel ready!' To himself he added, 'The noise won't matter once we get aboard!'

'*Sir!*' The stroke oar was pointing wildly. 'Look, sir! A guardboat!'

Bolitho cursed himself for his over-confidence. When he swung his head he saw the white splash of oars and heard the creak of rowlocks barely twenty yards away.

There were gasps of surprise from some of his men, but Bolitho said harshly, 'Now, bowman! The grapnel!'

The longboat swung clumsily across the sloop's stern even as the pronged grapnel soared up and bit into the bulwark.

Everything seemed to be happening at once. There were shouts and cries from the prowling guardboat, followed by a ragged volley of musket shots. The stroke oarsman beside Bolitho screamed and fell writhing over the gun-wale, his arms thrushing as he vanished below the dark water. Bullets thudded into the boat and into the sloop's side beyond.

The men faltered as a face appeared overhead and the longboat was briefly lit in the angry flash of a pistol. Belsey ducked and swore savagely, and another man fell whimpering, blood gushing from his shoulder.

Bolitho ran along the slewing boat and leapt for the sloop's rail. For a moment his feet kicked above the water and then he was up and over, the breath knocked out of him as a seaman followed him across the bulwark and fell on top of him.

He struggled to his feet as the rest of his depleted party scrambled up beside him. The sloop's one misguided defender lay open mouthed and staring in a widening pool of blood, and a second man who suddenly appeared naked at the open hatch gave a shriek of terror and fled below, slamming the hatch behind him.

Bolitho sheathed his sword and said calmly, 'It will save us the trouble of seeking them out.' Then as a further volley banged out from the guardboat he shouted, 'You know what to do, Belsey! Cut the cable, and put a hand at the wheel!'

His men were yelling and shouting like madmen as they scampered about the darkened deck as if it was an everyday occurrence. From astern Bolitho heard the raucous blare of a trumpet and then the strident rattle of a drum. He could imagine the panic and pandemonium as the sleep-fuddled crews tumbled from their hammocks in response to the call to arms.

'Cable's cut, sir!' A voice yelled from the bows.

'Very well, let the current take her!' Bolitho ran to the rail and peered through the gloom towards the nearest transport. There were more lights now, and he thought he could see the gunports being raised along the upperdeck. Their anger will give way to prudence in a moment, he thought wildly.

'Fire the ship, Belsey!' He pointed at the foremast. 'Start from there!'

Fascinated he watched Belsey's busy seamen as they upended the riding light across a deadly mixture of oil, loose cordage and spare canvas. The result was as swift as it was frightening. With a savage roar the flames soared up the shrouds and engulfed the whole forepart of the deck. Great tongues of fire lit up the whole anchorage, so that the other ships stood out stark and tall in the inferno. Rigging and cordage flamed and crackled as the fire reached through the tarred ropes and found the neatly furled sails. Spars and planking, sun-dried and well painted, flared like tinder, so that the roaring heat reached still further, consuming the sloop greedily as the men fell back, stunned by the extent of their destruction.

Bolitho clawed his way aft through the choking smoke and away from the searing heat. He was glad that Belsey had remembered to open the hatch, and noticed that most of the ship's crew had already jumped over the side and were either swimming or drowning while their world burned above them.

He leaned coughing on the taffrail and stared across at the big transport. Gone was the belligerence and awakened anger. Her decks seemed to be swarming with stampeding figures as officers and men dashed wildly to their stations, colliding with each other as they stared in horror at the approaching fireship.

The second transport was already slipping her cable, but the nearest ship stood no chance at all. Some of her men must have realised the inevitability of the collision, and Bolitho saw several small white splashes alongside as they jumped overboard. There were pistol shots too, and he guessed that the French officers were busy trying to restore calm and order to the last.

Belsey led his choking, wheezing men to the poop and

yelled, 'Time to go, sir!' He was grinning, and his eyes were streaming from the smoke.

Bolitho pointed down. 'The quarter boat is tied under the counter! Down you go, lads, and sharp about it! The magazine will blow up before long!'

One by one the sailors slithered down the rope and into the small boat below the poop. Bolitho went last, his lungs seared from the advancing fire, his eyes all but blinded.

Stockdale bawled, 'Out oars! Give way together!'

The boat pulled clear, each man's eyes white in the cruel glare as the burning sloop drifted past. Several French sailors were swimming nearby, and one tried to pull himself aboard the overcrowded boat. But Stockdale pushed him away, and Bolitho heard the man's cries fading piteously astern.

A seaman yelled, 'They've struck, by God!'

Sure enough, the sloop had reached the other vessel, and already the flames were racing up the transport's tall masts where the half-loosed sails vanished like ashes in a strong wind.

'Keep pulling, lads!' Bolitho turned to watch, satisfied but awed by the terrible success of his attack.

The sloop's magazine exploded, the shockwave making the little boat jump beneath Bolitho's chattering seamen. The little ship, which thirty minutes earlier had been riding quietly at her anchor, folded amidships and dipped spluttering and hissing below the surface. But the work was done. The transport was ablaze from stern to stern and with fore and main-masts already down in a welter of flame and dense smoke.

Of the second transport nothing was visible through the pall. But Bolitho knew that she had only two choices. To try to warp clear and risk the fate of her sister, or drift ashore to be left a useless ruin when the tide retreated.

Belsey said, 'There are lights at the end of the bay, sir! That must be where the troops are camped!'

Bolitho wiped his smoke-blackened face and nodded. 'There will be a hornet's nest about our ears shortly!' With their ships destroyed and no battery to protect them, the French soldiers would be all the more willing to die to avenge their disgrace, he thought grimly.

But it was done. And done far better than he had hoped. In future, people might remember this when they spoke the name of the *Phalarope*.

Lieutenant Matthew Okes stared down from the gun battery shocked and dazed by the raging holocaust and the echoing thunder of exploding powder. He could feel the hot breath of the burning ship across his sweating face, and his nostrils rebelled against the stench of charred timbers and other horrors he could only guess at.

Farquhar said sharply, 'Time to send the guns over!'

Okes nodded dumbly, his eyes still fixed on the blazing transport as it rolled slowly on to one side. Men were swimming and floating amongst the great mass of fragments and charred flotsam, and the glittering water was constantly pock-marked by falling wreckage from muffled explosions within the shattered hull. Faintly through the drifting smoke he could see the second transport already hard aground, her masts leaning at a dangerous angle.

Behind him he heard the rumble of chocks and then a ragged cheer as the sailors sent the first gun careering over the cliff edge and on to the rocks below. A second and then a third gun crashed after it, and he heard McIntosh yelling at his men to throw their weight against the others.

Okes could feel the strength draining from his limbs, and wanted to run from the scene of hell and destruction which lit the whole anchorage in a panorama of red flames and spark-dappled smoke. It was all sheer madness, something which none of them could control.

There was no sign of Bolitho, and even if he had

158

succeeded in escaping from his drifting fireship he would have a much longer passage to make back to the headland.

Farquhar said, 'Look sir! There are troops coming over the hill!'

As Okes tore his eyes away the transport took a final roll and plunged beneath the surface. Immediately the fierce light was extinguished like a candle and the anchorage was once more plunged into deep shadow. Okes blinked through the smoke and realised for the first time that the sky was already brighter and there was a tinge of grey along the ridge of hills beyond the anchorage. The fierceness of the blazing ships had hidden the dawn's stealthy approach, and now as he followed the direction of Farquhar's arm he saw with rising panic the faint glint of bayonets and the bright colours of a raised standard moving inexorably over the rim of the nearest hill like a mechanical caterpillar. His eyes darted from the marching troops to the bridge. From his own position on the battery to the end of the coast road. In a voice he no longer recognised he shouted, 'Prepare to blow the magazine, Mr. Farquhar!' He stared round like a trapped animal. 'I must see Rennie at once. You carry on here!'

He started to walk quickly away from the battery, ignoring the curious stares of the seamen and Farquhar's look of questioning contempt. His racing thoughts seemed to take over his feet, so that all at once he was running, his breath gasping painfully, his shoes skidding across stones and gorse alike as he ran blindly across the bridge, past the armed sailors on the far side and out along the open road. Here and there he could see the scarlet patches of crouching marines amongst the hillside bracken, and he was horrified to realise that he could already see the beach below and the jumble of houses beyond the pier. The growing daylight added to his sense of nakedness, and in his imagination he thought he heard the tramp of French soldiers as they marched steadily to cut his escape to the sea.

He rounded a bend in the road and almost fell on top of Captain Rennie, who was sitting comfortably on a small mound of grass, his cocked hat and sword lying neatly beside him. Cradled on his knees was a half-eaten pie, and even as Okes staggered to a halt Rennie glanced up at him and dabbed at his mouth with a handkerchief.

'Delicious.' He looked curiously past Okes. 'They sound busy back there.'

Okes stared round wildly. This was almost too much. He wanted to scream, to shake Rennie, to make him realise the enormity of the danger.

Rennie's eyes narrowed, but he said calmly, 'A chicken pie? I had almost forgotten what it was like.' He gestured over his shoulder, but kept his eyes on Okes' stricken face. 'Some Dutch folk from the village brought it for me during the night, y'know. Damn nice people really. It's a pity we're at war, isn't it.' He stood up and wrapped the remainder of the pie carefully in his handkerchief. Then he said quietly. 'You'd better tell me what is happening.'

Okes controlled his breathing with a savage effort. 'The French are coming! Over there, behind the hill.'

'I know. My men have already spotted them.' Rennie regarded him calmly. 'What did you expect them to do?'

The marine's obvious indifference gave Okes the little extra strength he still needed. 'You can start falling back. I've given orders to fire the magazine.' He dropped his eyes. 'I'm blowing the bridge as soon as McIntosh is ready!'

Rennie stared at him. 'But the captain! How in hell's name can he get back to us without the bridge?' He clapped on his hat and reached for his sword. 'I'd better go and have a look back there.'

Okes blocked his way, his eyes blazing. 'You know the orders! I'm in charge if anything happens to the captain! Your duty is to cover the withdrawal!'

Sergeant Garwood trotted round the bend, his half-pike

glittering in the growing light. 'Sir.' He ignored Okes. 'The Frogs is comin'! There's best part of a company movin' down on our flank. I think the rest will try and work round the village and take us from the rear.'

Rennie nodded, his face suddenly grave. 'Very well. I'll come at once.'

He turned back to Okes and said slowly, 'You'll wait a bit longer surely? It takes time to get a boat back to the headland!'

Okes swung on his heel as a ragged volley of musket fire echoed around the hills. 'Get back to your men, Captain Rennie. I hope I know *my* duty!'

Rennie shrugged and walked quickly up the sloping hillside towards the firing. When he looked back he could see the smoke from the anchorage drifting across the headland in a solid wall, and tried to picture the devastation beyond.

Against the hillside and the glittering water below the cliff Okes' running figure looked frail and lost. 'I hope you *do*, Mr. Okes!' Rennie spoke aloud to the empty hillside. Then he turned and began to run to his prepared positions and his men.

Okes found McIntosh already squatting on one side of the bridge, craning his head to peer down at one of the massive wooden trestles.

'Ready?' Okes could hardly stop himself from shouting. 'Well, are you?'

McIntosh nodded. 'Aye, aye, sir. A two-minute fuse. And a four-minute fuse to the magazine.' He rubbed his hard hands. 'Mr. Farquhar is waiting atop the battery to light it as soon as the cap'n gets back.'

Okes swayed and then controlled himself. 'Wait here!' He started to run again, and as soon as he had reached the outskirts of the battery he blew his whistle and yelled, 'Clear the headland! Fall back there!'

Startled, the seamen gathered up their weapons and

began to hurry towards the bridge. Most of them had seen the approaching soldiers and needed no second order.

A petty officer, his face stained with dirt and smoke, strode across to the panting lieutenant. 'Beggin' yer pardon, sir! The cap'n ain't come yet!'

'Yes, yes, I know that!' Okes glared at him glassily. 'You go with the others and get them across the bridge. Wait for me there, and be ready to move!' He peered through the smoke. 'Where is Mr. Farquhar?'

The man shrugged. 'Gone down the steps, sir. He said he'd get a better chance of seeing through the smoke from there.'

Okes strode to the battery wall and leaned against it for support. With the sailors gone and the gunports unoccupied and empty the place seemed strangely dead. He made himself walk to the top of the steps. There was no sign of Farquhar, of anybody in fact.

There was a fresh burst of firing, intermingled with wild cheering, and his limbs started to move as if he had already lost control of them. He walked to the open door of the magazine and stared for several seconds at the waiting fuse and the smouldering slow match beside it. It was not his fault, he told himself. There was nothing else he could do. He sank to his knees, his eyes filled with the fuse and the mental picture of Bolitho hurrying away towards the anchored sloop.

Damn them! Damn them all! He had to steady his wrist with his other and as he took the match and held it against the fuse.

He felt the nausea hard in his throat as he staggered to his feet and ran quickly towards the bridge.

McIntosh stared up at him, his eyes uncomprehending.

'Light it, you fool!' Okes was already halfway across the bridge. 'Or stay there and go up with the magazine!'

McIntosh fired the fuse and scrambled on to the bridge. He caught Okes up around the curve in the road and gasped, 'Where's Mr. Farquhar, sir? An' what happened to the captain?'

Okes snarled, 'Back to the beach! All of you!' To McIntosh he added, 'All dead! Like you'll be if the French catch you!'

There was a thunderous roar, followed almost immediately by a second, sharper explosion. The force of the detonations seemed to quell the musket fire and distant shouts, so that the whole island appeared to be stunned by the noise.

The growling rumble went on, and Okes heard a splintering crash as the bridge fell into the ravine like so much kindling wood.

Strangely, he found that he could walk now, his feet moving almost steadily as he followed his men down the road towards the pier and safety. He had acted in the only way possible. He kept his eyes fixed on the pier. The *only* way. Others would soon see that, too. He pictured his wife's face when she read the announcement in the *Gazette*.

'Lieutenant Matthew Okes, who carried the brunt of the responsibility of this daring raid after the death of his commanding officer, is to be congratulated on his valour and his keenness to press home an attack against impossible odds!'

He slowed to a halt as a group of marines burst through the gorse and took up positions on the road itself.

A marine yelled, 'Here they come, lads!'

Sergeant Garwood's voice boomed from beyond the hilltop. 'Hold your fire, my darlings! Ready, now! *Fire!*'

His last order came as a charging line of blue uniformed soldiers rose above the skyline and started to run down towards the beach. As the musket smoke drifted clear Okes saw the soldiers falling back, leaving others screaming and kicking in the low gorse.

'Reload! Take yer time!' Garwood sounded calm. 'Aim low, lads!'

Another sharp volley, but this time there were more soldiers, and they came on with fresh determination in spite of losses. And here and there a marine lay dead, and several others crawled slowly down the hillside after their comrades.

Okes could see Rennie standing imperturbably on a hillock, ignoring the sharpshooters as he controlled his thin line of retreating men. He felt his envy giving way to hatred. Rennie would never have acted as *he* had done! He would have waited for Bolitho and allowed everyone to die for nothing!

Okes shouted, 'To the lugger! Lively there!'

The sailors ran wildly to the pier, carrying their wounded companions and yelling encouragement to the marines. It seemed to Okes that another age passed before all his men were aboard and the last of the marines were falling back along the pier. There was a fresh morning breeze to fill the lugger's sails, and as the last marine scrambled gasping over the bulwark the boat idled clear.

With a maddened roar the French soldiers charged from cover and headed for the pier. From individual uniformed blobs they converged into a solid force, and as they surged on to the pier itself they merged into a single enemy.

McIntosh crouched in the bows and looked along the swivel gun. He ignored the sporadic musket fire, and waited until the soldiers were packed into a yelling, tangled throng before he jerked the lanyard. 'There, my beauties!' He stood up wildly in the pitching boat as the canister shot cut through the screaming soldiers like a scythe. 'That's fer the cap'n! An' all the others!'

Before the second wave of soldiers had reached the bloody, threshing carnage on the pier the lugger had gone about and headed out to sea. Aboard there was silence now, and even when the *Phalarope*'s raked masts rounded the headland and bore down on the small boat like a protective parent, the exhausted men could not even muster a cheer.

Okes looked back at the island, at the smoke, and the vague outline 'of the headland battery. It was over.

The lugger was to be abandoned after the raid, so Okes had it laid alongside the *Phalarope*, where many hands reached down for the wounded and the silent victors.

Captain Rennie stood aside to allow Okes to climb up the frigate's side. He said, 'After *you*, Mr. Okes. I'd not want to spoil your entrance this morning!'

Okes stared at him, his mouth hanging open to reply. Then he saw the cold hostility in Rennie's eyes and decided against it. He must expect jealousy, he told himself firmly. He must be prepared to deal with it.

He reached for the main chains and swung himself up and over the frigate's side. For a moment longer he stared around the familiar deck. He had survived.

9

Defeat

Bolitho did not actually remember hearing the exploding magazine. It was more like a sensation, or the ending of a nightmarish dream when a man awakes even more afraid of the waiting reality. He recalled sitting in the stern of the crowded and half-swamped boat, staring back at the hissing, writhing water where the transport had made her last dive to the bottom. His eyes ached from the blaze, and were now dulled by the ship's sudden disappearance and the shadow which reached across the high-sided anchorage to hide the pain and terror beneath.

His men were laughing and chattering with relief and excitement, but as Bolitho turned back to search for the treacherous rockfalls at the foot of the cliff the whole world seemed to explode in one gigantic tremor. Rocks rained down into the water, and as the men pulled desperately at the oars one large piece of splintered stone struck the stern like a hammer, and Bolitho staggered to his feet as the sea surged jubilantly into the listing boat.

It seemed as if the bombardment from above would never cease. He saw one man swept underwater by a complete section of cliff even as he tried to scramble up on to the rocks. Belsey, the master's mate, fell cursing into deep water, and when Stockdale heaved him bodily up on to the rocks he yelled in anguish. 'Me arm! God, me arm's broken!'

Bolitho's dazed thoughts were slowly returning to normal, and as he called encouragement to his half-drowned men his mind rebelled against what he knew to be true. Someone had fired the magazine without waiting for him and his party. He could find only small gratitude for the fact that had his boat returned minutes earlier they would have all been blasted skyward with the magazine and the battery.

He called, 'Follow me, lads! We'll climb along the water's edge on these rocks. The tide's dropping, so we should be able to reach the steps well enough.' He groped his way forward, knowing that they would follow. There was no choice. At the far end of the anchorage he could hear the frantic cries and the urgent notes of a trumpet. The French were too busy saving their own to care about the raiding party. But it would not last. Then the vengeance would be swift and final.

He staggered to a halt and blinked through the haze of acrid smoke. In the pale morning light which filtered down the steep ravine he could clearly see the remains of the bridge. There was no point in climbing the steps now. There was no way back to the beach.

A seaman ran dazedly past him and stared open mouthed at the wreckage. 'You bastards!' His voice shook with despair. 'You damn, cowardly *bastards*!'

'Silence!' Bolitho pushed the man back with the others. 'No doubt there was a good reason for blowing the bridge this early.' But he saw the look on Stockdale's face and knew that he had seen the lie in his eyes.

Belsey moaned and leaned against Stockdale for support. 'They left us to die! Ran to save their precious skins!'

Bolitho held up his hand. 'Quiet!' He cocked his head. 'Listen!'

A seaman said sharply, 'Over there, sir. I heard somethin', too.'

They scrambled over the smoking, splintered timbers until the first seaman fell back with a gasp of horror. Midshipman Farquhar was sitting propped against the ravine's rough wall, his body pinned in position by a great baulk of timber, and lying close by his side was a neatly severed leg.

Farquhar opened his eyes and croaked, 'Thank God, sir! I thought I was going to die alone!' He saw their expressions and managed a painful grin. 'It's not *my* leg, sir! It belongs to our Spanish prisoner!'

Bolitho glanced around him and then up at the brightening sky. 'Right. Lift that timber off him, and be very careful!' He knelt beside the midshipman and ran his hands swiftly beneath the massive beam, keeping his eyes on Farquhar's taut features as his fingers probed at his trapped body.

Farquhar said between his teeth, 'Nothing broken it seems!' He lay back and closed his eyes as the beam quivered and began to move. 'I was looking for you, sir. Then I returned to the magazine and saw that the fuse was almost burned through!' He sounded near breaking. 'I seized our Spaniard and ran for the bridge, but just as we reached it the whole thing blew up and dropped into the ravine.' He winced. 'And us with it!'

The beam was dragged clear, and Bolitho tightened his jaw as he saw the smashed remains of their prisoner. He asked harshly, 'How did it happen?'

Farquhar allowed himself to be lifted to his feet. Immediately his legs buckled, and Stockdale said gruffly, ''Ere, I'll take the young gentleman, sir!'

Farquhar clung to Stockdale's shoulder and said, 'Sorry about all this, sir. I'll be all right in a while.' He remembered Bolitho's question and said vaguely, 'I can't understand it, sir. I still can't believe it happened.'

Bolitho pulled the dirk from Farquhar's belt and handed it to one of the seamen. 'Here, make a good splint with this for Mr. Belsey's arm. It will suffice until we get back to the *Phalarope*.'

Belsey watched the men's awkward fingers and groaned. 'Watch what yer doin'! You're like a pair of blind whores!'

Bolitho walked slowly along the weed-encrusted stonework. Fourteen men including himself. One with a broken arm, and one already half delirious from a ball in his shoulder. Farquhar looked as if he might fall unconscious, too.

He tried to push the bitterness and suspicion to the back of his mind. That would keep. Right now he had to get these men to safety. No doubt the rest of the raiding party was already embarked in the lugger. He suddenly felt calmer. Whatever else happened, he had succeeded in his work. Two transports destroyed and a valuable sloop with them. And without a battery Mola Island would be useless to the French and their allies for a long while to come.

Stockdale called throatily. 'The second longboat, sir! It'll still be tied to the jetty where we left it!'

Bolitho scrambled across the wet stones and stared down at the remaining boat. It was not much of a craft. Patched and well used, and with only four oars and a mere scrap of canvas furled around the mast for every purpose. But no doubt the garrison had only used it for visiting the ships in harbour.

He said grimly, 'Get them aboard, Stockdale. We'll have to make the best of it.'

A ray of yellow sunlight lanced suddenly across the headland and glittered in the deep water. Without effort Bolitho could see the gleaming barrel of one of the battery's cannon almost below the swinging boat. A few feet this way and there would be no way out at all!

'Four of you man the oars! The rest of you take turns in baling and keeping a sharp lookout!'

Belsey struggled into a sitting position and peered at his splintered arm. The limb was tightly wrapped in an assortment of rags and strips of clothing, and stuck out in front of him like a club. He shook his head. 'Gawd! If I ever use this flipper agin I'll be surprised!'

'Shove off! Give way together!' Bolitho squatted on the gunwale and pushed the tiller hard over. As the boat moved swiftly with the current he stared up the blackened crest of the headland and wondered what had happened in those last minutes before Farquhar had been flung to almost certain death.

Farquhar moved weakly against the boat's side and snapped, 'Pull lively, Robinson! I'll flay you alive if you don't do your share!'

In spite of his misery Bolitho smiled to himself. Farquhar's experiences had not softened his attitude to duty.

The oars rose and fell steadily, and the boat moved further and further from the jutting headland with its attendant pall of drifting smoke.

A man in the bows spoke Bolitho's thoughts for him, and for once he could find no words to rebuke him. The sailor stared back along the labouring men and snarled, 'Gone! Look round, lads! The bloody ship's gone without us!'

Farquhar said bitterly, 'She must have gone around the island, sir. We'll never catch her now.'

'I know.' Bolitho shaded his eyes against the glare and looked thoughtfully at the stumpy mast. 'Get that sail broken out, lads. We'll get clear of Mola Island and make for the nearest friendly one.' His crisp tone hid the doubt and the anger.

Stockdale wiped the wounded seaman's forehead with a wet rag and muttered, 'A miracle would come in 'andy, sir!'

Bolitho stripped off his tattered coat and regarded him calmly. 'I'm afraid that is not my province, Stockdale, but I will bear it in mind.'

He settled against the tiller bar and steered towards the rising sun.

Lieutenant Thomas Herrick listened to the bell as it announced the end of the first Dog Watch and then resumed his pacing back and forth across the quarterdeck.

With a warm but fresh breeze from her quarter the *Phalarope* had made good time back to her patrol area, yet Herrick could find nothing but apprehension and a sense of loss at the speedy passage. He still could not accept what had happened, and felt the same inner anguish he had experienced when the weary raiding party had clambered up the frigate's side.

Even then he had been unwilling to accept that Bolitho was missing. Then he had seen Rennie's grim features and had felt the nervous uncertainty of the other returning sailors and marines. Only Okes had appeared unmoved by the disaster. No, Herrick frowned as he tried to relive exactly the moment Okes had stepped aboard, unmoved was not the proper description. There had been a sort of guarded jauntiness about him which was totally out of character. Herrick had gone to question him, but Vibart had summoned Okes to the quarterdeck where he had been brooding in silence since the landing party had left for the shore.

Rennie had been unusually reticent. But when Herrick had persisted, the marine had said shortly, 'It was a dangerous mission, Thomas. We must always expect such things to happen!' He had been watching Okes speaking jerkily to the first lieutenant and he had added bitterly, 'I was sent to this ship with my detachment to reinforce the discipline. To protect the officers from any new threat of mutiny.' His eyes had blazed with sudden anger. 'It now appears that the *Phalarope*'s officers must be protected from each other!' Rennie had ended, 'I must attend to my wounded. They at least have nothing of which to be ashamed!'

171

Herrick had then cornered McIntosh the gunner's mate. The latter had looked nervously at the quarterdeck before replying, 'How can I tell, sir? I just did my duty. Mr. Farquhar was the only one who must have seen what happened.' He had gestured wearily astern. 'And he's back there, dead with the rest!'

'But you think something went wrong, don't you?' Herrick's voice had been harsh.

'You know I can't afford to answer that, Mr. Herrick.' The man had looked back at the wounded and exhausted seamen from the lugger. 'It took a lot of pain and sweat to get where I am now. You know what would happen to me if I made accusations.'

Herrick had let him go, his eyes contemptuous, yet knowing in his heart that McIntosh was speaking the truth.

He stiffened as he heard Vibart's heavy step beside him.

'Pipe the hands aft, Mr. Herrick. I will tell them what is to be done.' Vibart looked composed and calm. Only his eyes betrayed a certain glitter which could be either excitement or triumph.

Herrick said, 'Are you sure there is nothing more we can do?'

Vibart stared past him at the ruffled water. 'I told you this morning, Mr. Herrick, just as I voiced my fears to the captain. The venture was dangerous and foolhardy. That it was a success is fortunate for all of us. But Bolitho knew the risk he was taking. There is nothing more to be said.'

Herrick persisted. 'But is Lieutenant Okes *sure*?'

'I am satisfied with his report.' There was a new edge to Vibart's tone. 'So that is enough!' He walked ponderously to the weather rail and sniffed loudly. 'At least we are back in our proper area. Now we can contact the flagship.'

Herrick spoke swiftly to Midshipman Neale and watched him scamper forward. Then he heard the boatswain's mates shouting. 'All hands! All hands! Lay aft!'

As the men poured up from below he crossed to Vibart

and said slowly, 'He was a good officer. I still think he could have escaped.'

'Then I will trouble you to keep your opinions to yourself, Mr. Herrick!' The deepset eyes were flecked with anger. 'You may have considered yourself one of his favourites, but I will have no such behaviour now.'

He turned away from Herrick's taut features as Quintal, the boatswain, touched his hat and rumbled, 'All present, sir.'

Vibart strode to the quarterdeck rail and stared down at the upturned faces. Herrick stayed by the helmsmen watching Vibart closely.

Vibart said, 'We are back on our patrol. We will shortly make contact with the admiral, and I will in due course tell him of our great success!'

Herrick felt himself tremble with anger. So it was a great success now, was it? When Bolitho was alive it had been foolhardy and dangerous, but now that Vibart stood to reap the full credit for it it was already a different picture.

'I am not satisfied with the recent slackness of discipline aboard, and I intend that this ship will return to a proper state of efficiency as of now!'

Vibart was staring round the assembled crew, his face flushed. Herrick felt sick. He is enjoying it, he thought. He is actually glad Bolitho is dead!

Herrick turned as Okes stepped through the cabin hatch and walked uncertainly towards him. Herrick took his sleeve and whispered fiercely, 'What did you tell Vibart, Matthew? For God's sake, what is the matter with you?'

Okes drew back. 'I told him nothing but the truth! Am I to be blamed for Bolitho's misfortunes?'

'And what of young Farquhar? Did you *see* him die?' Okes looked away. 'Of course I did. What the devil are you trying to imply?' But there was a shake in his voice, and Herrick was suddenly reminded of Okes' behaviour during the battle with the privateer. His fear, his complete terror. A man could not change overnight.

'I want to know, Matthew. You had better tell me now.'

Okes seemed to have recovered himself, and when he looked at Herrick his eyes were opaque and expressionless. 'I told the truth, damn you!' He tried to smile. 'But you should not worry too much. You'll be moving up to second lieutenant!'

Herrick stepped back and looked at him with disgust. 'And *you* will be first, no doubt! And both you and Vibart will be the heroes of the day!'

Okes' face drained of colour. 'How dare you! You were not there, so it is easy to be jealous and insulting! Bolitho was *only* a man!'

'And you are not fit to polish his shoes!' Herrick swung round as Vibart stepped between them.

'I will have no quarrelling aboard my ship, Mr. Herrick. Any more of it and I will make an entry in the log!' He looked hard at Okes. 'Come to the cabin. I have a few things to say to you.'

Herrick watched them go, sickened and helpless.

Little Neale asked quietly, 'What does it all mean, sir?'

Herrick looked down at him, his face grave. 'It means that we must watch our step in the weeks ahead, my boy. With the captain gone I feel no security here.'

He stiffened as he saw Evans, the purser, hurrying aft, an aggrieved expression on his ferret face. Behind him Thain, the master-at-arms, ushered two frightened-looking seamen, his face leaving Herrick in no doubt as to what would happen next. Floggings, and more floggings. All the old scores kept hidden while Bolitho had been in command would break into the open like festering sores,

He faced Evans and said sharply, 'Well? What is it now?'

Evans smiled nervously. 'Caught these men red-handed! Stealing rum they were!'

174

Herrick's heart sank and he called the men forward. 'Is that right?' He realised that both seamen had taken part in the raiding party.

One of the men said sullenly, 'Aye, sir. The rum was for one of our mates. 'E was wounded. We reckoned it would 'elp 'im' His companion nodded in agreement. Herrick took Evans aside. 'It could be true.'

'Of course it is true!' Evans stared at him in amazement. 'But that is hardly the point! Stealing is stealing. There is no excuse, and you know it.' He eyed Herrick with little disguised glee. 'So you had better inform Mr. Vibart.' He drew himself up importantly. 'Or I will, Mr. Herrick!'

'Don't you get stroppy with me, Evans!' Herrick's face was a mask of fury. 'Or I'll have you broken, believe me!' But it was only anger. There was nothing else he could do but inform Vibart.

He handed over the watch to Neale and went wearily below. The sentry opened the cabin door for him before he had reached it, and Herrick guessed that the marine had correctly foreseen his surprise. Vibart had moved into Bolitho's quarters already. It only added to Herrick's sense of nightmarish unreality.

Vibart looked up from the desk and stared at him.

'Two men for punishment.' Herrick saw Okes leaning against the stern windows, his face lost in thought.

Vibart leaned back in the chair. 'Say "sir" when you address me, Mr. Herrick.' He frowned. 'I can't imagine why you make such a point of worsening your position. He continued coldly, 'Make a report in the log, Mr. Herrick. Punishment at eight bells tomorrow morning. Two dozen lashes apiece.'

Herrick swallowed. 'But I have not told you their offence yet, sir!'

'No need.' Vibart gestured towards the open skylight. 'I happened to overhear your nonsensical conversation with Mr. Evans just now. And I must warn you I do not approve

175

of your apparent wish to toady with men who lie and steal!'

Herrick felt the cabin closing in around him. 'Is that all?' He swallowed again. '*Sir?*'

'For the present.' Vibart looked almost relaxed. 'We will alter course to the south'ard in one hour. Try and make sure that the men do not slacken off during your watch.'

'Aye, aye, sir.' Herrick contracted his stomach muscles into a tight knot.

Outside the cabin he turned momentarily and looked back. The door was shut again and the marine sentry stared blankly in front of him beneath the swinging lantern. It was just as if Pomfret had returned and now sat back there in the big cabin. Herrick shook his head and mounted the ladder to the quarterdeck. It was all moving so much to a pattern again that he found himself wondering if Pomfret had been the controlling influence which had made the *Phalarope* into a living hell!

When he returned to the deck he saw that the sun had already moved closer to the horizon. The sea was empty, a great desert of silver and purple hues, with an horizon like a knife edge.

Out here a ship's captain was God indeed, he thought bitterly. Only under Bolitho had he felt the meaning of purpose and understanding, and after Pomfret it had seemed like a new chance of life.

He looked aft to the taffrail as if expecting to see Bolitho's tall shape watching the trim of the sails or just waiting for the sun to reach the horizon. Herrick had never disturbed Bolitho at those moments, but had drawn on each occasion to better his own understanding of the man. In his mind's eye he could still see the strong profile, the firm mouth which could be amused and sad almost at the same instant. It did not seem possible that such a man could be wiped out like something from a slate.

He resumed his slow pacing, his chin low on his chest. In this world, he thought, you could never depend on anything.

To the tired men in the longboat the night seemed cold and cheerless, and even those who had cursed the blazing sunlight and bemoaned their urgent thirst found no comfort from the darkness.

Bolitho groped his way aft to where Farquhar was sitting beside the tiller. With Stockdale's assistance he had just dropped a dead seaman over the side while the other men had watched in silence. The sailor in question had been spared the worst of his wound and the suffering of pain and thirst by remaining almost unconscious from the moment he had been shot down by the sloop's deck watch. The longboat was moving so slowly under her small sail that it seemed to take an age for the corpse to bob astern. There was not even an anchor to weight the man's body. In fact there was not much of anything. Just a cask of rancid water and little more than a day's ration of a cup per man.

Bolitho sank into the sternsheets and stared up at the glittering ceiling of stars. 'Keep her due south if you can.' He felt dry and aching with fatigue. 'I wish we could get a bit more wind in this wretched sail.'

Farquhar said, 'I think the boat would sink, sir! It feels rotten and worm-eaten!'

Bolitho eased his legs and thought back over the long, slow passage of time. If that was only the first day, he pondered, what would happen in the next? And the next after that?

The men were quiet enough, but that too could be dangerous. The first relief at escaping from the French could soon give way to mistrust and recriminations. The misery of being a prisoner of war might soon appear comfort itself compared with a living death without food or water.

177

Farquhar said absently, 'In Hampshire there will be snow on the hills now, I expect. All the sheep will be brought down to their feed, and the farm workers will be drinking good ale by their firesides.' He licked his lips. 'A few will be thinking of us maybe.'

Bolitho nodded, feeling his eyelids droop. 'A few.' He thought of his father in the big house and the row of watchful portraits. After this there would be no heir to carry on the family's name, he thought dully. Maybe some rich merchant would buy the house when his father died, and would find time to wonder at the portraits and the other relics of deeds and men soon forgotten. He said, 'I am going to try and sleep for an hour. Call me if you need anything.'

He closed his eyes and did not even hear Farquhar's reply.

Then he was aware of his arm being tugged and of the boat swaying and rolling as the listless seamen came to life and crowded excitedly in the bows. For a moment longer he imagined that he was dreaming. Then he heard Farquhar shout, 'Look, sir! She came to look for us after all!'

Bolitho staggered to his feet, his sore eyes probing over the heads of his men as he tried to pierce the darkness. Then he saw it. It was more an absence of familiar stars than an actual outline, but as he stared he began to see the contours of something darker and sharper. A ship.

He snapped, 'Make a light, Stockdale! Fire some of those rags!'

The sliver of moon struck silver from the distant sails, and against the night's dark blackcloth Bolitho could see the darker tracery of raked masts and rigging. It was a frigate right enough.

The makeshift flare sizzled and then burst into flames, so that once more the eyes were blinded and limited to the small confines of the boat. Some men were cheering, others merely hugged each other and grinned like children.

'Now we shall get an answer to the mystery, Mr. Farquhar.' Bolitho pushed the tiller over as the ship changed shape and moved silently above them. He could hear the creak of yards, the sudden flurry of canvas as the frigate started to back her sails and heave to. He thought he heard a distant hail and the sound of running feet.

He said, 'Lower the sail, Stockdale! You men forrard, get ready to catch a line!' But nobody needed any encouragement from him.

The bowsprit swung dizzily barely feet away, and as Stockdale lit another crude flare Bolitho felt the grip of ice around his heart. The frigate's figurehead danced and flickered in the light as if it was alive. A gilt-painted demon wielding a pair of furnace irons like weapons of war.

Stockdale threw the flare into the water and turned to stare at Bolitho. 'Did you see, sir? Did you *see*?'

Bolitho let his arm go limp. 'Yes, Stockdale. It is the *Andiron*!'

The cheers and jubilation in the longboat died as suddenly as the flare, and the men stood or sat like stricken beings as lanterns shone down from the frigate's deck and a grapnel bit into the boat's gunwale.

His men stood aside to let Bolitho pass as he made his way to the bows and reached out for the dangling ladder which had suddenly appeared. He was still too fatigued and too stunned by the change of events to mark a clear sequence of what was happening. His mind would only record brief, unreal images, magnified and distorted by patches of light from the circle of lanterns. Glittering bayonets, and pressing, curious faces.

As he stepped into the lamplight he heard a mixture of gasps and comments. An Irish voice called, 'It's an English officer!' Another with a twangy colonial accent broke in. 'Hell it is! It's a *captain*!'

179

One by one the *Phalarope*'s men climbed up the side and were pushed into line against the ship's gangway. An officer in a dark coat and cocked hat pushed through the packed crowd and regarded Bolitho with amusement.

'Welcome aboard, Cap'n! A real pleasure!' He turned and shouted, 'Put the men under guard and drop a round shot through that coffin of a boat!' To a massive Negro he added, 'Separate any officers amongst them and take 'em aft!' Then to Bolitho he made a mock bow. 'Now if you will come with me, I am sure the captain will be glad to make your acquaintance.'

Even in the uncertain light of the lanterns Bolitho was able to distinguish the old, familiar details of the privateer's main-deck. He recalled with sudden clarity the last time he had visited the ship to see his friend Captain Masterman, a grave but friendly officer, who unlike many of his contemporaries had always been willing to share his knowledge and experience, and pleased to answer Bolitho's constant stream of questions,

The memory helped to drive back some of the gnawing despair, so that he automatically straightened his shoulders and was able to feel some bitter satisfaction at the scars and crudely repaired damage left from the *Phalarope*'s broadsides. The *Andiron*'s captain must have been heading for Mola Island to complete the repairs, he thought. Maybe the captured lugger's contents of spars and canvas had been earmarked for the *Andiron* alone.

He ducked his head as the officer led the way below the wide quarterdeck. At each step of the way he saw curious groups of the frigate's crew as they gathered to watch him pass. They were a mixed crew sure enough, he decided. Some were openly hostile and called insultingly as he strode by. Others dropped their eyes or hid their faces, and Bolitho guessed that they were probably English deserters, some even members of the *Andiron*'s original crew. There were Negroes and olive-skinned Mexicans.

Loud-mouthed Irishmen and dark faced sailors who must have breathed their first breaths by the Mediterranean. But it was obviously a close-knit company, if only because of their mutual danger and the hazards of their chosen trade.

The officer opened a heavy door and stood aside to let Bolitho enter a small, sparsely furnished cabin.

'You can wait here. We have to get under way now, but I guess the captain'll want to see you soon.' He held out his hand. 'I'll take the sword.' He saw Bolitho's look of resentment and added, 'And in case you start getting ideas of glory, there is a guard right outside the door.' He took the sword and turned it over in his hands. 'A pretty ancient blade for an English captain?' He grinned. 'But then I imagine things are getting a bit difficult for you all round?'

Bolitho ignored him. The officer was goading him. There was no point in pleading or asking favours. He watched the lamplight shining dully on his father's sword and then deliberately turned his back.

He was a prisoner. He must save his energy for later. The door slammed and he heard the officer's feet moving away.

Wearily Bolitho slumped down on a sea chest and stared at the deck. Farquhar and Belsey would be kept apart like himself. No doubt the *Andiron*'s commander would wish to question each one separately. As he himself would have done. It was strange to realise that it was only two days since he had been questioning the terrified Spaniard aboard his own ship. And in the following period so much had happened that it was almost impossible to trace the pattern of time and events.

One thing was sure. He had lost his ship, and for him the future was an empty ruin.

The stuffy air in the cabin aided by the heavy fatigue in his body eventually took effect. As the deck canted slightly and the ship once more gathered way, Richard

Bolitho leaned back against the cabin bulkhead and fell instantly asleep.

He was awakened by someone shaking his arm, and for a few more moments he found himself hoping it was all part of a terrible dream. Perhaps he could go back and take up reality again, even in the cramped uncertainty of the longboat. But it was the same officer who had escorted him to the cabin, and as Bolitho sat up on the chest he said, 'I thought you were dead!'

Bolitho realised with a further start that there was daylight in the passage outside the door, and as his mind accepted the reality of his position he heard the busy sounds of holystones and the sluice of water across the upperdeck.

'What time is it?'

The officer shrugged. 'Seven bells. You've been asleep for nearly seven hours at that!' He beckoned to a seaman in the passageway, 'There is some water for shaving and a razor.' He eyed Bolitho coldly. 'My man here will stay with you to make sure you don't cut your throat!'

'You are very considerate.' Bolitho took the bowl of hot water and ignored the seaman's look of fascinated interest. 'I would hate to die and miss seeing you hang, Lieutenant!'

The officer grinned calmly. 'You sure are a little firebrand, I'll say that for you.' He spoke sharply to the seaman. 'Just watch him, Jorgens! One false move and I'll expect you to deal with him, got it?'

The door slammed and the sailor said, 'The cap'n wants to see you when you's ready.' He licked his lips. 'He's havin' your breakfast got ready.' He sounded amazed at such treatment.

Bolitho continued with his shaving, but his mind was as busy as his razor. Perhaps it would be better to do as the officer had implied, he thought bitterly. One slash with the razor and his captors would be left with neither a ready victim nor a possible source of information,

He remembered Herrick's face when he had told him, 'Information. Out here the lack of it could lose a war,' Now his own words were coming back to mock him,

Then he thought of Farquhar and the others, and the look on Stockdale's battered face when the privateer's men had pulled them apart. It had been an expression of trust and quiet confidence. At that terrible moment it had done more to hold back Bolitho's final despair than any words or deeds imaginable.

He wiped the razor and laid it on the chest. No, there was more to living than a man's own private hopes, he decided.

He pulled his torn uniform into shape and brushed the dark hair back from his forehead. 'I'm ready,' he said coolly. 'Perhaps you will lead the way?'

He followed the seaman along the passageway, and in the filtered daylight he saw more evidence of the brief battle. Smashed timbers shored up with makeshift beams, and telltale red blotches which so far had defied weeks of scrubbing.

An armed sailor stood aside and opened the main cabin door, and as Bolitho entered the once familiar place he was momentarily blinded by the dazzling reflections from sea and sky as the morning sunlight blazed across the wide stern windows.

The *Andiron*'s captain was leaning out over the stern bench, his body a dark silhouette against the glittering water, but Bolitho's eyes fastened instead on his own sword which lay in the centre of the polished table.

He waited, standing quite still, his feet automatically braced against the ship's easy plunge and roll. Even this cabin was not spared from the *Phalarope*'s wounded anger. More scars, and deeply gouged gaps left by flying splinters. *Andiron* must have spent little time in harbour, he thought.

The officer at the window turned very slowly, so that

the light played across his face for a few moments before becoming once more a dark silhouette. For the second time in twenty-four hours Bolitho's reserve almost broke. It took all his strength to keep him from crying out in disbelief, but when the other man spoke, he knew that this too was no fantasy.

'Welcome aboard the *Andiron*, Richard! When my second lieutenant brought me this sword I knew it had to be you!'

Bolitho stared at his brother, feeling the years dropping away, his brain reeling with a thousand memories. Hugh Bolitho, the son about whom his father had spoken so bitterly, yet with so much anxiety. Now commanding an enemy privateer! It was the culmination of every worst possible belief.

His brother said slowly, 'It had to happen of course. But I hoped it might be otherwise. At some other place perhaps.'

Bolitho heard himself say, 'Do you know what you have done? What this will do to . . .?' He faltered, even unable to accept that they were both sons of the same man. He added quietly. 'So you were in command when we fought your ship last month?'

Hugh Bolitho seemed to relax slightly, as if he considered the worst was now over. 'Yes. And that was a real surprise, I can tell you! We were just closing for the kill when I caught sight of you through my glass!' His face crinkled as he relived the moment. 'So I hauled off. You were lucky that day, my lad!'

Bolitho tried to hide the pain in his eyes and said shortly, 'Are you saying that my being there made a difference?'

'Did you think you had won the day, Richard?' For a moment longer Hugh Bolitho studied his brother with something like amusement. 'Believe me, in spite of your chain shot I could still have taken the *Phalarope*!' He

184

shrugged and walked to the table and stared at the sword. 'I was taken off guard. I had no idea you were returning to the Indies.'

Bolitho watched his brother closely, noting the grey streaks in his dark hair, the lines of strain about his mouth. He was only four years older than himself, but there could have been ten years between them.

He said, 'Well, I am your prisoner now. What do you intend to do with me?'

The other man did not answer directly but picked up the sword and held it against the sun. 'So he gave it to *you*!' He shook his head, the gesture both familiar and painful. 'Poor Father. I imagine he believes the worst of me?'

'Are you surprised?'

Hugh Bolitho placed the sword on the table and thrust his hands deeply into his plain blue coat. 'I neither asked for nor expected this encounter, Richard. You may think as you please, but you know as well as I do that events out here are moving too quickly for a display of sentiment.' He watched his brother narrowly. 'When I saw you standing on your deck with that wretched crew of yours going to pieces around you, I could not bring myself to close the combat.' He waved one hand vaguely. 'Just like the old days, Richard. I could never find it easy to take what you thought was yours.'

Bolitho replied evenly, 'But you always did, didn't you?'

'Those days are past.' He pointed at a chart spread across another table. 'We are sailing for St. Kitts. We will make a landfall before night.' He watched the doubt in Bolitho's eyes. 'I know you so well, Richard. I can see the same old look of mistrust there!' He laughed. 'St. Kitts has already fallen to our ally. Sir Samuel Hood has pulled out to lick his wounds!' He waved across the chart. 'It will soon be over. Whether your government believes it or not, America will be an independent nation, perhaps sooner than they think!'

Bolitho felt his fingers locking together behind his back. While he was here being confronted with his past, his own world was falling apart. St. Kitts gone. Perhaps the French were already massing for an attack elsewhere. But where? They had the whole Caribbean to choose from.

His brother said quietly, 'If you are trying to make some scheme to foil my own plans you can forget it, Richard! For you the war is over.' He tapped the table with his fingertips. 'Unless?'

'Unless what?'

Hugh Bolitho walked round the table and stared him in the face. 'Unless you come in with us, Richard! I am well considered by the French. I am sure they would give you a ship of sorts! After what you did at Mola Island I am sure they would not deny your tenacity!' He smiled at some secret thought. 'It might even be the *Phalarope*.

He studied Bolitho's unsmiling face and then walked back to the window. 'These are *our* waters now. We get our intelligence from many sources. Fishermen, trading boats, even slavers when we get the chance. With St. Kitts fallen your ships will draw further south to Antigua and beyond. There are not many patrols in this area now. It is too wasteful for your admiral, am I right?' He smiled sadly. 'Just one ship perhaps. Just one.'

Bolitho thought of the *Phalarope* and tried to imagine what Vibart would do.

'Your ship, Richard. The *Phalarope*! We need every frigate we can get. It is the same in all navies. And I have made sure that your admiral, that pompous fool, Sir Robert Napier, will be *informed* of our movements. I am quite sure that he will be so drunk with your success at Mola Island that he will soon despatch the *Phalarope* to find us! The admiral will surely be eager to avenge the loss of the *Andiron* from his command, eh?'

'You must be mad!' Bolitho watched his brother coldly.

'Mad? I think not, Richard. I have interrogated your

men. They have told me how their ship was punished by Admiral Napier for letting *Andiron* escape. They told me also of the trouble there was aboard before you took command.' He spread his hands. 'I am afraid that most of your men have thrown in their lot with me. But do not distress yourself, it was wise of them. There is a whole new world opening up out here, and they will be part of it. When the war is over I will sail for England just to claim my inheritance, Richard. Then I will return to America. I have proved my worth out here. The past holds nothing for me.'

Bolitho said calmly, 'Then I pity your new nation! If it depends on traitors for existence it has a difficult course to steer.'

His brother remained unmoved. 'Traitors or patriots? It depends on a point of view! In any case, the *Andiron* will anchor off St. Kitts tonight. Not in the main harbour, but in a quiet little bay which I think would be considered quite ideal for recapturing her!' He threw back his head and laughed. 'Except that the *Phalarope* will be the one to step into the net, my brother!'

Bolitho stared at him without expression. 'As far as you are concerned I am a prisoner. I do not wish to tarnish either the name of my family or my country by being called a brother!'

Just for an instant he saw the barb go home. Then his brother recovered himself and said flatly, 'Then you will go below.' He picked up the sword again. 'I will wear this in future. It is mine by right!'

He banged the table and a sentry appeared in the doorway. Then he added, 'I am glad you are aboard my ship, Richard. This time, when the *Phalarope* comes creeping under my guns, I will have nothing to forestall me!'

'We will see.'

'We shall indeed.' Hugh Bolitho walked across to his

chart. 'If I have the temper of your crew rightly, Richard, I think they will soon be eager to follow *Andiron*'s orders!'

Bolitho turned on his heel and walked back past the guard.

'Behind him the *Andiron*'s captain stayed watching the door, his hand still holding the tarnished sword like a talisman.

10

The Red Baize Bag

For Richard Bolitho each day of captivity seemed longer than the one before, and the daily routine aboard the *Andiron* dragged into a slow torture. He was allowed the comparative freedom of the frigate's poop, from where he could watch the regular comings and goings of shore boats, the casual routine of a ship at anchor. At night he was returned to the solitude of a small cabin, and only joined Farquhar and Belsey for meals. Even then it was difficult to talk freely, because one of the privateer's warrant officers always waited close at hand.

It was a week since the *Andiron* had dropped her anchor, but to Bolitho it felt like an eternity. As each day passed he seemed to withdraw more and more into himself, going over his predicament again and again until his mind felt as if it was bursting.

From his small piece of deck he could see Belsey sitting gloomily on a hatch cover beside Farquhar, both apparently engaged in staring at the empty sea. Like everyone else aboard they were waiting, he thought bitterly. Waiting and wondering when *Phalarope* would approach the island and fall into the trap. He noticed that Belsey had a fresh bandage on his arm, and thought back to that first and only petty triumph when he had been allowed to join the other two after his meeting with his brother.

It was obvious at the time that both Farquhar and Belsey had already been told who the *Andiron*'s captain really was, just as it was equally plain to see their pitiful relief at his reappearance. Did they really believe that he would desert them and give his allegiance to the enemy? Even now he was surprised and faintly pleased to find that he was angry at the idea.

Belsey had been moving his bandaged arm painfully and had said, 'The ship's surgeon is goin' to have a look at it, sir.'

It had been then, and only then that Bolitho had remembered Farquhar's dirk which still lay hidden and used as a splint beneath the crude bandages. Hardly daring to speak, and watched by the others, he had broken a piece of wood from the cabin chair, and with Farquhar's help had replaced the dirk with a piece of polished mahogany. Once Belsey had yelped aloud and Bolitho had snapped, 'Keep quiet, you fool! We may have use for this later on!'

The dirk now lay hidden in his own bedding below decks, but after the agonising passing of days he could no longer view the possession of such a puny weapon with much hope.

He had seen little of his brother, and for that he was thankful. Once he had caught sight of him being rowed ashore in his gig. And on other occasions he had watched him staring at the tall mass of headland which towered above the anchored ship.

Bolitho had examined and thought over that one conversation in the stern cabin until he could see meanings where there were none. But he was sure of one thing. Hugh Bolitho was not bluffing. He had no need to.

The *Andiron* was anchored off the southern tip of the Island of Nevis, a smaller subsidiary of the main island, St. Kitts. Bolitho knew from experience that this small, oval-shaped island was separated by The Narrows, a mere two miles or so from St. Kitts itself and a full fifteen miles from the main town of Basseterre where Hood had successfully stood siege until forced to cut his cables and retire to Antigua.

Nevis had been a good choice, Bolitho conceded grimly. During his endless walks up and down the poop he had watched the rapid preparations, the careful cunning which had gone into laying a perfect trap for any ship attempting to seize the *Andiron*.

The sheltered piece of water was commanded by the jutting promontory of Dogwood Point, while inland and towering like a miniature volcano was the bare outline of Saddle Hill. From either position even a wall-eyed lookout could quickly spot any unusual or suspicious approach and send a report down to both ship and shoreline.

It was so simple that Bolitho had to admit he would have used the same method himself. Perhaps it was because it was his own flesh and blood which was working out the plan, and a mind like his own was laying the snare.

If Sir Robert Napier had been informed of *Andiron*'s presence here, it was not unreasonable to expect him to take some sort of offensive action. A swift frigate attack would not match up to the smarting loss of St. Kitts, but it would do much for the morale of the embattled British fleet. It did not have to be the *Phalarope*, of course.

Bolitho discounted the idea immediately. His brother had been right about that, too. Admiral Napier would have few ships at his disposal now that Hood was back in the saddle. In addition, he would see *Phalarope*'s success as an act of justice to purge her name and avenge the memory of his own son.

He tried again to put himself into the position of an attacking captain. He would make a slow approach, just to make sure that the information about the *Andiron* was not suspect, and in order that the lookouts ashore should not see any sign of a masthead before sunset. Then under cover of darkness he would close the shore and drop a full boarding party of perhaps three or four boats. It would not be easy, but a ship foolish enough to anchor away from the defended base might be expected to fall after a swift struggle. He closed his eyes tightly and tried to blot out the picture of the attacking ship at the moment of truth and realisation.

There was a hidden battery of artillery already sighted and ranged across the whole area below the headland. And although to all outward appearances the *Andiron* was resting confidently below a friendly island, Bolitho had seen the preparations and the care his brother had gone to, to make sure of a victory.

Guns were loaded with grape and depressed behind their closed ports. Boarding nets were already slung, suitably slack to prevent a quick inrush of any who lived through the first holocaust of fire. The *Andiron*'s men slept at their stations, each one armed to the teeth and eager to complete his captain's strategy.

Rockets were rigged on the quarterdeck, and as soon as the boarders were engaged the rockets would be fired. From further inshore the signal would be passed to a waiting French frigate and the battle would be all but over. The attacking ship would stand no chance if caught without the best part of her crew. And if she closed to give the boarding party support the shore artillery would pound her to fragments before she realised her mistake.

And if it was the *Phalarope* there was one further despairing thought. Vibart would be in command. It was hard to see his mind working fast enough to deal with such a situation.

Bolitho gritted his teeth and walked slowly to the side. The island looked at peace. The defenders had settled down now and were waiting like himself. Except that when the time came *he* would be battened below, helpless and wretched as he listened to the death of his own ship. Or worse, her capture, he thought for the hundredth time.

He felt a fresh pang of inner pain as he saw one of the *Andiron*'s cutters unloading fruit alongside. There was no mistaking the bulky shape of Stockdale straddle-legged on the gunwale tossing up the nets of fruit as if they were weightless.

Strangely, that had been almost the hardest thing to bear. Stockdale of all people. Whether he had been eager or reluctant, Bolitho did not know, but he had gone over with the privateer's crew, and like sheep the other men from his raiding party had followed suit. He knew he could not blame them. If Stockdale, the captain's trusted coxswain, could change colours, why not they?

Stockdale looked up, squinting against the sun. Then he threw a mock salute, and some of the men laughed delightedly.

The American officer of the watch said dryly: 'Sometimes I think there's no such thing as loyalty, Captain! Just a *price*!'

Bolitho shrugged. 'Perhaps.'

The officer seemed glad of a chance to break Bolitho's brooding silence. 'I can't get over your being our captain's kin. It makes it kind of unnerving. But then I guess it's that way with you?'

Bolitho glanced quickly at the officer's tanned features. It was a friendly face. And that of a man lonely and tired by war, he thought. He said evenly, 'Have you been with him long?'

'A year or so.' The man frowned. 'It seems longer now. He came aboard as first lieutenant, but soon got command when the skipper was killed in a fight with one of your ships off Cape Cod.' He grinned. 'But I hope I'll be able to go home soon. I've a wife and two boys waiting for me. I should be tending my farm, not fighting King George!'

Bolitho recalled his brother's firm promise that he was

returning to Cornwall to claim his rightful inheritance, and felt the same savage bitterness as when he had heard the words the first time.

He controlled his rising emotion and asked quietly, 'Do you really think it will be that simple?'

The man stared at him. 'What could happen now? I don't mean to add insult to injury, Captain, but I don't really think the British stand much of a chance to regain America.'

Bolitho smiled. 'I was thinking more of the French. If as you say American independence will be ratified by all those concerned, do you imagine the French will be prepared to sail away and leave you alone? They have done most of the fighting, remember. Without their fleet and supplies do you think you would have succeeded thus far?'

The American scratched his head. 'War makes strange allies, Captain.'

'I know. I have seen some of them.' Bolitho looked away. 'I think the French will want to stay out here, as they tried to do in Canada.' He shook his head. 'You could easily exchange one master for another!'

The officer yawned and said wearily, 'Well, it's not for me to decide, thank the Lord!' He shaded his eyes and peered towards the dark shadow below Saddle Hill. A white and blue dot was moving rapidly down the rough track from the summit in a cloud of dust.

The officer looked meaningly at Bolitho and said briefly, 'Horse and rider! That means one thing, Captain. The bait has been accepted. It will be tonight, or not at all!'

There was a shout from the forecastle as a blinding needle of light stabbed out from the bleak headland. Someone was using a heliograph, and from further inland Bolitho heard the eager beating of drums.

He asked, 'How did they get a signal?'

The officer closed his mouth and then said not unkindly, 'There is a chain of fishing boats out there, Captain. They pass the sighting reports from boat to boat. The nearest one is well in sight of the hill lookouts.' He looked embarrassed. 'Why not try and forget it? There's nothing you can do now. Any more than I could do if the situation were reversed!'

Bolitho looked at him thoughtfully. 'Thank you. I will try to remember that.' Then he resumed his pacing, and with a shrug the officer returned to the opposite side of the poop.

The short truce was over. They were no longer fellow sailors. The flashing heliograph had made them enemies once more.

'It'll be sunset in one hour!' Daniel Proby, the *Phalarope*'s master, scribbled slowly on his slate and then ambled across to join Herrick by the weather rail. 'But in all my experience I've not seen one like this!'

Herrick brought his mind back to the present and followed Proby's mournful gaze across the vast glittering waste of open sea.

For most of the afternoon and early evening the frigate had pushed her way steadily north-east, and now as she lay close-hauled on the port tack, every mast and spar, every inch of straining canvas shone with the hue of burnished copper. The sky, which for days had remained bright blue and empty, was streaked with long cruising clouds, streaming like trails of glowing smoke towards the far horizon. It was an angry sky, and the sea was reacting to the change in its own way. Instead of short, choppy whitecaps the surface had altered to advancing lines of hump-backed rollers, one behind the other in neatly matched ranks which made the ship heave and groan as her figurehead lifted to the sky and then plunged forward and down in drawn-out, sickening swoops.

Herrick said, 'Maybe a storm is coming through from the Atlantic?'

The master shook his head, unconvinced. 'You don't get much in the way of storms at this time of year.' He glanced aloft as the sails thundered as if to mock his words. 'All the same, we will have to take in another reef if it don't improve a bit.'

In spite of his gloom Herrick was able to smile to himself. He could not see Vibart being happy about that. For two days, since he had received his new orders, he had been driving the ship like a madman. He thought back again to the moment a lookout had sighted the distant sail. For an instant they had all imagined it was a patrolling frigate or the *Cassius* herself. But it had been a fast-moving brig, her low hull smothered in spray as she had gone about and run down towards the *Phalarope*.

Her arrival had been an unexpected but welcome diversion as far as Herrick was concerned. The tension aboard the frigate was getting bad enough to *feel*, like something with a soul of its own. In a matter of days there had been seven floggings, but instead of settling the crew into dumb servility it had only helped to drive a firm wedge between quarterdeck and forecastle. There was little chatter or laughter any more between decks, and when an officer passed close by a group of seamen, the latter would lapse into sullen silence and turn their faces away.

Midshipman Maynard had reported. 'The brig is *Witch of Looe*, sir! She has despatches for us!'

Vibart had waited importantly on the quarterdeck, alone and aloof, saying nothing and watching everything.

A boat had skipped across the choppy water, and soon a young lieutenant had climbed aboard carrying the inevitable canvas envelope.

Herrick had been standing nearby, straining his ears and trying to imagine what was happening. He had heard Vibart asking about the flagship and the lieutenant's brief reply.

'These orders are from the admiral, sir. I have nothing

to add.'

The reply had been too brief, almost insolent, and Herrick had guessed that the young lieutenant was high enough on the admiral's list of favourites to afford such rudeness.

Vibart had started to tell the brig's messenger about the raid on Mola Island and had then clamped his jaw tightly shut. He had turned on his heel, merely adding for Herrick's benefit, 'Get the ship under way again, Mr. Herrick. I have work to do!'

He was always the same now, Herrick pondered. Fluctuating between ponderous self-importance and fits of blind rage. From one hour to the next you could never be sure of his reactions, and it was doubly bad because he was always in evidence. Watching and criticising and bawling out fresh orders to overrule those of his subordinates.

Herrick had stopped the lieutenant at the entry port and had tried to get more information.

The officer had regarded him thoughtfully. 'St. Kitts has fallen. The fleet is falling back and regrouping. I am on my way to Antigua now.' He had stared across at his own ship. 'But Rodney is said to be on his way back from England with twelve ships of the line. I hope to God he will be in time.' Then he added quickly, 'Where is your Captain?'

'Dead.' Herrick's tongue had lingered on the word. 'We lost him at Mola Island.'

'Well, I don't care much for your new commander, my friend.' The lieutenant had paused above his swaying boat. 'We have been searching for the *Phalarope* for two days! The admiral will not be pleased that you were off your station, Mola Island or not!' He had rolled his eyes. 'Sir Robert is a stickler for routine.'

Herrick's mind shifted to the next part in the sequence of events which had sent the *Phalarope* on her new course

197

towards the islands. Vibart had called a meeting in the stern cabin. Every officer and warrant officer had been present, and it was somehow typical of Vibart that while he sat comfortably in his chair, all the others were kept standing.

'Sir Robert Napier has received information that the *Andiron* is lying off Nevis.' He had plunged into what sounded very like a carefully rehearsed speech. 'She is apparently carrying out repairs and awaiting fresh orders, but there is no saying how long she will remain there.' He had looked slowly around their faces. 'Sir Robert requires that we make our way to Nevis forthwith to sink or cut-out the *Andiron*.' His words had dropped in the cabin like stones in a pool. 'We will make as quick a passage as possible.' He had glared meaningly. 'So make sure there are no mistakes, Mr. Proby!'

Herrick had been studying Vibart during his announcement, and had been surprised by his apparent eagerness to begin the operation. It might be a false piece of intelligence, but if not, it would not be an easy matter to cut-out an anchored ship close inshore to a hostile island.

Then, as Vibart had droned on about details and timing, he had realised that Vibart's demeanour owed much to his own uncertainty. So far, although he had been in command since Bolitho's loss, Okes stood in the best position to gain full credit for past successes against the enemy. He still had to ensure the firmness of his own control, and this new operation was the obvious opportunity.

It was odd that he had sent no despatches across to the *Witch of Looe*, Herrick thought. It was just as if he wanted to save the whole record for the admiral's ear alone. Sir Robert might be angry about *Phalarope* being off station, but the destruction of the Mola Island battery and transports, and a victory over the privateer *Andiron* would do much to placate anyone but the devil himself.

But now that Vibart had time to consider the full implications of his orders he had changed yet again. As the ship drove towards the chosen rendezvous he had grown nervous and edgy, and more than once had let his impatience get the upper hand. Only that morning he had had a man flogged for letting a marline-spike fall from the foreyard. It had struck quivering in the deck within feet of Packwood, a boatswain's mate. Vibart had been brooding on the quarterdeck, watching the boats being checked and moved ready for instant lowering. Packwood's startled shout had given him yet one more outlet for his unpredictable temper.

'Get that man down here!' His voice had stopped all work on the maindeck. 'I saw what he did! That was meant to fall on Packwood!'

Even the boatswain's mate had voiced a protest. 'It's lively aloft today, sir. It was an accident.'

Vibart's face had gone scarlet. 'Silence! Or I'll see your backbones, too!'

Again the dread pipe. 'All hands lay aft to witness punishment!'

Again the agonising passage of time while the grating was rigged and the marines had made a scarlet rectangle on the quarterdeck.

The seaman in question was a man called Kirk. He was a thin, hollow-eyed sailor who had gone almost deaf after the encounter with the *Andiron*, his ears apparently permanently damaged by the thundering crash of broadsides.

Mr. Quintal, the boatswain, had walked slowly aft, the familiar red baize bag swinging from his wrist as the silent company parted to allow him through.

Up to the last moment, even as Vibart closed the Articles of War and announced harshly, 'Four dozen, Mr. Quintal!' Herrick doubted if Kirk had heard a single word.

Only when the boatswain's mates seized him and

stripped his thin body and spread-eagled him across the grating like a writhing crucifix did he start to scream and protest.

Most men took their punishment in silence. The tremendous force of a single blow from the cat-o'-nine-tails was enough to drive the wind from the lungs and left little to cry on.

Kirk's cries continued as his wrists were tied in position so that his feet were only just touching the deck, and the boatswains mates exchanged quick glances, momentarily unnerved by the man's terror.

Quintal drew the lash from the red bag and handed it to Packwood. Gruffly he had said, 'Two dozen. Josling can do the other two.' Under his breath he had added, 'If he lives that long!'

Vibart had replaced his hat and nodded curtly. 'Carry on!'

Herrick had seen plenty of floggings, and had steeled himself to accept what was part of naval life. But this one had seemed different, and unfair because of Vibart's obvious eagerness.

The marine drummer had struck into a quick roll, and Packwood had drawn back his thick arm.

'One!' The lash came down with a swishing crack.

As usual Herrick had been sickly fascinated by the time it took to show its mark. For a moment there was nothing on the man's naked back, not even a bruise, but even as the lash swung back for the second stroke the whole area of taut skin from the shoulder to the waist opened and shone in a criss-cross of fine cuts.

'Two!' Kirk screamed and wriggled helplessly on the grating, and Herrick saw blood on his chin and knew that he had bitten through his tongue.

'Three!' Packwood faltered and hit again, his eyes glassy as Kirk's back began to shred into a tangle of bloody flesh.

Vibart's voice had cut through the roll of the drum.

'Harder, Packwood! Don't go easy on the scum, unless you wish to change places with him!'

And so it had continued. Stroke by stroke, to the inhuman rattle of the drum. Kirk had fallen silent and limp after the first dozen, but when Ellice, the surgeon, had pronounced grimly, "E's still alive, sir, but not takin' it well!' Vibart had snapped, 'Carry on with punishment!'

Herrick had seen Midshipman Neale holding Maynard's sleeve as if for support as the grisly flogging had continued.

Kirk had little flesh to begin with, and after eighteen strokes Herrick thought he could see the gleam of bone and muscle through the man's butchered skin.

Josling had taken the lash from his fellow boatswain's mate and had run it through his fingers to clear it of flesh and gristle. With a quick glance upwards at Vibart's expressionless face he had carried on with the second two dozen.

At the twentieth stroke Mr Quintal had knocked up Josling's arm and had said firmly, 'That's enough, sir! He's dyin'!'

Kirk's bloodied body had been cut down and carried below, but only after Ellice had backed up the boatswain's quick intervention. He had muttered vaguely, 'Might live. Can't say. I think his kidneys have burst.'

Herrick had looked for some sign of pity or even triumph on Vibart's heavy features. But there had been nothing but stony indifference. Captain Pomfret had watched floggings like a man will watch a spectacle of sport, and at each bloody conclusion he was almost elated, as if he had just experienced some perverted sexual act. But not Vibart. There was nothing at all which Herrick could recognise as feeling of any sort.

He turned away swiftly as Vibart appeared at the cabin hatch and sniffed at the wind. Vibart studied the strange copper sky and remarked slowly, 'Wind's freshened.

We'll shorten sail in ten minutes.' He glanced at Proby. 'Now, are you sure of our position? Our *exact* position?'

Proby nodded gloomily. 'Aye, sir. Nevis bears nor'-east, near on fifteen miles.'

Vibart regarded him searchingly. 'I hope for your sake that is so, Mr. Proby.' He contented himself with another quick bark at the helmsman, 'Watch her head, you fool! Keep her close to the wind!'

Herrick glanced aloft and knew that the ship was running perfectly. Vibart was obviously getting more and more on edge as they drew nearer the island. Not afraid. He had never shown a sign of fear at any time. No, it went far deeper, to the lurking possibility of failure.

Vibart saw Herrick watching him and snapped, 'Have you detailed the cutting-out parties?'

'Aye, sir. All the boats except the gig are prepared. The gig is unsuitable for this work.'

'I know that, Mr. Herrick!' Vibart's eyes were flecked with red. 'You will take over-all charge of the boarders with Maynard, Packwood and Parker in charge of the other three boats.' He looked darkly at the men working on deck. 'As a master's mate, Parker will be ideal for getting sail on the *Andiron* if you succeed in your attack.'

'Yes, sir.' Herrick knew all this. He had detailed each man personally, and had already decided on his set plan. He asked, 'Do you expect much opposition, sir?'

'We are committed now. It doesn't matter what I think!'

Proby consulted his massive watch and said, 'Call all hands! Prepare to shorten sail!'

Herrick wondered why Vibart had left it so long. Several times he had seen fishing boats in the far distance. There was no point in advertising the *Phalarope*'s haste by her obvious press of sail.

The seamen were already climbing the shrouds and pulling themselves out along the swaying yards. With the ship's uncomfortable motion the business of taking in sails was all the more dangerous to the unwary.

Vibart growled, 'This will make us harder to see. And with the wind rising all the time it will save us the trouble of shortening later on.' He seemed to be thinking aloud.

Proby cupped his hands and yelled hoarsely, 'Tops'ls and jib's all we need! Lively there!'

Followed by Vibart's eyes and the urgent shouts of their petty officers the men aloft fought at the thrashing canvas, cursing the wind and the treacherous sails which tried their utmost to hurl the men from the yards to the deck beneath.

Herrick felt the ship's motion ease slightly as top gallants and courses contracted and finally submitted to the struggling seamen. He watched the long cruising rollers and gauged the distance between them. It would be more sheltered below Nevis's lee, he thought, but even so it would not be easy to keep the raiding boats together. He caught sight of Okes standing at the lee rail, and found himself wondering why Vibart had not chosen him for the cutting-out expedition. If Okes was so changed and reliable, he was the obvious choice.

Captain Rennie sauntered across the quarterdeck and remarked quietly, 'Congratulations, Herrick. I hope you do well tonight. I wish I could come with you, but marines are hardly suitable for falling about in boats!'

Herrick smiled. 'Thank you.'

Rennie gestured towards Okes. 'It would seem that our commanding officer knows more than we thought, eh? He will not trust this attack to a man who is as weak as water!'

Herrick glanced quickly at the open skylight. 'Keep your voice down! Your remarks might be taken seriously!'

Rennie shrugged but dropped his voice. 'I feel past caring. Like a man walking on ice. It can only take so much!'

He walked away, and Herrick stood watching the

seamen shinning down from the work aloft. If only Bolitho were here to inspire and carry them all, he thought heavily. He could imagine the *Phalarope* sailing into Antigua with Vibart expanding with pleasure as cheers and congratulations marked their return to the fleet and to glory. It would make victory all the more bitter, he thought. But for Bolitho the *Phalarope* would never have got this far, and if Vibart retained his command the future was bleak indeed.

Tobias Ellice rolled aft and mounted the quarterdeck ladder, touching his shabby hat and belching simultaneously. 'Kirk's dead,' he grunted abruptly. 'I'm having him sewn up nice an' neat like!'

Herrick replied, 'Very well. I'll put it in the log.' He could smell the rum on the surgeon's breath and wondered how the man was able to perform his duties.

Ellice said, 'You can also put in the log that I'm sick of this ship and the whole bloody lot of you!' He swayed tipsily and would have fallen but for Herrick's arm. He muttered, 'Treat 'em like dogs!' He shook his head vaguely. 'No, not dogs, they live like kings by comparison.'

Herrick regarded him wearily. 'Have you finished?'

Ellice took a giant red handkerchief from the tail of his coat and blew his nose loudly. 'You can sneer, Mr. Herrick! You're off to gain glory tonight and to test your steel against the enemy.' He bared his teeth and tried to focus Herrick in his rheumy eyes. 'But you'll change yer tune when you're down below waiting for the saw to lop off your pretty arm or take away a leg or two!'

'Only two?' Herrick eyed him with sad amusement. Ellice became suddenly serious as his rum-sodden mind grappled with Herrick's question. 'You can live without 'em, boy! I've seen it many a time.' He dropped his voice. 'But watch out for your wedding-tackle! A woman'll forgive much, but lose that lot and you might as well be food for the fish!'

Herrick watched him go and then strode aft to the taffrail. Another man dead. Whose turn would it be next?

Bryan Ferguson took another cutlass from the deep chest and handed it to old Ben Strachan. The latter peered quickly along the heavy blade and then bent over the grindstone and began to run the cutlass back and forth across the spinning stone, his eyes gleaming brightly in the flying sparks.

Ferguson looked at the berth deck and at the leaping shadows cast by the madly swinging lanterns as the ship rolled and staggered beneath his feet. It was strange how he was now able to retain his balance, and even his stomach seemed able to resist the lurking agony of seasickness.

The low-beamed berth deck was strangely deserted by comparison with its usual appearance of crowded humanity, he thought. Apart from the men selected for the boarding parties, all other available hands were on deck preparing the ship for action. As he watched Strachan concentrating on his sharpening he could hear the menacing rumble of gun trucks as the main armament was carefully loaded and then lashed once more behind sealed ports. The decks were already sanded, and he could hear Mr. Brock, the gunner, yelling some last-minute instructions to his magazine party.

There was a strong smell of neat rum pervading the berth deck, and he turned to stare at the huddled groups of seamen who remained below enjoying a small moment of rest before taking to the boats.

He said quietly to Strachan, 'What will happen, do you think?'

Strachan tested the blade and laid it carefully on the pile beside him. 'Hard to tell, mate. I've been on a few cuttin' out raids meself. Sometimes it was all over with a few prayers and a few "Oh my Gods" an' afore you knew what 'ad 'appened you was back aboard none the worse! An' other times you was shocked to be still alive!'

Ferguson nodded, unable to picture the nerve-wrenching horror of a raid in total darkness. His new duties as clerk kept him away from that sort of danger and had somehow thrown him further apart from his companions.

It was all he could do to stay clear of trouble with the first lieutenant. Vibart read every order and account at least twice, and he never failed to follow up a complaint with a threat of punishment.

Ferguson thought back to the floggings and the last one in particular. He had wanted to hide his face, yet was stricken and mesmerised by the relentless punishment so that he had watched it to the end. Kirk had died in the sickbay, but his sobbing cries still seemed to hover in the space which had once been his home,

Strachan remarked, 'It's gettin' pretty rough up top. I wouldn't like to be takin' part!' He shook his grey head. 'It was as black as a pig's belly when I last took a look!'

Onslow, the big seaman from the *Cassius*, sauntered across and stared thoughtfully at Ferguson for several seconds. In his checked shirt and tight canvas trousers he looked even taller and more formidable than usual, and his thick hair was tied to the nape of his neck with a piece of red ribbon.

He said, 'You'll be staying aboard then?' He smiled. 'And quite right, too.' He rested his hand on Ferguson's thin shoulder. 'You save your energy, my lad. I'll want to be knowing what is happening down aft in the cabin.'

Ferguson stared at him. 'I—I don't understand?'

Onslow yawned and spread his arms. 'It's always just as well to know what the officers are planning next, y'see. That's what stops men like us staying rabble. With knowledge,' he tapped his forehead meaningly, 'we are equal to them, and *ready*!'

Lugg, a gunner's mate, ran down a ladder and squinted through the gloom. 'Right, you lot! On deck and lively about it! Each man take a cutlass and muster aft!'

Onslow eyed him calmly. 'What, no pistols?'

Lugg replied coldly, 'I'll pistol you if you don't learn some manners!'

There was a rasp of steel as each hurrying figure took a cutlass, and once or twice Ferguson spoke to a passing familiar face, but each time he received no answer.

Strachan wiped his hands and muttered, 'Save yer breath, mate. They're thinkin' of what lies ahead. There'll be talk enough later, I shouldn't wonder!'

John Allday hung back to the last. Then he picked up a cutlass and swung it slowly in the lamplight. Quietly he said, 'Be careful of Onslow, Bryan. He is a born trouble-maker. I don't trust him an inch!'

Ferguson studied his friend with surprise and something like guilt. Since his unexpected change of jobs to captain's clerk he had seemingly drifted away from Allday's quiet protection, and whenever he had resumed to the berth deck it had always been Onslow or his friend Pook who had dragged him into a tight circle of chatter and speculation.

Allday saw the uncertainty on Ferguson's face and added, 'You saw the flogging, Bryan. Be warned!'

'But Onslow is on our side, surely?' Ferguson wanted to understand. 'You heard him talking today. He was as sickened as the rest of us!'

'I heard him.' Allday's mouth twisted in a grim smile. 'But he only talks. He is never the one who goes to the gratings!'

Old Strachan mumbled, 'I seen a lad like 'im in the old *Gorgon*. Stirred up the men till they never knew which way ter jump. They 'anged 'im in the end!'

'And they'll hang all of us if he keeps up this mutinous talk!' Allday's eyes flashed. 'We are here, and we must

207

make the best of it!'

Lugg peered down the ladder and bellowed, 'Come up on deck, you idle bugger! You're the last as usual!' But there was no real anger in his voice. He was as tense and jumpy as everyone else aboard.

Ferguson called, 'Good luck!' but Allday was already running on deck, his eyes momentarily blinded in the darkness which enclosed the pitching hull like a cloak.

Overhead there were few stars, and then only occasionally visible between the low scudding clouds.

Petty officers were bawling names, and slipping and cursing the seamen pushed into separate parties near the boats which were already clear of their chocks and ready to be swayed outboard.

Allday saw the white lapels of Lieutenant Herrick's coat gleaming faintly against the dark sky and was strangely glad he was going with his boat. Midshipman Maynard seemed a likeable enough youngster, but he lacked both experience and confidence. He could see him now whispering furtively to his small friend Neale below the quarterdeck.

Herrick said sharply, 'Now listen to me, lads! I will lead in the launch. The cutter will follow close astern and then the pinnace. Mr. Parker will stay last in the jolly boat.' He had to shout above the moaning wind, and Allday glanced uneasily at the creaming water alongside and the rising spectres of blown spray. It would be a hard pull, he thought, and automatically spat on his hands.

He pricked up his ears as Parker, the master's mate, reported, 'All present, Mr. Herrick. Sixty-six men all told!'

'Very good. I will inform the . . .' He faltered and added harshly, 'I will tell Mr. Vibart!'

Allday bit his lip. There was no love lost between Herrick and the new captain, he thought.

He saw Onslow leaning negligently against a pike rack and remembered Ferguson's uneasiness. It was odd how

208

eager Onslow had been to see Ferguson appointed as clerk, he decided. And how convenient it had been that Mathias, Bolitho's original clerk, had died in the hold.

'Sway out the cutter!' Mr. Quintal groped his way towards the tackle. 'Hoist away there!'

Allday faltered, his mind suddenly filled with one, stark picture. He had been masthead lookout the morning Mathias had fallen to his death. It was strange how he had not thought of the connection before. He had seen the clerk climbing through the small inspection hatch shortly before he had been found unconscious and dying. But there had already been someone else in the hold before that! He looked quickly at Onslow, remembering the exact moment and the fact that it had been Onslow who had reported the clerk's fall.

He felt Quintal's hard hand on his shoulder and threw his weight against the tackle with the others. All at once the sea seemed to become rougher and the *Phalarope* seemed to shrink by comparison.

Through his racing thoughts he heard Onslow say casually, 'We'll give the buggers a taste of steel!'

But who did he mean? Allday wondered.

11

Fortune of War

The *Phalarope*'s heavy launch, packed as she was with additional men for the cutting-out raid, began to ship water within minutes of leaving the security of the frigate's side.

Herrick wedged himself in one corner of the stern and peered over the heads of the straining oarsmen, his vision hampered by both darkness and a continuous stream of bursting spray. He tried to concentrate on the set plan of attack, but as time dragged by and the boat's swooping motion became more pronounced he found that half of his mind dwelt on the realisation that things were already moving against him. The wind had gained in force, and he didn't need to consult his small compass to know that it had also veered more to the east, so that what cover there might have been from the island was lost in an angry welter of tossing whitecaps and great swirling patterns of backwash from partially hidden rocks.

Every so often he looked astern and was thankful to see the cutter riding in his wake, her banks of oars slashing one moment at wave crests and then buried to the rowlocks as the boat dropped into another sickening trough.

Ryan, a seasoned quartermaster, swung the tiller bar and yelled, 'She'm takin' it poorly, sir! The lads are all but wore out!'

Herrick nodded but did not reply. It was obvious from the slow, laboured stroke that the men were already exhausted and in no shape for carrying out any sort of attack. More and more Herrick was nagged by the thought that Vibart had dropped the boats too soon. Nevis Island was still only a darker patch in the night's angry backcloth, and there was no sign at all of the chosen landmarks.

He felt a surge of anger when he remembered Vibart's brusqueness when he had last seen him. All he had wanted was to get the boats away. No second plan, no arrangements for possible discovery had even been discussed.

The *Andiron* was supposed to be anchored below Dogwood Point, but even allowing for better shelter inshore, it was still likely that her captain had called extra hands to watch for possible dangers in the rising wind. Herrick had a sudden picture of his exhausted boats' crews arriving at the ship's side to be met with a murderous fire from the awakened and eager gunners.

Ryan was shouting again. 'There's a strong drift, y'see! It'll carry us clear of the 'eadland, sir!' He sounded bitter. 'It'll be a long pull to clear the point at this rate.'

As if to back his words there was an anonymous rumble of voices from the darkened boat. Someone muttered, 'We should turn back. There's no chance now!'

Herrick glared down the boat. 'Silence! Do you want the whole island to hear us?'

Ryan whispered, 'Could we not lie beneath the point, sir?' He sounded slightly ashamed. 'We could rest the men a bit an' then try again.'

Herrick nodded, another plan forming in his brain. 'Good idea. Signal the cutter, Ryan.' He took the tiller as the quartermaster opened the shutter of his lantern and blinked it twice astern. To the oarsmen he snapped, 'Keep the stroke! *Together*, now!' There was no muttering, but he could sense them all watching him in the darkness. He

211

added, 'The rest of you keep baling, and watch the oars. I want 'em muffled at every pull!'

Ryan said, 'Cutter's turning, sir. I can see the pinnace back there, too.'

'Well, thank God for that!' Herrick forgot the grumbling seamen as the skyline hardened into a jagged overhanging cliff. It was Dogwood Point well enough, but they had drifted further than he had feared. They were not below it, but on the wrong side altogether. As he stared wretchedly at the land's hostile outline he felt the boat's motion begin to ease and heard the oars pick up a steadier time as the launch thrust into more sheltered water.

He said quietly, 'Oars! Easy with those blades now! You sound like a lot of damn cattle!'

The boat rode uneasily in the inshore swell while the weary sailors fell across their oars and sucked gratefully at the damp air. The pinnace moved out of the gloom and lay close by, and then the cutter crossed to the other side and paddled nearer so that Midshipman Maynard could make himself heard.

'What shall we do, Mr. Herrick?'

'Lie here for a bit!' Herrick spoke slowly to give himself time to sort out his hazy ideas. He wished Maynard would not sound so lost and bewildered in front of his men. Things were already bad enough. He added, 'Where is Mr. Parker and the jolly boat?'

Maynard shrugged, and Packwood, the boatswain's mate, called quickly from the pinnace, 'We've lost sight of him long since, Mr. Herrick!'

Herrick controlled his reply with an effort. 'Maybe he turned back!'

A seaman murmured, 'Sunk more likely!'

Herrick made up his mind. 'Come alongside! But get some fenders out!'

He waited, holding his breath as the two boats sidled against the launch. At each creak and thud he expected to hear shouts from ashore, or the ominous rattle of musket fire. But only the wind and the hissing spray interrupted his words as Maynard and Packwood craned to hear him.

'If we pull around the point we shall be too late to make an attack.'

Maynard muttered petulantly, 'We were given too far to row in my opinion. It was impossible from the start!'

Herrick snarled, 'No one is asking for your opinion, so just listen to me will you?' Herrick was surprised at the savagery in his own voice but hurried on, 'There should be a bit of foreshore below the point, so we'll head for it now. Mr. Packwood will wait with half a crew per boat and lie as close as possible to the rocks.' He waited, feeling the tension dragging at his patience. 'Understand?'

They nodded doubtfully and he continued, 'Mr. Maynard will accompany me ashore with thirty men. If we scale the point we should be able to see down the other side. If the *Andiron* is still there we might try an attack even now, especially if she looks peaceful enough and is close to the headland. Otherwise we will head back to the picking-up area.' He had a brief picture of Vibart's scorn and rage when he returned to announce the failure of the attack. He again felt the same unreasonable anger at the mission. The admiral should have sent a heavier force. Even the *Cassius* would have helped just by adding her strength and availability for the final withdrawal.

Perhaps it was his own fault after all. If he had not trusted Vibart's complacency and had checked the distance from the shore more carefully. If only he had allowed for the change of wind and the savage offshore drift. He shook himself angrily. It was too late now. The present was all that counted.

But he still found time to imagine Bolitho in these circumstances. The mental picture of that impassive face helped to steady him and he said in a level voice, 'Bear off and head for the rocks. But not a sound, *any* of you!'

One by one the boats moved inshore, and when almost hemmed in by dark-fanged rocks the first men leapt slipping and cursing into shallow water.

There was no point in trying to split the party into groups now, Herrick decided. It would take too long, and they had taken enough chances already. He watched the three boats move clear and then snapped, 'Mr Maynard, come with me. McIntosh will take charge down here.' He groped through his mind to remember the carefully listed names. 'Allday and Martin follow me!'

Allday seemed a capable man, and Martin, who had once earned a rare living as a Dorset poacher, was as nimble and quiet as a rabbit.

As they climbed in silence up the steeply sloping cliff Herrick again thought of Bolitho and his dashing attack on Mola Island. There he had had to deal with every sort of danger, yet he had succeeded at the cost of his own life. Compared with Mola Island this escapade was nothing, he thought grimly.

And why had he made a point of suggesting an alternative to the attack? Was he perhaps already preparing to slip away to the waiting *Phalarope* without even attempting to complete the mission?

He stumbled and almost fell to the rocks below, but a hand seized his wrist and he heard Allday say, 'You must watch this sort of cliff, sir! It feels secure, but the stones are only caked in soil. There's no real grip in them.'

Herrick stared at him. Of course, Allday had been a shepherd as well as a sailor. After Cornwall's rocky cliffs and hills this was probably child's play to him.

As if reading his thoughts Allday murmured, 'Many's the time I've been down this sort of thing after a wandering lamb.'

They both froze into silence as Martin hissed, 'Sir! There's a sentry up yonder!'

Herrick stared. 'Where? Are you sure, man?'

Martin nodded vehemently. 'Thirty yards or so over there! I heard his boots. *There*!' His eyes gleamed excitedly. 'Did you hear 'em?'

'Yes, I did.' Herrick sank down on a ledge of wet grass. A sentry up here. What was the point of it? No man could see much beyond the edge of the cliff at night-time. He said, 'We'll crawl closer and take a look!'

Holding their weapons clear of the treacherous stones they wriggled across the side of the headland, their eyes smarting from straining and watching.

Herrick said at length, 'Martin, get away to the left. Allday, take the seaward side.' He watched them crawl away. We'll push on up this slope, Mr. Maynard. I feel that something is not quite right here.'

Allday came back first, his body bent double as he ran quickly from bush to bush. 'The *Andiron*'s there right enough, sir! She's just on the other side of the point. She's in complete darkness. Not a light or a sound from her!'

Maynard muttered, 'They must be damn confident!'

Allday said, 'The crew could be ashore, sir.'

'Unlikely.' Herrick tried to find the cause of his uncertainty. 'Their anchorage must be a good one.' He stiffened and then relaxed as Martin slithered down the slope on his scrawny buttocks.

Martin waited to regain his breath. 'Them's soldiers up there, sir!'

'What are they doing?' Herrick forced himself to remain calm.

'Sleepin' by the looks of it, sir!' Martin picked a thorn from his bare foot. 'They'm got a sentry at each end, but the rest is just lyin' about.' He shrugged. 'Sleepin' like I said!' He sounded scornful.

Herrick asked sharply, 'What did you mean, Martin, "at each end"?'

'Oh, I forgot, sir.' Martin grinned. 'They've got six pieces of artillery along the side of the cliff.'

Herrick felt strangely relaxed. Not knowing the odds was always worse than actually facing them. Almost to himself he said, 'Just two sentries, you say?'

Martin nodded. 'Aye, sir. An' about thirty men lyin' beside the guns.' He chuckled. 'I could'a cut their throats easily!'

Herrick said, 'You may have to.' Suddenly it was quite clear what he had to do. The *Andiron* slept at anchor because she was well protected by firmly mounted field pieces. No doubt each gun was already loaded and ranged to cover the whole anchorage. It was not an uncommon arrangement where no proper harbour was available.

He felt suddenly cold at the thought of what would have happened if his boats had made their planned attack. The casualties and the noise would have killed any chance of success.

He said flatly, 'Get to the beach, Mr. Maynard. Send every available man up here as fast as you can. Anchor the boats and let the remaining men swim ashore. Tell McIntosh and the others that I intend to rush the guns and put 'em out of action. Then we'll take to the boats and go for the *Andiron* as planned!'

They all watched him in silence. Then Maynard said, 'And you, sir?'

Herrick patted Martin's shoulder. 'Our poacher is going to earn his keep tonight, Mr. Maynard!'

Martin pulled a knife from his belt and handed his heavy cutlass to Allday. He said cheerfully, 'Easy, sir! It don't seem fair, do it?'

When Martin and Maynard had slithered back into the darkness Herrick said quietly, 'Those soldiers must be silenced as they sleep. Killed or clubbed, I don't care. But they must be kept from raising the alarm!'

Allday winced as Maynard's dirk clattered on a rock below and then said, 'It's them or us, isn't it, sir?'

*

'How is your arm, Mr. Belsey?' Bolitho heard the master's mate move somewhere in the pitch darkness and knew he had asked the question merely to break the nerve-jarring silence. With Belsey and Farquhar he had been hustled below and locked unceremoniously in a tiny unused storeroom somewhere beneath the *Andiron*'s forecastle, and after a short attempt at conversation each man had lapsed into silence and the apprehension of his own thoughts.

Belsey said, 'Fair enough, sir. But this motion is makin' me sweat!'

The ship's uneasy movement had certainly increased even during the last hour. The storeroom was below the *Andiron*'s water-line, and the savage jarring of the anchored hull was all the more apparent. The crew had already paid out more hawse to compensate for the sudden change of wind which now swept across the once protected anchorage with mounting ferocity.

Belsey added, 'Maybe the *Phalarope* will stand out to sea agin, sir? Surely they'll not send boats out in this lot?'

Bolitho was glad the others could not see his face. A change of weather would make little difference to Vibart's determination to produce a victory, he thought. From the moment the signal had been flashed down the hillside to the hidden defenders he had felt a growing despair, the fretting certainty of calamity and destruction for the *Phalarope* and her company. And he was powerless to help a single man.

He felt a sudden pressure at his shoulders as the ship heeled in a deep swell. She was snubbing at her cable at regular intervals now, and he could feel the deck lifting and then sliding back with each shuddering jerk.

He found himself thinking again of his brother, and wondered what he was doing at this moment. His earlier eagerness at the proposed massacre of *Phalarope*'s boarding party must have given way a little to the anxiety for his own ship's safety. At any other time he would have made sail and headed for the more sheltered side of the island. It was strange how the unexpected change of weather had taken a part in the game. Not that it could have any final effect. It merely prolonged the misery of waiting.

Farquhar said absently, 'I wish something would happen! This waiting is getting on my nerves!'

Bolitho shifted his position to stare at the brightly lit crack in the storeroom door. Occasionally a shadow blotted out the tiny sliver of light as a sentry moved his position in the narrow passageway beyond. As he rearranged his cramped limbs Bolitho felt the warm touch of steel against his leg and remembered the hidden dirk. For all the use it was now he could have left it in the cabin, he thought wearily.

It was strange that the guards had not bothered to search him. But they were so openly confident, and with such good reason, that it was only to be expected. Even his brother had found time to see him just as he was being led below to the storeroom.

Hugh Bolitho had been wearing his father's sword, as well as a brace of pistols, and seemed to have gained new life and excitement from the impending battle.

'Well, Richard. This is your last chance.' He had stood easily on the swaying deck, his head on one side as he had watched his brother with something like amusement. 'Just one decision, and it is yours to make!'

'I have nothing to say to you. Not now. Nor ever!' Bolitho had tried not to stare at the sword. It had been like a final insult.

'Very well. After this I may see little of you. I will have much to do.' He had stared up at the angry sky. 'The wind is rising, but I expect to have visitors none the less!' He had added in a harder tone, 'You will have to take your chances with the French authorities. I must take *Andiron* to join the combined fleets.'

He had seen his brother's immediate caution and had continued calmly, 'I can tell you now, Richard. For you will be unable to take part. The French admiral, de Grasse, will join with a Spanish squadron. Together with our ships they will attack Jamaica.' He had made a curt gesture as if to demonstrate the finality of the campaign. 'I am afraid King George will have to find fresh fields to conquer elsewhere!'

Bolitho had said to his guard, 'I wish to go below.'

His brother had called after him, 'You are foolish, Richard. And what is worse, you are *wrong*!'

As he sat in the swaying storeroom Bolitho found plenty of time to relive the bitterness and the sense of defeat.

There was a scraping of metal as the bolts were drawn from the door, and Belsey groaned. 'Comin' to gloat again! God rot their bloody souls!'

But as the lamplight flooded the storeroom and seared their eyes Bolitho could only stare with surprise. Stockdale stood blinking in the doorway, a heavy boarding axe swinging from his hand.

Bolitho struggled to his feet and then caught sight of the sentry sprawled below the swinging lantern, the back of his head smashed in like an eggshell.

Stockdale said humbly, 'I am sorry it took me so long, Captain! But I had to win their confidence.' He grinned sheepishly. 'Even now I'm not sure I done as you expected.'

Bolitho could hardly speak. He gripped the man's massive arm and muttered, 'You did rightly, Stockdale. Have no fear of that!' To the others he said, 'Are you with me?'

Farquhar replied dazedly, 'Just tell me what to do, sir!'

'Quick, Stockdale!' Bolitho stepped into the passage-way and peered into the darkness beyond the lantern. 'Tell me what is happening!'

The ex-prizefighter answered thickly, 'They're getting

worried up top, sir. No sign of an attack, an' the ship's taking the wind badly.' He thought for a moment. 'Maybe we could swim for the beach, sir?' He nodded with rare excitement. 'Yes, we could do it with luck!'

Bolitho shook his head. 'Not yet. They will be watching like hawks. We must not think of ourselves. We must try to save the *Phalarope* before it is too late!'

Stockdale glanced at the corpse by his feet. 'They change the guard in half an hour, sir. There's not much time!'

'I see.' Bolitho tried to stifle the excitement and urgency in his mind and think more clearly. 'We cannot fight the whole crew, but with luck we might still surprise them!'

Belsey said, 'I'd like to take a few of the buggers with me!'

Bolitho drew the dirk from his breeches and held it glinting in the lamplight. 'Lead the way, Stockdale. If we can get to the forecastle there is something which we can do to provide a diversion!'

Farquhar picked up the dead guard's cutlass and murmured bleakly, 'Are you thinking of the cable, sir?'

Bolitho shot him a swift glance of approval. 'The ship is already dragging hard at her anchor. If we could cut the cable she would be in serious danger. Our men are out there somewhere, and they will soon pull clear when they see *Andiron* drifting towards the point!'

Belsey broke in excitedly, 'The *Andiron*'ll have to make sail, sir! Even then she might not be in time! She'll run hard aground with the wind in this quarter.'

'Begging your pardon, sir.' Stockdale looked at Bolitho sadly. 'They've already got a strong anchor party in the bows looking out for trouble!'

Bolitho smiled coldly. 'I'm not surprised.' He gestured to the others. 'Come, we have little time.' As they crept along the passageway he added, 'Remember that nine-pounder on the forecastle, Mr. Farquhar?'

Farquhar nodded, his eyes gleaming. 'Yes, sir. One of the bow-chasers!'

Bolitho paused below a narrow ladder, straining his eyes towards the hatch above. It might just work. They would all die for their efforts, but he knew that each man now understood that well enough.

He said quietly, 'The gun was lashed there while the rail was being repaired from *Phalarope*'s mauling. If it were cut loose now, in this gale, it would run amuck like a maddened bullock!'

Belsey sucked his teeth. 'My God! A nine-pounder weighs well over a ton! It'd take a bit of holding down!'

Bolitho said, 'If I cut the lashings, Stockdale, could you . . .?'

The man grinned down at him. 'Say no more, Captain!' He swung the heavy axe. 'Just a few minutes is all I'd need!'

'A few minutes are all you'll get, my lad!' Bolitho eased himself up the ladder and peered through the hatch. Again the whole deck area was deserted. He stared up the next and final ladder and then said, 'You can stay behind, Belsey. You can't fight with one arm.'

'Nor can I sit an' do nothin', sir!' Belsey eyed him stubbornly. 'Never mind me, sir. I can still do a bit.'

Any sound made by their stealthy footsteps was drowned by the creak of spars and the thrumming rattle of shrouds and rigging. Bolitho peered quickly at the nearest line of lashed guns and the shadowed shapes of their crews. Most of the men were lying on the deck or resting against the bulwark, and only a few were still on their feet. And they were watching outboard, their eyes only just raised above the hammock nettings.

Bolitho saw the solitary nine-pounder, its long outline jutting aft towards the maindeck. He could hear it creaking gently, as if angered by the lashings which held it tethered and impotent beside the capstan.

Bolitho brushed the sweat from his eyes and cursed the painful beating of his heart against his ribs. It was now or never. At any moment they would be seen for what they were and the gesture would have been in vain. While the others watched him with fixed fascination he stood up and sauntered openly towards the gun. Then he seated himself noisily on the deck and folded his arms across his chest as if trying to sleep.

Farquhar said between his teeth, 'God, look at him! Surely one of those men will realise who he is?'

But the very openness of Bolitho's movements seemed to have killed any immediate interest, and while the *Andiron* rolled from one sickening arc to another the ship's forecastle remained quiet and undisturbed.

Belsey turned on his side by the hatch coaming and croaked, 'Look! There's an officer coming!'

They watched in stricken silence as the blue and white shape of a ship's lieutenant made its way slowly forward from the maindeck towards the forecastle ladder. The officer had to pause halfway up the ladder as a heavier squall than usual struck the ship's side with a crash of spray which made the foremast vibrate like a young tree.

Then Stockdale who had turned his gaze back to Bolitho said, 'He's done it!'

As the frigate's bows lifted and yawed against her anchor cable the nine-pounder began to move. At first the movement was hardly noticeable, then with its small chocks squealing it thundered down the full length of the forecastle to smash with shivering force against the foot of the foremast.

Everyone was yelling and shouting at once. Some of the shouts changed to cries of fear as the gun swung malevolently as if controlled by invisible hands and then charged crazily back across the sloping deck.

The lieutenant called, 'You men! Get handspikes and fresh lashings! Lively there, or it'll smash through the side!'

The anchor watch rose from their concealed positions and ran back from the bows to join the stampede of men at the break of the forecastle. In the centre of the confusion, jubilant and deadly, the long nine-pounder turned its muzzle as if to sniff out new havoc, and then careered squeaking and rumbling towards the opposite side. It crashed against another gun and scattered a shot rack like loose pebbles. The rolling cannon balls added to the pandemonium, and some could be heard thudding on the deck below.

A braver seaman than some leapt across the gun's breech, his hands already fastening a rope's eye around the muzzle. But as the gun trundled back again he screamed and fell against the bulwark to receive the twenty-six hundredweight of wood and metal full on his chest.

Bolitho seized Farquhar's arm and snapped, 'Look! They've got a wedge under the carriage! We've not long now.'

Even as he spoke some of the seamen around the gun turned and stared, their expressions of shock and disbelief changing to cold fury. Bolitho and his two companions slowly retreated towards the bows, the wind and sea at their backs, a converging mass of men driving towards them, all the more terrible because of their complete silence.

Then, to break the spell, a man bellowed, 'Kill them! Cut the bastards down!'

Pressed on by the men behind, the whole mob swept forward, only to sway to an uncertain halt as something like a gunshot echoed around the deck, followed instantly by Stockdale's great shout of triumph.

'It's parted! The cable's cut!'

For a moment longer the *Andiron*'s seamen started at one another, and then as the realisation of their unexpected peril dawned on their minds they hesitated no longer. An officer was yelling from the maindeck, and the cry was carried forward by men who had still managed to keep their heads.

'Hands aloft! Hands aloft! Loose tops'ls!'

From aft Bolitho heard his brother's voice magnified and hardened by his speaking trumpet. 'Man the wheel there!' And then as the ship trembled from stem to stern like a released animal he shouted, 'Mr. Faulkner! Drive those men to the braces!'

Bolitho leaned against the rail, his dirk still held across his body as the frigate heeled still further and began to fall away. Men were running wildly up the shrouds, and already a small patch of canvas was billowing and flapping against the dark sky.

The speaking trumpet called again. 'Cover those men on the fo'c's'le! Shoot them down if they try to escape!'

Belsey wiped his forehead and muttered, 'If our lads *is* out there they'll not want to try an' board!' He peered at Bolitho's tense face. 'I can die in peace now, sir! I reckon we did right well tonight!'

Bolitho saw his face light up with a bright orange glow, and as he turned in surprise the air around him seemed to come alive with the searing whine of gunshot. Stays and halyards parted, and beyond his feet the deck planking splintered and cracked as a thousand balls swept across the forepart of the ship.

Farquhar pointed. 'Look! The battery has fired on us!' He waved his hat. 'The stupid fools have fired on their own men!'

Bolitho pulled him down. 'And us! So keep your head lowered, Mr. Farquhar. You may have use for it still!'

There was no further gunfire, but the one, carefully loaded salvo was sufficient. The prompt action of the *Andiron*'s officers and the quick response of her more level-headed sailors might have taken her clear of danger. But as the whining barrage of grapeshot swept her shrouds and yards free of men and cut down some of the hands still cramming her maindeck, the last opportunity was lost. The black outline of Dogwood Point appeared to grow double in size until the ship was dwarfed beneath it. Even then it looked as if the wind and tide would carry her clear, but as Bolitho pulled his gaping companions to the deck the *Andiron* gave a long-drawn-out shudder, followed instantly by a tremendous crash which threw the remaining seamen from their feet.

Belsey stared up at the sky and crossed himself. 'The mainmast is fallin'! My God, so is the mizzen!'

Fascinated, Bolitho watched the two great masts shiver and then bow very slowly towards the starboard side. Then as stays parted and the angle became more acute the masts thundered down in a flapping tangle of spars and torn sails to plunge eventually into the white-crested water alongside.

Another crash and yet another shook the hull, and while the deck tilted more and more towards the sea Bolitho dragged himself to his feet and shouted, 'She's hard on the sandbar! She'll break her back and capsize in minutes!'

He could hear guns tearing themselves from their lashings and charging across the deck to carve through the screaming, struggling remnants of their late masters. There was no hope of lowering a boat, and nobody even attempted it. Already some were leaping overboard, to be swept away instantly in the strong current. Others ran below as if to find safety, in the darkness, and all around voices cried and pleaded, threatened and cursed as their ship broke up beneath them.

The foremast splintered some four feet from the deck and followed the rest into the sea. From a trim frigate the *Andiron* was changed into a lolling, dismasted hulk, already a thing of ugliness and horror.

Belsey shouted above the din, 'There's a hatch cover, sir! Look, floating by the bowsprit!' He watched Bolitho wildly. 'We could jump for it!'

Bolitho turned to watch as the deck shivered yet again and another released gun charged through a group of crawling seamen. Then he saw his brother standing alone by the quarterdeck rail, his body appearing to be at a forty-five-degree angle on the reeling deck. He was not calling any more, but was standing quite motionless, as if to share the agony of his ship to the last.

For a moment longer Bolitho stared towards him, separated from the other man by far more than a length of deck. He could feel a sudden surge of understanding, even pity, knowing full well how he himself would have felt at such a time.

Then he said sharply, 'Over you go, lads! Jump well clear!'

Belsey and Farquhar leaped together, and he saw them struggling towards the listing square of timber. Stockdale said hoarsely, 'Here, Captain, I'll jump with you!'

As he gripped the rail Bolitho heard a cry behind him and got a vague glimpse of an officer dragging himself up the canting deck towards him. He saw blood on the man's face and recognised him as the lieutenant who had shared his lonely captivity on the poop. The man who had spoken of his farm and the impossible freedom of peace.

Then he saw the pistol in the lieutenant's hand, and even as he tried to pull himself over the rail the deck lit up with a blinding flash, and something like a white-hot iron exploded across his ribs.

Stockdale tore his eyes from Bolitho and gave a short, animal cry. It was as if it had been torn from his very soul. With all his strength he cleaved outwards with his axe, the force of the blow almost decapitating the American officer, so that the man seemed to bow forward in a grisly salute.

Bolitho was vaguely aware of being gathered bodily in Stockdale's arms and then falling through the air. His lungs were bursting and his throat was filled with salt water, and when he tried to open his eyes there was only stinging darkness.

Then he was being hauled up and across the little raft, and he heard Belsey gasp, 'Oh the bloody bastards! They've done for the captain!'

Then Farquhar's voice, shaking but determined. 'For God's sake watch out! There's a boat! Keep down and stay silent!'

Bolitho tried to speak, but could only stare up at Stockdale's misty face framed against the low, scudding clouds. He could hear oars, the swish of a boat cutting through water. But captivity or death were not in vain. Not this time! He listened to the distant boom of surf across the wrecked frigate, the small cries of those who still clung to the shattered hull.

Then, as if from right overhead he heard a sharp cry followed instantly by the click of a flintlock. It was still a dream, and nothing seemed to affect him personally. Only when a loud, English voice called, 'Them's some of the devils down in th' water, sir!' did the slow realisation begin to break through the mist and the pain.

Farquhar stood up yelling, 'Don't shoot! Don't shoot, we're English!'

Then everyone seemed to be shouting at once, and as another boat pulled nearby Bolitho heard one familiar voice as if from far away.

'Who have you got there, Mr. Farquhar?' Herrick's question was shaking with emotion, as if he still mistrusted what he saw.

Farquhar replied, 'It's the captain!'

Bolitho felt hands lifting him up over the gunwale, and saw distorted faces swooping above him in vague, unreal patterns. Hands moved across his ribs, and there was the stabbing fire of fresh pain. Then the muffling comfort of a bandage, and all the time the excited chatter of the men around . . . His men.

Herrick had his face very close, so that Bolitho could see the brightness in his eyes. Somehow he wanted to say something, to reassure Herrick, to make him understand.

But he could no longer find the strength even for that. Instead he squeezed Herrick's hand, and then allowed the waiting darkness to gather him in like a cloak.

12

'Confusion to Our Enemies!'

The high afternoon sun blazed down on the sheltered
water and threw a dancing pattern of reflections across the
deckhead above Bolitho's small desk. Just by turning his
head he could see the lush green hillsides of Antigua and
a few scattered dwellings around the smooth stretch of St.
John's harbour. He had to force himself back to his task of
completing his report in readiness for the admiral's
scrutiny.

He leaned his forehead against the palm of his hand,
feeling the weakness moving through his veins, willing
him to rest, to do anything but attend to the waiting duties
and orders. Beneath his shirt he could feel the stiff
embrace of the bandage, and allowed his mind to move
back in time, as he had done so often since his unexpected
return to the *Phalarope*.

Like everything else which had happened, it was
difficult to separate fact from vague delirious pictures
which had come and gone with the stabbing agony of his
wound. By the merest chance the pistol ball had passed
cleanly between his ribs, leaving a deep and ragged scar
which made him wince with every sudden movement.

From the moment he had been dragged aboard the
frigate and the boats had been hastily hoisted on deck his
memory was blurred and disjointed. The savage and
unheralded storm had only helped to add to the nightmare

quality of his recollections, and for two weeks the ship had driven south-west ahead of the screaming wind, unable to do other than run before it under all but bare spars. Then as he had struggled to avoid the surgeon's clumsy care and the vague comings and goings of his officers, the wind had moderated and *Phalarope* had at last gone about to beat her way back to Antigua and make her report.

He stared down at the carefully listed descriptions and the mentions of individual names. Nothing must be left out. There was never time for second thoughts.

Each name brought back a different memory and gave him the strange sensation of being an onlooker.

Midshipman Charles Farquhar, who had behaved in a manner far exceeding his actual experience and authority and in the best interests of the Service. A sea-officer who would one day merit senior command.

Arthur Belsey, master's mate, who in spite of his injured arm did everything possible to assist the final destruction of the *Andiron*.

Bolitho tapped his pen thoughtfully against Belsey's name. That last wild leap to safety from the *Andiron*'s shattered hull had finished any hope he might have had for return to proper duty. His broken arm was now beyond repair, and he would be a weakened cripple for the rest of his life. With luck, a good mention in the report, plus Bolitho's commendation, might ensure his quick discharge with some suitable recognition for his long service. He would probably return to Plymouth and open a small inn there, Bolitho thought sadly. Every seaport was full of such men, broken and forgotten, but still clinging to the fringe of the sea which had discarded them.

Of Lieutenant Herrick's assault on the artillery there was little to add to the bare facts. If he had tried to embroider the truth, to give Herrick more of the praise which he so richly deserved, the admiral would be quick to see the other side of the coin. That it was largely luck, added to a goodly portion of impudence.

There were so many 'ifs', Bolitho thought moodily.

If the cutting-out party had been dropped closer inshore every man would be either dead or imprisoned. If the tide had not been too strong for Herrick's oarsmen he would have pressed on with his impossible mission, instead of taking the secondary path of his own making.

And what of Stockdale? Without his aid and unshaken loyalty none of these things would have come about at all. In his fight-dulled brain he had worked out each careful move, unaided and without guidance from anyone. And again his last action had been to save Bolitho's life.

But what could he do for him? There was no promotion open to him, no reward which made any sense. Once when he had pattered into the cabin to tend Bolitho's wound he had asked the giant seaman what he would most cherish as payment for his bravery and his devotion.

Stockdale had not even hesitated. 'I'd like to go on serving you, Captain. I don't have no other wish!'

Bolitho had been considering the idea of getting Stockdale discharged ashore as soon as the ship returned to an English port. There with a little help he might be able to settle down to live his life in peace and security. But as what? Stockdale's prompt and simple reply had driven the suggestion from his mind. It would only have hurt the man.

He wrote: 'And of my coxswain, Mark Stockdale, I can only add that without his prompt action the entire mission might have ended in failure. By cutting the *Andiron*'s cable and thereby allowing her to drift beneath Lieutenant Herrick's fire he ensured the total and complete destruction of the ship with a minimum loss to our own side.' He signed his name wearily across the bottom and stood up. Pages of writing. It was to be hoped that they would be read by those unbiased against the *Phalarope*'s name.

231

At least Farquhar's uncle, Vice-Admiral Sir Henry Langford, would be pleased. His faith would be sustained, and given time his hopes for his nephew would certainly materialise.

Bolitho leaned out of the stern window and let the warm air caress his face. He could hear the creak of tackles and the steady splash of oars as boats plied back and forth to the shore. The ship had dropped anchor in the early morning, and all day the boats had been busy gathering fresh stores and taking the wounded to more comfortable quarters in the town.

He watched the impressive line of anchored ships, the growing might of the West Indies fleet. Perhaps their presence had dwarfed what might have otherwise been a triumphant return for the *Phalarope*. He frowned at his recurring thought. Maybe the *Phalarope* was still to be treated with shame and mistrust?

Bolitho let his eyes move slowly along the great ships with their towering masts and lines of open gunports. There was the *Formidable*, ninety-eight, fresh out of England with Sir George Rodney's flag at her truck. There were others, too, their names already well known in the face of war. *Ajax* and *Resolution*, *Agamemnon* and *Royal Oak*, and Sir Samuel Hood's flagship *Barfleur*. And there were some he did not recognise at all, no doubt reinforcements brought by Rodney from the Channel Fleet. And they were all gathering for one purpose. To seek out and destroy the great French and Spanish fleet before it in turn drove the British from the Caribbean for good.

He turned his head to look towards his own small squadron on the other side of the anchorage. The elderly *Cassius* dwarfing the little *Witch of Looe*. And one other frigate, the *Volcano*, a vessel very similar to the *Phalarope*.

There was still no summons from the admiral. Just a brief message brought by a pink-faced midshipman to state that Bolitho's report was required before sunset. The frigate was to complete reprovisioning and await further orders. Nothing more.

Nothing more until something even stranger had happened.

Halfway through the forenoon a boat had put off from the *Cassius* and within minutes a dapper lieutenant had reported himself to Bolitho. He had said, 'Rear-Admiral Sir Robert Napier sends his compliments, sir. He wishes to inform you that he will be willing to accept an invitation for dinner tonight aboard your ship. He will be bringing our captain as an additional guest.' The officer had watched the consternation on Bolitho's features and had added helpfully, 'Is there anything I can do to help, sir?'

Bolitho had been stunned by the wording of the message. It was unusual for flag officers to dine aboard their less impressive ships. It was *unknown* for them actually to word their own invitations!

Bolitho had thought of his dwindling provisions and the crude results produced from the galley.

The lieutenant from the *Cassius* had obviously been well briefed. 'If I may make a suggestion, sir?'

Bolitho stared at him. 'Anything you can say would be a great help at this moment.'

'My captain is sending some stores from his own pantry, sir. In addition there will be some quite drinkable wine arriving within the hour.' He had ticked off the items on his fingers, his face wrapped in thought. Bolitho had guessed that the young man was not unused to the strange behaviour of his admiral. 'If I may suggest some lean pork, sir? It is in goodly supply in St. John's, and the cheese is newly arrived with Admiral Rodney's ships from England.'

Bolitho had sent for Vibart and the purser, Evans, and explained what was due to happen. For once Vibart seemed too surprised to make any comment, and Bolitho had said curtly, 'See to it, Mr. Vibart. And tell my servant to clean out the cabin and lay a full table.' He had felt suddenly reckless. 'Sir Robert Napier must not expect a flagship's fare aboard a mere frigate!'

Now, looking back, he knew that the momentary reck-lessness was more likely to have been a result of too much sun on the open quarterdeck and the weakening pain of his wound.

Well, it could not be helped. It was more than obvious what the admiral intended. With Rodney back at the reins he would not wish to lambast *Phalarope* in public. He would not even risk an open argument aboard his own flagship. No, he would come to the *Phalarope* in person, like God coming down to smite a sinner, Bolitho thought bitterly. No success would wipe away his first displeasure or recompense his son's death. If the *Andiron* lay under guard beneath the guns of his own flagship the admiral might have felt differently. But the privateer was now less than nothing. A mere pencilled mark on a chart.

Bolitho sat down heavily on the stern bench, suddenly tired and irritable. He stared at the waiting report and then called, 'Sentry! Pass the word for Mr. Herrick!'

The report could go across to *Cassius* now, he thought angrily. Whatever else happened, he wanted to make sure that his men received recognition and had their efforts properly recorded.

Herrick entered the cabin and stood alertly beside the desk. 'Take this envelope over to the flagship.' Bolitho saw the immediate concern on Herrick's open face and became more irritated. Try as he might he could not keep the dullness from his voice, and knew that in spite of all his efforts his fatigue was wearing him down, so that every word seemed to drag from his lips.

Herrick said carefully, 'May I suggest that you take a rest, sir? I think you have been doing too much.'

'Kindly attend to your duties, damn you!' Bolitho

looked away, angry with Herrick but more so with himself for the unfairness of his attack.

'Aye, aye, sir.' Herrick seemed unmoved and said, 'May I ask if this is the full report about the *Andiron*, sir?'

Bolitho turned coldly. 'Of course it is! Were you afraid I'd not included your efforts in this escapade?'

Herrick eyed him steadily. 'I am sorry, sir. It's just that—' He swallowed hard. 'Well, we feel, those of us who took part,' he began to stammer. 'You are the one who should take all the credit, sir!'

Bolitho looked at the deck, the blood singing in his ears. 'You have a happy knack of making me feel ashamed, Mr. Herrick. I would be obliged if you would refrain from doing so in the future!' He looked up sharply, remembering with sudden clarity the sound of Herrick's voice in the darkness, the touch of his hands on his wound. 'But thank you.' He walked slowly to the desk. 'The attack on the *Andiron* was a series of lucky occurrences, Mr. Herrick. The end result may seem to some to justify this. But I must admit that I am still dissatisfied. I believe in luck, but I know that no man can *depend* upon it!'

'Yes, sir.' Herrick watched him closely. 'I just wanted you to know how we all feel.' His jaw jutted stubbornly. 'Whatever lies in store for us, we'll feel all the better for your being in command, sir.'

Bolitho ruffled the papers on his desk. 'Thank you. Now for God's sake go to the *Cassius*, Mr. Herrick.' He watched Herrick duck through the door and heard his voice calling for the quarter boat.

It was odd how easy it was to tell his fears to Herrick. Stranger too that Herrick was able to listen without taking advantage of this confidence.

His eye fell on the punishment book, and again he felt the tired glow of anger. While he had been a prisoner of his own brother the old disease had broken out again. Floggings and more floggings, with one man dying of his

235

agony under the lash. Maybe there would be time to heal the damage, he thought grimly. He must accept Vibart's sullen explanations, just as he had had to recognise Okes' report on the attack on Mola Island. He must back up his own officers. And if they were weak and stupid, then *he* must take the blame for that also.

He thought too of Vibart's attitude since his return to command. Due to his wound and the swirling darkness of pain and sickness he had not seen his face at the actual moment of return. But in the days which had followed, the days and nights of creaking timbers and thundering seas against the hull, he had seen him several times. Once when he had been delirious and sweating in his swaying cot he had seen Vibart standing over him and had heard him ask, 'Will he live? Tell me, Mr. Ellice, will he *live*?'

Perhaps he had only imagined it. It was hard to tell now. But for a brief moment he was sure he had heard the true resentment in Vibart's voice. He wanted him to die. Just as his return from the dead was still leaving him resentful and bitter.

The door opened and Stockdale said throatily, 'I've told Atwell to lay out your best uniform, sir. And he'll be in here shortly to prepare the table.' He stared at Bolitho's worn features and then said flatly, 'You'll be taking a rest now, I expect?'

Bolitho glared at him. 'I have *work* to do, damn you!'

Stockdale said, 'I'll just turn your cot down. A couple of hours until the Dog Watches will do you a power of good.' He ignored Bolitho's expression and added cheerfully, 'I see the *Formidable*'s here, sir! She's a fine big ship an' no mistake! But then you'd need a big ship to hold an admiral like Rodney!' He stood a moment longer, one hand resting on the cot. 'Are you ready now, sir?'

Bolitho gave in. 'Well, just two hours. No more.'

He allowed Stockdale to help him into the cot and felt the tiredness closing in on him once more. Stockdale picked up his shoes and said to himself, 'You rest there. We'll need a good captain tonight to meet the bloody admiral!'

As he turned Stockdale's eye fell on Bolitho's empty rack above the cot, and for a moment he felt strangely unnerved. The sword was back there somewhere in the wrecked *Andiron*. If only he could have got it back. If only . . .

He stared down at Bolitho's face relaxed in sleep. And he wanted to do something for *me*! He pulled the curtain to shade Bolitho's face from the reflected sunlight and then ambled slowly towards the door.

The tall stone jetty threw a welcome rectangle of dark shade across the *Phalarope*'s cutter as it rested easily alongside the steps. Packwood, the boatswain's mate, paused at the top of the steps and looked down at the lolling seamen in the boat. 'You can take a break. But nobody leaves the cutter, got it?'

Onslow squatted comfortably on the gunwale and pulled a short clay pipe from his shirt. Under his breath he murmured, 'Right, Mr. bloody Packwood! We do all the work, and you go off an' fill your belly with rum!'

Most of the other men were too weary to comment. All day they had pulled the cutter back and forth to the anchored frigate, the first excitement of seeing a friendly port again soon giving way to grumbling complaint.

Packwood was in charge of their party, and although a capable man and considered to be fair in his allocation of work, was plagued by a complete lack of imagination. If he had told the men that the work was essential, not only to the *Phalarope*'s efficiency, but more important, to the welfare of the crew once she returned to sea, some of the bitterness might have been dulled. As it was, Packwood had been too long in the Navy to seek for unnecessary explanations to anything. Work was work. Orders would be carried out at all times without question.

Pook, Onslow's constant companion, raised himself on his scrawny legs and peered towards the distant houses. He breathed out slowly. 'Mother of God! I kin see women!'

Onslow grimaced. 'What did you expect? Bloody clergymen?' He watched the men from beneath lowered lids. 'The officers will be doing themselves well enough. You see if I'm not right, lads!' He spat over the side. 'But just one of you try an' lay a little foot on the shore an' see what happens!' He gestured towards a red-coated marine who was leaning contentedly on his grounded musket. 'That bloody bullock'll place a ball between your eyes!'

John Allday lay across the oars and watched Onslow thoughtfully. Every word the man spoke seemed to be carefully weighted and fashioned before it was uttered. He turned as another seaman named Ritchie spoke up from the bow.

Ritchie was a slow-thinking Devon man, with an equally slow manner of speech. 'When we was at Nevis Oi didn't see yew runnin' off, Onslow!' He blinked his mild eyes against the glittering water. 'Yew had plenty of time to go an' join your rebel friends!'

Allday watched Onslow, expecting a flash of anger. But the tall seaman merely eyed Ritchie with something like pity. 'An' what good would that do? If I went over to the rebels or to the Frogs, do you think we'd be any better off?' He had their full attention now. 'No, lads. We'd be exchanging one master for another. A fresh flag, but make no mistake, the lash feels the same in any navy!'

Ritchie scratched his head. 'Oi still don't see what yew'm gettin' at!'

Pook sneered, 'That's because you're stupid, you great ox!'

'Easy, lads.' Onslow dropped his voice. 'I meant what I said. Out here or in the Americas a man can live well. A new life, with a chance to make something for himself!'

He gave a small smile. 'But to start off right a man needs more than hope. He needs money, too!'

Nick Pochin stirred himself and said uneasily, 'If the war ends an' we gets paid off, we can go back to our homes.'

'And who'll want to remember you there?' Onslow looked down at him coldly. 'You've been away too long, like all the rest of us. There'll be nothing for you but begging on the streets!'

Pochin persisted. 'I was a good ploughman once. I could do it again!'

'Aye, maybe you could.' Onslow watched him closely, his eyes full of contempt. 'You can push your furrow for the rest of your stupid life. Until the furrow is deep enough for some fat squire to bury you in!'

Another voice asked cautiously, 'Well then? What's the point of arguing about it?'

'I'll tell you the point!' Onslow slid from the gunwale like a cat. 'Soon we'll be at sea again. You've seen the fleet mustering here. There'll be no rest for the likes of us. The buggers always need an extra frigate!' He pointed at the *Phalarope* as she swung gently at her anchor. 'There is our chance, lads! The price of our future!' He lowered his voice again. 'We could take the ship!' He spoke very slowly to allow each word to sink in. 'Then we could use her to bargain for our own price!' He looked around their grim faces. 'Just think of it! We could parley with the other side and name our own amount! Then with the money and a free passage we could split up and go our own ways, every one of us richer than he ever thought possible!'

Pochin sat up with a jerk. 'That's mutiny! You mad bugger, we'd all be caught and hanged!'

Onslow grinned. 'Never! After the war is over, who will have time to care about us?'

Pook added gleefully, 'He's right! We'd be rich!'

239

Allday said, 'And we'd never see England again!'

'And who cares about that?' Onslow threw back his head. 'Do you think we have any chance at present? You saw what they did to Kirk? You've seen men die week by week from disease or the lash. From battle or falling from aloft! And if you escape all that, it's more than likely that you'll get shipped off in some other ship, as *I* was!'

Allday felt a chill at his spine as the uneasiness and resentment moved through the boat like a threat. He said quickly, 'Do you think Captain Bolitho would stand for your ideas?' He looked at the others. 'I've been through the mill, but I trust the captain. He's a brave and fair man. He'll not let us down!'

Onslow shrugged. 'Suit yourself.' He added tightly, 'Just so long as you keep your thoughts *to* yourself, mate! If what I said gets out, we'll know where to come a'hunting!'

There was a scattered murmur of assent from the boat, and Allday realised with sudden shock that Onslow's little speech had already gone deep. It was strange that nobody had noticed before how Onslow had persisted in his efforts to rouse the men to mutiny. Perhaps because his words were carefully chosen and without the blind malice of a wronged sailor. The latter was too common to rouse much more than jeers.

He thought too of Mathias's death in the hold and Onslow's careful manœuvring to get Ferguson the job as captain's clerk. The pattern was like a slow but deadly disease. When the symptoms came to light the victim was already beyond hope.

He said, 'You'll find me ready enough, Onslow! Just you keep out of *my* way!'

Pochin muttered, 'Watch out! 'E's comin' back!'

Packwood stood at the top of the steps, his face sweating profusely from a hasty tankard of rum. 'Right, my babies! Stand by to take on some more casks!' He swung his rattan casually. 'After this trip you can go to your sty and get cleaned up. The admiral is coming to see you all this evening!'

Pook nudged his friend. 'That Allday! Is he safe?'

Onslow ran his fingers around the loom of his oar. 'The men like him. It must be handled carefully. It needs thinking about.' He watched Allday's naked back rippling in the sunlight. 'But *handled* it must be!'

Punctual to the minute, Rear-Admiral Sir Robert Napier stepped through the *Phalarope*'s entry port and removed his hat to receive his due respects. As the shrill pipes faded into silence and the marine guard presented arms the frigate's small drummer, accompanied by two reedy fifes, broke into a frail but jaunty march, and with a final glance around the upperdeck Bolitho stepped forward to meet his admiral.

Sir Robert nodded curtly to the assembled officers, and as the marines banged their muskets to the deck he carried out a brief but searching inspection of the guard, followed at a discreet distance by Rennie and Captain Cope of the *Cassius*.

Bolitho tried to gauge the admiral's mood or his real reason for his visit from the man's profile, but Sir Robert's pinched face remained sphinxlike and unchanging, even when he fired the occasional question or comment to Rennie about the bearing of the marines.

At the end of the double line of men he paused to survey the maindeck. 'You keep a smart ship, Bolitho.' There was nothing in his dry tone to suggest either praise or suspicion.

'Thank you, sir.' Bolitho wished that he was alone aboard the flagship in the great stern cabin. There he could face and deal with anything Sir Robert chose to say. These circumstances kept every comment on a formal and controlled level which made his nerves raw with uncertainty.

Whatever the admiral really thought of the ship, Bolitho was certainly satisfied with her appearance. Long before a frantic messenger had reported a flurry of activity aboard the flagship and the smartly crewed barge had pulled swiftly towards the *Phalarope*'s side, Bolitho had been round his ship to make absolutely sure that Sir Robert would find no fault with her at least.

The ship's company had manned the side, every eye on the small, gold-laced figure in the stern of the barge, and now as the admiral stood in silent contemplation there was an atmosphere of nervous expectancy which defied even the fifes and drum on the quarterdeck.

The admiral said, 'You may dismiss the hands, Bolitho.'

At the prearranged signal the men poured from the maindeck, and with a clash of weapons the marines wheeled and followed suit.

Then he said, 'I have read the report, Bolitho. It had a great deal to say.' His wintry eyes drifted across Bolitho's set features. 'I was particularly interested in the part about the *Andiron*'s captain.' He saw Bolitho stiffen and continued calmly, 'As a matter of fact I had received information as to his identity, but I thought it best to let you carry out your task.' He shrugged, the movement painful beneath his heavy uniform. 'Of course, what I did not know was that you were in fact already a prisoner at his hands.'

'And if you had known, sir?' Bolitho tried to keep his tone relaxed.

'I am not sure. Your first lieutenant is apparently capable in many ways, but I fear he will always be a man who takes orders. A *born* subordinate!'

From the corner of his eye Bolitho saw Captain Cope being ushered below by his own officers, and waited for the admiral to continue. He did not have long to wait.

'*Andiron* is finished. Her very existence was a challenge and an insult to every man in our fleet. I have already passed my views on the matter to the Commander-in-Chief, and I have no doubt you will receive due recognition.' He faced Bolitho squarely. 'However, the fact that your own brother once commanded her and is obviously still alive may in some quarters be taken as some sort of connivance on your part.' He walked to the side and stared at the *Cassius*. 'I do not happen to take that view myself, Bolitho. I gave you the task, not in spite of the *Andiron*'s captain but because of him! You and your ship behaved very well indeed. I have told Sir George Rodney as much.' He added slowly, 'But had your brother been killed it might have been better all round.'

'I think I understand, sir.'

'Of course you do!' The admiral's old testiness was breaking through. 'To be killed is to be forgotten. But if he is taken in the future, he will have no defence. A public trial and hanging will follow. And I think you realise that such disgrace can smear a whole family!'

'Yes, sir.'

Sir Robert rubbed his hands. 'Well, enough of that. You carried out your orders as best you could. That will have to suffice for the present. You did in fact find out about the enemy's intentions. If it is true, it will weigh heavily in your favour.'

He looked up at the gently moving flag and murmured, 'We could do with a little good fortune at the moment!'

Sir Robert lapsed into silence until Bolitho had guided him below to his cabin where the other officers were already seated. With the table fully extended and ten officers already crammed round it, the cabin seemed to be full to capacity, and Bolitho found time to wonder why the admiral had bothered to make this journey away from the comparative luxury of his own quarters.

The officers rose to their feet and then sank expectantly into their seats again as Bolitho and the admiral squeezed around the head of the table.

Bolitho also realised for the first time that this was the only occasion he had sat down to dine with all his officers. As Atwell and two hastily recruited messmen began to serve dinner he glanced round the table marking the strange difference which seemed to have come over the familiar faces. They were like embarrassed strangers, he thought vaguely.

Apart from his lieutenants and Captain Rennie he had arranged for the three midshipmen to be present also. As representatives of the ship's warrant officers Proby, the master, and Tobias Ellice, the surgeon, sat in stiff discomfort, their eyes on their plates.

Still the admiral gave no sign of relaxing. In almost complete silence the dinner went on. But with it came the wine, this time brought by the admiral's personal steward, a tall, disdainful man in a scarlet jacket. It was then that Bolitho began to realise what Sir Robert was doing. Coupled with the tension and the unaccustomed richness of the excellent dinner, the wine began to take effect. When Bolitho noticed that the admiral had hardly eaten more than a bird's share of the food and made a point of keeping the same glass of wine at his elbow, he fully understood.

Voices grew louder, and while Sir Robert sat calmly at Bolitho's side the officers began to talk more freely. Bolitho did not know which he felt more. Annoyance or admiration. Not content with a bald report, no matter how concise, Sir Robert was here to hear for himself. From the men who until now had been mere names from Bolitho's pen.

Some of the strain seemed to drain out of him. Right or wrong, the admiral's sly methods were now beyond his control.

Slowly the story began to unfold. Each phase being taken up and polished by a different officer. The attack on Mola Island and the taking of the battery. The more eloquent elaborated on the plan as a whole, the less capable ones contenting themselves on painting the smaller parts to the overall picture.

There was humour too in some of the recollections. Like the story of Parker, the master's mate, who had commanded the jolly boat during the attack on the *Andiron*. Separated from the other boats by the rising sea, he had returned to the *Phalarope* only to have his discomfort further increased by a volley of musket fire from some vigilant marines. And the story of Captain Rennie conducting the retreat from Mola Island with his sword in one hand and half a chicken pie in the other. But this sort of reminiscence did not last.

Sir Robert snapped suddenly, 'And you, Mr. Farquhar, were left behind with the Spanish prisoner?'

Farquhar eyed him carefully, and for a moment Bolitho felt the tension returning to the crowded table. But Farquhar kept his head. Even the fact that it was well known that Sir Robert normally made a point of never addressing anyone below the rank of lieutenant failed to ruffle him.

'Yes, sir. I joined the captain and together we went into captivity.'

The admiral swung round in his chair and peered at Okes, who until now had remained almost silent. 'Your part in this business seems to have kept you very busy, Mr. Okes?

The lieutenant looked up startled. 'Er, yes, sir. I did what I had to do. There was no other way!'

Sir Robert sipped his wine and eyed him coolly. 'For an officer who has gained nothing but glory you sound remarkably guarded, Mr. Okes. A modicum of modesty is welcome these days, but not when it sounds remarkably like guilt!' For a second longer he held Okes' pale face with his cold eyes, and then he laughed. It was a humourless sound, but it helped to break the sudden and unhappy silence.

'And you, Mr. Herrick?' Sir Robert craned round his own captain to stare along the table. 'Your exploits at Nevis seem a trifle haphazard? But against that you obtained the result you intended no doubt?'

Herrick gave a broad grin. 'Captain Bolitho has already pointed out to me the pitfalls of too much luck, sir!'

'Did he indeed?' The admiral's eyebrows rose slightly. 'I am gratified to hear it.'

And on it went in the same vein. The admiral would question and listen, or when that failed would openly provoke the luckless officer into some excited and unguarded reply.

The loyal toast was called for by the junior officer present. Midshipman Neale, dwarfed on either side by Proby and Ellice, squeaked, 'Gentlemen, the King!' and then sank into a blushing silence.

Bolitho noticed that the admiral's right hand was curled like a claw around his goblet, and when the latter saw him looking at it the admiral snapped petulantly, 'Damned rheumatism! Had it for years!'

For a few moments Bolitho took time to appreciate the man sitting by his side. Not the admiral, with all his petty foibles, his unfair uses of privilege and rank, but the actual man.

He was old, probably in his sixties, and to Bolitho's knowledge had not set foot ashore for more than a few days at a time in the last ten years. He had shifted his flag from ship to ship, dealing with problems and strategy which Bolitho could only half imagine.

The admiral was looking at him unwinkingly. 'Are you still wondering why I came, Bolitho?' He did not wait for an answer. 'I commanded a frigate myself many years ago. The happiest time in the Navy for me. Life was easier in many ways then. But the stakes were not so high.' The shutter dropped again. 'I came because I wanted to see what you have *made* of this ship.' He tugged at his chin as if to seek some way of avoiding a compliment. 'What I find does not displease me entirely.' He dropped his voice, so that it was almost lost in the newly awakened conversation around the table. 'Most of your officers appear to have great respect for you. I know from experience that it is very hard to come by!'

Bolitho gave a small smile. 'Thank you, sir.'

'And you can remove that stupid smile from your face!' The admiral shifted beneath his coat. 'I like to know the men whom I command! When I see a sail on the horizon I don't wish to know the size of her guns or the state of her paintwork. I want to know the mind of the man in control, see?' He stared over the heads of the lolling officers. 'England is fighting for her life. It is a war of defence now. The attack will come later, perhaps years later, after I am dead and buried! But until that time England depends on her ships, maybe only a couple of hundred ships which are in a position to act to full advantage!' He tapped on the table, so that the others fell silent and turned to listen. 'And those ships depend on their captains and no one else!'

Bolitho opened his mouth to speak but the admiral said testily, 'Hear me out! I know your reputation now. You are an idealist in many ways. You have hopes for better conditions for your men, so that they can make the sea an honourable career again.' He waved a finger. 'When I was younger I wanted all those things and more beside. But a good captain is the one who accepts all these difficulties as they stand and still manages to run an efficient ship, one worthy of honour and praise.'

He glared round the table. 'Well, gentlemen, did I make myself understood?'

Bolitho followed his gaze. Vibart, flushed and unsmiling. Herrick, still grinning and unquenched by the admiral's earlier sarcasm. Rennie, stiff-backed but with eyes so glassy that they were beyond focus. Old Daniel

247

Proby, humbled by being with such illustrious company, yet whose face was stiff with sudden pride, as if he had heard a deeper meaning in the admiral's words. And Ellice, the bucolic surgeon, who had been drinking without pause since they had arrived at table. Bolitho could find time to pity Ellice. Poorly paid, like all ships' surgeons, it was no wonder he was more of a butcher than a doctor. It was a race which would win. Drink or a fatal mistake, it was merely a matter of time.

Okes, still smarting from the admiral's keen appraisal of the half-remembered attack on Mola Island. Bolitho noticed how he kept darting quick, desperate glances towards Farquhar, who by comparison was calm and impassive, his thoughts perhaps far away. Maybe still back there below the shattered bridge where he had been left to die by the man who now sat watching him. The fact that Farquhar had made neither comment nor complaint must be all the more worrying for Okes, Bolitho thought grimly.

And the two other midshipmen, Maynard and Neale. Excited and untouched by the deeper channels of comment and thought around them. Bolitho was suddenly very aware of his responsibility to all of them.

The admiral stood up and lifted his glass. 'A toast!' His pale eyes flashed below the low beams. 'Death to the French!'

The glasses came up as one and the voices rumbled the reply, 'And confusion to our enemies!'

The admiral called to his captain, 'Time we were going, Cope!'

Bolitho followed him to the upperdeck, only half listening to the scamper of feet and the hurried creak of oars alongside. It was over. The admiral would never admit a mistake, but Bolitho knew that the worst was behind him. *Phalarope* was free of disgrace at last.

He lifted his hat as the admiral crossed to the port and

waited until he had vanished to the waiting barge. Then he clamped on his hat and began to pace the deserted quarterdeck, his hands clasped behind him.

The admiral had also made it plain in his own way that if the ship was free of disgrace it was up to her captain to keep her so.

He looked at the riding lights dancing across the water and listened to the plaintive scrape of a violin and the accompanying sadness of an old shanty. If the men could still sing there was hope for all of them, he thought.

13

Danger from Within

The pipes shrilled in salute as Richard Bolitho stepped through the ornate entry port and on to the *Formidable*'s wide deck. Automatically he doffed his hat to the quarter-deck, and as he returned the greeting of the flagship's officer of the watch he allowed his eyes to move swiftly up and around him, taking in the busy activity, the seemingly endless deck space and the long lines of gleaming guns.

An impeccable midshipman in white gloves crossed the deck at a trot, and under the beady eye of the duty officer led Bolitho aft towards the great stern cabin, to which every available captain had been summoned at an hour's notice.

Bolitho had been toying with his lonely breakfast, pondering on the previous night's strange dinner party and Sir Robert Napier's persistent questions, when Maynard had hurried into his cabin with news of the signal. As he had hurriedly changed into his best uniform Bolitho had wondered why Sir Robert had not mentioned this meeting with the Commander-in-Chief. He must have known about it. As Bolitho had stared unseeingly at his reflection in the bulkhead mirror he had wondered if Sir Robert was making just one more private test. He probably kept his glass trained on the *Phalarope*'s deck from the moment *Formidable* had hoisted her general signal.

He almost cannoned into the midshipman and realised that they had reached the great cabin. The youngster called, 'Captain Richard Bolitho of the *Phalarope*!'

But only those officers standing near the door took any notice, and soon returned to their own busy conversation. For that Bolitho was grateful. He made his way to one corner of the cabin, and as one messman took his hat another placed a tall glass of sherry in his hand. Neither spoke a word, and Bolitho guessed that it was no easy matter to remain calm and unruffled when serving the Commander-in-Chief.

He sipped at his glass and carefully studied the other officers. There must be about thirty captains present, he decided. Captains of every size and shape, of every age and seniority. After the first scrutiny Bolitho decided that he must be the most junior, but just as he had reached this conclusion he felt a movement at his elbow and turned to meet the gaze of a tall, gangling lieutenant whom he vaguely remembered as the commander of the little brig, *Witch of Looe*.

The latter raised his glass and said quietly, 'Your health, sir! I was coming across to see you and tell you how glad I am of your safe return.'

Bolitho smiled. 'Thank you.' He shrugged. 'I am afraid your name has escaped me.'

'Philip Dancer, sir.'

'I will remember it in future.' Bolitho saw the lieutenant loosening his neckcloth with one finger and suddenly realised that he was actually nervous. It was not easy to be so junior in such an illustrious gathering. He said quickly, 'I expect this seems a bit luxurious after your little brig?'

Dancer grimaced. 'Just a bit!'

They both looked at the great stern windows with the wide gallery beyond where the admiral could take an undisturbed walk above the ship's own wake. There were long boxes of potted plants too, and on the handsome

251

sideboard Bolitho caught a glimpse of gleaming silver and cut glass below a fine painting of Hampton Court Palace.

Then the buzzz of conversation died away, and every man turned to face a side door as the small procession entered the cabin.

Bolitho was shocked to see the change which had come over Sir George Rodney since he had last seen him some two years earlier. Beneath the resplendent uniform with its bright ribbon and decorations the admiral's once upright figure appeared bent and drooping, and his mouth, now set in a tight line, betrayed the illness which had plagued him for so many months. It was hard to picture him as the same man who had overwhelmed a powerful enemy force only two years ago to break through and relieve the besieged fortress of Gibraltar, or who had attacked and sacked St. Eustatius and taken over three million sterling back to England as a prize.

But the eyes were the same. Hard and steady, as if they drew and contained all the energy of his being.

At his side his second in command, Sir Samuel Hood, made a sharp contrast. He looked calm and composed as he studied the assembled officers, his features dominated by his large, arrogant nose and high forehead.

Behind his two superiors Sir Robert Napier looked almost insignificant, Bolitho thought.

Sir George Rodney lowered himself into a tall chair and folded his hands in his lap. Then he said curtly, 'I wanted you all here to tell you that it now seems likely the French and their allies will attempt a final overthrow of English forces in this area.' He coughed shortly and dabbed his mouth with a handkerchief. 'Comte de Grasse has assembled a strong force of ships of the line, the most powerful vessels ever gathered under one flag, and were I in his fortunate position I would have no hesitation in preparing to do battle.'

He coughed again, and Bolitho felt a tremor of

uneasiness transmit itself through the watching officers. The strain of years of planning and fighting were paring Rodney away like a knife blade. When he had sailed for England there was not an officer in his fleet who did not believe it was his last journey and that another would return to take his place. But somewhere within that tired body was a soul of steel. Rodney intended to see no replacement in the West Indies to take either the fruits of his hard and unsparing work or the shame and misery of possible defeat.

Sir Samuel Hood said evenly, 'Intelligence has reached us that there is more to de Grasse's intentions than a mere sea victory. He has been gathering seasoned French troops, as well as supplying arms and assistance to the American colonials. He is a shrewd and dedicated strategist, and I believe he intends to exploit whatever successes he has already made.' He looked suddenly across the nearest heads and fixed his heavy lidded eyes on Bolitho.

'The captain of the frigate *Phalarope* has added to this informatioin in no little amount, gentlemen!'

For a few seconds every head in the cabin turned to stare at him, and caught off guard by this turn of events Bolitho felt a tinge of confusion.

In those few seconds he got a vague impression of faces and the reactions of their owners. Some nodded approvingly, and some merely eyed him with barely masked envy. Others studied his face as if to search out some deeper meaning from the admiral's comment. A small item of praise from Hood, and therefore condoned by the great Rodney himself, could immediately mark Bolitho as a firm rival in the ladder of promotion and reward.

Hood added dryly: 'Now that you all know each other, we will continue! From this day forward our vigilance must be stepped up. Our patrols must make every effort to watch each enemy port and spare no efforts to pass information back to me. When de Grasse breaks out it will be swift and final. If we cannot call his challenge and close him in battle we are done for, and make no mistake about it!'

His deep, booming voice filled the crowded cabin, so that Bolitho could almost feel the import of his words like a physical force.

The admiral went on tirelessly and methodically to outline the known whereabouts of supply ships and enemy forces. He showed neither strain nor impatience, and there was nothing at all in his manner to betray the fact that he had only recently returned to Antigua after holding St. Kitts against the whole French military force and their attendant fleet.

Sir George Rodney interrupted, 'I want every one of you to study and familiarise yourselves with my signal requirements.' He looked sharply around the cabin. 'I will not tolerate any officer misunderstanding my signals, any more than I accept excuses for failing to execute same!'

Several captains exchanged quick glances. It was well known that when Rodney had tried to close the French admiral de Guichen off Martinique, and had not succeeded because some of his captains had failed either to understand or react to his signals, he had been quite ruthless. More than one captain now lived on miserly half-pay in England with nothing but disgrace and bad memories for comfort.

Rodney continued in a calmer tone, 'Watch for my signals. Wherever, and on whatever ship my flag flies, *watch for my signals*!' He leaned back and stared at the deckhead. 'This time there will be no second chance. We will win a great victory, or we will lose everything!'

He nodded to Hood, who added briefly, 'Orders will be issued immediately to senior officers of squadrons. From the moment you leave here the fleet will be in all respects ready for sea. It is up to our patrolling frigates and sloops to watch the enemy's lairs like hounds.' He pounded the table with his fist. 'Give the Commander-in-Chief the scent and the kill is assured!'

There was a murmur of approval, and Bolitho realised that the meeting was over.

Lieutenant Dancer said quietly, 'I wonder where our squadron will be sent? I would hate to miss the final scene when it comes!'

Bolitho nodded, mentally smiling at the picture of the tiny *Witch of Looe* engaging de Grasse's three-deckers. Aloud he said, 'There are never enough frigates. In every war it is the same story. Too little too late!' But he could say it without bitterness. *Phalarope* would be needed more than ever now. With the vast sea areas, the complex hiding places amongst the lines of scattered islands, every frigate would have more than enough to do.

He realised with a start that a sharp-faced flag-lieutenant had crossed the cabin to stop him leaving with the others.

'Sir George Rodney wishes to speak to you.'

Bolitho hitched up his sword and walked across the thick carpet. By the table he halted, half listening to the retreating scrape of footsteps. He heard the door close and the distant shrill of pipes speeding the exit of the fleet's captains, and for a terrible moment he thought he had misunderstood the flag-lieutenant's words.

Rodney was still sitting in his chair, his eyes half closed as he stared at the deckhead. Hood and Sir Robert Napier were completely engrossed in a chart on a nearby desk, and even the messmen seemed busy and oblivious to the young captain by the table.

Then Rodney lowered his eyes and said wearily, 'I know your father, Bolitho. We sailed together, of course. A very gallant officer, and a good friend.' He let his gaze move slowly across Bolitho's tanned face and down the

255

length of his body. 'You have a lot of him in you.' He nodded. 'I am glad to have you under my command.'

Bolitho thought of his father alone in the big house, watching the ships in the bay. He said, 'Thank you, sir. My father wished to be remembered to you.'

Rodney did not seem to hear. 'There is so much to do. So few ships for the task.' He sighed deeply. 'I am sorry you had to meet your only brother in such a fashion.' His eyes were suddenly fixed and unwavering.

Bolitho saw Sir Robert Napier stiffen beside the chart and heard himself reply, 'He believes what he is doing is right, sir.'

The eyes were still hard on his face. 'And what do *you* believe?'

'He is my brother, sir. But if we meet again I will not betray my cause.' He hesitated. 'Or your trust, sir.'

Rodney nodded. 'I never doubted it, my boy.'

Sir Samuel Hood coughed politely, and Rodney said with sudden briskness, 'Return to your ship, Bolitho. I hope that both you and your father will be spared further hurt.' His eyes were cold as he added, 'It is easy to do your duty when there is no alternative. Yours was not an easy choice. Nor will it be if your brother is taken!'

He lapsed into silence, and the flag-lieutenant said impatiently, 'Your hat, sir! And I have just called for your boat!'

Bolitho followed the harassed officer into the sunlight, his mind still dwelling on the admiral's words. So the whole fleet would now know about his brother. In the confined, monastic world of ships permanently at sea he would be discussed and measured against past exploits and future events.

He ran down the gangway to the waiting boat and stared across at the anchored *Phalarope*. Once she had been on trial. Now it was the turn of her captain.

*

On the evening of the same day that Bolitho had attended the conference aboard the *Formidable*, and with a minimum of fuss or ceremony, the *Phalarope* weighed and headed for the open sea.

The following morning found her a bare fifty miles to the south-west, her full set of sails drawing on the gentle breeze which did little to ease the growing power of the sun.

But this time she was not completely alone. Even from the deck it was possible to see the *Cassius*, her tall pyramids of canvas golden in the early sunlight as she moved on a ponderous and slow parallel course. Somewhere beyond her, hidden below the lip of the horizon, was the frigate *Volcano*. Invisible, and ahead of the slow-moving formation, Lieutenant Dancer's tiny *Witch of Looe* alone enjoyed a certain freedom of movement beyond the scrutiny of her admiral.

Lieutenant Herrick had just taken over the forenoon watch and stood relaxed by the the quarterdeck rail as he idly watched the men at work on the maindeck. Earlier the swabs and holy-stones had made the planking wet and pliable, but now as the heat slowly mounted above the gently swaying hull the decks shone in shimmering whiteness while the normal business of splicing and running repairs was carried out.

It was a peaceful scene, and the combination of warmth and a good breakfast left Herrick drowsy and at ease. Occasionally he cast an eye towards Midshipman Neale to make sure he had his glass trained on the distant flagship, and *Phalarope* was keeping as good a station as the wind allowed.

He could see Lieutenant Okes inspecting the starboard battery of twelve-pounders with Brock, the gunner, and wondered, not for the first time, what was going on behind his strained features. Ever since the raid on Mola Island,

Okes had been a changed man. And the admiral's casual comments across the dinner table had made him withdraw even more into himself.

As for Farquhar, it was quite impossible to tell what he was thinking. Herrick was not sure if he envied the midshipman's aloof reserve or admired him for it. It was strange how Farquhar's manner had always made him feel on the defensive. Perhaps it was because of his own humble beginnings, he decided. Even here, cooped up in a small frigate, Farquhar retained his distance and individuality.

Herrick tried to imagine what he would have felt if, as Rennie had suggested, Okes had retreated from the raid without care or interest, and had left *him* to die. He pictured himself reacting as Farquhar had done, but instantly in his heart he knew he was deceiving himself. More than likely it would have ended in an open conflict, with a court martial to round it off.

The helmsman coughed warningly, and Herrick turned quickly as Bolitho came up the cabin hatch. He touched his hat and waited as Bolitho walked first to the compass and then stood looking up at the masthead pendant. Then he relaxed slightly as Bolitho crossed to his side and looked down at the busy seamen on deck.

'Another fifty miles to our patrolling station, Mr. Herrick. At this speed we will need another day!' There was impatience in his tone, and a touch of irritation which Herrick was now able to recognise immediately.

Herrick said, 'But still it is comforting to see the *Cassius* abeam, sir. If de Grasse ventures out this way we will not be alone!'

Bolitho stared at the distant gleam of sails, but there was no response to Herrick's forced cheerfulness. 'Ah yes, the flagship.' He gave a bitter smile. 'Forty years old, and so much weed on her bottom that she crawls even in a strong gale!'

Herrick looked quickly at the *Cassius*. Up until this moment size and seniority had represented safety and a ready shield. He replied, 'I did not know, sir.'

'She was a Dutch prize, Mr. Herrick. Look at the rake of her beakhead!' Then as if realising that he was speaking from memory of things which were of no importance he added harshly, 'My God, this crawling makes me sick!'

Herrick tried another tack. 'Our orders, sir. May I ask what is expected of us?'

He immediately regretted his impulse and checked himself as Bolitho turned his head away to watch a slowly circling gull. But from the set of the captain's shoulders and the way his hands were locked on the rail he knew that he had struck on something uppermost in Bolitho's mind.

But Bolitho's voice was calm as he answered, 'We will take up our station fifty miles to the west'rd of Guadeloupe and keep contact with our' – he waved his hand towards the open sea – 'with our squadron!'

Herrick digested this information slowly. The excitement and frantic preparations at Antigua had left him in little doubt of an impending battle, and he knew that even now most of those proud ships he had watched with an undiminished fascination would have weighed and set sail to complete Rodney's plan to seek out and confront the Comte de Grasse.

Bolitho continued absently, 'There is a chain of ships up and down the Caribbean. One good sighting and the chase will be on.' But there was no excitement in his voice. 'Unfortunately, Martinique is another hundred miles to the south of our patrol area, Mr. Herrick. De Grasse will be there with the bulk of his ships. He will bide his time and then make a dash for Jamaica.' He turned swiftly and stared at Herrick's frowning face 'And when Rodney's frigates report that the French have sailed, the fleet will attack him!' He shrugged, the gesture both angry and despairing. 'And we shall still be on our station, as useless as a signpost in a desert!'

'But the French may come this way, sir.' Herrick felt Bolitho's bitterness changing his own eagerness to gloom. As he spoke he realised the reason for Bolitho's earlier scorn of the elderly *Cassius*. It was obvious that Rodney was using Admiral Napier's small squadron for the least important part of his overall plan.

'And pigs may lay eggs, Mr. Herrick!' said Bolitho evenly. 'But not in our day!'

'I see, sir.' Herrick was at a loss for words.

Bolitho studied him gravely and then touched his arm. 'Cheer up, Mr. Herrick. I am bad company this morning.' He winced and fingered his side. 'I am thankful that ball missed anything vital. But I could well do without its reminder.'

Herrick watched him thoughtfully. 'You should take more rest, sir.'

'I find it hard even to sit down, Mr. Herrick.' Bolitho shaded his eyes to watch the set of the sails. 'There is so much happening. History is being made all around us!' He suddenly began to pace, so that Herrick had to fall in step to keep up with him. 'De Grasse will come out, I'm sure of it!' He was speaking quickly in time with his steps. 'You saw that freak gale which gave you your chance to rake the *Andiron*? Well, it was rare indeed for this time of year. But later,' he smiled grimly at some hidden memory, 'later in the year the hurricanes hit the West Indies in profusion. From August to September they follow one another like messengers from hell itself!' He shook his head firmly. 'No, Mr. Herrick, de Grasse will come out soon. He has much to accomplish before that time.'

Herrick said, 'But which way will he go?'

'Maybe through the Martinique Passage. But either way he will head straight for the central Caribbean. There are a thousand miles between him and Jamaica. You could lose a whole fleet in such an area. If we fail to make contact when he sails we will never catch him again until it is too late!'

Herrick nodded, at last understanding the full reason for Bolitho's apprehension. 'He has troops and guns. He can occupy any territory he chooses to take.'

'Quite so. The men and stores we dealt with at Mola Island were just a part of his strength. He had hoped to tie down the fleet while he drove on to Jamaica unimpeded. Now he knows we are alerted. His urgency will be all the keener.'

He stopped in his tracks and stared fixedly at the naked horizon. 'If only we knew! If only we could go and find out for ourselves!' Then he seemed to realise that he was showing his own despair and he added briefly, 'You may return to your watch, Mr. Herrick. I have some thinking to do.'

Herrick walked back to the rail, but as the sun beat down on the tinder-dry decks, he was constantly aware of Bolitho's shadow. Back and forth, up and down.

When Herrick had been a midshipman he had dreamed of the time when he might attain the impossible heights of a lieutenant. From then on he had watched the slow path to promotion, gauging his own progress by the experience or the incompetence of his superiors. And all the time, nursed in the back in his mind like some precious jewel, was the idea that one day he might at last hold a command of his own.

But now, as he watched Bolitho's restless shadow and imagined the fretting thoughts which kept it company, he was not so sure.

Halfway through the forenoon the pipes shrilled, 'Stand easy!' With varying degrees of relief the frigate's seamen threw themselves into patches of shade to make the most of the short break in routine.

John Allday stayed where he had been working, with his legs astride the larboard cathead, his bronzed body

261

sheltered from the sun by the jibsail. In the foremost part of the ship he had been engaged in cleaning and scraping one of the great anchors, and as he squatted comfortably above the small bow wave he rested one foot on the anchor's massive stock, feeling its warmth against the bare skin. At his back the other members of the working party lounged in various stages of abandon, while above their heads the air was tinged with a slow-moving vapour of smoke from their long pipes.

Old Ben Strachan picked up a new rope and examined the eye-splice which one of the ship's boys had just completed. 'Not bad, youngster. Not bad at all.' He sucked noisily at his pipe and peered aft the length of the *Phalarope*'s deck. 'Is that the cap'n pacin' up an' down?'

Pochin, who was lying with his head cradled on his thick arms, muttered, 'Course it is! Must be mad to be in this 'eat when 'e could be down in 'is cabin!'

Allday swung one leg and stared thoughtfully at the clear water below him. Pochin was still worried about Onslow's words in the cutter. He was edgy, as if he realised his own guilt. Just listening to such talk made a man liable to be labelled a conspirator.

He turned slightly to look aft, and across the length of the ship he saw Herrick, watching him from the quarter-deck. The lieutenant gave him a brief nod of recognition before returning to his own contemplation, and Allday suddenly remembered that moment on the crumbling cliff when he had stopped Herrick from falling to the rocks below. In spite of his original intention to stay apart from internal affairs in the *Phalarope*, and to keep clear of loyalty to either faction, Allday was beginning to realise that such neutrality was impossible, even dangerous.

Allday liked Herrick, and recognised what he was trying to do. He was always ready to listen to complaints from his division, and was never quick to award punishment. But he was no fool, and few took advantage of his humane manner a second time.

Allday could see the captain still pacing the quarterdeck at the weather rail, coatless with his shirt open to his chest and his dark hair pulled back to the nape of his neck. He was a harder man to know, Allday thought, but it was strangely reassuring to see him back at his familiar place on the poop. Allday, perhaps better than most, knew the reputation of the Bolitho family. On his visits to Falmouth he had often heard them discussed in the taverns, and had even seen the house which was the captain's home. It was strange to realise that he had a brother fighting on the other side. Allday wondered how he would have felt. Not only that, but Bolitho's brother was said to have deserted from the Navy, a crime which could only be wiped out at the end of a rope.

He came back from his thoughts as Ferguson climbed up from the maindeck and walked across to the rail. He looked strained and self-conscious in his clean clothes, a marked contrast to the tired and sweating seamen who had once been his companions.

Ferguson fidgeted for a few moments and then said, 'Do you think we will see any more fighting?'

Pochin turned his head and growled, 'You should know! Aren't you in the captain's pocket?'

Allday grinned. 'Don't pay any attention to Nick.' He dropped his voice. 'Has Onslow been after you again?' He saw Ferguson's pale eyes flicker.

'Not much. He just passes the time with me sometimes.'

'Well, remember my warning, Bryan!' Allday studied him closely. 'I've not told a living soul aboard, but I believe he had a lot to do with Mathias's death.' He saw the disbelief in Ferguson's face and added sharply, 'In fact, I'm sure he had!'

'Why should he do a thing like that?' Ferguson tried to smile, but his mouth remained slack.

'He's a bad one. He knows no other life but this. He

came to the fleet as a child. His world is bounded by the sides of a wooden hull.' He ran his hands along the carved cathead. 'I've met a few of his kind before, Bryan. They're as dangerous as wolves!'

Ferguson said, 'He'll not make trouble. He wouldn't dare!'

'No? And why do you think he keeps asking about the cabin? He's biding his time. His sort have a lot of patience.'

'The captain'd not stand for any more trouble!' Ferguson showed his agitation in the quick movements of his hands. 'I've heard him telling Mr. Vibart about taking care of the men. About how he wants them treated.'

Allday sighed. 'You see? You're even telling me what you've heard. If you want to stay safe you'd better keep what you know to yourself.'

Ferguson stared at him. 'You don't have to tell me!' He tightened his month with sudden anger. 'You're just like the others. You're jealous because of my job!'

Allday turned away. 'Suit yourself.'

He waited until he heard Ferguson moving aft again. Then he turned to watch as Onslow stepped from beside the mainmast to stop his passing. He saw Onslow grinning and patting Ferguson on the shoulder.

Pochin's hard voice interrupted his thoughts. 'What d'you reckon? D'you think Onslow is right?' He sounded worried. 'If there is more trouble aboard this ship we'll all be in it. We'll have to take sides!'

Allday replied flatly, 'You'd be a fool to pay heed to that one!' He tried to put some value to his words. 'Anyway, the captain'll make short work of him if he tries anything!'

Pochin nodded doubtfully. 'Maybe. Dyin' under a French broadside is one thing, but I'll not cough out blood for 'im or the buggers like Onslow!'

The pipes shrilled again, and the men stirred themselves

264

back to work.

Allday kept his eyes down to his task as Quintal, the boatswain, and Josling, one of his mates, walked forward to inspect the forecastle. He heard Josling say, 'I see that the old *Cassius* was signalling just now, Mr. Quintal?'

Quintal replied in his deep voice, 'Aye, lad. We'll be hauling off shortly to our own little patrol area. It'll be a long job, I wouldn't wonder, so see that you keep the hands busy. There's nothing worse for discipline than too much free time.' The rest of his comments were lost to Allday as the two men moved up towards the bowsprit, but he had heard enough.

Phalarope was to be alone again, and out of sight of the flagship. The boatswain was right. With the heat and the dull monotony of an empty patrol, Onslow would find a good breeding ground for more trouble if he could.

He looked sideways at his silent companions, each man apparently engrossed in his own task, yet each no doubt thinking of that green patch of land which they had just left behind.

No ordinary seaman had set foot ashore. Some of the crew had not left a deck for years. It was hardly surprising that men like Onslow could find a ready audience.

He shaded his eyes and stared towards the horizon. Already the distant two-decker seemed smaller, her hull lost in the heat haze below the clear sky. Her sails had merged into one shining pyramid, and as he watched she appeared to sink lower in the glittering sea. Another hour and she would have vanished altogether.

After that, he thought coldly, you could trust no man.

Deep below the forecastle deck where Allday sat immersed in his own thoughts was the *Phalarope*'s cable tier. In harbour it was a spacious, empty place, but now, as the frigate moved listlessly on the calm water, it was packed to the deckhead with the massive anchor cables.

Coil upon coil, the great, salt-hardened ropes added to the sour stench of the bilges and the richer smells of tar and hemp. Stout upright pillars on either side of the shelving hull held the cables clear of the timbers to allow easy access to the ship's fabric at all times. These 'carpenter's walks' as they were named ran the full length of the hull below the water-line to afford inspection and, if necessary, repairs in time of battle. Little wider than a man's body, they were usually in total darkness.

But now, as the bow wave swished dully against the timbers and furtive rats continued their endless search for food, a small, shaded lantern cast an eerie light against the piled cable and threw a distorted reflection back to the faces of the men squeezed in the narrow passageway.

Onslow held the lantern higher and peered at the waiting men. He only had to count them to be sure. He knew each man's face and name without need for further examination.

'We must be quick, lads! We'll be missed if we stay too long!'

Like an echo he heard Pook's voice. 'Just pay heed to wot 'e says!'

Onslow's teeth gleamed in the darkness. He could feel his legs shaking with wild excitement, like the effect of rum on an empty stomach. 'We're pulling away from the other ships. I think the time has almost come to carry out our plan.'

He heard a dull murmur of agreement and grinned even broader. Just by saying *our* instead of *my* acted on these men like the crack of a whip.

'From what Ferguson has told me Bolitho intends to run to the south'rd. The *Phalarope*'ll be on the end of the patrol line. No chance of meeting any of the others, y'see?'

A voice asked from the darkness. ''Ow can we take the ship on our own?' He broke off with a yelp as Pook drove

266

his elbow into his ribs.

Onslow said calmly, 'Leave that part to me. I'll tell you how and when.' He looked at the crouching line of dark figures. All the ones who had come with him from the *Cassius*, and several more recruited in the *Phalarope*. It was far more than he had dared to hope.

'We must get rid of the bloody bullocks. Without their red coats athwart the quarterdeck it'll be easy.'

Pook asked. 'Wot about Allday an' the like?'

'Ah yes.' Onslow smiled crookedly. 'Master John Allday.'

Pook added gloomily, 'The lads *listen* to 'im!'

'And if anything happened to Allday we'd get a lot more on our side, eh?' Onslow's brain was moving ahead of his words. 'But it has to be clever. If it looks like our doing we might as well hang ourselves!'

They all froze as heavy footsteps sounded overhead. Then as they died away Onslow continued easily, 'I think Allday guesses what happened to Mathias. He's too clever to live, is that one!' He reached out and gripped Pook's arm. 'So we'll make him a bloody martyr, shall we?' He gave a rumbling laugh. 'Now we can't do fairer than that!'

The same uncertain voice tried again. 'We'll be cut down afore we can raise a finger, I say!'

'*I'll* cut you down, you bugger!' For a moment Onslow's good humour retreated. Then he added more calmly, 'Now listen to me, all of you! We must wait a bit longer to get the lads more worried. Then when the time's ripe I'll tell you what I want. That fool Ferguson can keep an eye on the captain's log for me, just so that I know where we are. When we get a bit nearer some land, I'll be ready.'

He snapped his fingers. 'Those weapons we brought off from Mola Island. Have you got 'em safely stowed?'

Pook nodded. 'Aye, they'll not be discovered!'

'Right then. Get back to your work now, lads. And stay out of trouble. You're all marked men anyway, so don't give the bastards a chance to nail you!'

He watched them creeping away into the darkness beyond the dim lantern and felt satisfied. Now, just as he had told those poor sheep, it was just a matter of time.

14

Blood and Fresh Water

Tobias Ellice, the *Phalarope*'s surgeon, arose wheezing from his uncomfortable stooping position and threw the sweat-stained bandage out of the open stern window. 'Right, sir. You kin stand up now if you like.' He stepped away from the bench seat as Bolitho threw his legs over the side and lifted himself to his feet.

Ellice mopped his streaming face and peered closely at the rough scar across Bolitho's ribs. 'Not a bad job of work, if I says so meself!' He beamed and licked his lips. 'It's thirsty work, an' no mistake!'

Bolitho touched the scar with his fingertips and then stood facing the open windows to allow the tiny breeze to play across his bare skin. It was good to be rid of the bandage, he thought. Its very embrace was a constant reminder of the *Andiron* and all that had gone before. It was well to leave it all in the past. There were troubles enough to deal with today and the next day after that.

It was a full fourteen days since they had sailed with the squadron from Antigua, and almost every one of them had been like this one. Hardly a lick of air which could seriously be called a breeze to fill the hungry sails or even to ventilate the ship. And all the time a broiling sun which seemed to bleach the colour from the sky itself. The nights brought little respite. Between decks the air remained humid and heavy with damp, and the seamen were further

269

wearied by the constant calls to trim sails, only to be dismissed cursing and despairing as the wind died before a single sheet could be handled.

It was enough to break even the sturdiest heart, Bolitho thought heavily. And coupled with the fact that they had not sighted a single sail, and knew nothing of events beyond the mocking horizon, he found it was all he could do to restrain his own mounting impatience.

'How are the men?' He reached for a clean shirt and then relented. The old one would have to do. There was little point in badgering his servant to wash more clothes than necessary.

Ellice shrugged. 'Not happy, sir. 'Tis bad enough as it is without hungering after a drink all the time.'

'Water is precious, Mr. Ellice.' It was now reduced to a pint a day per man, which was less than adequate. But there was no telling how long it would be before their senseless vigil was broken. He had increased the daily ration of *Miss Taylor*, as the rough white wine from the victualling yard was named, but its satisfaction was only temporary. Within a few hours the drinker would be left as dry as before. He added as an afterthought, 'They must get as much fresh fruit as we can spare. It is the only thing to keep down disease out here.'

It was odd how much clamour and argument there had been in Antigua when he had insisted on a full cargo of fruit to be shipped for his crew. Maybe that was what the admiral had meant when he had said, 'You are an idealist in many ways!' But to Bolitho's practical mind it was only being sensible. Even though he had paid for the fruit from his own pocket he knew it was more of a good investment than a method of arousing favouritism with his men. A fit and healthy sailor was worth far more than a basket of fruit. In fact, the normal wastage did not stop there. Other men were used to care for their sick comrades, and their work had to be taken on by still more men. And so it went on, yet there were still plenty of captains who could see no further than their prize money as a measure of success.

He tucked his shirt into his breeches and said, 'Take a glass if you will, Mr. Ellice.' He looked away ashamed as the big, untidy man shambled quickly to the sideboard and slopped a generous portion of brandy into his goblet. Ellice's hand shook as he poured and downed a second glass before mumbling, 'Thankee, sir. That's the first today!'

Bolitho glanced at the shadow of the stern, close to the barely moving wake. The sun was high in the sky. It was more than likely that Ellice had already consumed a goodly portion from his private store.

'I did not see you go ashore in Antigua, Mr. Ellice? You had only to ask.'

Ellice licked his lips and shot a quick glance at the decanter. 'I never go on land now, sir, thankee all the same. At first I used to wander like a lovesick girl amongst the grass and weep when the shoreline dropped over the sea's edge.' He saw Bolitho nod towards the decanter and hurriedly poured another drink. 'Now when the ship sails I hardly looks up.' He shook his head as if to restore some broken memory. 'Anyway, I've seen it all!'

There was a tap at the door, but before Bolitho could call it burst open and Lieutenant Vibart stamped into the cabin. He looked strained and angry, and wasted no time in breaking his news.

'I have to report that we are almost out of fresh water, sir.'

Bolitho studied him for a few seconds. 'What do you mean?'

Vibart glanced round the cabin. 'I have the cooper outside, sir. It might save time if *he* told you!'

Bolitho ignored Vibart's insolent manner. 'Send him in.' He was glad that the sea's reflected glare kept his face in deep shadow. At every turn events seemed to twist and

271

mock at his efforts. Now this, the one predominant worry, had been fanned alight even as he had been openly discussing it with Ellice.

Mr. Trevenen, the *Phalarope*'s cooper, was an undersized warrant officer who was known for his extremely bad eyesight. Too long in too many darkened holds had left him half blind, like some creature of the night. Now, as he stood blinking and shifting uneasily under Bolitho's stare he looked small and defenceless.

Bolitho stifled his usual feeling of pity which inevitably arose on the rare occasions of meeting the cooper. 'Well, spit it out, man! What the hell have you discovered?'

Trevenen gulped miserably. 'I've been doin' my rounds, sir. You see I always does 'em on a Thursday. If you build up a system of inspections you can . . .'

Vibart bellowed, '*Tell* him, you old fool!'

The cooper said in a small voice, 'Two thirds of me casks are foul with salt water, sir.' He peered at his feet. 'I don't understand it, sir. In all my years afloat I never seen nothin' like it.'

'Hold your damned tongue!' Vibart looked as if he would strike the wretched man. 'Admit that you made a mistake at Antigua. You're so bloody blind you don't know the difference! If I had my way I'd . . .'

Bolitho made himself speak slowly to give his mind time to recover from the shock. 'If you please, Mr. Vibart! I think *I* can evaluate the extent of this information!' He turned again to Trevenen. 'Are you sure now?'

The wrinkled head nodded violently. 'No mistake about it, sir!' He looked up, his faded eyes filling his face. 'In all my years, sir, I never . . .'

'I know, Mr. Trevenen, you just told us.' Bolitho added to Vibart sharply, 'Have the casks checked for yourself, Mr. Vibart. Separate the fresh ones from the others, and see that the salt water is drained away and the wood cleaned off.'

He strode to the chart and leaned across it, his face set in a deep frown. 'We are here.' He tapped the chart with the heavy dividers. 'Fifty miles south-west of Guadeloupe, give or take a mile.' He picked up his ruler and ran it across the thick parchment. 'There are some small islands to the south of us. Uninhabited and useless except for wrecking the unwary sailor.' He made a small cross on the chart and stood up. 'Call the hands and prepare to wear ship, Mr. Vibart. This breeze, slight though it is, will suit our purpose.'

He looked across at Trevenen. 'Whatever the reason for this, be it seepage or sheer carelessness, we must have water, and quickly! So prepare your party to take on a fresh supply.'

Trevenen blinked at him. He looked like a man who had just heard of a miracle at first hand.

Bolitho continued, 'We should make a landfall within two days, sooner if the wind finds us again. I have visited these islands before.' He touched the scar beneath the dark forelock of hair. 'There are streams and quite reliable pools on some of them.'

Vibart said heavily, 'The admiral gave no orders about leaving our station, sir.'

'Would you have the men die of thirst, Mr. Vibart?' Bolitho stared down at the chart again. 'But if you are worried I will have my clerk make an entry in the patrol report today.' He smiled wryly. 'Should I vanish again, you will have the necessary shield from Sir Robert's anger!'

Ellice said dreamily, 'I was in a ship once when this 'appened. Two of the seamen ran amuck for want of water!'

Vibart snarled, 'Well you at least will be untroubled by *that*, I imagine!'

Bolitho smiled in spite of his troubled thoughts. 'Carry on, Mr. Vibart. Have the hands mustered to their stations.

273

I will be up directly.' He watched the door quiver in its frame and then said to Ellice, 'You asked for that, Mr. Ellice!'

The surgeon was unmoved. 'With all due respect to the first lieutenant, sir, but he was too long aboard a slaver, if you ask me. To 'im men is just bloody extra cargo!'

'That will do, Mr. Ellice.' Bolitho glanced at the decanter. As if by magic it had emptied during his talk with Trevenen. 'I suggest you take a turn around the maindeck.'

Ellice peered at him uncertainly. Then he grinned. 'Aye, sir. So I will. It'll give me a fair appetite!' He ambled away, his shabby coat hanging around him like a sack. Rain or fine, sun or sheeting squalls, Ellice was never dressed differently. Some had even suggested he slept in his clothes.

Bolitho dismissed him from his mind as the pipes shrilled and the decks thudded with bare feet as the men ran to their stations for wearing ship.

Within an hour the *Phalarope* had gone about, her sails flat and listless in the relentless glare. But in spite of the outward stillness there was enough power in the breeze to cause a small ripple beneath her gilt figurehead, and at the mainmast truck the commissioning pendant flapped and whipped with lonely agitation, as if it commanded the only strength the wind had to offer. Lieutenant Herrick walked slowly aft along the maindeck, his eyes moving from side to side as he watched the men flaking down ropes and putting a last tautness in sheets and braces. He knew that they were discussing the news about the contaminated water, and other things beside, but as he passed even the usually friendly ones fell silent. The past two weeks of heat and dull discomfort were showing their teeth now, he decided. No one complained or grumbled any more. That was the worst sign of all.

He halted as Midshipman Maynard appeared below the quarterdeck and leaned heavily on a twelve-pounder. Beneath his tan his thin features were as pale as death, and his legs looked as if they were near collapse.

Herrick crossed to his side. 'What is it, lad? Are you ill?'

Maynard turned and stared at him, his eyes opaque with fear. For a moment he could not speak, then the words poured from his dry lips in a flood.

'I've just come from below, sir.' He screwed up his face. 'I was sent down to the orlop to fetch Mr. Evans.' He swallowed hard and tried to speak coherently. 'I found him in his cabin, sir.' He retched and swayed against the gun.

Herrick gripped his arm and whispered fiercely, 'Go on, lad! What the hell is wrong?'

'Dead!' The word was wrung from his lips. 'My God, sir! He's been cut to pieces!' He stared at Herrick's grim features, reliving the nightmare of his discovery. He repeated faintly, 'Cut to pieces.'

'Keep your voice down!' Herrick struggled to control his shocked thoughts. In a calmer tone he called, 'Mr. Quintal! Take Mr. Maynard aft and see that he is kept alone!'

The boatswain, caught in the act of reprimanding a seaman, stared from one to the other. He touched his forehead and said gruffly, 'Aye, aye, sir.' Then he asked quietly, 'Is somethin' up, sir?'

Herrick looked at Quintal's broad, competent face and answered flatly, 'It seems that the purser is dead, Mr. Quintal!' He saw the quick start of alarm in the man's eyes and added, 'Show no sign! This ship is like a tinderbox as it is.'

Herrick watched the boatswain leading the young midshipman into the shadow of the quarterdeck and then glanced quickly around him. Everything looked as it had two minutes earlier.

Lieutenant Okes had the watch and was standing at the quarterdeck rail, his eyes up at the topsails. Further aft Herrick could see the captain in conversation with Vibart and Rennie, while at the wheel the two helmsmen looked as if they had been at their posts since time began.

Herrick walked slowly towards the lower cabin hatch. He made himself move calmly, but his heart felt as if it was in his throat.

With all hands employed trimming sails the lower deck was deserted and strangely alien. A few lanterns swung on their hooks, and as he began to climb down the second and last ladder Herrick could sense an air of menace and danger. Even so, he was totally unprepared for the sight in the purser's tiny cabin.

Deep in the hull of the ship the stillness was all the more apparent, and the solitary lantern on the low deckhead cast a steady circle of light on a scene which made Herrick's throat choke with bile. Evans, the purser, must have been secreting a bag of flour for his own private uses when his assailant had struck him down. He lay spread-eagled on the upended sack, his eyes bright in the lamplight, while from his severed throat a great torrent of dark blood seeped and congealed in the scattered flour. There was blood everywhere, and as Herrick stared with fixed horror at the corpse at his feet he saw that Evans had been stabbed and slashed as if by some crazed beast.

He leaned against the door and touched his face with his hand. His palm felt cold and clammy, and he thought of young Maynard alone with this appalling spectacle. No one could have blamed him if he had rushed screaming to the upperdeck.

'My God!' Herrick's voice hung in the gloom in a mocking echo. He almost cried out again as a foot rasped on the ladder behind him, but as he groped blindly for his pistol he saw that it was Captain Renme, his scariet coat like a reflection of the blood on the cabin deck.

276

Rennie brushed past him and stared fixedly at the corpse. Then he said coldly, 'I'll put two of my best men on guard here. The cabin must be sealed until there has been an investigation.' He eyed Herrick meaningly. 'You know what this means, don't you?'

Herrick felt himself nod. 'I do.' He pulled himself together. 'I'll go and tell the captain.'

As he climbed up the ladder Rennie called quietly, 'Easy, Thomas. There will be at least one guilty man watching your face on deck!'

Herrick glanced back at the open cabin door, making himself form a final picture of the murdered man. 'I suppose I was expecting something like this.' He bit his lip. 'But when it comes, it's still a shock.'

Rennie watched him go and then stepped carefully over the glaring corpse. Ignoring the thing by his polished boots he began to search methodically amongst the scattered souvenirs of the purser's life.

Herrick's face was like stone as he crossed to the weather side of the quarterdeck to where Bolitho was still speaking with Vibart. He touched his hat and waited until Bolitho turned to face him.

'Well, Mr. Herrick?' Bolitho's smile of welcome faded. 'Is it more trouble?'

Herrick looked quickly around him. 'Mr. Evans has been murdered, sir.' He spoke in a tight, clipped voice which he no longer recognised. 'Maynard found him a few minutes ago.' He ran his hand across his face. It was still cold, like the mark of death.

Bolitho said slowly, 'What have you done so far, Mr. Herrick?' There was nothing in his question to betray what he must be feeling, and his features were composed in an impassive mask. 'Take your time. Just tell me what you saw.'

Herrick moved closer to the rail, his eyes on the

277

glittering water. In a slow, flat voice he described the events from the moment Maynard had appeared on deck to the actual second of realisation.

Bolitho listened in complete silence, and at Herrick's side Vibart stood swaying with the ship, his hands opening and closing from either anger or shock at Maynard's discovery.

Herrick concluded heavily, 'He had not been dead long, sir.' He found himself repeating the midshipman's words. 'He has been cut to pieces.'

Captain Rennie marched across the deck and said crisply, 'I have put some men on guard, sir.' He saw Bolitho looking at his boots and bent quickly to wipe a bright stain from the polished leather. He added calmly, 'I've had a good look round, sir. Evans' pistols are missing. Stolen most likely.'

Bolitho eyed him thoughtfully. 'Thank you, gentlemen. You have both behaved very well.'

Vibart said vehemently, 'What did I tell you, sir? Softness with these scum is no use! They only understand a hard hand!'

Bolitho said, 'His pistols, you say?'

Rennie nodded. 'He had two small weapons. He was very proud of them. Gold-mounted and quite valuable, I believe. He said he got them in Spain.' He fell silent, as if he, like the others, was thinking of the dead man as he had once been. One of the most disliked men in the ship. A man with grudges and hates more than most. It was not difficult to understand that he would have an equal number of enemies.

Proby climbed the ladder and touched his hat. 'May I dismiss the watch below, sir?' He seemed to realise that he was intruding and muttered, 'Beggin' your pardon, sir!'

Bolitho said, 'Have the hands stay at their stations, Mr. Proby.' They all looked at him. There was a new coldness in Bolitho's voice and an unfamiliar hardness in his eyes.

To Rennie he continued, 'Post sentries at every hatch. Nobody will go below.'

Vibart murmured, 'So you'll see it *my* way, sir?'

Bolitho swung round. 'Someone is guilty, Mr. Vibart. But not the whole ship! I don't want this man to escape, or his actions to contaminate the rest of our people!' In a calmer tone he said, 'Mr. Herrick, you will take the berth deck with Mr. Farquhar and the boatswain. Captain Rennie will search the rest of the ship with his own men.' He looked down at the waiting seamen on the decks and gangways. 'Mr. Vibart, you will take the upperdeck yourself with Mr. Brock. Look in every locker and beneath each gun, and be as quick as you can!'

He watched them troop down the ladder and then returned his attention to the crowded maindeck. Every sailor was now fully aware that something was wrong. He saw one nudge his companion, and another fell back fearfully as Vibart and the gunner pushed through the watching men.

Perhaps Vibart was right after all? He gripped his hands together behind him with such force that the pain helped to control his whirling mind. No, he must not think like that. Without faith there was nothing. Nothing at all.

As the minutes dragged on a growing wave of apprehension moved across the crowded maindeck like smoke from an uncontrollable fire. The seamen at the foot of the mainmast parted to allow Vibart and the gunner to move through and then shuffled together as if for mutual support.

Pochin rubbed his tarry hands on his trousers and glared angrily after Vibart's bulky figure. 'What the hell's happenin'?' He reached out as a boatswain's mate made to pass him. 'Do *you* know, Mr. Josling?'

Josling darted a quick glance at the quarterdeck. 'The purser. 'E's dead!'

A new ripple of uneasiness broke over the waiting men, and Pochin stared across at Allday who was leaning watchfully against the mast. 'Did you hear that, man?'

Allday nodded and then slowly turned his head to look at Onslow. He was standing a bit apart from the others, his legs relaxed, his brown arms hanging loosely at his sides. But there was an air of animal watchfulness about the man, betrayed in the flat hardness of his eyes and the excited dilation of his nostrils. Allday released his breath very slowly. In his own mind he had no doubt as to where the finger of accusation would point.

Old Strachan muttered, 'Looks bad, don't it? I got a feelin' that we're in for another squall!'

There was a sudden burst of activity from the quarter-deck, and as every head turned aft Captain Rennie's marines trooped up the ladders and formed a solid scarlet barrier athwart the deck. Sergeant Garwood dressed the ranks and then took his place beside the small drummer. Captain Rennie stood coolly ahead of his men, one hand resting on his sword hilt, his face empty of expression.

From the side of his mouth the sergeant rasped, 'Fix bayonets!' Every hand moved as one, the blades rippling along the swaying front rank before clicking into place on the long muskets.

On deck the tension was almost unbearable. Every man watched transfixed, afraid to speak or turn his head for fear of missing some part of this new drama. Here and there a hand moved to dash away the sweat, and some-where in the packed throng a man began to cough nervously.

Allday saw the captain speaking with Lieutenant Herrick and the boatswain, and watched as Bolitho shook his head at something one of them had said. It might have been anger or disbelief. It was impossible to tell.

Vibart had realised that the search was over, and moved slowly aft, his hands pushing the silent men aside like reeds, his red-rimmed eyes fixed on the little group behind the marines.

Pochin whispered, 'We'll soon know now!'

Allday darted another glance at Onslow. For a moment he felt something like pity for him. He had been so long penned up in a ship he had known no other life but the ceaseless battle of the lower deck.

Captain Bolitho's voice broke into his thoughts, and when he looked aft again he saw him at the quarterdeck rail, his hands resting on the starboard carronade as he stared down at the assembled seamen.

'As most of you know by now, Mr. Evans the purser is dead. He was killed in his cabin a short while ago, without pity, and without reason.' He broke off as Herrick descended one of the ladders to speak to the first lieutenant. Then he continued in the same even tone, 'Every man will stand fast until the culprit has been taken!'

Pochin's scarred face was streaming with sweat. He said in a hoarse voice, ''E's got some 'opes! Every bastard in the ship 'ated the bloody purser!'

But no one responded or even gave him a glance. Every eye was on Vibart as he moved purposefully along the maindeck with Brock at his back.

Even the sound of sea and canvas seemed stilled, and as Vibart halted below the mainyard Allday could hear his heavy breathing and the squeak of his sword belt.

For a few seconds longer the aweful suspense continued. Then, as Vibart ran his eye slowly around the watching faces, Brock stepped forward and lifted his cane.

'That's him, sir! That's the murderous cur!'

The cane fell in a tight arc, and Allday reeled back, half stunned from the blow.

The weeks and months dropped away, and he was back on the cliff road with Brock lashing out at his face with the same cane while the other members of the press gang crowded round to watch. He could feel the blood stinging the corner of his mouth, and there seemed to be a great roaring in his ears. Voices were calling and shouting all around him, yet he felt unable to move or defend himself as Brock struck him once more across the neck with his cane. Vibart was staring at him, his eyes almost hidden by his brows as he watched Brock pull him from the mast and away from the other men.

Old Strachan croaked, ' 'E was with me! 'E never done it, Mr. Vibart!'

At last Vibart seemed to find his voice. But his words were strangled, as if his body was so taut with insane anger that he could hardly get himself to speak. 'Silence, you stupid old fool!' He thrust the man aside, 'Or I will take you, too!'

Some of the men had recovered from the first shock and now surged forward, pressed on by those at the rear. Instantly there was a barked command from the quarter-deck, and a line of muskets rose above the rail. There was no doubting their intent, or the gleam in Sergeant Garwood's eyes.

Bolitho was still at one side of the rail, his figure dark against the pale sky. 'Bring that man aft, Mr. Vibart!'

Old Strachan was muttering vaguely, ' 'E was with me. I swear it!'

Brock pushed Allday towards the quarterdeck and snapped, 'Were you, Strachan? *All* the time?'

Strachan was confused. 'Well, all but a minute, Mr. Brock!'

Brock's voice was harsh. 'It only takes a minute to kill a man!'

Allday made another effort to clear his dazed mind as he was pushed up a ladder and past the grim-faced marines. He felt like another person, someone on the outside untouched by the cruel reality of events. Even his limbs felt numb and beyond his control, and the cuts from

Brock's cane had neither pain nor meaning. He saw Lieutenant Herrick watching him like a stranger, and beyond him Proby, the master, looked away, as if he could not bear to meet his eye.

Captain Bolitho seemed to appear from nowhere, and as they faced each other across three feet of deck Allday heard him say, 'John Allday, do you have anything to say?'

He had to move his numb lips several times before the words would come. 'No, sir.' An insane voice seemed to cry from the depths of his soul. Tell him! Tell him! He tried again. 'It wasn't me, sir.'

He tried to see beyond the shadow which hid the captain's face. He could see the lines at the corners of his mouth, a bead of sweat running from beneath the dark hair. But there was no reality. It was all part of the same nightmare.

Bolitho said, 'Do you recognise these?'

Someone held out a pair of small pistols, bright and evil looking in the sunlight.

Allday shook his head. 'No, sir.'

'Or this?' Bolitho's voice was quite empty of emotion. This time it was a knife, the tip broken off by the force of savage blows, its worn handle dark with congealed blood.

Allday stared. 'It's mine, sir!' He clapped his hand to his belt, his fingers brushing against an empty sheath.

Bolitho said, 'The pistols were found amongst your possessions below. Your knife was discoverd beneath Mr. Evans' locker.' He paused to let the words sink in. 'Where it was dropped after the struggle.'

Allday swayed. 'I didn't do it, sir.' The words seemed to hang in his throat. 'Why would I do such a thing?'

As if from a long way off he heard Vibart's harsh voice. 'Let me run him up to the yard now, sir! It will give others of his sort something to think about with him dancing from a halter!'

Bolitho snapped, 'I think you have said enough, Mr. Vibart!' He turned back to Allday. 'After your behaviour since you first came aboard, I had high hopes for you, Allday. Mr. Herrick has already spoken on your behalf, but on this occasion I can find no reason for leniency.' He paused. 'Under the Articles of War I could have you hanged forthwith. As it is, I intend that you should be tried by court martial as soon as the opportunity arises.'

There was a low murmur of despair from the maindeck, and Allday knew that in everyone's eyes he was already a dead man.

Bolitho turned away. 'Place him in irons, Mr. Vibart. But any unnecessary brutality will be answerable to me!'

Dazed, and stumbling like a drunken man, Allday allowed himself to be led below.

Deep below the maindeck there were two tiny cells, each just large enough to contain one man. Allday watched dumbly as the rough manacles were snapped around his wrists and ankles, but only when the door was slammed and bolted behind him and he was left in total darkness did the true realisation close on him like a vice.

By the time the *Phalarope* returned to port, and a necessary number of officers was available for a court martial, no one would remember or even care if he was guilty or not. He would be used as an example to others. A dancing, kicking puppet on the end of a rope as he was hauled slowly to the mainyard to the accompaniment of a drum's mournful beat.

He smashed his fists against the door, and heard the sound echo and vibrate in the stillness of the hull. Again and again, until he could feel the blood running across his fingers and taste the angry tears on his lips.

But when he fell exhausted and gasping behind the door, there was nothing but silence.

The deep, empty silence of a tomb.

*

284

Lieutenant Herrick rested his shoulder against an empty hammock netting and stared moodily along the frigate's deserted decks. An hour of the middle watch had passed, and in the bright moonlight the sails and rigging gave off an eerie glow, like those of some phantom vessel.

Try as he might, he could not put the thought of Allday and the murdered purser from his mind. He should have been able to tell himself that it was over and done with. Just one more item in the log to be talked over for a time and then forgotten. Evans was dead, and his killer was penned below in irons. That at least should be some small satisfaction to everybody. An undetected murderer, at large to terrorise the lower deck or to strike again, would have been far more to worry about.

He tried to picture Allday standing over that hideous corpse, crazed enough to rip at the man's body until it was hardly human, yet calmly able to steal a pair of pistols and secrete them in his own quarters. It did not make any sense at all, but Herrick knew that had it been anyone else but Allday he would never have questioned such evidence.

Just before coming on watch Herrick had made his way below to the darkened cells, and after sending the marine sentry to the top of the ladder, had opened the door and held a lantern inside.

Allday had crouched against the opposite side, his hands shading his eyes from the light, his feet skidding in his own filth. Any disgust or anger Herrick may have felt faded in that instant. He had expected loud denials of guilt, or dumb insolence. Instead there was only a pathetic attempt at pride.

He had asked quietly, 'Have you anything more to tell me, Allday? I have not forgotten that you saved my life on the cliff. Perhaps if you tell me the full circumstances I will be able to do something to attract clemency on your behalf?'

Allday had made as if to brush his long hair from his

eyes, and then looked down at the heavy manacles. In a barely controlled voice he had replied, 'I did not do it, Mr. Herrick. I cannot find a defence for something I *did not do*!'

'I see.' In the silence Herrick had heard the scampering rats, the strange, unknown creaks of a ship at sea. 'If you change your mind, I . . .'

Allday had tried to step towards him and had fallen forward on Herrick's arm. For a few seconds Herrick had felt the touch of his bare skin, damp with fear, had smelt his despair, like the odour of death.

Allday had said thickly, 'You don't believe me either! So what's the point?' His voice had gained some small inner strength. 'Just leave me alone! For God's sake leave me *alone*!'

But as Herrick had been about to rebolt the door Allday had asked quietly, 'D'you think they'll send me home for court martial, sir?'

Herrick knew that the Navy would have other ideas. Justice was swift and final. But as he had stared at the heavy studded door he had heard himself reply, 'Maybe they will. Why do you ask?'

The answer had been muffled, as if Allday had turned his face away. 'I would like to see the green hills again. Just once. Even for a few minutes!'

The sadness and despair of those last words had dogged Herrick for the rest of the day, and now during his watch they were with him still.

'Damn!' He spoke aloud with sudden anger, and the two helmsmen jerked upright by the wheel as if he had struck them.

The senior man watched anxiously as Herrick walked towards the wheel and said quickly, 'Full an' bye, sir! Course south by east!'

Herrick stared at him and then at the gently swinging compass card. Poor devils, he thought vaguely. Scared sick because I swore aloud.

A dark figure moved from the lee rail and walked slowly towards him. It was Proby, his heavy jowls glowing faintly from his short clay pipe.

Herrick said, 'Can't you sleep, Mr. Proby? The breeze is slight but steady now. They'll be nothing for you to attend to tonight.'

The master sucked noisily at the stem. 'It's the best time of the night, Mr. Herrick. You can look into the wind's eye and think about what you've done with your life!'

Herrick looked sideways at Proby's crumpled features. In the pipe glow his face looked like a piece of weather-worn sculpture, but there was something reassuring about him all the same. Timeless, like the sea itself.

He said at length, 'Do you think we have heard the last of Evans' death?'

'Who can say?' Proby shifted on his flat feet. 'It takes time to clean such a deed from a man's memory. Aye, it takes a long time.'

The pipe glow suddenly vanished in the palm of Proby's beefy hand, and he said tersely, 'The captain is on deck, Mr. Herrick!' Then in a louder, matter-of-fact tone he said, 'We should make a good landfall tomorrow if this wind holds. So I'll bid you good night, Mr. Herrick!'

Then he was gone, and Herrick moved towards the lee rail. From the corner of his eye he could see Bolitho standing straight against the weather rail, the moonlight sharp across his white shirt as he stared at the glittering reflections beyond the ship.

Bolitho had not left the quarterdeck for more than an hour at a time, and ever since Allday's arrest he had been seen by the taffrail, either pacing the deck or just staring out to sea, as he was now.

Earlier Herrick had overheard the master speaking to Quintal, the boatswain, and now as he watched Bolitho's motionless figure the words came back to him. Quintal had said in a hoarse whisper, 'I didn't know he felt like

287

that about Evans. He seems fair troubled by it all!'

Old Proby had weighed his words before replying. 'It's the deed which bothers the captain, Mr. Quintal. He feels betrayed, that's what is wrong with *him*!'

Herrick saw Bolitho touch the scar on his forehead and then rub the tiredness from his eyes. Proby was right, he thought. He feels it more than we realise. Whatever any of us does, he shares it like his own burden.

Before he realised what he was doing, Herrick had crossed the deck to Bolitho's side. Instantly he regretted his action. He half expected Bolitho to turn and reprimand him, and even that might have been better than the complete silence. He said, 'The wind is holding well, sir. The master has prophesied a quick landfall.'

'I think I heard him.' Bolitho seemed to be deep in his own thoughts.

Herrick saw that the captain's shirt was dark with thrown spray and clung close to his body like another skin. There were deep shadows beneath his eyes, and Herrick could almost feel the inner torment which was keeping Bolitho on deck instead of the privacy of the cabin.

He said, 'Would you like me to call your servant, sir? Perhaps a hot drink before you turn in for the night?'

Bolitho twisted round at the rail, his eyes bright in the moonlight. 'Spare me this small talk, Mr. Herrick! What is it which bothers you?'

Herrick swallowed hard and then blurted out, 'I have been speaking with Allday, sir. I know it was wrong, but I feel partly responsible for him.'

Bolitho was watching him closely. 'Go on.'

'He is one of my men, sir, and I think there may be more to what happened than we think.' He finished lamely, 'I know him better than most. He is not the sort to change.'

Bolitho sighed. 'Only the stars never change, Mr. Herrick.'

Herrick said stubbonly, 'Even so, he may be innocent!'

'And you think this is important?' Bolitho sounded tired. 'You believe that the life of one man, a man almost certain to be found guilty, is worth consideration?'

'Well, as a matter of fact, I do, sir.' Herrick felt Bolitho's eyes fixed on his face in a cold stare. 'The authorities will not listen to half a story . . .'

Bolitho shifted with sudden impatience. '*We* are the authority out here, Mr. Herrick! And I will decide what is to be done!'

Herrick looked away. 'Yes, sir.'

'As it happens, I entirely agree with you.' Bolitho pushed the lock of hair back from his forehead, ignoring Herrick's open astonishment. 'But I just wanted to hear it from one other person!'

He became suddenly brisk. 'I think I will go below now, Mr. Herrick, *without* a hot drink. Tomorrow we will search for fresh water and attend to the matter of fighting a war.' He paused momentarily by the rail. 'I will also think about what you have said tonight. It may be important for all of us.'

Without another word he turned on his heel and descended the cabin stairway. Herrick stared after him, his jaw hanging open.

'Well, I'll be damned!' He shook his head and grinned. 'Well, I'll be *double*-damned!'

15

The Storm Breaks

Surprisingly the wind did hold, and twenty hours after Proby's prophecy the *Phalarope*'s anchor splashed down into deep, clear water amidst a huddle of low, desolate islets.

Apart from lowering boats and filling them with water casks in readiness for the following morning, it was pointless to attempt a landing with night so close at hand, but at the first hint of daylight, long before the sun was able to burnish an edge to the horizon, the first boatloads of men grated up the narrow shelving beach of the nearest islet.

Bolitho climbed through the tangle of dark scrub at the top of the beach and stared round at the busy preparations behind him. The boats had already shoved off to collect more men, and the ones already landed were standing huddled together, as if conscious of the island's bleak inhospitality. One or two of the sailors were staggering like drunken revellers, their legs so used to the pitch and toss of a ship's deck that the unfamilar land destroyed their sense of balance.

Petty officers bawled orders and checked their lists of names, and as the next batch of men arrived to join the swelling mass of sailors at the water's edge the first parties picked up their casks and tools and began to stumble inland.

Lieutenant Okes appeared on the ridge and touched his hat. 'All working parties ready, sir.' He looked harassed.

Bolitho nodded. 'You have your orders, Mr. Okes. Just follow the rough map I made for you and you should find fresh water without difficulty. Keep the men moving fast before the sun comes up. You'll need every available man to carry the full casks down to the beach, so see they don't wander off.'

He saw Trevenen, the cooper, scurrying ahead of another party accompanied by Ledward, the carpenter, the latter ever hopeful of replenishing his stock of spare timber. He'd not find much here, Bolitho thought grimly. These islets were useless and left well alone, but for occasional fresh-water parties. Underfoot the ground was hidden by layer upon layer of rotten vegetation, its heavy stench well mixed with seagull droppings and small bright patches of fungus. Further inland there were a few hump-backed hills, from the top of which a man could see the sea in every direction.

Okes walked off after his men, and Bolitho caught sight of Farquhar's slim figure outlined against the green scrub, before he too vanished over the far side of the ridge. Bolitho had deliberately ordered the midshipman to join Okes in command of the main party. It would do them both good to work together, if only to break down the strange air of watchful tension between them. It seemed as if Farquhar was playing some sort of game with Okes. Ever since his escape from the *Andiron* Farquhar had made a point of not speaking to Okes, but his presence alone seemed more than enough to reduce the lieutenant to a state of permanent agitation.

Okes had acted hastily during the retreat from Mola Island, but unless he made an open admission there was little point in pursuing the matter, Bolitho thought. He could sympathise with Farquhar, and wondered what he himself might have done under the same set of circumstances. Farquhar's built-in sense of caution had obviously taught him that there was more to a career than gaining petty triumphs. Also his breeding, the security of a powerful family, as well as his own self-confidence, gave him the ability to bide his time.

Herrick strode up the slope and said, 'Shall we return to the ship, sir?'

Bolitho shook his head. 'We'll walk a little further, Mr. Herrick.'

He pushed through a line of sun-scarred bushes and headed away from the beach. Herrick walked beside him in silence, no doubt thinking of the strangeness of the land around him. The sea's gentle hiss was gone and the air was heavy with alien smells and a thick, clinging humidity.

Bolitho said at length, 'I hope Okes can get the men working quickly. Every hour may be precious.'

'You are thinking of the French, sir?'

Bolitho wiped the sweat from his face and nodded. 'De Grasse may have sailed by now. If he behaves as Sir George Rodney believes he will, his fleet will already be striking west for Jamaica.' He looked up fretfully at the limp leaves and cloudless sky. 'Not a breath of wind. Nothing. We were lucky it held long enough for us to reach here!'

Herrick was breathing heavily. 'My God, sir, I'm feeling this!' He mopped his face. 'I have not set foot ashore since Falmouth. I had almost forgotten what it was like.'

Falmouth. Again the name brought back a flood of memories to Bolitho as he strode unseeingly through the thick scrub. His father would still be waiting and wondering, nursing the hurt which Hugh had left with him. Bolitho wondered momentarily what would have happened if he had seen and recognised his brother on the *Andiron*'s poop on that first savage encounter. Would he have pressed home his attack with such fervour? If he had caused Hugh's death it might have eased the minds of the Navy, but in his heart Bolitho knew that it would only have added to his father's grief and sense of loss.

Perhaps Hugh already had another ship. He dismissed the idea at once. The French would not trust another prize to a man who had allowed *Andiron* to fall into her own snare. And the American rebel government had few ships to spare. No, Hugh would have his own problems in plenty at this moment.

He thought too of Vibart, left behind in charge of the frigate. It was strange how Evans' murder had affected him. Bolitho had always thought Evans to be more of a toady than a friend of the first lieutenant. Yet his death seemed in some way to have deprived Vibart of something familiar and reliable, the last outlet from his own isolation. Bolitho knew that Vibart blamed him for Evans' death, as much as he hated Allday for the deed. Vibart viewed humanity like sentiment. To him both were useless hindrances to duty.

He also knew that he would never see eye to eye with Vibart whatever happened. To Bolitho the humane treatment of his men, the understanding of their problems, and the earning of their loyalty, were as precious as gold. Equally he knew he must uphold this difficult and bitter man, for commanding a ship of war left little room for personal animosity amongst officers.

Bolitho halted with a jerk and pointed. 'Is that a marine?'

Herrick stood beside him breathing deeply. A red coat flashed between the dull foliage and then another, and as Bolitho started forward, Sergeant Garwood appeared at the head of a file of sweating marines.

Bolitho asked sharply, 'What are you doing ashore, Sergeant?'

Garwood stared fixedly over Bolitho's shoulder. 'Mr. Vibart 'as sent all the marines across, sir.' He swallowed hard. 'The prisoner Allday 'as escaped, sir. We've been sent to catch 'im again!'

Bolitho heard Herrick catch his breath and glanced quickly at his streaming face. He could see the shock and disappointment plain on the lieutenant's features, as if he was personally involved.

'I see.' Bolitho controlled the sudden rise of anger and added calmly, 'Where is Captain Rennie?'

'T'other side of the island, sir.' Garwood looked unhappy. 'The relief sentry found the cell guard clubbed senseless an' the prisoner gone, sir. 'Is manacle 'ad been struck off too, sir.'

'So someone else was involved?' Bolitho stared hard at the sergeant's bronzed features. 'Who else is missing?'

The marine gulped. 'Yer clerk, Ferguson, sir!'

Bolitho turned away. 'Very well, I suppose you had better carry on now that you are here.' He watched the man clump gratefully away and then said tightly, 'Mr. Vibart was over hasty to send all the marines ashore. If the ship was surprised at her anchor by another vessel, there would be insufficient men to repel an attack.' He turned abruptly. 'Come, we will go back to the beach.'

Herrick said wretchedly, 'I am sorry, sir. I feel to blame more than ever. I trusted Allday, and I was the one who chose Ferguson as your clerk.'

Bolitho replied flatly, 'It has proved that we were both wrong, Mr. Herrick. An innocent man does not run!' He added, 'Mr. Vibart should not have allowed his anger to blind his judgement in this matter. Allday will surely die if he is left here. He will go mad on this island once the ship has sailed, and will not thank Ferguson for his rescue from a cell!'

They hurried across the beach, and the drowsing gig's crew jerked into life as the two officers climbed aboard.

Bolitho shaded his eyes to look at the anchored frigate as the gig moved slowly across the placid water. The sun was only just showing above the nearest hump of land, and the *Phalarope*'s yards and topmasts were shining as if coated with gilt.

Herrick asked quietly, 'If the marines catch Allday, sir. What will you do?'

'I will hang him this time, Mr. Herrick. For the sake of discipline I have no choice now.' He glanced back at the land. 'For that reason I hope they do not find him.'

The bowman hooked on to the chains, and Bolitho pulled himself through the entry port.

At his elbow Herrick snapped, 'Why did you not hail the gig, man?' His own unhappy thoughts put an unusual edge to his voice.

The seaman at the entry port blinked and stammered, 'I'm sorry, sir. I – I . . .' His voice trailed away as he stared up at the quarterdeck.

There was a tight group of seamen beneath the quarterdeck, and as the cold realisation seeped into Bolitho's brain, they pushed out into the growing sunlight which shone and reflected on their raised muskets.

Herrick thrust Bolitho aside and reached for his sword, but a giant sailor with a pistol snapped, 'Stay where you are, Mr. Herrick!' He pointed up at the quarterdeck rail. 'Otherwise it will go hard with that one!'

Two more men appeared from behind the cabin hatch, between them carrying the small, struggling figure of Midshipman Neale. One man drew a knife from his belt and laid it across Neale's throat, grinning down at the two officers as he did so.

The tall seaman, whom Bolitho now recognised as Onslow, stepped slowly across the maindeck, his pistol trained on Herrick. 'Well, Mr. Herrick? Do you drop your sword?' He grinned lazily. 'It's all the same to me!'

Bolitho said, 'Do as he says, Mr. Herrick.' He had seen the brightness in Onslow's eyes, and knew that the man was eager, desperately eager to kill. He was only just keeping his pent up madness in check. One false move and there would be no more time left to act.

The sword clattered on the deck. Onslow kicked it aside and called sharply, 'Take the gig's crew forrard and batten 'em down with the other pretty boys!' He tapped his nose with his pistol. 'They'll all join us later, or feed the fish!'

Some of the men laughed. It was a wild, explosive sound. Brittle with tension.

Bolitho studied Onslow, the first shock giving way to sudden caution. Every captain dreaded such a moment. Some had earned it, others had fallen foul of uncontrollable circumstances. Now it had happened to him. To the *Phalarope.*

It was mutiny.

Onslow watched as the gig's crew was bundled below deck and then said, 'We'll up anchor as soon as a likely wind blows. We have the master below, and either he or you will take the ship to open waters.'

Herrick said hoarsely, 'You're mad! You'll swing for this!'

The pistol barrel came down sharply, and Herrick dropped to his knees, his hands across his forehead.

Bolitho saw the blood bright across Herrick's fingers and said coldly, 'And if the wind fails to arrive, Onslow? What will you do?'

Onslow nodded, his eyes searching Bolitho's face. 'A good question. Well, we have a good little ship beneath us. We can sink any boat which tries to board us, do you not agree?'

Bolitho kept his face impassive, but realised that Onslow had good reasons for confidence. Outnumbered by the rest of the crew and Rennie's marines, Onslow was still in the position of king. Even a handful of men could keep boats at bay with the frigate's guns loaded with grape. He glanced at the sun. It would be hours yet before Okes started on the long march back to the beach.

He said slowly. 'So it was you all the time.'

Another man, small and stinking of rum, capered round the two officers. 'He's done it all! Just as 'e said 'e would!'

Onslow snarled, 'Stow it, Pook!' Then more calmly, 'Your clerk told me when the ship was nearing land. All I had to do was foul the fresh-water casks with salt.' He laughed, amused by the very simplicity of his plan. 'Then, when you headed this way, I killed that rat Evans.'

Bolitho said, 'You must have been very afraid of Allday to incriminate him with murder!'

Onslow glanced along the deck and then said calmly, 'It was necessary. I knew if the bullocks were still aboard some of my white-livered friends might not be so willing to seize the ship!' He shrugged. 'So I had Allday released, and the bullocks went charging off after him. Just as I *knew* they would!'

'You've damned yourself, Onslow!' Bolitho kept his voice level. 'But think of these other men with you. Will you see them hanged?'

Onslow shouted, 'Shut your mouth! And think yourself lucky I've not had you strung up at the mainyard! I'm going to barter the ship for our freedom! No bloody navy'll catch us after that!'

Bolitho hardened his tone to hide his rising despair. 'You are a fool if you believe that!'

His head jerked back as Onslow struck him across the face with the back of his hand. '*Silence*!' Onslow's shout brought more men pressing around. Herrick was dragged to his feet and his hands were pinioned behind him. He was still dazed, and his face was streaming with blood.

Bolitho said, 'You can send the officers ashore. They are nothing to you, Onslow.'

'Ah now, Captain, you're wrong there!' Onslow's good humour was returning. 'Hostages. You may fetch a good price, too!' He laughed. 'But then you must be getting used to that!'

Pook yelled, 'Why not kill 'em now?' He waved a cutlass. 'Let me have 'em!'

Onslow looked at Bolitho. 'You see? Only I can save you.'

'What have you done with the first lieutenant?' Bolitho saw Pook nudge another seaman. 'Have you killed him, too?'

Pook sniggered. 'Not likely! We're savin' 'im for a bit o' sport later on!'

Onslow flexed his arms. 'He's flogged enough of us, Captain. I'll see how he likes the cat across *his* fat hide!'

Herrick muttered between his clenched teeth, 'Think of what you're doing! You are selling this ship to the enemy!'

'You're my enemy!' Onslow's nostrils flared as if he had been touched with a hot iron. 'I'll do what I like with her, and with you, too!'

Bolitho said quietly, 'Easy, Mr. Herrick. There is nothing you can do.'

'Spoken like a true gentleman!' Onslow gave a slow grin. 'It's best to know when you're beaten!' Then sharply he called, 'Lock them below, lads! And kill the first bugger who tries anything!'

Some of the men growled with obvious disapproval. Their lust was high. They were all committed. Bolitho knew that Onslow's careful plan was only half clear in their rum-sodden minds.

Onslow added, 'As soon as the wind gets up, we're off, lads! You can leave the rest to Harry Onslow!'

Herrick and Bolitho were pushed along the deck and down into the dark confines of a small storeroom. A moment later Midshipman Neale and Proby, the master, were thrust in with them and the door slammed shut.

High up the side of the cabin was a small circular port, used to ventilate the compartment and the stores it

298

normally contained. Bolitho guessed that the mutineers had already dragged the contents elsewhere for their own uses.

In the darkness Neale sobbed, 'I – I'm sorry, sir! I let you down! I was on watch when it all happened!'

Bolitho said quietly, 'It was not your fault, boy. The odds were against you this time. It was just ironic that Onslow stayed aboard because he could not be trusted *off* the ship!'

Neale said brokenly, 'Mr. Vibart was in his cabin. They seized him and nearly killed him! Onslow stopped them just in time!'

Herrick said bleakly, 'Not for long!' Then with sudden fury, 'The fools! The French or the Spanish will never bargain with Onslow! They won't have to. They'll seize the *Phalarope* and take the whole lot prisoners!'

Bolitho said, 'I know that, Herrick. But if the mutineers began to think as you do, they'd have no reason for sparing our lives!'

'I see, sir.' Herrick was peering at him in the gloom. 'And I thought . . .'

'You imagined that I had given up hope?' Bolitho breathed out slowly. 'Not yet. Not without a fight!'

He stood up on an empty box and peered through the small vent hole. The ship had swung slightly at her cable and he could see the far end of the little beach and a low hill beyond. There was no sign of life. Nor had he expected any.

Proby muttered, 'Two of the mutineers I know well. Good men, with no cause to follow scum like Onslow and Pook!' He added thickly, 'It'll do 'em no good. They'll be caught and hanged with the rest!'

Herrick slipped and cursed in the darkness. 'Damn!' He groped with his fingers. 'Some old butter! Rancid as bilge water!'

Bolitho cocked his head to listen to the sudden stamp of

feet and a wave of laughter. 'They've taken more than butter, Mr. Herrick. They'll be too drunk to control soon!' He thought of the knife's glitter across Neale's throat. Soon the second phase would be enacted. The mutineers would get bored with merely drinking. They would have to prove themselves. To kill.

He said, 'Can you come up here beside me, Neale?' He felt the midshipman struggling on to the box. 'Now, do you think you could get through that vent?'

Neale's eyes flickered in the shaft of sunlight. He replied doubtfully, 'It's very small, sir.' Then more firmly, 'I'll try.'

Proby asked, 'What do you have in mind, sir?'

Bolitho ran his hands around the circular hole. It was barely ten inches across. He controlled the rising excitement in his heart. It *had* to be tried.

He said, 'If Neale could slip through . . .' He broke off. 'The butter! Quick, Neale, strip off your clothes!' He reached out for Herrick. 'We'll rub him with butter, Herrick, and ease him through, like a sponge in a gun barrel!'

Neale pulled off his clothes and stood uncertainly in the centre of the storeroom. In the faint glow from the vent hole his small body shone like some discarded statue. Bolitho took a double handful of stinking butter from the deck and ignoring Neale's cry of alarm slapped it across his shoulders. As Herrick followed suit Bolitho said quickly, 'The loyal men, Neale, where are they?'

Neale's teeth were beginning to chatter uncontrollably but he replied, 'In the cable tier, sir. The surgeon and some of the older hands as well.'

'Just as I thought.' Bolitho stood back and wiped his palms on his breeches. 'Now listen. If we get you through this hole, could you climb along the forechains?'

Neale nodded. 'I'll try, sir.'

'The others will be locked in the tier by staple. If I can

distract the guards you open the door and release them.'
He rested his hand on the boy's shoulder. 'But if anyone
sees you, forget what I said and jump for it. You could
swim ashore before anyone could catch you.'

He turned to the others. 'Right, lend a hand here!'

Neale felt like a greasy fish, and at the first attempt they
nearly dropped him.

Herrick suggested, 'One arm first, Neale, then your
head.'

They tried again, with the room plunged into total
darkness as the struggling, wriggling midshipman was
forced into the vent hole.

The boy was gasping with pain, and Proby said, 'Lucky
he ain't no fatter.'

Then, with a sudden rush he was through, and after a
few agonising seconds, while they all waited for a shouted
challenge from the deck, his eyes appeared outside the
vent hole. He was scarlet in the face and his shoulder was
bleeding from the rough passage.

But he was strangely determined, and Bolitho said
softly, 'Take your time, boy. And no chances!'

Neale vanished, and Herrick said heavily, 'Well, at least
he's out of it if the worst happens.'

Bolitho looked at him sharply. It was almost as if
Herrick had read his own thoughts. But he replied calmly,
'I'll blow this ship to hell before I let it fall to the enemy,
Mr. Herrick! Make no mistake about that.'

Then, in silence, he settled down to wait.

John Allday leaned against a tall slab of rock, his chest
heaving from exertion as he fought to regain his breath. A
few paces away, lying like a corpse with his head and
shoulders in a small pool, Bryan Ferguson drank deeply,
pausing every so often to give a great gasp for air.

Allday turned to look back through the tangled mass of
small trees through which they had just come. There was

301

still no sign of pursuit, but he had no doubt that the alarm was now under way.

He said, 'I've not had time to thank you, Bryan. That was a rash thing you did!'

Ferguson rolled on to his side and stared at him with glazed eyes. 'Had to do it. Had to.'

'It's your neck as well as mine now, Bryan.' Allday studied him sadly. 'But at least we're free. There's always hope when you have your freedom!'

He had been lying in his darkened cell listening to the familiar sounds of boats filling with men and pushing off from the frigate's hull. Then, as the emptied ship had fallen into silence, there had been a cry of alarm and the thud of a body falling against the door.

Ferguson had wrenched it open, his mouth slack with fear, his fingers trembling as he had unlocked the shackles and gabbled out some vague ideas of escape.

The dawn was still a dull smudge in the sky as they had slipped quietly over the side into the cool water. Like many sailors Allday could hardly swim a stroke, but Ferguson, driven by the desperation of fear, had helped him, until choking and gasping they had both staggered on to the safety of the beach.

Hardly speaking they had run or crawled through dense brush, had climbed over fallen rocks, never pausing to either look back or listen. Now they were between two low hills, and exhaustion had pulled them both to a halt.

Allday said, 'Come on, we'd better get ourselves moving again. Up this hill. We'll be safe there. You should be able to see miles from the top.'

Ferguson was still staring at him. 'You were right about Onslow. He is a bad man!' He shuddered. 'I thought he was just trying to be friendly to me. I told him things about the captain's log. About what the ship was doing!' He staggered to his feet and followed Allday slowly up the side of the hill. 'No one will believe me now. I'm as guilty as he is!'

'At least you know I didn't kill the purser!' Allday squinted up at the sun. It would soon be time to stop and hide.

'Onslow boasted about it!' Ferguson gave another shudder. 'After you had been taken to the cells I overheard him talking with some of the others, Pook and Pochin. He boasted how he had killed Evans!'

Allday pulled him into a bush. 'Look!' He pointed across to a distant hillside at a slow-moving line of red dots. 'The bullocks are out looking for us already.'

Ferguson gave a low cry. 'I'll never get back home! I'll never see Grace again!'

Allday looked at him gravely. 'Hold on, Bryan! We're not finished yet. Maybe another ship will call here one day, and we'll pretend we're shipwrecked.'

He turned to watch the distant marines as they moved away to the right. Marines in their heavy boots and equipment were no match for this sort of game, he thought. Even on a bare Cornish hillside he could have evaded them. Here it was easier, because of the heavy tangle of scrub all around them.

He said, 'It's all right. They're over the other side now. Come on, Bryan!'

They continued up the hillside until Allday found a sheltered clump of bushes which jutted from a great fallen slide of rock. He threw himself down and stared out at the great empty waste of water.

'We'll be safe here, Bryan. When the ship puts to sea we'll build a shelter like I had outside Falmouth. Don't worry about it.'

Ferguson was still standing, his eyes wide as he peered down at his friend. 'Onslow intends to take the ship!' His mouth quivered. 'He told me. He knew I couldn't do anything. He said that I was as guilty as the rest of them!'

Allday tried to grin. 'You're tired!' He tried again. 'Look, how can Onslow seize a frigate?' His grin faded into a look of shocked horror as the true implication dawned on him. He jumped to his feet and seized Ferguson's arm. 'Do you mean Onslow planned all of this? The fresh water, the murder, and my escape?' He did not wait for a reply. The expression on the other man's face was enough.

He gave a hollow groan. 'My God, Bryan! What are we going to do?'

Ferguson said weakly, 'I wanted to tell you. But there was no time! They'd have killed you anyway.'

Allday nodded heavily. 'I know, Bryan. I know.' He stared at the ground. 'I warned them about this.' He ran his fingers through his hair. 'Mutiny! I'll have no part of it!' He looked at Ferguson with sudden determination. 'We must go back and warn them.'

'It'll be too late!' Ferguson clasped his hands together. 'Anyway, I couldn't go! Don't you see? I'm one of them now!' Tears began to pour down his face. 'I couldn't take the lash, John! Please, I *couldn't*!'

Allday turned his back to hide his face from the other man. He stared out to sea, at the hard horizon line which seemed to represent the impossibility of distance. You poor little bugger, he thought. It must have cost a lot of pluck to knock down the sentry and open the cell. Over his shoulder he said calmly, 'I know, Bryan. But give me time to think things out.'

So it was all wasted after all. The determination to take life as it came, to accept danger and hardship in order that he should one day return home, had all come to nothing. It was curious that Ferguson, the one man aboard who had the most to lose, had been the one to spring off the disaster of mutiny.

And disaster it would be, he told himself grimly. They never gave up a search for a mutineer. No matter how long

304

it took. He remembered seeing some of them hanging in chains at Plymouth. Rotting, eyeless remnants left to the gulls as a warning to others.

Far out on the flat, glittering water something moved to break the calm emptiness of the horizon. Allday dropped on one knee and shaded his eyes with both hands. He blinked to clear the moisture and then looked again. Months at sea as a masthead lookout had given him the sailor's instinct to interpret more than was merely visible to the naked eye. He turned his head slightly. There was another one. Much smaller. Probably a mile beyond the first.

Ferguson seemed to realise something was happening. 'What is it?'

Allday sat down on the rock at his side and stared at him thoughtfully. 'There are two frigates out yonder, Bryan. Big ones, probably Frogs by the look of 'em.' He let the words sink in and then asked quietly, 'Tell me about your wife back at Falmouth. Grace, isn't that her name?'

Ferguson nodded dumbly, still not understanding.

Allday reached out and took his hand firmly in his own. 'She'll not want to remember you as a mutineer, Bryan?' He saw the quick shake of the head, the unheeded tears on his sunburned cheeks. Then he continued, 'Nor will she want to remember you as the man who let his ship fall to the enemy without lifting a finger to help her.' He stood up slowly and pulled Ferguson to his feet. 'Take a look at those ships, Bryan, and then tell me what to do. You saved my life. I owe you that at least!'

Ferguson stared at the dancing reflections, too blinded with tears to see beyond Allday's quiet words. 'You want me to go back with you?' He spoke in a small voice, yet unable to stop himself. *'To go back?'*

Allday nodded, still keeping his eyes on Ferguson's agonised face. 'We have to, Bryan. You can see that, can't you?'

He touched Ferguson's arm, and after a momentary hesitation began to walk down the side of the hill. He did not have to look back to know that Ferguson was following him.

Bolitho felt the hair stirring against the nape of his neck, and stood up to face the small vent hole. After a moment he said, 'Do you feel it? The wind is returning!'

Herrick replied uneasily, 'Okes will never be back in time. And even if he is . . .'

Bolitho touched his lips. 'Quiet! Someone's coming!' He bent down and with a quick jerk thrust Neale's clothes out through the vent hole.

The door grated back and Pook peered in at them. He gestured with a heavy pistol. 'On deck! All of you!' His eyes were very bright, and his shirt was well stained with neat rum. Then he stared past Bolitho and shouted, 'Where's that brat gone, for Christ's sake?'

Bolitho said calmly, 'Out through the port. He swam ashore.'

Pook muttered, 'It'll do 'im no good! 'E can stay with the others to starve!'

Cursing and muttering to himself he drove the three officers on deck, where Onslow and some of his trusted men were assembled beside the wheel.

Bolitho whispered to Herrick, 'Don't provoke him. He looks too dangerous to trifle with!'

Onslow was certainiy showing signs of strain, and as Bolitho and the others reached the quarterdeck rail he snapped, 'Right then! You can get the ship under way!' He levelled his pistol at Herrick's stomach and added meaningly, 'I shall shoot him if you try and trick me!'

Bolitho glanced along the maindeck, feeling his spirits sinking. There were some twenty men staring up at him. All the ones who had been sent from the *Cassius* and some others he recognised as old and trusted men of the original

306

Phalarope crew. As he had remarked to the unhappy Neale, it was just bad luck that all these men had stayed together aboard the frigate while other, more reliable elements had been sent ashore with the water casks. Normally it would not have mattered. He bit his lip and stared beyond the bowsprit where a small islet seemed to be swinging on its own momentum as the wind tugged at the anchored ship. Now it made the difference between life and death to all of them.

He nodded to Proby. 'Tops'ls and jib, Mr. Proby.' To Onslow he said, 'We will need more men to break out the anchor.'

Onslow showed his teeth. 'A good try, but not good enough. I will cut the cable!' He waved the pistol. 'I have enough men here for the sails!' He hardened his jaw. 'Try that sort of trick again and I will kill the lieutenant!' He cocked the pistol and pointed it again at Herrick. 'Carry on, *sir*!'

Bolitho felt the sun beating down on his face and tried to shut out the overwhelming sensation of defeat. There was nothing he could do. He had even put young Neale's life in danger now.

Quietly he said, 'Very well, Onslow. But I hope you live long enough to regret this.'

A man yelled from forward, 'Look! There are some men on the beach!'

Onslow swung round, his eyes glinting. 'By God, there's a boat shoving off!'

Bolitho turned to watch as the *Phalarope*'s jolly boat idled clear of the sand and began to move across the water. There were only two men in it, and he guessed that the landing party must have broken into panic at the sight of the frigate preparing to sail without them. Several mutineers were already aloft, and a jibsail flapped impatiently in the rising breeze. He could see many more men further along the green ridge and the glint of metal on a drawn sword.

Onslow said slowly, 'Let the boat get near enough to rake with a nine-pounder!' He was grinning. 'And fetch up Mr. bloody Vibart! We'll give those bastards something to remember us by!' To Bolitho he said, 'It will be a hanging after all, and who better?'

It took four men to drag the first lieutenant from the cabin hatch. His clothes were in ribbons, and his face was scarred and battered almost beyond recognition. For several seconds he stared up at the running noose which was already being passed down from the mainyard to eager hands on deck. Then he turned and looked up towards the quarterdeck, seeing Bolitho and the others for the first time. One of his eyes was closed, but the other stared straight at Onslow with neither fear nor hope.

Onslow called, 'Now, Mr. Vibart! Let us see you dance to our tune!' Some of the men laughed as he added, 'You'll get a good view from up there.'

Bolitho said, 'Leave him! You have *me*, Onslow, isn't that enough?'

But Vibart shouted, 'Save your pleadings for yourself! I don't want your damn pity!'

Suddenly a voice shouted, 'Look! In the jolly boat! It's Allday and Ferguson!'

Several men ran to the side, and one even started to cheer.

Onslow rasped, 'Stand by that gun! We don't need them here!'

Bolitho watched narrowly as another big seaman, the one called Pochin, pushed past the wheel and growled, ''Old on! It's Allday! 'E's a good mate, an' always 'as bin.' He looked down at the maindeck. 'What d'you say, lads?'

There was a rumble of agreement from some of the watching men, and Pochin added, 'Call the boat alongside.'

Bolitho could feel his heart pounding against his ribs as

the boat bumped against the hull, and in sudden silence Allday and Ferguson climbed up through the entry port.

Pochin leaned over the rail and shouted, 'Welcome back, John! We'll sail together after all!'

But Allday stayed where he was below the starboard gangway, the sunlight bright across his upturned face. Then he said, 'I'll not sail with him!' He pointed straight at Onslow. 'He killed Evans and put the blame on me! I would have ended on a gallows but for Bryan here!'

Onslow replied calmly, 'But now you're free. I never intended you to die.' There was sweat on his forehead, and the knuckles around the pistol were white. 'You can stay with us, and welcome.'

Allday ignored him and turned to the men on deck. 'There are two French frigates out yonder, lads! Will you let the *Phalarope* fall to them because of the word of that murdering swine?' His voice grew louder. 'You, Pochin? Are you such a fool that you cannot see your own death?' He seized another seaman by the arm. 'And you, Ted! Can you live with this for the rest of your life?'

A babble of voices broke out, and even the men from aloft swarmed down to join the others in noisy argument.

Bolitho shot a glance at Herrick. It was now or never. He had seen two armed seamen walk aft to see what was happening. They had to be the sentries guarding the rest of the prisoners.

But it was Vibart who acted first. Broken and bleeding, his head sunk dejectedly in his shoulders, he was momentarily forgotten by the men around him.

With a sudden roar he lashed out and knocked his guards sprawling.

Bolitho yelled, 'Neale! *Now*, for God's sake!'

As he shouted he threw himself bodily sideways into Onslow, and together they rolled kicking and fighting across the deck.

Pook screamed with fury and had his feet kicked from

under him by Herrick, who scooped up his pistol, cocked it and fired in a matter of seconds. The force of the shot lifted Pook from his knees and smashed him back against a carronade, his jaw and half his face blown to bloody fragments.

Somehow Onslow managed to fight himself free, and with one great bound cleared the rail to land amidst the other seamen. The sudden pistol shot had left the men standing like statues, but as Onslow hit the deck he snatched up a cutlass and yelled, 'To me, lads! Kill the bastards!'

Bolitho seized Onslow's pistol and fired point-blank at a man by the wheel, and then gasped, 'Go aft, Mr. Proby! Get weapons!'

There was a ragged volley from the forecastle, and the stunned mutineers reeled back across the maindeck as another handful of seamen surged up from below led by Belsey, the master's mate, his injured arm strapped across his body, but wielding a boarding axe with his good hand.

Herrick shouted, 'The boats are coming, sir!' He hurled his empty pistol at another shadowy figure and grabbed a cutlass from Proby. 'My God, the boats are coming at last!'

Bolitho snapped, 'Follow me!' Swinging the unfamilar cutlass like a scythe he dashed down the ladder, hitting out with all his strength as a man charged across the deck with a long pike. He felt the hot blood spurt across his face as the massive blade sliced through the man's bulging neck artery as if it had been thread.

Faces loomed up, ugly and distorted, but faded into screams as he slashed his way across the deck to where Vibart was fighting with his bare hands against three mutineers. As he drove his cutlass into the nearest man's shoulder he saw the sun gleam on a knife, and heard Vibart's great bellow of agony. Then he was down, and as the released men from the cable tier charged into the fray, some of the remaining mutineers dropped their weapons and held up their hands. Bolitho slipped in some blood and felt someone lifting him to his feet. It was Allday.

He managed to gasp, 'Thank you, Allday!'

But Allday was staring past him, to the far side, where encircled by levelled weapons and abandoned by his fellow conspirators, Onslow stood with his back against a gun, his cutless still held in front of him.

Allday said, 'He is *mine*, sir!'

Bolitho was about to answer when he heard Vibart calling his name. In three strides he reached the man's side and knelt on the stained planking where Ellice and Belsey were holding Vibart's shoulders clear of the deck. There was a thin ribbon of blood running from the corner of Vibart's mouth, and as he lay staring up at Bolitho's grave features he looked suddenly old and frail.

Bolitho said quietly, 'Rest easy, Mr. Vibart. We'll soon have you comfortable.'

Vibart coughed, and the blood dribbled down his chin in a growing flood. 'Not this time. They've done for me this time!' He made as if to move his hand, but the effort was too much. From behind his shoulders the surgeon gave a quick shake of his head.

Bolitho said, 'It was a brave thing you did.'

There was a clash of steel across the deck, and Bolitho turned to see Allday and Onslow encircling each other with bared cutlasses. The other men stood watching in silence. This was no court martial. This was the justice of the lower deck. Bolitho looked again at Vibart. 'Is there anything I can do for you?'

The dying man grimaced as a fresh agony ran through his body. 'Nothing. Not from you. Not from anybody!' He coughed again, but this time the torrent did not stop.

As the returning boats ground alongside and the gangways became alive with breathless men, Vibart died. Bolitho stood up slowly and stared at the dead man. It was somehow typical and right that Vibart had remained unflinching and unshaken to the end.

He saw Captain Rennie and Midshipman Farquhar stepping over some wounded seamen, their faces drawn and ashen by what they saw. He clasped his hands behind him to hide his emotion from them.

'Put these men under guard, Mr. Farquhar. Then carry on at once with loading the fresh water. We sail as soon as it is completed.' He walked slowly across to the opposite side, and as the men parted to let him through he saw Onslow staring up at him, his eyes already glazed in death.

All at once Bolitho felt sick and unclean, as if the mutiny had left him with another, deeper scar.

He said harshly, 'I hope we can match the French as well as we can fight each other!' Then he turned and strode aft.

16

A Special Sort of Man

Midshipman Maynard tapped on the door of Bolitho's cabin and reported breathlessly, 'Mr. Herrick's respects, sir, and we have just sighted two sail on the starboard bow.' He darted a quick glance at the other officers who were standing beside Bolitho's desk. 'It's the flagship, and the frigate *Volcano*.'

Bolitho nodded, his face thoughtful. 'Thank you. My compliments to Mr. Herrick. Tell him to tack the ship to intercept.'

He paused. 'And have the prisoners ready to be sent across to *Cassius*.'

He listened to Maynard's feet scurrying up the cabin ladder and then turned back to the other officers. 'Well, gentlemen, at last we have found the flagship.'

It had been two days since the *Phalarope* had crept away from the small islets. Two long days in which to think back on mutiny and murder. Bolitho had broken his normal practice of appearing regularly on the quarterdeck, and had spent long, brooding hours in his cabin, reliving each moment, torturing himself with regrets and recriminations.

He looked down at the chart and said slowly, 'From what Allday described, I would say that the French are out in force. The two frigates were probably feelers from de Grasse's main fleet. If so, they have changed their plans.'

He tapped the chart with one finger. 'De Grasse would never waste frigates at a time like this. It looks to me as if he intends to avoid all the main channels and will use the Dominica passage. That way he might well bypass our patrols.' He stopped thinking aloud, and with sudden briskness rolled up the chart and laid it to one side.

He said, 'I shall go over to the *Cassius* and speak to the admiral.' He glanced at the neat pile of reports on the desk. 'There is much that Sir Robert will wish to know.' How trite it sounded, he thought bitterly. Like items in the ship's log, bald of feeling or humanity. How could he describe the atmosphere on the maindeck when he had spoken a prayer before the shrouded corpses had slid over the side?

Lieutenant Vibart's body, alongside those of the dead mutineers. The rest of the crew had gathered round in silence. Not just a silence of respect or sadness, but something much deeper. It was like an air of shame, a combined feeling of guilt.

He stared at the watching officers beside him, Okes and Rennie, Farquhar and Proby.

Bolitho continued in the same curt tone, 'You all showed great resource and courage. I have made a full report and I trust it will receive proper attention.' He did not add that without such a report from the ship's captain the story of the brief, savage mutiny would overshadow all else with the admiral and his superiors. As it was it might still be insufficent to save the ship's name from further harm.

He looked hard at Okes. 'You will take over as first lieutenant of course, and Mr. Herrick will assume your duties forthwith.' He switched his gaze to Farquhar. 'I do not have to add to what I have put in my report about you. You are appointed acting lieutenant immediately. I have no doubt whatever that it will be confirmed with equal speed.'

Farquhar said, 'Thank you, sir.' He looked round as if expecting to see an immediate change in his surroundings. 'I am very grateful.'

Okes said nervously, 'I still can't believe that Mr Vibart is dead.'

Bolitho eyed him impassively. 'Death is the only thing which is inevitable, Mr. Okes. Yet it is the one thing we can never take for granted!'

There was a tap at the door and Stockdale peered in. 'Flagship is signalling, Captain. For you to report on board as soon as possible.'

'Very well, Stockdale. Call away my boat's crew.' He added to the others, 'Remember this, gentlemen. The *Phalarope* was nearly lost by mutiny.' He allowed his tongue to linger on the word. 'What we have to decide now is whether we have gained anything by a reprieve. He saw their quick exchange of glances and continued, 'The ship is either cleansed of evil or smeared by shame. The choice is ours. Yours and mine!' He looked around their grave faces. 'That is all. You may go.'

Stockdale reappeared as the officers filed out, and busied himself getting Bolitho's hat and sword. He said, 'Allday is waiting to see you, Captain.' He sounded disapproving.

'Yes, I sent for him.' He listened to the squeal of blocks as the gig was hoisted out, and remembered Stockdale's stricken face as he had returned with the rest of the shore party. He had stared round the stained deck at the corpses and then at his captain. He had said brokenly, 'I should never have left you, Captain! Not for an instant!' It was as if he believed he had failed Bolitho. He seemed to think that if he had stayed aboard the mutiny could never have happened.

Bolitho said quietly, 'Send him in. He is a good seaman, Stockdale. I wronged *him*, not the other way about!'

Stockdale shook his head, but shambled away to fetch the man who had broken the mutiny.

And what a risk he had taken, Bolitho thought. He had walked back towards the searching marines, knowing full well that they were unaware of his innocence, and that any man might shoot him down without waiting for an explanation. Allday had found Okes and Farquhar, and together it seemed they had decided it best for Allday to try to reach the ship unsupported by anyone but Ferguson. It was a right decision, and a brave one. If Onslow had seen a boatload of men approaching the ship the balance would have tipped in his favour.

There was a tap at the door and Allday stepped into the cabin. Dressed in white trousers and checked shirt, his long hair tied back with a length of codline, he looked every inch the landsman's idea of a sailor. On his cheek and neck there were two diagonal scars where Brock had struck with his cane.

Bolitho faced him for several seconds. Then he said, 'I called you here to thank you properly for what you did, Allday. I wish I could say something which would help clean away the wrong which was done you.' He shrugged. 'But I know of no such reward.'

Allday relaxed slightly. 'I understand, sir. As it was, it all turned out for the best.' He grinned self-consciously. 'I was a bit scared, I can tell you, sir.' His eyes hardened. 'But when I saw Onslow, that was enough! I'm glad I was able to kill him!'

Bolitho studied Allday with new interest. He had a clean-cut, intelligent face, and but for his total lack of education might have gone far and done well by himself.

'Onslow should be a lesson to all of us, Allday.' Bolitho walked to the stern windows, his mind going back over the thought which had nagged him most since the mutiny. 'He was doomed by his life and circumstances. It is up to us not to make any more Onslows through cruelty or lack of understanding.' He swung round. 'No, Allday, I failed with Onslow. He was just a man like the rest of us. He never stood a real chance from the day he was born!'

Allday stared at him with surprise. 'There was nothing you could have done for him, if you'll excuse me saying so.' He spread his hands. 'He was a bad one, and I've seen a few in my time!'

Maynard peered in the door. 'Closing the flagship now, sir. Ready to lower the gig.'

'Very good.' Bolitho looked at Allday. 'Is there anything I can do for you?'

Allday shifted uncomfortably. 'There is one thing, sir.' Then he lifted his chin, his eyes suddenly clear and determined. 'It's about Ferguson, your clerk, sir. Are you sending him over with the other mutineers?'

Bolitho spread his arms to allow Stockdale to buckle on his sword. 'That was the intention, Allday.' He frowned. 'I know he came back with you, and did much to repair the damage he had done by his complicity with Onslow. But,' he shrugged, 'there are several charges against him. He aided the mutineers with confidential information, without which any sort of uprising might have been impossible. He attacked a sentry and released a prisoner, the guilt or innocence of whom had not been decided.' He picked up his hat and stared at it. 'Do you think he should warrant complete pardon?'

Allday said quietly, 'Remember what you said about Onslow, sir? Ferguson's no real sailor, and never will be.' He smiled sadly. 'I've looked after him since we were pressed together. If you do this to him I shall feel I've let him down. I shall feel as you do now over Onslow!'

Bolitho nodded. 'I will have to think about it.' He walked to the ladder, ducking below the beams. Then he said, 'Thank you, Allday. You put a forceful argument.'

He ran up into the sunlight and looked quickly across at the *Cassius*. She looked big and reliable against the blue

317

water, and he could see the other frigate hove to beyond her.

Herrick touched his hat. 'Gig ready, sir.' He glanced questioningly at the silent group of manacled men by the entry port. 'Shall I send 'em over while you're with the admiral?'

'If you please, Mr. Herrick.' Bolitho caught sight of Allday's tall figure beside the cabin hatch and added sharply, 'But have Ferguson kept aboard. I will deal with him myself.'

Herrick looked mystified. 'Ferguson, sir'?'

Bolitho eyed him coldly. 'He *is* my clerk, Mr. Herrick! Have you forgotten so soon that you chose him for me?' He gave a brief smile and saw the relief flooding across the other man's face.

'Aye, aye, sir!' Herrick strode to the rail. 'Man the side there! Stand by for the captain!'

The pipes trilled and Bolitho vanished down into the boat.

Herrick looked round as old Proby mumbled, 'How old is he? Twenty-five or six?' He gave a deep sigh. 'I'm twice his age and more beside, and there are others like me aboard the *Phalarope*.' He watched the little gig skimming through the whitecaps towards the swaying ship of the line. 'Yet he's like a father to all of us!' He shook his head. 'Have you seen the way the crew look at him now, Mr. Herrick? Like children caught out doing wrong. They know how he *feels* what has happened, how their shame is more'n doubled for him!'

Herrick stared at him. It was rare for the master to say so much all at once. 'I never realised that you admired him, too!'

Proby pouted his pendulous lower lip. 'I'm too old for admiration, Mr. Herrick. It's deeper'n that. Our captain is a special sort of man.' He frowned and then added, 'I'd die for him, and willingly. I can't say more'n that!' He turned

318

with sudden anger. 'Blast me, Mr. Herrick! How can you let me go on like that?' He shuffled noisily across the quarterdeck like an untidy spider.

Herrick crossed to the rail, his mind still dwelling on Proby's words. Below, watched by armed marines, the remnants of Onslow's conspirators stood awaiting passage to the *Cassius*. Herrick did not share Bolitho's shame on their behalf. He would willingly have hanged each one of them single-handed, if only to lift the despair from Bolitho's shoulders.

He remembered his own exultation when Okes and Rennie had boarded the frigate and he had realised that the mutiny's sudden fire had been quenched. It was then that he had seen through Bolitho's careful mask and had penetrated to the man within. Yes. Proby was right. He was a very special sort of man.

Midshipman Neale crossed to his side and trained his glass on the flagship. Herrick glanced down at the small midshipman and remembered his frantic struggles as they thrust his greased body through the vent hole. Neale's sudden appearance had made quite a sensation when he had flung open the doors of the cable tier. As Ellice, the surgeon, had said later, 'There we all was, Mr. 'Errick, thinkin' of death or worse, an' suddenly the doors come flyin' open like the gates of 'eaven itself!' The surgeon's crimson face had crinkled into a grin. 'When I saw this little naked cherub with the sun behind 'im I thought I was already dead without knowin' it 'ad 'appened!'

Herrick smiled to himself. Neale seemed to have grown in stature since that dreadful day. He said, 'In a few years you'll be getting promoted like Mr. Farquhar if you go on like this.'

Neale considered the suggestion and then replied, 'I never doubted it, sir.' He flushed and added quickly, 'Well, not often!'

*

319

Sir Robert Napier walked stiffly to a small gilt chair and sat down. For several seconds he stared at Bolitho's tense features and then said dryly, 'You are a very erratic and unpredictable young man, Bolitho.' He tapped his fingertips together. 'But there is one thing to be said in your favour. You are never dull!'

Bolitho did not trust himself to smile. It was still far too early to know exactly how his ideas had been received. With fretting impatience he had waited in an adjoining cabin while the admiral read his reports, and after what seemed like an hour he was ushered into the great man's presence. There were two other captains already present. Cope of the *Cassius*, and a thickset, unsmiling man Bolitho recognised as Fox of the frigate *Volcano*.

The admiral said, 'It seems to me that you are getting unnecessarily excited about the French frigates which one of your men men sighted.' He waved one hand across his big coloured chart. 'Look for yourself, Bolitho. The Leeward and Windward Islands are like a broken chain running from north to south. If the French fleet is out in force, and I say *if*, Sir George Rodney's frigates will have reported the fact, and both sides will have engaged already. That being so, what further can I do in the matter?' He leaned back, his eyes fixed on Bolitho's face.

Bolitho glanced quickly at the other officers. Cope, being Sir Robert's flag captain, would naturally stay non-committal until he knew his master's intentions. Fox was the man to convince. He was said to be a hard man, and as he was somewhat old for his rank, inclined to be over-cautious.

Bolitho took his own chart and laid it carefully across the admiral's. He started quietly. 'The whole plan to contain and engage the French fleet is based on one main theme, sir. We know that de Grasse has his strongest force at Martinique to the south. To meet with his Spanish ally

320

and to reach Jamaica, his first necessity is to *avoid* any damaging action with us.'

The admiral said irritably, 'I know that, dammit!'

Bolitho continued, 'I believe that the two frigates were part of a scouting force, ahead of the main fleet.' He ran his finger along the chart. 'He could sail north from Martinique, and if necessary deploy his ships amongst the scattered islands en route. Then, at his most suitable moment he could swing west to Jamaica as planned.' He looked at Fox who met his eyes without expression. He added urgently, 'Sir George Rodney is depending on a quick engagement, sir. But suppose de Grasse avoids that first contact, or, even worse, he makes a feint attack on our ships and *then* heads north?' He waited, watching the admiral's pale eyes moving across the chart.

Sir Robert said grudgingly, 'It could happen, I suppose. De Grasse could skirt any hostile land and then keep close inshore of more friendly territory, Guadeloupe for instance.' He puckered his lower lip. 'He would thereby avoid a running battle in open water, like the Martinique Passage.' He nodded, his face suddenly grave. 'Yours is a dangerous supposition, Bolitho.'

Captain Cope said uneasily, 'If the French can get ahead of Rodney we're done for!'

Bolitho asked, 'Could I suggest something, sir?' He tried to gauge the extent of his own forcefulness. 'If I am wrong, there can be no real harm in my idea.'

The admiral shrugged. 'I cannot find it in my heart to dampen such rare enthusiasm, Bolitho.' He wagged one finger. 'But I do not promise to abide by it!'

Bolitho leaned across the chart. 'My ship was down here in search of fresh water . . .'

The admiral interrupted, 'And well off her allotted station incidentally!'

'Yes, sir.' Bolitho hurried on. 'Allowing for perhaps a day without wind, and a further two days to regain contact

321

with their admiral, the two French frigates would have had ample time to examine the full *extent* of this Channel.' He stood back slightly as the other two captains craned over to look. 'There is a whole cluster of small islands to the north of the Dominica Passage.' He paused. 'The Isles des Saintes. If I were de Grasse, that is where I would make for. From that point he could swing west to Jamaica, or run for safety at Guadeloupe if Rodney's fleet is too close on his heels.' He swallowed and added, 'If our squadron moved south-east we might be in a better position to observe, and if necessary to report to Sir George Rodney what is happening!'

Sir Robert rubbed his chin. 'What do you think, Cope?'

The flag captain shifted uncomfortably on his feet. 'It's hard to say, sir. If Bolitho is right, and I am sure he has considered the matter most carefully, then de Grasse will have chosen the most unlikely route to slip past our blockade.' He added unhelpfully, 'But of course, if he is wrong, then we will have left our allotted station without good cause!'

The admiral glared at him. 'You do not have to remind me!' He turned his gaze on Fox, who was still leaning over the chart. 'Well?'

Fox straightened his back. 'I think I agree with Bolitho.' He paused. 'However, there is one point which he seems to have overlooked.' He jabbed at the pencilled lines with his finger. 'If Sir George Rodney flushes de Grasse away from the Dominica Passage the Frogs will certainly have the advantage. The wind is too poor to allow our fleet time to re-engage before de Grasse dashes for open water.' He drew his finger slowly across the chart in a straight line. 'But our squadron might be right across their line of escape!'

The admiral stirred in his chair. 'Do you think I had not considered this?' He glared at Bolitho. 'Well, what do *you* say?'

Bolitho answered stubbornly, 'I still say we shall be in a better position to report and, if necessary, shadow the enemy, sir.'

The admiral stood up and began to pace with sudden agitation. 'If only I could get some real news! I sent the brig *Witch of Looe* away days ago to try and gain intelligence, but with this damn climate what can you expect?' He stared through the open stern windows. 'Sometimes we are becalmed for days on end. The war could be over for all I know!'

Bolitho said, 'I could take the *Phalarope* to the south'rd, sir.'

'No!' The admiral's voice was like a whipcrack. 'I will have no captain of mine taking what should be my responsibility!'

He gave a frosty smile. 'Or was it your intention to force me into this decision?' He did not wait for a reply. 'Very well, gentlemen. We will make sail and proceed south-east immediately.' He stared at each of them in turn. 'But I want nothing foolhardy! If we sight the enemy we will retire and report our findings to Sir George Rodney.'

Bolitho masked his disappointment. He must be content. He had not even expected Sir Robert Napier to agree to leaving the present area, let alone to commit himself to what might well be a pointless and time-wasting venture.

As he turned to follow Fox the admiral added sharply, 'And as to that other matter, Bolitho.' He rested his hand on the open envelope. 'I will deal with that in my own way. I do not wish the reputation of my ships to be tarnished by mutiny. I intend that it should stay within the squadron.' He was looking impatient again. 'As for Lieutenant Vibart, well, I suppose it cannot be helped now. A dead officer is no use to me, no matter how he died!'

Bolitho tried to think of a suitable reply. 'He died bravely, sir.'

The admiral grunted. 'So did the Christians in Rome! And damn little good it did anybody!'

Bolitho backed from the cabin and then hurried on deck to summon his boat. The sea was still speckled with small whitecaps, and the admiral's flag was streaming bravely in the freshening breeze. It was good sailing weather, he thought. And that was too rare to waste at any time.

With the ponderous two-decker between them, the frigates spread their sails and hauled off on either beam. By nightfall the wind had fallen slightly, but was still sufficient to make the sails boom with unaccustomed vigour as the yards were braced round to keep all three ships on a slow starboard tack.

Before the night fell completely to hide one vessel from another there was a final unhappy incident. Bolitho had been striding up and down the weather side of the quarterdeck when he heard Okes snap, 'Mr. Maynard! Lively there! Train your glass on the flagship. She seems to be hoisting a signal.' Bolitho had crossed the deck to watch the midshipman fumbling with his long telescope. It was strange for the admiral to be sending signals in such poor visibility. A flare would have been more effective.

Maynard had lowered his glass and looked round at the two officers. He had looked sick, as he had on the day he had discovered Evans' body. 'It's no signal, sir!'

Bolitho had taken the glass from the youth's hands and trained it across the hammock netting. Coldly he had watched the small black dot rising towards the *Cassius*'s mainyard. It had twisted as it made its slow journey. Twisted and kicked, so that in his imagination Bolitho had thought he could hear the drum's staccato roll and the steady tramp of bare feet as the selected men had hauled the choking mutineer slowly up to the yard.

Maynard was wrong about one thing. It *was* a signal to every man who saw it.

Bolitho had returned the glass and said, 'I am going below, Mr. Okes. See that you have the best lookouts aloft, and call me if you sight *anything*.' He had glanced quickly at Maynard and added quietly, 'That man, whoever he was, knew the price of his folly. Discipline demands that it be paid in full!'

He turned on his heel and walked below, despising himself for the cold unreality of his words. In his mind he seemed to hear Vibart's thick, accusing voice, still jeering at him for his weakness. What did one more death matter? Fever and unaccountable accident, the cannon's harvest or the end of a rope, it was all the same in the end.

He threw himself across his cot and stared at the deckhead. A captain had to be above such things, to be able to play God without thought for those who served him. Then he remembered Allday's words and the blind trust of men like Herrick and Stockdale. Such men deserved his attention, even his love, he thought vaguely. To use power as a tyrant was to be without honour. To be without honour was to be less than a man.

With that thought uppermost in his mind he fell into a deep sleep.

'Captain, sir!' Midshipman Neale rested his hand anxiously on Bolitho's arm and then jumped back in alarm as the cot swayed violently to one side.

Bolitho swung his legs to the deck and stared for a long moment while his mind sought to recover from the nightmare. He had been surrounded by screaming, faceless men, and his arms had been pinioned while he felt a noose being tightened around his neck. Neale's hand had only added to the nightmare's reality, and he could still feel the sweat running across his spine.

He said harshly, 'What is it?' The cabin was still in darkness, and it took him several more seconds to recover his composure.

Neale said, 'Mr. Herrick's respects, sir.' He thinks you should know we've heard something.' He fell back another pace as Bolitho lurched to his feet. 'It sounded like gunfire, sir!'

Bolitho did not pause to find his coat but ran quickly to the quarterdeck. It was almost dawn, and already the sky was painted in a pale blue strip beyond the gently corkscrewing bows.

'What is it, Mr. Herrick?' He moved to the rail and cupped his hands to his ears.

Herrick stared at him uncertainly. 'I could be mistaken, sir. It might have been thunder.'

'Most unlikely.' Bolitho shivered slightly in the cool dawn breeze. 'Can you see the *Cassius* yet?'

'No, sir.' Herrick pointed vaguely. 'There's a mist coming up. It'll be another hot day, I'm thinking.'

Bolitho stiffened as a low rumble echoed sullenly across the open water. 'Maybe hotter than you think, Mr. Herrick.' He glanced up at the jerking canvas. 'The wind seems to be holding.' He was suddenly aware that there were several figures already standing on the maindeck. Everyone faced forward, listening and wondering.

Bolitho said, 'Call the hands.' He peered upwards again. In the dim light he could just see the masthead pendant whipping out like a pointing finger. 'Take out the second reef, Mr. Herrick. And set the fores'l and spanker.'

Herrick called for a boatswain's mate, and seconds later the ship came alive to the call of pipes and the stamp of running feet,

Then Herrick said, 'I still can't see the flagship, sir.'

'We won't wait for her!' Bolitho watched the men swarming aloft and listened to the harsh bark of commands. 'That is gunfire ahead. Make no mistake about it!'

Proby came on deck buttoning his heavy coat. He seemed half asleep, but as the big spanker filled with wind and the deck canted obediently to the wind's eager thrust

326

he contained any comment he might have felt and crossed to the wheel.

Bolitho said calmly, 'Alter course two points to larboard, Mr. Proby.' The ship's sudden response to wind and sail had swept away the strain and sleep from his mind. He had been right. The waiting was almost over.

He looked sideways at Herrick and saw his face was clearer in the growing light. He looked worried and not a little startled by the swift chain of events.

Bolitho said quietly, 'We will investigate, Mr. Herrick.' He pointed at the men swarming back along the yards. 'I want chain slings fitted on every yard. If we are called to action our people have enough to contend with at the guns. I don't want them crushed by falling spars.' He halted the lieutenant in his tracks. 'And have nets spread above the maindeck, too.' He made himself stand quite still by the rail, his hands resting on the worn and polished wood. He could feel the ship trembling beneath his palms, as if his thoughts were being transformed into new life, and the life was flowing through the *Phalarope* even as he watched.

From newly awakened chaos the ship had already settled down into a purposeful rhythm. All the weeks of training, the hours of persistent instruction were giving their rewards.

Stockdale joined him by the rail. 'I'll get your coat, sir.'

'Not yet, Stockdale. That can keep for a moment longer.' He turned as Okes appeared at the ladder, his face still crumpled from sleep. 'I want the hands to eat well this morning, Mr. Okes. I have a feeling that the galley fire will be out for some time to come.' He saw the understanding spreading across the officer's face. '*This* time we will be ready!'

Like a living creature the *Phalarope* lifted her bows and smashed jubilantly into each succeeding rank of low waves, the spray bursting back over her forecastle in long white streamers.

Herrick reported, 'Chain slings rigged, sir.'

'Very well.' It was an effort to speak calmly. 'Have the boats swung out for towing astern. If we fight today there will be enough splinters flying without the boats adding to them!'

Okes managed to ask, 'The gunfire, sir? What do you make of it?'

Bolitho saw several men pausing to listen to his reply. He said slowly, 'Two ships. One much smaller than the other by the sound of the firing. We can be sure of one thing, Mr. Okes. They cannot both be enemies!'

Herrick was back again. 'What now, sir?'

'I am going down to shave and wash. When I return I will expect to hear that the men have been fed.' He smiled. 'After that, we shall have to see!'

But once back in his cabin it was almost more than he could bear to take time to shave and change his clothes. The breakfast which Stockdale hurriedly laid on the cabin table he could not even face. By tonight, or perhaps within the next few hours, he might be dead. Or even worse, screaming for mercy under the surgeon's knife. He shuddered. It was pointless even to think of it. More, it was harmful.

Stockdale said, 'I have laid out a fresh shirt, sir.' He looked searchingly at Bolitho. 'I think you should wear your best uniform, too.'

'For heaven's sake why, man?' He stared at the coxswain's battered face in surprise.

Stockdale replied gravely, 'This is the day, sir. I have the same feeling I had with you once before.' He added stubbornly, 'And the men will be looking to you, sir. They'll want to *see* you.' He nodded as if to settle the matter. 'After all that's happened they'll need to know you're with them.'

Bolitho stared at him, suddenly moved by the man's halting, broken voice. 'If you say so, Stockdale.'

328

Ten minutes later a voice echoed faintly above the sounds of sea and canvas. 'Deck there! Sail on the starboard bow!'

Bolitho made himself wait just a few more seconds as Stockdale buckled on his sword, and then walked to the cabin ladder. The quarterdeck seemed crammed with figures, all pointing and speaking at once. Every voice fell silent as Bolitho walked to the rail to take a telescope from Maynard.

Through the frigate's criss-cross of rigging he could see the distorted patterns of tossing whitecaps beyond her bows. The sky was already clear, but the water seemed to writhe in the grip of a slow-moving sea mist, and for once the new day felt drained of warmth.

Then he saw them. Two ships close together, their hulls hidden in a dense cloud of smoke and mist, their tattered sails hanging disembodied above the hidden battle below.

But the flags were easily visible. One blood red, like that which flew above him. The other clear and white. The flag of France.

He closed the telescope with a snap. 'Very well, Mr. Okes. Beat to quarters and clear for action!'

His eyes held them a moment longer. 'We must give well of ourselves today, gentlemen. If our people see us doing our best, they will be willing enough to do *their* duty!'

He half listened to the distant thunder of gunfire. 'Carry on, Mr. Okes!'

They all touched their hats and then looked at one another, as if each man realised that for some, maybe for all of them, it would be the last time.

Then the drum began to rattle, and the small moment was past.

17

Form Line of Battle!

Within ten minutes of the drum's urgent tattoo the *Phalarope* was cleared for action. Decks were sanded and buckets of water stood within reach of every gun. Over the whole ship there had fallen a strange, gripping stillness, broken only by the uneasy slap of canvas and the steady sluice of water around the stern.

Bolitho shaded his eyes and watched the sun's unearthly orange glow as it tried to filter through the unending wall of sea mist. The bang and clatter of gunfire had become more uneven and sporadic with each dragging minute, and now as the distance fell away between the *Phalarope* and the other ships there came new sounds, more vicious, and somehow more personal. Bolitho could hear the sharp cracks of muskets and pistols, the jarring scrape of steel against steel, and above all the mingling cries of men fighting for their lives.

Okes wiped his face with the back of his hand and said quickly, 'This damn mist! I can't see what's happening!'

Bolitho glanced at him briefly. 'It is a godsend, Mr. Okes. They are too busy to see us!' He lifted his hand to the quartermaster. 'Starboard a point!' Then he walked to the rail and looked down at Herrick's upturned face.

'Have the guns loaded, but do not run out until I tell you.'

He saw the gunners push the fresh charges down the

gaping muzzles, followed by the round, gleaming shot. The more experienced gun captains took time to fondle each ball, weighing it almost lovingly to make sure that the first salvo would be a perfect one.

He heard Herrick shout, 'Double-shotted and grape, lads! Let 'em *feel* it this time!'

A stronger breath of wind rolled aside the mist around the entangled ships, and Bolitho tightened his lips into a thin line. Almost stern on to the *Phalarope*'s swift approach was a French frigate, and alongside, listing and battered almost beyond recognition, was the little brig, *Witch of Looe*. One mast was already gone, and the other seemed to be held upright only by the remaining stays. He thought of her commander, the young Lieutenant Dancer he had met aboard the flagship, and marvelled at the man's pluck or wasted courage which had made him match his ship against this powerful opponent. His little pop-guns against the still-smoking twelve-pounders.

Okes said, 'They've seen us, sir!' He swallowed hard as something like an animal growl floated across the water. 'My God, look at them!'

The *Witch of Looe*'s shattered deck seemed to be swamped in French sailors, and as the drifting gun-smoke parted momentarily to allow the sunlight to play across the carnage, Bolitho saw the small knot of defenders, still fighting back from the brig's small quarterdeck. In a few more minutes they would be swamped completely.

The gunports along the French frigate's disengaged side suddenly opened, and to the steady rumble of trucks the guns appeared like a line of bared teeth.

Bolitho shut his ears and mind to the victorious shouts from the French frigate and concentrated his thoughts on the narrowing strip of water between them. Less than a cable's length to go, with neither ship able to fire. *Phalarope* was almost dead in line with the other ship's stern, so that if she held her course her bowsprit would drive straight through the stern windows. On one side of the enemy frigate lay the listing, riddled brig, and on the other the guns waited to claim another victim.

Bolitho called sharply, 'Run out the starboard battery!'

He watched as his men threw themselves against the tackle falls, and in a squealing, protesting line the guns trundled up the slight slope of the deck and out through the open ports.

There was a great bellow of noise from the French ship, wild and inhuman. The sound gained from killing and madness. *Phalarope*'s own men remained tense and cold, their eyes unblinking as the enemy's pockmarked sails grew higher and higher above the bows.

Bolitho placed his hands on the rail and said slowly, 'Now send your men across to the larboard battery, Mr. Herrick!' He saw the quick mystified glances and added harshly, 'In another minute I am going to turn to starboard and go alongside the *Witch of Looe*. She is low in the water, our broadside should pass right above her!'

Herrick's frown gave way to a look of open admiration. 'Aye, aye, sir!'

Bolitho's voice stopped him in his tracks. 'Quietly there! I don't want the Frogs to see what we're doing!'

Crouching almost on their knees the gunners scuttled across to the opposite side, their excitement instantly quelled by hoarse threats from the gun captains.

Nearer and nearer. A few musket balls whined harmlessly overhead, but for the most part the French captain was prepared to wait. He could match gun for gun, and as *Phalarope*'s bows and foremast would take the first punishment he could afford to feel confident. His own ship was drifting slowly downwind and his gunners could thank the *Witch of Looe*'s weight alongside for a steadier platform beneath their feet. There was a faint ripple of cheering, drowned instantly by a fresh outburst of musket fire.

Proby muttered. 'The brig's people are cheering us, sir!'

Bolitho ignored him. One error now and his ship would change into a shambles. Fifty yards, thirty yards. Bolitho lifted his hand. He saw Quintal crouching like a runner, one beefy hand resting on the nearest seaman at the braces.

Bolitho shouted, '*Now*!'

At his side Proby added his weight to the wheel, as with a scream of blocks the yards began to swing, the sails flapping in protest, but answering the challenge of wind and rudder.

'Run out!' Bolitho felt ice cold as the larboard battery squealed across the sanded planks. 'Fire as your guns bear!'

He pounded the rail, counting each frantic second. For a moment he thought that he had mistimed the change of course, but even as he waited, holding his breath and hardly daring to watch, the bowsprit swung lazily across the French ship's high stern, almost brushing away a small group of sailors which had gathered above the hammock nettings.

Herrick ran from gun to gun, making sure that each successive shot went home. Not that he need have troubled. As the French gunners ran dazedly from the opposite side the first shots went crashing home. The *Phalarope* shuddered as she ground against the little brig, but maintained her way steadily down the ship's side, her guns belching fire and death above the heads of the stunned boarders and the remaining members of the brig's crew.

Bolitho winced as the quarterdeck nine-pounders joined in the din. But still there was no answer from the French ship. Bolitho had guessed correctly that the guns which stared impotently at the *Phalarope*'s smashing attack would have been in action right up to the moment of grappling and boarding the little brig.

He watched as great pieces of the frigate's bulwark

caved in and fragments of torn planking rose above the smoke as if thrown from an invisible hand. An axe flashed dully, and Bolitho yelled, 'He's trying to free himself!' He drew his sword. 'Over you go, lads! Boarders away!'

As the *Phalarope* ground to a sluggish halt, her bows locked into the brig's fallen rigging and spars, Bolitho ran down the port gangway and clambered on to the *Witch of Looe*'s tilting deck. For a moment nobody followed him, and then with a great roar, half cheer and half scream, the waiting seamen swept over the bulwark behind him.

Most of the French sailors, caught between the *Phalarope*'s savage gunfire and the revived members of the brig's crew, threw up their hands in surrender, but Bolitho thrust them aside, his sword raised high towards his own men. 'Come on, lads! We'll take the frigate!' There would be time enough for the boarders later, he thought vaguely.

Once up the frigate's shot-pitted side the resistance became fierce and deadly. Wild, crazed faces floated around Bolitho as he hacked his way aft towards the poop, and his feet barely supported him in the heel-thick layer of blood which seemed to cover the deck like fresh paint. The enemy's upperdeck had been crammed with men. Some were boarders recalled from the *Witch of Looe*, and others were gunners caught off guard by the *Phalarope*'s sudden change of course. This tangled, momentarily disorganised mass of men had received the full force of the broadside. All the *Phalarope*'s larboard twelve-pounders and the quarterdeck battery as well, every one double-shotted and loaded with grape for good measure. It looked as if a maniac had been throwing buckets of blood everywhere. Even the lower edges of the sails were speckled in scarlet, and fragments of men hung from upended guns and splintered bulwarks alike.

A French officer, hatless and bleeding from a scalp wound, leapt in front of Bolitho, his thin sword red to its hilt. Bolitho lifted his own sword, but felt it parried aside, and saw the French officer's expression change from anxiety to sudden exultation. Bolitho tried to draw back, but the struggling press of figures prevented it. He could not lift his sword in time. He saw the man's arm come round, heard the swish of steel, and waited for the shock of the thrust.

Instead the Frenchman's face twisted with alarm as a battle-crazed marine burst through the throng, his fixed bayonet held in front of him like a spear. The sword swung round yet again, but it was too late. The momentum of the marine's charge impaled the officer on the bayonet and threw them both against the poop ladder. The marine screamed with wild delight and stamped his boot on the Frenchman's stomach, at the same moment wrenching out the dripping bayonet. The French officer sank slowly to his knees, his mouth opening and shutting like a dying fish. The marine stared at him as if for the first time and then thrust the bayonet home again.

Bolitho caught his arm. 'That's enough! For God's sake, man!' The marine did not seem to hear him, but after a brief startled look at his captain's face he charged off into the battle once more, his expression one of concentration and hatred.

The frigate's captain lay on the poop, his shoulders supported by a young lieutenant. Someone was tying a crude tourniquet around the shattered stump of one leg, and the captain was only just hanging on to his senses as fighting, stabbing seamen reeled and staggered across his body.

Bolitho shouted, 'Strike! *Strike*, Captain! While you still have some men left!' He did not recognise his own voice, and his hand around the hilt of his sword was wet with sweat. He thought of the crazed marine and knew that he too was in danger of giving way to the lust of battle.

The French captain gestured faintly, and the lieutenant gasped, 'We strike! M'sieu, we strike!'

But even after the white flag had fluttered to the deck and men had been hauled bodily from the work of killing, it took time to make the *Phalarope*'s men realise they had won.

The first to congratulate Bolitho was Dancer of the *Witch of Looe*. Bleeding from several wounds, his arm tied across his chest with a piece of codline, he limped over the splintered, bloodstained deck and held out his good hand. 'Thank you, sir! I was never more pleased to see any man!'

Bolitho sheathed his sword. 'Your own ship is sinking, I fear.' He looked up at the frigate's tattered sails. 'But you sold her dearly.'

Dancer swayed and then gripped Bolitho's arm. 'I was trying to warn Sir Robert! The French are out, sir!' He squinted his eyes as if to restore his dazed thoughts. 'Three days ago de Grasse met up with Rodney's fleet, but after a quick clash at long range, broke off the battle.' He pointed vaguely through the smoke. 'I have been trying to shadow the Frogs, and this morning I saw the whole fleet nor'-west of Dominica!' He shook his head. 'I think Sir George Rodney has managed to engage them again, but I cannot be sure. I was caught by this frigate before I could get back to the squadron.' He smiled ruefully. 'Now I have no ship at all!'

Bolitho frowned. 'Have you enough men to take this frigate as prize?'

Dancer stared. 'But she is *your* prize, sir!'

'We can discuss the share of financial reward at a later and more convenient time, Lieutenant!' Bolitho smiled. 'In the meantime I suggest you herd these prisoners below and make as much speed as you can with these rags for some port of safety.' He peered up through the smoke. 'The wind has veered slightly to the south-east. It should carry you clear of any impending battle!'

Herrick blundered through the mess and tangle of corpses, his sword dangling from his wrist. He touched his hat. 'We have just sighted the *Cassius*, sir!'

'Very well.' Bolitho held Dancer's hand. 'Thank you for your news. At least it will justify Sir Robert's leaving his proper station!' He turned on his heel and climbed back across the sinking brig towards his own ship.

Still deep in thought he clambered over the bulwark and walked along the gangway. The gunners were standing below him, their faces upturned as he passed. The marine marksmen high in the tops and the little powder monkeys by the magazine hatch, all stood and stared at the slim solitary figure framed against the torn sails of the vanquished Frenchman.

It had been a swift and incredible victory. Not a man injured let alone killed in the attack, and no damage to the *Phalarope* at all. Some good men had died in the fight aboard the enemy ship, but the success far outweighed any such loss. A frigate taken as a prize, the *Witch of Looe* revenged if not saved, and all within an hour.

Yet Bolitho thought of none of these things. In his mind's eye he could see his well-worn chart, and the enemy's fleet moving in an irresistible tide towards the open sea, and Jamaica the prize.

Then a voice yelled out from the maindeck and Bolitho turned startled and caught off guard.

'Three cheers, lads! Three cheers for our Dick!'

Bolitho stared round at the quarterdeck as the air was split with wild, uncontrollable cheering. Herrick and Rennie were openly grinning at him. Neale and Maynard waving their hats to the men on deck below. Bolitho felt confused and entirely unprepared, and as the three cheers extended to a frenzied shouting Herrick crossed to his side and said, 'Well done, sir! Well *done*!'

Bolitho said, 'What is the matter with everyone today?'

337

Herrick replied firmly, 'You've given them more than a *victory*, sir! You've given 'em back their self-respect!'

The cheering died away as if from a signal, and Herrick said quietly, 'They want you to tell them, sir.' He dropped his eyes.

Bolitho moved to the rail and stared slowly around the familiar faces. These men. His men. The thoughts chased one another through his mind like shadows. Starve them, beat them. Let them face scurvy and disease, and death a hundred different ways. But still they could cheer. He gripped the rail hard and stared above their heads. When he spoke his voice was quiet, and those men furthest away leaned forward to hear it better.

'This morning we fought and beat a French frigate!' He saw some of the men nudging each other and grinning like children. 'But more important to me is the fact that we fought as a single unit, as a King's ship should, and must fight!' A few of the older seamen nodded soberly, and Bolitho tried to steel himself for what he had to tell them.

It was no use just telling men to fight. They had to be led. It was an act of mutual trust. He cleared his throat. 'When you see an enemy ship abeam and the balls begin to fly overhead, you all fight for many reasons.' He looked around their tanned and expectant faces. 'You fight out of comradeship, to protect each other, and avenge well-loved friends who have already laid down their lives. Or you fight out of fear, a fear which breeds a power of hatred for the enemy who is always faceless yet ever present. And above all we fight for our ship!' He waved his arm around him. 'This is our ship, and will remain so, as long as we have the will to live and die for what is right!'

Some of the men started to cheer again, but he held up his hand, his eyes suddenly sad. 'But this short fight today was only a beginning. I cannot tell you how our small deeds will fit into the great pattern of battle, for I do not know. I only know that it is our common duty to fight today, and to fight as we have never done before!'

He had their full attention now, and he hated himself for the truth which had to be told. 'This morning we had luck on our side. But before this day dies we will need much more than that.'

As he paused the air seemed to give a sullen shudder, which as every man turned to stare across the captured ship alongside extended into a low, menacing rumble, like thunder across distant hills.

Bolitho continued steadily, 'Over there, lads, lies the enemy!'

He watched each man in turn, his heart suddenly dreading what was to come. He had brought them all to this. For no matter what reason, or how justified his efforts might be seen by others, he had committed his ship and his men to the inevitable.

He felt a sudden gust of warm wind at his neck, and as he watched the low, writhing bank of morning mist began to move clear. One minute the two frigates with the sinking wreck of the *Witch of Looe* between them made up their own small world. To one beam lay the sun-tinted mist, and to the other the open sea, where night had already crossed the hard horizon, and the top-sails of the labouring *Cassius* showed above its edge, gleaming in the sunlight like a pink shell. Then, as the mist rolled away that small world broke up for ever.

Shrouded in haze to the south-east Bolitho could see the low wedge of Dominica, while away to the north the scattered islands which were called the Saintes. But between these two there was no horizon. It was a sight so vast and so terrible that nobody said a word. From side to side, as far as the eye could reach, the blue water was topped with an unbroken line of ships. There seemed to be no gap between each towering crop of sails, and as the growing sunlight reflected across the apparently motionless panorama of armed might, Bolitho was reminded of

339

an old painting he had seen as a child. The armoured knights at Agincourt, their great horses bedecked in standards and gleaming mail, the proud pennants and banners streaming from lances as they gathered to charge the flimsy line of English archers.

Almost desperately he looked down at his spellbound men. 'Well, lads, what do you say?' He pointed towards the great shimmering line of ships. 'Beyond that fleet lies England, across five thousand miles of open sea. At our back is Jamaica.' He pointed down between his feet. 'And below us is a thousand fathoms to the bottom!' He leaned forward, his eyes flashing with sudden urgency. 'So which is to be, lads?'

The new sound of distant gunfire was drowned in the sudden wave of wild and uncontrolled cheering which swept across the *Phalarope*'s maindeck, to be caught and carried by those aboard the captured frigate. Even wounded men who were being carried below shouted with the rest, some not knowing why, or even having heard Bolitho's words. It was as if all the bitterness and pent-up frustrations were being swept away by their great chorus of voices.

Bolitho turned away, and Herrick who was nearest saw the strange sadness and disbelief in his eyes. He said quickly, 'There's your answer, sir!' He was excited like the others, even jubilant.

When Bolitho turned to look at him he studied the lieutenant as if he was a stranger. 'Tell me, Mr. Herrick, have you ever seen a sea battle?' He waved towards the horizon. 'Like this one will be?' He did not wait for a reply. '*I* have. There is no dash and madcap victory. No hit-and-run when the game gets too rough.' He gripped his hands behind him and stared unseeingly past the other officers. 'The sky is so dark with smoke that it is like hell. Even the ships cry out, did you know that?' His voice became harsher. 'They cry because they are

340

being torn apart, like the fools who man them!'

He swung round as Midshipman Maynard said hoarsely, 'Flagship's signalling, sir.'

Bolitho walked to the weather side and stared down at the listing brig. The water was already lapping over her bulwark, and only discarded corpses lolled on her battle-torn deck. He snapped, 'Do not acknowledge, Mr. Maynard!' To Herrick he added, 'Cast off from the brig and get under way.' He looked up at the masthead. 'We will steer due east!'

Herrick asked, 'What of the flagship, sir?'

'Sir Robert is a gallant gentleman, Mr. Herrick. But his seniority will have made him more careful than I.' He gave a short smile. 'And *his* men may not be so keen to die on this fine day!' His smile vanished. 'Now get those men to their stations, and stop this damn cheering!'

The *Phalarope* idled clear from the wreckage, and as the captured frigate cast off her grappling irons the little brig rolled slowly on to her beam, the bursting air bubbles tinged with scarlet as the creeping water surged triumphantly across her battered hull.

Bolitho lifted his glass as the yards went round and the deck canted slightly to the wind. He could see the frigate *Volcano*'s topmasts beyond the *Cassius*, and wondered how her captain would react to this awesome sight. Sir Robert Napier still had time to retire. One definite signal would take them all out of danger, mute witnesses as the French burst from the battle and headed for their goal.

Bolitho made up his mind. 'Mr. Maynard, make a signal to the *Flag*.' He saw Herrick look at Rennie and shrug, as if his captain's actions were now quite beyond his ability to keep up. 'Enemy in sight!'

He did not watch the flags soaring up the yards, but made himself walk back and forth across the quarterdeck, followed by the eyes of Rennie's square of marines. This was the decisive moment. Sir Robert was an old man, and past his best. To try to delay the French ships would give him nothing but glory he would never see. It might even be so futile that his action would be remembered with scorn which could overshadow and despoil his whole career.

Maynard called, '*Flag* has acknowledged, sir!'

Bolitho bit his lip and continued his pacing. He could imagine the admiral's rasping voice as he dictated his signals, the uncertainty of the flag-captain, and the cautious confidence of Fox in the *Volcano*.

Maynard said suddenly, 'I can just make out her hoist, sir!' His eye was pressed to the end of the big telescope. '*Flag* to *Volcano*. Prepare for battle!'

The word flashed along the quarterdeck and down to the men waiting by the guns. Again the cheering, and again the cheer taken up across the water aboard the French ship. Bolitho waved absently as he saw Lieutenant Dancer's limping figure by the taffrail as the captured ship braced her yards and spread her tattered sails abreast the low wind.

Herrick said excitedly, '*Cassius* is making all sail, sir! My God, what a sight!' He seemed more impressed by the flagship's sudden activity than the fleet at his back.

Bolitho said, 'Have every man armed, Mr. Herrick. Put cutlasses and tomahawks at each gun. There will be plenty of fighting before long!'

Maynard lowered his glass, his voice shaking as he stared across at his captain. 'From *Flag*, sir! General signal.' He sounded as if he was trying to feel each word. '*Form line of battle!*'

Bolitho nodded slowly. 'Shorten sail, Mr. Herrick. We will bide here and allow the *Cassius* to meet up with us.' He sniffed the air. 'I feel we will lose the wind very soon. Dominica will act as a lee, I am afraid.'

He moved to the weather side and raised his glass across the nettings. Very slowly he moved the lens from side to side. In the small magnified picture he could see the dull flash of cannon fire, the brave flags and the gleam of sails as ship after mighty ship wheeled ponderously into line. He could feel the sweat at his spine, as he had after his nightmare. But this was real, yet harder to comprehend. God, there were three deckers in plenty, perhaps sixty sail of the line. British and French, gliding together for a first, inexorable embrace.

He said sharply, 'Pass the word for Mr. Brock!' He did not lower his glass until the gunner reached the quarter-deck.

'Mr. Brock, I want both carronades taken to the forecastle. Put your best hands in charge of them, and see that their slides are freshly smeared with tallow.' He closed the glass and studied the gunner's dour face. 'The carronades are the only weapons we possess which the French lack.' He stared down at the nearest weapon, snub-nosed and ugly, and lacking either the grace or the proportion of a proper deck gun. Yet a carronade could throw a massive sixty-eight-pound shot at short range, the power of which was devastating. Each circular shot burst on impact to deluge everything nearby with murderous cast-iron balls. One shot had the lethal quality of grape, added to which was the weight of a much heavier weapon.

He walked slowly to the rail and looked down at the neat decks. Had he forgotten anything? He ignored Brock and his stripped working party struggling and cursing the heavy carronades. He had to concentrate his full being on the task ahead. He must trust each officer and man. If they failed now, it was his fault for some earlier lapse in judgement.

Suddenly the restless, crowded figures below each gangway took on another meaning. Bolitho felt the pain of loss, as if he was looking at faces already dead. Quintal, the boatswain, spitting on his hands and pointing aloft for the benefit of the men who waited to sail the ship into action. Farquhar, slim and self-contained, walking abreast his battery of guns, his eyes moving over each weapon and every man in its crew. And the seamen themselves. Tanned and healthy in spite of their discomforts. Some faces standing out more than others. Here a man who had done well at Mola Island. There another who had fled from his station when they had met the *Andiron*.

He let his eyes move up the shrouds, to the men like Allday still at work aloft, and the marines kneeling in the tops with their long muskets loaded and ready.

Then aft, here to the quarterdeck. With its nine-pounders, and Neale's tiny figure dwarfed by that of a pigtailed gunner's mate. And Proby, old Proby, waving his arms like some fat scarecrow as he gave his instructions to the helmsmen. One of the men at the wheel Bolitho recognised as Strachan, the oldest sailor in the company. Too old to work a gun to Brock's satisfaction, he was still keen enough to stand his trick at the helm, and when the hell of battle swept this very deck, Bolitho knew a man like Strachan would never falter. Not because he was brave or stupid, but because it was part of his life. The only life he had known, and had been trained for.

Bolitho saw Okes watching him, his fingers playing nervously with the scabbard of his sword. Inwardly he wished it was Herrick at his side, but the latter would have his work cut out handling the ship's firepower. And anyway, Bolitho thought with sudden irritation, Okes was now first lieutenant. Vibart was dead. Not even a memory any more.

By the cabin hatch Stockdale saw Bolitho's grave face and gave a slight nod. He saw the captain's eyes catch the gesture and then move. But Stockdale was satisfied. Bolitho knew he was there. And that was enough.

Close-hauled, and making heavy weather of the faltering breeze, the three ships tacked into line. Just as they had rehearsed it so many frustrating times under the pitiless sun and beneath the eye of this same querulous admiral.

Bolitho raised his hat as the *Volcano*'s sails billowed with sudden power and the lean frigate took her station in the lead. *Cassius* followed heavily in her wake, and as more flags soared aloft, Bolitho said sharply, 'Take station astern the *Flag*, Mr. Okes!'

He watched the men scampering to the braces, and then looked at the two-decker, as like an elderly but experienced warrior she opened her double line of ports and ran out her guns.

A voice pealed out suddenly, 'Deck there! Ships on the starboard bow!' A pause while every eye peered up at the tiny figure in the main crosstrees. 'Two ship o' the line! An' two frigates!'

Bolitho tried to control his impatience. At the rear of the small line *Phalarope* would engage last. By then, it might all be decided, he thought bitterly.

The sails flapped dejectedly, and he heard the helmsmen curse as the wheel went slack. 'Wind is backing to the east, sir!' Proby looked mournful.

'Very well.' Bolitho lifted his glass and tried to see the nearest enemy ships. The gunfire was louder and unending, but the main battle fleets seemed stationary as before. It was of course an illusion.

Beyond the *Cassius*'s flapping main course he saw a brief picture of the ships indicated by the lookout. Two big ones very close in line. With two smaller sails, one on either beam. But the falling wind was playing havoc with his own men, he thought angrily. They had cheered, expecting to fight or die in glory. But this waiting, this agonising waiting, while all the time that slowly advancing fleet grew and grew, until the once exuberant seamen seemed too stunned to move, or drag their eyes from the smoke-shrouded ships.

Bolitho said, 'I am going aloft, Mr. Okes.' Without a

glance at the sweating lieutenant he strode to the starboard gangway and made his way to the main shrouds. Even as a young midshipman Bolitho had never achieved a good head for heights, but after a quick look at the listless sails he started on the long climb to the main topmast.

As he swung through the lubber's hole of the main-top the waiting marines stared at him without speaking, and then turned their eyes back to the embattled fleets. The air was dinning with noise, and Bolitho's nostrils seemed full of the smell of powder and burned wood.

He found a solitary seaman perched in the crosstrees, and waited to regain his breath before opening his glass to stare over and beyond the slow-moving *Cassius*.

It was impossible to tell one line of battle from the other. The main British and French squadrons were practically ship to ship, yardarm to yardarm, their masts and sails enveloped in a dense pall of trapped gunsmoke.

He shifted the glass and tried not to look at the deck far below his dangling legs. Then he stiffened. The ships which this lookout had reported minutes earlier were breaking away from the main battle. The two ships of the line were in fact linked by a stout cable, and as he peered through the forerigging he realised that the furthest vessel, a big three-decker, was partially disabled and without either bowsprit or foremast.

The towing ship, hampered by her massive consort, yawed from side to side, her sails puffing and then falling slack in the sluggish wind. As she swung the sunlight threw strange shadows on her tall side, and on the gleaming rows of guns already run out and prepared to fight.

Bolitho nodded to the lookout. 'Keep a good eye on them.'

The man grinned. 'Got nothin' else to do, zur!' He leaned over to watch Bolitho's careful descent and then settled down at his post. As Bolitho made his way down the rough, vibrating ratlines he heard the man humming.

He found Okes and Rennie waiting for him beside the wheel. Bolitho said flatly, 'Two big ships right enough. But one of them is disabled. Probably in a collision during the night.' He rubbed his chin. 'The towing ship is flying a command flag. White over blue,' He forced a smile and called to Maynard, 'What do you make of that, my lad?'

The midshipman lowered his glass for a moment. 'Part of the French van, sir.' He looked uneasy.

'Right.' Bolitho walked to the rail. 'De Grasse will be worried about his transports. To mount an attack on Jamaica he will need more than fighting ships. He'll have troops and supplies in other craft, like the ones we burned at Mola Island.'

Okes said, 'While the fleet is engaged, de Grasse will try and force his transports this way!'

Bolitho nodded grimly. 'Right again.' He snapped his fingers. 'Part of the French van has been detached to clear the way for them!' He looked up at the listless sails. 'And three ships only bar their way.' He turned to Rennie who was swinging his sword idly against his polished boots. 'If we can turn the enemy's van, gentlemen, Sir George Rodney will do the rest!' He slapped his palms together. 'Like rabbits in a trap!'

Okes stared at the slow-moving ships ahead of the *Cassius*. 'In this case the rabbits are bigger than the hunters, sir!'

But Bolitho had already moved away. He paused beside the minute drummer boy and asked calmly, 'Give us a tune on your fife, boy.' He spoke loudly, so that the men at the nine-pounders could hear him.

The boy peered up from beneath his shako and swallowed hard. His lips were pale, and Bolitho could see his hands shaking against his tunic. 'Wh-what shall I play, sir?'

Bolitho looked around at the strained, watchful faces.

347

'What about "Hearts of Oak"? We all know that, eh, lads?'

And so with the overwhelming roar of battle drumming in their ears, the *Phalarope*'s sailors picked up the fife's feeble lilt.

Bolitho walked back to the weather side and lifted his glass. Even aboard the *Cassius* the men might hear the *Phalarope*'s sailors singing the well-used words and gain some slight confidence.

'Come cheer up my lads,
'Tis to Glory we steer . .

Bolitho watched the great rolling bank of black smoke as it moved steadily towards the three British ships. It was like a living thing, he thought coldly. Writhing, and alight with angry red and orange flashes. Yet he was grateful for its presence. At least it hid the horror and the gruesome scenes beyond.

He looked down at this men, their faces momentarily engrossed in their singing. *They* would not have much longer to wait.

18

A Tradition of Victory

John Allday tied his neckerchief tightly around his head and ears and then dashed the sweat from his face with one forearm. Right forward on the frigate's tapered forecastle he had an uninterrupted view of the *Cassius*, and ahead of her he could just see part of the *Volcano*'s upper rigging. Deliberately he turned his back on them and on the smoke-shrouded tangle of ships beyond. He looked down at McIntosh, the gunner's mate, who was on his knees beside one of the carronades as if in prayer.

As Allday had slithered to the deck from the mainyard, Brock, the gunner, had halted him with a sharp, 'Here you!' For a moment they had faced each other once again. Allday, the pressed seaman, whose skin still bore the scars of Brock's cane, and who had nearly hanged because of another's treachery and cunning. And the gunner, hard-faced and expressionless, who rarely showed any trace of his inner feelings, if he had any.

Brock had gestured with his cane. 'Up forrard, you! Join the crews on the carronades!'

Allday had made to run off but Brock had added harshly, 'I was wrong about you it seems!' It was not an apology. Just a statement of fact. 'So get up there and do your best!' His thin mouth had moved in what might have been a smile. 'My God, Allday, your sheep would be proud of you today!'

He smiled at the recollection and then looked round with surprise as Ferguson scrambled up beside him. His eyes were bright with fear, and he clung to the hammock nettings as if he would fall without their support.

McIntosh grunted, 'What do *you* want here?'

'I-I was sent, sir.' Ferguson licked his lips. 'I'm no use for anything else.'

McIntosh turned back to his inspection of the training tackles. 'Christ Almighty!' was his only comment.

'Don't look at the ships, Bryan.' Allday picked up his cutlass and ran it through his belt. The hilt felt warm against his naked back. 'Just don't think about 'em. Keep down behind the nettings and do as I do.' He forced a grin. 'We have a fine view from here!'

Ritchie, the stolid Devon seaman, ran his fingers over the shot rack and asked vaguely, 'Wot are we to shoot at, Mr. McIntosh?'

The gunner's mate was edgy. 'The captain hasn't told me yet! When he does, I'll tell *you*!'

Ritchie shrugged. 'Us'll roast they devils!' He peered at the *Cassius*. 'The Frogs'll turn an' run!'

Kemp, one of the loaders, grimaced. 'When they sees *you* they will!'

Ferguson lowered his head against his arm. 'It's madness! We'll all be killed!'

Allday studied him sadly. He is right, he thought. Nothing can live against such a force. He said kindly, 'It's April, Bryan. Just think how it looks in Cornwall, eh? The hedgerows and the green fields . . .'

Ferguson stared at him. 'For God's sake, what are you talking about?'

Allday replied calmly, 'Have you forgotten already what nearly happened to us, Bryan?' He hardened his voice, knowing that Ferguson was at breaking point. 'Remember Nick Pochin?' He saw Ferguson flinch, but carried on.

'Well, he's dead, hanged aboard the *Cassius* with the other fools!'

Ferguson hung his head. 'I-I'm sorry.'

Allday said, 'I know you're afraid. And so am I. And so is the captain, I shouldn't wonder.'

At that moment Lieutenant Herrick stepped on to the forecastle and walked briskly to the carronades. 'Everything well, Mr. McIntosh?'

The gunner's mate stood up and wiped his palms on his trousers. 'Aye, sir.' He studied the lieutenant and then added, 'Mola Island seems a long time ago now, Mr. Herrick.'

Herrick stared aft along the maindeck to the raised quarterdeck where Okes stood stiffly beside the captain. Would Okes crack this time? he wondered. Which way would his private shame make him react? He replied, 'It does indeed.'

Okes' voice, distorted by his speaking trumpet, echoed above the rumble of gunfire. 'Another pull on the weather forebrace there! Mr. Packwood, take that man's name!'

Herrick hid his dismay from McIntosh. Okes was so much on edge that he had to say something. Anything.

McIntosh said dryly. 'Promotion does not seem to solve *everything*, Mr. Herrick!'

Herrick swung round as flags broke from the *Cassius*'s yards. A moment later he heard Maynard yell, 'Engage the enemy, sir!' Then, in a slightly steadier voice, 'Tack in succession!'

The pipes trilled. 'Lee braces. Jump to it!'

Keeping time with the ponderous two-decker the frigates tacked slowly to the south-east. Herrick shaded his eyes as the sun lanced down between the sails, and saw the nearest enemy ships less than a quarter of a mile away. They were in no apparent order, but with their yards braced round were tacking on a converging course with the British squadron. The big three-decker hid her gaping

351

ranks of guns in deep shadow as she swung slightly up wind. The two had been cast off, and the leading ship of the line, unhampered by her massive consort, heeled easily in the breeze, her command flag pointing directly at the *Cassius*.

Herrick tried to clear the dryness from his throat. 'Carry on, Mr. McIntosh. I must attend my duties!'

He had to force himself to walk slowly down to the maindeck. As he passed an open hatch where a marine sentry leaned on his musket he saw the surgeon's scarlet face grinning up at him.

'Yer 'ealth, Mr. 'Errick!' He waved a tankard.

Herrick felt slightly mad. 'Damn you, Tobias! You'll not have my body today!'

Some of the men at the nearest guns chuckled. 'That's right, sir! You tell 'im!'

Herrick strode on to take up his position in the centre of the deck. Farquhar was below the quarterdeck, his haughty features slightly pale but determined. Herrick gave him a nod, but Farquhar did not seem to see him,

There was a crashing boom, all the more startling because every man had been expecting it. It was followed instantly by a ragged salvo, and another.

Bolitho's voice broke through Herrick's stricken thoughts. 'Note it in the log, Mr. Proby! We have engaged the enemy!' His voice was muffled as he turned away. 'Cut those boats adrift, Mr. Neale! They'll act like a damn sea anchor in this poor wind!'

Herrick looked at his hands. They were quite steady, yet he felt as if every bone and muscle was quivering uncontrollably. He could imagine the *Phalarope*'s boats drifting astern, and thought of Bolitho's earlier words to the crew.

'. . . below us it is a thousand fathoms to the bottom!' Herrick winced as another thunderous broadside sent a dull vibration through the planks at his feet. A thousand fathoms, and now not even a boat to save the survivors!

He looked up and saw that Bolitho had returned to the quarterdeck rail and was staring at him. He did not speak, but gave a strange, lingering smile, as if he was trying to convey some personal message to him.

Then Bolitho called sharply, 'Mr. Neale, do not run like that! Remember our people are watching you today!'

Herrick turned away. The message could have been for him, he thought. He felt strangly calmed by this realisation and walked to the larboard battery and looked down the line of guns. In a few minutes every one of them would be firing. In a few minutes. He studied the faces of the men beside them and felt suddenly humble.

'Well, lads, this is better than practice, eh?'

Surprisingly they laughed at his stupid joke, and in spite of the cold fingers around his stomach Herrick was able to join them.

Bolitho blinked in the reflected sunlight and peered across the weather rail. Ahead of the *Phalarope* the flagship was holding her course, but the frigate *Volcano* which had been leading the line was pulling away to larboard. breaking the pattern as two French frigates drove down towards her.

Rennie gasped, 'He's done for! We cannot give him any help!'

The sea's surface, shimmered as another crashing broadside rippled along the *Volcano*'s gunports. Gun by gun, each one carefully aimed and fired in rapid succession.

Undeterred, the two frigates, with the wind in their favour, swept down on either beam.

Proby said sharply, '*Volcano*'s luffing!'

Bolitho breathed out painfully. Fox was no fool, and as wily as his name. As the two enemy frigates swept downwind for a quick kill the *Volcano* swung lazily into the wind, her sails flapping in violent protest. The nearest French ship realised her mistake just too late. As her yards started to swing, the *Volcano* presented her opposite side and fired a full salvo. The French ship seemed to stagger as if dealt a body blow. Across the water Bolitho could hear the crash of falling spars and the sliding thunder of overturned cannon. All else was hidden in the billowing clouds of smoke, but above it he could see *Volcano*'s ensign and all three masts still standing.

'Flagship signalling! "Close on *Flag*!"' Maynard ran to hoist an acknowledgement.

Bolitho tore his eyes from Captain Fox's lithe frigate as it went about to take the wind's advantage from the two Frenchmen. *Cassius* was heading straight for the powerful two-decker with the command flag. She would need all the help she could get. Fox would have to manage for himself for a while.

'Starboard a point!' Bolitho ran to the rail and leaned out as far as he could. Then he saw the towering sails of the ship of the line as it drove down on a converging course with the flagship. They should pass port to port, he thought. He shouted to the maindeck, 'Stand by, Mr. Herrick!'

Okes yelled, 'The Frenchman's changing his tack, sir!' He was jumping with agitation. 'God in hell, sir! He's turning across the *Cassius*'s bows!'

Either the French captain was unwilling to face a gun for gun contest, or he hoped to rake the *Cassius*'s bows and masts as he crossed her course, Bolitho was not quite sure which. But either way he had not allowed for the extra sail carried by Admiral Napier's elderly flagship.

Instead, the two ships crossed their bowsprits and then met at right-angles with a sickening crash. As they locked together both ships opened fire, the arrowhead of water between them erupting in a great sheet of flame and black smoke.

Bolitho watched in chilled silence as *Cassius*'s foremast and main topgallant leaned drunkenly and then smashed down into the all-enveloping smoke. He could see rigging and spars ripping away the sails and scattering men from the tops like dead fruit.

Another broadside split the air apart, and Bolitho knew that the *Cassius*'s forward guns were within feet of the enemy's. Yet still they stayed locked together, their splintered bowsprits and jib booms entangled like the tusks of two crazed beasts from a nightmare.

Bolitho cupped his hands. 'Both carronades to starboard!' He waved his hand at Proby. 'We will put her across the enemy's stern, if we can!' He half ducked as a ball screamed overhead and slapped through the driver leaving a ragged tear. A stray shot from the giants, but just as deadly, he thought grimly.

All around him men were coughing and wiping their eyes as the smoke reached out and over the frigate's decks.

The helmsman cursed as the *Cassius*'s torn sails loomed over the fog like some great spectre. But Bolitho gauged the set of the flagship's masts and knew he was on the right course. The fog closed in again, and he saw the double lines of flashes as both fired salvo after salvo at pointblank range. He could hear the two hulls grinding together, the screams and cries of the wounded and dying, mingled with the unbelievable sound of the admiral's drum and fife band. It was impossible to tell what they were playing, or how a man could live, let alone think of an empty tune in that holocaust.

But Bolitho shouted, 'A cheer, lads! Give a cheer to the *Flag*!'

Muskets banged through the smoke, and Bolitho heard the balls thudding into the bulwarks and whining against the nine-pounders.

Rennie bellowed, 'Marksmen! Shoot down those bastards!' And from aloft came an answering volley.

The wind seemed to have gone altogether, although in the dense smoke it was impossible to gauge either speed or distance. Then out of the flickering, choking fog Bolitho saw the stern of the two-decker. It seemed to hang above the *Phalarope*'s starboard bow like an ornate cliff, and he could see the flash of musket fire from her stern windows as marksmen directed their attention to the frigate's forecastle.

Bolitho banged the rail with his hands, ignoring the whining balls and the cries from forward. In his mind he was picturing the enemy ship's lower gundeck. Cleared for action it was one long battery which ran from one end of the ship to the other. Bolitho had been a midshipman in a ship of the line, and he knew that there must be upwards of three hundred men in there, stooping in semi-darkness, choking in the acrid fumes, and firing their guns more from familiarity than accuracy.

He shouted, 'The carronades, Mr. McIntosh! Fire as we cross her stern!'

Rennie grinned and wiped his face with his sleeve. 'That'll kill a few, sir!'

Bolitho bit his lip as the sound of a mast thundering across smashed and broken rigging broke through the roar of combat. *Cassius* was a very old ship. Much more of this punishment and she would either break up or sink as she fought!

He wondered what had happened to the *Volcano*, and worse, the crippled three-decker. If the latter was able to engage, it would be over in minutes. Her lower gundeck was crammed with thirty-two pounders. One of those could smash through two and a half feet of solid oak at maximum range. Bolitho tried not to picture what would happen to the *Phalarope*'s frail timbers.

'Ready, sir!' McIntosh was yelling like a madman.

Bolitho drew his sword. 'Larboard a point, Mr. Proby!' He watched the jib flapping and dropped his sword.

'*Fire!*'

Herrick felt the deck shudder beneath him as both carronades fired almost together. As the thick muzzle smoke eddied clear he stared up at the French ship's stern momentarily forgetting the battle which raged around him. A few seconds earlier he had watched the tall stern emerge from the fog of gunfire and had seen the great cabin windows with their life-sized figures on either quarter, full-breasted nymphs carrying tridents with the vessel's name, *Ondine*, in scarlet and gilt across the wide counter between them, and had marvelled at the ship's overpowering appearance of grandeur and indestructibility. As the smoke moved clear he gaped at the black jagged holes which left the stern like the entrance of a fire-scarred cave. At the horror and chaos beyond he could only briefly imagine, for as a fresh gust of wind moved busily through the *Phalarope*'s sails the deck tilted, and with her helm hard over she swung in a tight arc around the enemy ship's larboard quarter.

He shouted hoarsely above the din, 'Ready, lads!' He peered along the crouching line of gun captains. 'Fire as you bear!'

The first guns of the starboard battery fired as one, and in ragged succession the others followed as lanyard after lanyard was pulled taut, and the double-shotted charges crashed into the trapped smoke alongside.

A few men were cheering, their cries broken by coughs and curses as the smoke swirled back through the open ports.

Herrick yelled, 'Reload! Reload and run out!' He watched narrowly as the frigate moved down the other ship's beam, barely twenty yards clear. He could see the crowded heads on the high bulwark, the stabbing yellow flashes of muskets from her tops, but from the lower gundeck with its line of powerful guns there was not a single shot in reply. The carronades' lethal attack must have swept through the crowded gundeck like a scythe through a field of standing corn.

But as he watched he saw the first guns on the upper-deck lurch back at their ports, and then in the twinkling of an eye the whole upper battery erupted in one deafening broadside.

Herrick fell back, half stunned by the volume of the combined sounds of exploding guns, following instantly by the demoniac scream of balls above his head. The nets which Bolitho had ordered to be placed over the maindeck jumped and vibrated to falling wreckage, blocks, severed rigging and whole strips of blackened canvas. But Herrick stared up with amazement as he realised that the ill-aimed broadside had missed everything vital to *Phalarope*'s movements. Not a mast or spar had fallen. Had it been the lower battery, he knew that the frigate's starboard side and gunports would now be a shattered ruin.

He heard the gun captains shouting like demons. 'Run out! Heave on the tackles! Stand clear!' Then with the jerk of trigger lines the guns rumbled back to the full extent of their tackles.

A musket clattered by Herrick's feet, and as he stared upward he looked into the dead eyes of a spreadeagled marine who had pitched down from the maintop on to the net below.

But he forgot the marine immediately as something more terrible took his attention. Through the smoke, falling like a giant tree, he saw the *Ondine*'s mizzenmast. It was impossible, but it was happening. Mast, top and topgallant, with all the attendant weight of sails, rigging and yards, hung in the air as if caught in a strong wind. Then, amid the screams and desperate cries of those men caught like flies in the shrouds, it crashed down across the

Phalarope's quarterdeck. The hull quivered as if the frigate had hit a reef, and as Herrick ran aft to the ladder he felt the *Phalarope* shake from truck to keel and then begin to swing slowly to starboard. Like an unyielding bridge the *Ondine*'s severed mast held both ships together, and as a fresh burst of musket fire struck foot-long splinters from the deck, Herrick fought his way up the ladder and stared with dismay at the destruction around him.

A complete yard had fallen amongst Rennie's marines, and he turned away from the smashed, writhing remains as Sergeant Garwood roared, 'Stand to! Leave those men alone!' He was glaring at the remainder of his marines. 'Rapid fire on her poop, my lads!' He vanished in a fresh cloud of smoke as the frigate's guns fired again, the shots crashing into the *Ondine*'s hull, which at the nearest point was ten feet clear.

Herrick pushed past the struggling seamen who were trying to hack away the French rigging and dropped on one knee beside Bolitho. For a moment he thought the captain had been hit by a musket ball, but as he slid his arm beneath his shoulders Bolitho opened his eyes and struggled into a sitting position. He blinked at Herrick's anxious face and said, 'Keep the guns firing, Herrick!' He peered up at the enemy ship alongside and pulled himself to his feet. 'We must stop them boarding us!'

He groped for his sword and shouted harshly, 'Cut that wreckage away!'

Okes staggered through the smoke, his breeches and coat splashed with blood and torn flesh. His eyes seemed to fill his face, and although he appeared to be shouting, Herrick could hear nothing.

Bolitho pointed with his sword. 'Mr. Okes, clear the larboard battery and prepare to repel boarders!' He reached out and shook the lieutenant like a dog. 'Do you hear me, damn you?'

Okes nodded violently, and a long thread of spittle ran down his chin.

Bolitho pushed him to the ladder, but Herrick said quickly, 'I'll do it, sir!'

'No you won't!' Bolitho looked wild. 'Get your guns firing! It is our only chance!'

At that moment the *Ondine*'s guns banged out once again, and Herrick flinched as the salvo seared his face like a hot wind. He saw a party of sailors hacking away at a length of broken shrouds. In the next instant there was nothing but a squirming mass of pulped flesh and bones, with a gaping gash in the lee bulwark beyond.

Bolitho shouted in his ear, 'We'll not be so lucky next time!'

Herrick ran down the ladder, closing his eyes and ears to the horror beside him as more great blows shook the frigate's hull like hammers on an anvil. He walked through the smoke, his eyes streaming, his throat like sand, as he shouted wild and unheeded encouragement to the powder-blackened gunners.

Farquhar caught his arm and shouted, 'They'll never cut that mast away in time!' He pointed towards the *Ondine*'s lower gundeck. 'They'll not be silent for ever!' Herrick did not reply. With the wind at her beam, and held aft by the broken mast, the *Phalarope*'s bows were starting to swing inwards towards the *Ondine*'s hull. Through the smoke he could see men running along the two-decker's side towards the point of contact, the filtered sunlight playing on raised weapons.

He saw Okes groping towards the forecastle, his sword still in its sheath. He snapped, 'Go with him, Mr. Farquhar! He looks in a bad condition!'

Farquhar's eyes gleamed coldly. 'It will be a pleasure!'

Herrick flinched as a complete section of the starboard gangway splintered skyward and one of the twelve-pounders lurched on to its side. A seaman screamed as a severed head landed at his feet, and another ran from the gun, his eyes blinded by flying splinters.

Herrick called, 'Take those men below!' But as he shouted he heard the sudden clank of pumps and knew that it was probably just as safe on deck.

He tried to shut it all from his mind and made himself walk back along the line of guns. Men were falling all around him but he knew he must not falter, and shouted, 'Keep hitting 'em, lads!' He waved his hat. 'If you want to see England again, keep those guns firing!'

On the forecastle the men from the unemployed guns gathered below the nettings, their hands gripping cutlasses and boarding axes as the bowsprit quivered against the enemy's forerigging. Okes croaked, 'Over you go, lads! Keep those swine off our bows!'

Some of the men cheered and began to scramble out along the bowsprit, others fell back as a flurry of musket shots cut through the eager sailors and sent their corpses spinning into the water below.

Farquhar said urgently, 'You must lead them! My God, you're asking the impossible!'

Okes swung round, his mouth slack. 'Hold your tongue! *I'll* give the orders!'

Farquhar eyed him coolly. 'I have said nothing in the past, Mr. Okes! But I will say it now as it seems we will all die today!' His hat was plucked away by a musket ball but he did not drop his eyes. 'You are a cheat, a coward and a liar! If I thought you were worth it, I would discredit you here and now in front of these men, whom you are too squeamish to lead!' He turned his back on Okes' stricken face and shouted, 'Follow me, you ragged heroes!' He waved his sword. 'Make way for a younger man!'

They laughed like lunatics and slapped his shoulders as he crawled over the nettings and clambered on to the smooth bowsprit. Shots whined all around him, but he was breathless with a mixture of relief and madness. All this was worth it, if only for telling Okes what he thought of him for his cowardice at Mola Island.

Okes stared back at the quarterdeck and whimpered as a seaman crawled past him, half disembowelled by a great sliver of torn planking. Bolitho was still at the quarterdeck rail, a speaking trumpet in one hand, his sword in the other. His uniform seemed to shine in the frail sunlight, and Okes could see the hammock nettings jumping as hidden marksmen tried to find the *Phalarope*'s captain.

Okes cried, 'I hope they kill you! I hope they kill all of you!'

He sobbed and groped for his sword. Nobody listened to his wild words, or even heeded his presence on the blood-spattered forecastle. He thought of the stinging words and the contempt in Farquhar's eyes.

'*Never!*' He pulled himself towards the bowsprit where already some of the men were clashing steel with the enemy seamen. 'I'll show the lot of you!' Heedless of the curses and screams he pulled himself over the clinging sailors and hacked at a French petty officer with his sword. He saw the man's shocked surprise as a great gash opened across his neck and he fell between the grinding hulls. Then he was up and over, pushing Farquhar aside in his frenzied efforts to reach and strike at the enemy.

Farquhar saw the madness on Oke's face and tried to pull him back. But it was useless. Encouraged by the apparent bravery of their officers the British sailors swarmed on to the *Ondine*'s bulwark.

Okes snarled, 'Are you afraid, Mr. Farquhar?' He threw back his head and emitted a shrill laugh. 'Your uncle won't like that!'

Farquhar parried a thrusting pike and followed Okes down on to the wide deck. It was every man for himself now.

Bolitho strained his eyes through the smoke and watched

362

his men changing from defenders to boarders. Whoever had decided to board the *Ondine* had made the right guess, he thought grimly. He heard the axes ringing on the tangle of wreckage behind him and knew it was impossible to free *Phalarope* from its embrace before the *Ondine*'s heavy guns were brought back into action.

He crossed the deck and said to Rennie, 'We must board her from aft, too!' He saw the marine nod. 'Get some men together immediately!'

He heard someone sobbing and saw Neale on his knees below the lee rail. Midshipman Maynard was lying on his back, one hand held upright entangled in a signal lanyard, his eyes wide and unseeing and strangely peaceful. Neale was holding his hand and rocking back and forth, oblivious to the crash of gunfire and the slapping musket balls which had already claimed his friend.

Bolitho reached down and pulled Neale to his feet. The boy's last reserve seemed to collapse, and with a frantic cry he buried his face in Bolitho's coat, his body shaking with convulsions of grief. Bolitho prised him away and lifted his chin with the hilt of his sword. For a moment he stared down at him, then he said gravely, 'Take a grip on yourself, Mr. Neale!' He saw the stunned look in Neale's eyes and shut his mind to the fact that he was talking with a terrified thirteen-year-old child who had just lost his best friend. 'You are a King's officer, Neale!' He softened his voice. 'I said earlier, our people are watching you today. Do you think you can help me now?'

Neale brushed his eyes with his sleeve and looked back at Maynard's body by the bulwark. As the halyard jerked in the breeze his arm moved as if he still held on to life. Then Neale turned back to Bolitho and said brokenly, 'I'm all right now, sir!'

Bolitho watched him walk back to the shouting gunners, a small figure half hidden in the smoke and flame of this savage battle.

Rennie reappeared, a cut above one eye. 'Ready, sir!' He swung his curved sword. 'Shall I take 'em across?'

Bolitho looked around the battered quarterdeck. There seemed to be more corpses than live men, he thought wearily. He faltered as a shot crashed against the quarterdeck ladder and tore into the planking like a plough. With disbelief he saw Proby put his hands to his face and watched his fingers clawing at the sudden torrent of blood. The master staggered against the wheel, but as Strachan left the spokes to hold him he fell moaning on to his side and lay still. His hands thudded on the planking, and Bolitho saw that his face had been torn away.

'We must take the *Ondine*!' The words were wrung from his lips. 'If the French see their command ship strike, they'll . . .' He faltered and stared again at Proby's body. I've done for the lot of them! He felt the anguish changing to helpless anger. I have sacrificed the ship and every man aboard just for *this*!

But Rennie eyed him evenly and said, 'It is the right decision, sir!' He straightened his hat and said to his sergeant, 'Right, Garwood, do you feel like a little walk?'

Bolitho stared at him. It was as if the marine had been reading his mind. He said, 'The *Cassius* will support us.' He looked at the waiting marines. They crouched like animals, wild and beyond fear or even anger. It's us or them, lads!'

Then, as the men shouted and cheered he jumped on to the *Ondine*'s broken mast and began to claw his way across. Once he looked down at the water below him. It was littered with broken woodwork and sodden corpses, French and British alike.

As he reached the *Ondine*'s poop he felt the balls whining past him and heard screams at his back as men fell to join the waiting corpses below. Then as he reached the scarred bulwark he hacked away the remains of the French boarding nets and leapt down on to the deck. Dead and dying lay everywhere, but when he glanced quickly across the far side he felt a further sense of shock as he saw the *Cassius*. She was not alongside anymore, but drifting away in the smoke of her own wounds, a mastless hulk, battered beyond recognition. From every scupper he could see long, glistening streams of blood, which poured down the ship's side to colour the water in one unbroken stain. It was as if the ship herself was bleeding to death. But from the stump of her mizzen the ensign, pitted and torn with shot holes, still flapped in defiance, and as Rennie's marines swept across the *Ondine*'s poop there was a burst of cheering from the *Cassius*'s deck. It was not much of a cheer, for there could not be many left to raise it, but to Bolitho it acted like the stab of a spur.

He ran across the littered deck, cutting down two seamen with hardly a pause, propelled on by the cheering and the battle-crazed men at his back. He could see his men on the *Ondine*'s forecastle, almost encircled by an overwhelming mass of French seamen, their stubborn resistance faltering as they were forced back towards the rail.

Bolitho yelled, 'Hold on *Phalarope*'s!' He saw the Frenchmen falter and turn to face this new threat. 'To me, lads! Cut your way through 'em!'

More men were swarming from the frigate now, and he saw Herrick's uniform through the smoke as he waved his men forward.

He turned as Okes slashed a path for himself in the press of figures, his sword gleaming red as he cut down a screaming midshipman and went on towards a man who was reloading a swivel gun beside the quarterdeck. Okes was bleeding from a dozen wounds, and as he reached the ladder the swivel gun exploded with a dull roar. The packed grapeshot lifted Okes like a rag doll and flung him lifeless into the fighting men below the ladder. The gunner fell a second later, cut down by a swinging cutlass.

Then, all at once it was over. The deck clattered with the weapons thrown down by the *Ondine*'s seamen, and Bolitho realised that their cries of defiance had changed to pleas for quarter. He knew he could not hold his men back if they wanted to complete the slaughter. It fell to some unknown sailor to break the spell of destruction and killing.

'A cheer for the *Phalarope*!' The voice cracked with relief and jubilation. 'An' a cheer for Mad Dick!'

Bolitho climbed down the ladder, past the dazed Frenchmen and the mangled litter of entwined corpses.

'Captain Rennie!' He paused beside the remains of Lieutenant Okes. 'Hoist our flag above the French ensign!' He felt his hands shaking. 'Let them all see what you have done today.'

Sergeant Garwood said gruffly, 'The cap'n is dead, sir!' He unrolled the flag carefully. 'But I will do it!'

'Dead?' Bolitho stared after him. 'Rennie, too?' He felt Herrick pulling his arm and asked heavily, 'What is it?'

'The ship is ours, sir!' Herrick was shaking with excitement. 'The gundeck is like a slaughterhouse! Our carronades did more than . . .' He broke off as he saw Bolitho's face.

'Very well, Mr. Herrick. Thank you.' His voice shook. 'Thank *all* of you!' He turned away as more cheering echoed round the bloody decks.

Herrick shook his head as if he was beyond understanding. 'A two-decker, sir! What a victory!'

Bolitho replied quietly, 'We have a tradition of victory, Mr. Herrick.' He seemed to be speaking to himself. 'Now gather our people and send them back to the ship. They have cut the wreckage away.' He stared dully at the *Phalarope* and let his eyes move slowly along her length. There were great gaping holes in her once-trim hull, and she was well down by the head. It sounded as if the pumps were only just containing the inrush of water. All three topmasts had gone, and the sails flapped in the breeze in long canvas streamers. He could see bodies hanging in the tops, the great patches of scarlet across the smashed and buckled planking below. Intruding for the first time since their battle had begun came the distant thunder of that other great fight. Still far away and impersonal.

Bolitho made another effort to pull himself together. 'Lively, Mr. Herrick! The battle is still not over!'

If only his men would stop cheering. If only he could get away and be with himself.

Herrick waved his arm. 'Clear the ship, lads! We can take this wreck later in our own good time!'

Bolitho walked to the bulwark. Across the gap he could see Neale standing just where he had left him beside the wheel. He said, 'Tell my coxswain to take Mr. Okes and Captain Rennie over to the ship.' He saw Herrick's sudden anxiety and felt despair closing in again. 'Not Stockdale, Mr. Herrick?'

Herrick nodded 'He fell as you were fighting on the poop, sir. He was defending your back from the marksmen.' He tried to smile. 'I am sure that was what he would have wished!'

Bolitho stared at him. Stockdale dead. And he had not even seen him fall.

Farquhar pushed forward, his features wildly excited. 'Captain, sir! The lookouts report that our fleet has broken the enemy's line in two places!' He stared round the stained, watching faces. 'Rodney has broken the French line, do you hear?'

Bolitho felt the breeze across his cheek, feeling its way through the battle's stench like an awed stranger. So de Grasse was beaten. He stared at the listing frigate below him, feeling the prick of emotion behind his eyes. Was all this sacrifice for nothing after all?

Herrick took his arm and said thickly, '*Look*, sir! Over yonder!'

As the freshening wind pushed away the curtain of smoke from the embattled and shattered ships, Bolitho saw the tall outline of the big three-decker. Her guns were still run out, and her paintwork was gleaming and unscarred by any cannon. Throughout the fighting she had lain impotent or unwilling to face the holocaust of close combat, and no British blood had been given to her massive armament.

Yet in spite of all these things there was another flag flying above her own. The same that flew on the dismasted *Cassius* and aboard the *Ondine*. The same as the *Phalarope*'s own ensign and the victorious *Volcano* which now pushed her way through the last rolling bank of smoke.

Herrick asked soberly, 'Do you need more than that, sir? She's struck to *you*!'

Bolitho nodded and then climbed over the bulwark. 'We will get the ship under way, Mr. Herrick. Though I fear she may never fight again!'

Herrick said quietly, 'There'll be other ships, sir.'

Bolitho stepped down on to the *Phalarope*'s gangway and walked slowly above the spent and sweating gunners.

'Other ships?' He touched the splintered rail and smiled sadly. 'Not like this one, Mr. Herrick.' He tilted his head and looked up at the flag.

'Not like the *Phalarope*!'

Epilogue

Lieutenant Thomas Herrick pulled his boat cloak closer around his shoulders and picked up his small travelling bag. The houses around the cobbled square were thickly covered in snow, and the wind which blew strongly inland from Falmouth Bay and seemed to pierce his bones to the marrow, told him that there was more to come. For a moment longer he watched the ostlers guiding the steaming horses into the inn yard, leaving the slush-stained coach which Herrick had just vacated isolated and empty. Through the inn windows he could see a cheerful fire and hear voices raised in laughter and busy conversation.

He was suddenly tempted to go inside and join these unknown people. After the long journey from Plymouth, and four days on the road before that, he felt drained and weary, but as he looked up at the mist-shrouded hump of Pendennis Castle and the bleak hillside beyond he knew he was only deluding himself. He turned his back on the inn and started up the narrow lane from the square. Everything seemed smaller than he remembered it. Even the church with its low wall and the leaning stones within the graveyard appeared to have shrunk since that last and only visit. He stepped sideways into a mound of muddy snow as two shouting children dashed past him dragging a homemade sledge. Neither gave Herrick a glance. That too was different from the last time.

Herrick ducked his head as a strong gust whipped the snow from a low hedgerow and across his face, and when he looked up again he saw the old house, square and grey, facing him like a picture from all those past memories. He quickened his pace, suddenly nervous and unsure of himself.

He heard the bell jangling within the house, and even as he released the heavy iron handle the door swung open, and a neat fair-haired woman in a dark dress and white cap stood aside to greet him.

Herrick said uncertainly, 'Good day, ma'am. My name is Herrick. I have just driven from the other side of England.'

She took his cloak and hat and stared at him with a strange, secret smile. 'That's a long journey, sir. The master is expecting you.'

At that moment the door at the far side of the hall swung open and Bolitho stepped forward to meet him. For a long moment they both stood still, their hands clasped in an embrace which neither wanted to break.

Then Bolitho said, 'Come into the study, Thomas. There is a good fire waiting!'

Herrick allowed himself to be placed in a deep leather chair, and let his eyes stray over the old portraits which lined the panelled walls.

Bolitho watched him gravely. 'I am glad you came, Thomas. More glad than I can say.' He seemed nervous and ill at ease.

Herrick said, 'How it all comes back to me as I sit here. It is a year and a month since we weighed anchor from Falmouth and sailed for the West Indies together.' He shook his head sadly. 'Now it is all finished. The peace is signed at Versailles. It is over.'

Bolitho was staring into the fire, the dancing reflections playing across his dark hair and his grey, steady eyes. He said suddenly, 'My father is dead, Thomas.' He paused as

370

Herrick jerked upright in his chair. 'And so is Hugh, my brother!'

Herrick did not know what to say. He wanted to find some word of comfort, something to ease the pain from Bolitho's voice. Without effort he could throw his mind back over the months, to the aftermath of the battle when the listing, battered *Phalarope* had limped painfully to Antigua for repairs. Herrick had known that Bolitho was offered an immediate passage home to England, for a better and bigger command. But he had stayed with the frigate. Nursing her through every indignity of the dockyard, and watching over the care and treatment of her sick and wounded men.

October had arrived, and with her refit only half completed the *Phalarope* was ordered home to England. The Battle of the Saintes, as it was soon to be known, was the last great struggle of that unfortunate war. As the frigate dropped her anchor at Spithead, England rejoiced at the sounds of peace. It was an unsatisfactory agreement, but for England the war had been too long on the defensive. And as Pitt had remarked to the House of Commons, 'A defensive war can only end in inevitable defeat.'

Bolitho had left the ship at Portsmouth, but only after every man had been properly paid off and letters of credit had been sent to the dependants of her many dead. Then with hardly a word he had left for Falmouth.

As first lieutenant, Herrick had stayed to hand over the ship to the dockyard, then he too had gone to his home in Kent.

Bolitho's letter had arrived within a few days, and Herrick had set off for Cornwall, hardly knowing if the invitation was genuine or just common courtesy.

But as he looked at the big, shadowed room and Bolitho's slim figure before the fire, he began to understand for the first time. Bolitho was now completely alone.

371

He said quietly, 'I am sorry. I had no idea.' Bolitho said, 'My father died three months ago.' He gave a short, bitter smile. 'Hugh went a few months after the Saintes battle. He was killed by accident. A runaway horse, I believe.'

Herrick stared at him, 'How do you know all this?'

Bolitho opened a cupboard and then laid a sword on the table. In the firelight it gleamed with sudden brightness which hid the tarnished gilt and well-worn scabbard.

Bolitho said quietly, 'Hugh sent this to my father. To give it back to me.' He turned back to the fire. 'He wrote that he considered it to be mine by right.'

The door opened, and the fair-haired woman entered with a tray of hot punch.

Bolitho smiled. 'Thank you, Mrs. Ferguson. We will dine directly.'

As the door closed again Bolitho saw the question on Herrick's face. 'Yes, that is the wife of Ferguson, my clerk. He works for me, too.'

Herrick nodded and took one of the goblets. 'He lost an arm at the Saintes. I remember.'

Bolitho poured himself a drink and held it to the firelight. 'His wife did not die after all. And Ferguson is quite a hero in the town!' It seemed to amuse him. and Herrick saw the old smile playing at the corners of his mouth. Bolitho added, 'Now the war is done, Thomas. You and I are on the beach. I wonder what lies ahead for those like us?'

Herrick replied thoughtfully, 'This peace will not last.' He lifted his goblet. 'To old friends, sir!' He paused, seeing the memories all over again. 'To the ship, bless her!'

Bolitho drained his drink and gripped his hands behind him. Even that unconscious gesture stabbed Herrick's memory like a knife. The screaming shot, the crash and thunder of battle, with Bolitho pacing the quarterdeck like a man deep in thought.

'And you, sir? What will you do now?'

Bolitho shrugged. 'I have the chance to become a landowner, I suppose. And a magistrate like my father.' He looked up at the portraits. 'But I can wait. For another ship.'

The door opened, and a man in a green apron asked, 'Will you be requiring any more wine from the cellar, Captain?'

Herrick jumped to his feet. 'My God! Allday!'

Allday grinned self-consciously. 'Aye, Mr. Herrick. 'Tis me right enough!'

Bolitho looked from one to the other. 'After Stockdale died, Allday here said he wanted to change his mind about leaving the Service.' He smiled sadly. 'So if the chance comes we will go back to sea together.'

Bolitho picked up the sword and held it in both hands. Over his shoulder he added quietly, 'When that time comes I will want a good first lieutenant, Thomas.' He turned and looked straight into Herrick's eyes.

Herrick felt the warmth flooding back through his body, sweeping away the doubt and the sense of loss. He raised his goblet. 'It is not far to Kent, sir. I'll be ready when you give me the word!'

Bolitho turned his face away and watched the snow whipping across the windows. For a while longer he looked at the grey sky and scudding clouds, and imagined he could hear the wind whining through shrouds and taut rigging, with the hiss of thrown spray rising above the lee bulwark.

Then he faced his friend and said firmly, 'Come, Thomas, there is much to talk about!'

Allday watched them go into the dining room, and then with a quiet smile he placed the sword carefully back in the cupboard.

Relentless Pursuit

Alexander Kent

It is December 1815 and Adam Bolitho's orders are unequivocal. As captain of His Majesty's Frigate *Unrivalled* of forty-six guns, he is required to *'repair in the first instance to Freetown Sierra Leone, and reasonably assist the senior officer of the patrolling squadron'*. But all efforts of the British anti-slavery patrols to curb a flourishing trade in human life are hampered by unsuitable ships, by the indifference of a government more concerned with old enemies made distrustful allies, and by the continuing belligerence of the Dey of Algiers, which threatens to ignite a full-scale war.

For Adam, also, there is no peace. Lost in grief and loneliness, his uncle's death still avenged, he is uncertain of all but his identity as a man of war. The sea is his element, the ship his only home, and a reckless, perhaps doomed attack on an impregnable stronghold his only hope of settling the bitterest of debts.

'As ever, Kent evokes the blood and smoke of battle in crimson-vivid prose'
Mail on Sunday

'A splendid yarn'
The Times

arrow books

Success to the Brave

Alexander Kent

Spring, 1802

Richard Bolitho is summoned to the Admiralty to receive his orders for a diffcult and thankless mission . . .

The recent Peace of Amiens is already showing signs of strain as old enemies wrangle over colonies won and lost during the war. In the little 64-gun *Achates*, Bolitho sails west for the Caribbean, to hand over the island of San Felipe to the French.

But diplomacy is not enough . . .

'One of our foremost writers of naval fiction . . .'
Sunday Times

arrow books